THE End of the World RUNNING CLUB

ADRIAN J WALKER

5 7 9 10 8 6

Del Rey, an imprint of Ebury Publishing
20 Vauxhall Bridge Road,
London SW1V 2SA

Del Rey is part of the Penguin Random House group of companies whose addresses can be found at global.penguinrandomhouse.com

Originally self-published in 2014 by Adrian J Walker
This edition published in 2016 by Del Rey

www.eburypublishing.co.uk

A CIP catalogue record for this book is available from the British Library

ISBN 9781785032660

Typeset in India by Thomson Digital Pvt Ltd, Noida, Delhi

Printed and bound in Great Britain by Clays Ltd, St Ives PLC

Penguin Random House is committed to a sustainable future for our business, our readers and our planet. This book is made from Forest Stewardship Council® certified paper.

Adrian J Walker was born in the bush suburbs of Sydney, Australia in the mid '70s. After his father found a camper van in a ditch, he renovated it and moved his family back to the UK, where Adrian was raised. Ever since he can remember, Adrian has been interested in three things: words, music and technology, and when he graduated from the University of Leeds, he found a career in software.

He lives in London with his wife and two children. To find out more visit: www.adrianjwalker.com

'Ridiculously gripping straight from the start' Jenny Colgan

'A page-turning thriller with a pace as relentless as the characters' feet hitting the pavement. A deft look into the mind of a man who needs the near-destruction of the world to show him what truly matters' Laura Lam, author of *False Hearts*

'A really fun, engaging, exciting and compassionate take on a familiar scenario: the apocalypse ... Highly recommended' David Owen, Carnegie longlisted author of *Panther*

For Debbie,
Bailey and Joseph

Belief

Beliefs are strange. Things of certainty about things uncertain. Take mine, for example. I believe there are graves in the field next to the house where I live. I stop at the fence every morning and I look at three lashed crosses standing crooked against the sea, and I believe I know who is buried beneath them.

But I can't be sure. So I believe instead. I suppose I could dig them up, but, as I see it, there are only two ways that little enterprise can end and neither of them is particularly palatable. Besides, if you have to go round digging up graves to prove your own sanity then you've probably already lost it.

This house, and the cliff to which it clings, is falling down. I believe that I came here on a road that was drowning in mud, that I climbed stairs from a deserted beach to join that road, that I swam to that beach from a small boat and sat there shivering beneath a gathering storm, watching the boat sail back the way it had come. I believe that I arrived at that boat after following a series of roads through a country that was torn apart, washed away and burned down to its raw rock. I believe that I wasn't alone.

My memory stretches into the past like this, filament thin, a string of flickering flames, each one connected to the next. Some burn strong and bright, others barely glimmer.

The line between any two points in your life is liable to be strange and unfathomable, a tangle of chance and tedium.

But some points seem to have clearer connections, even ones that are far from each other, as if they have a direct line that bypasses the normal run of time. I remember things that no longer make any sense; events from yesterday that may as well have happened to a different person. Other things from many years ago still seem to be echoing now. I can smell Beth's perfume in that crowded party and feel the warmth of her knee as she pressed it mischievously against mine, telling me that this was going to lead somewhere else, that her face was going to be a part of my life from then on. I can still hear the clatter of metal and the squeak of the hospital bed as Alice was passed to me, still feel the bucket inside of me emptying, the panic rising in my breath as Beth's was filled with relief in her final contractions.

I can still feel the sun of an English summer, smell the warm grass that brushed against my boyhood face, hear my mother's voice calling beneath the gentle hum of a single-engined aeroplane.

I believe what I believe to make life less terrifying. That's all beliefs are: stories we tell ourselves to stop being afraid. Beliefs have very little to do with the truth.

I don't know. Belief, memory, fear – these things hold you back, weigh you down, stop you moving. And I need to get moving. I need to stop thinking about this stuff. That's what Harvey would say – *stop thinking, keep moving*. But it's hard to stop thinking when there's nobody else but you and a candle and an old house on the crumbling coast of a ruined country. Maybe that's why I'm writing this down – so I can stop thinking about it and get moving.

So I need a place to start. I may as well start at the end.

The End

I heard my name called. Once, twice, then a third time louder. I jerked awake. I was sitting down; my arms were folded, stiff with inaction. The air was full of noise and movement. Screams, colours flashing by, something tugging at my trouser leg. I tried to focus. A red, urgent face was looking down on me, shouting.

'*Ed!*'

I croaked something, prised my lips apart and tried to work some moisture back into the foul pit that was my mouth. Beth gradually came into focus. She sighed and looked me up and down, blew a wet ringlet of hair from her forehead. A vague mixture of disappointment and disgust flickered across her face.

'Look after Arthur,' she said. I frowned. 'Our son,' she said. 'Your *heir*.' She pulled back her lips on this last word. I glanced down at Arthur, halfway up my shin, eyes wide as he prepared to attach his gums to my knee. 'I'm taking Alice on the big slide.'

It was Saturday afternoon, the day before it happened. I was badly hungover from after-work beers and we were at Cheeky Monkeys, probably the worst place to find yourself in such a state. Cheeky Monkeys was a vast indoor soft-play arena of gigantic foam climbing frames, nets, plastic slides and – most notably – children. A hundred or more of them, fully fuelled, fully wired, clambering, crawling, clawing and yowling up ladders, across rope bridges and around the padded maze. Parents trailed behind them, lumbering on all fours through the hot fug of their own offspring like damned souls in some long-forgotten circle of hell. Others, those who had been temporarily spared this doom, stood about in groups drinking tea and energy drinks; women with dark-ringed eyes compared notes and cackled, packs of men grinned like loons, as they rushed to take photographs of their little ones on their phones, their bellies bursting through T-shirts designed for teenagers.

Or men sat in the corner, like me, trying to sleep off the nine pints of strong lager that were still dribbling through an empty stomach.

I picked up Arthur and got to my feet, and was immediately hit by a head rush that sent me careering into a table of three scowling teenage mothers. One tutted. I mumbled some apology and staggered away from them, dropped Arthur into the baby's section and fell back into my seat again, breathless. I watched him. He looked around for a bit, then crawled over to another little boy and began a wordless dispute over a plastic hammer. Another child cried as she was pushed head first off a bean bag by a red-faced sibling. Everywhere I looked there was some kind of conflict, infants disagreeing, trying to lay their own boundaries, little souls crashing together. All that noise and clamour; life beginning as it meant to go on – a struggle. Fighting down my own stale bile, I watched it all and wondered what any man might wonder at any given moment of his life: how the hell did I get here?

The truth was that I was thirty-five and caught in my own headlock. I believed that I – Edgar Hill, husband, father of two young children, homeowner, Englishman, full-time employee of a large, self-serving corporation, the name of which was soon to be scorched forever from its office walls – was the product of a sick environment, a civilisation that had failed beyond hope. I wondered daily how we had ever even made it this far. It was a joke, pointless. How could we look after a planet when we couldn't even look after our own countries, our own towns, our own communities?

Our own families. Our own selves.

Our own bodies. Our own heads.

I was only halfway to the age when it's OK to feel lethargic, cold, bitter and confused, and yet I felt those things every minute of every day. I was overweight. I ate double portions, drank double measures, avoided exercise. I was inflating like a balloon on an abandoned gas cylinder. My world perplexed me – every day was a haze of confusion. My job grated my very core. My marriage gave me vertigo. And my kids … well … I wasn't what you'd call the most-engaged father. I went through the motions alright, but let's just say there are lots of urgent things you can find to do around the home and it's amazing how long it can take sometimes to put out the bins. Don't get me wrong, I loved my wife and I loved my kids, but that doesn't mean to say I had to be happy about it. For me, then at least, being a husband and father meant being simultaneously exhausted and terrified. I was like a man on a cliff edge, nodding off.

Love my wife. *Love* my kids. You have to take care with your tenses when the world ends.

Later, after the hell of Cheeky Monkeys, we drove home on roads shimmering with heat. The sky had that bright and colourless sheen that you only see in cities during the summer. The volume of traffic had tripled for the weather. We got stuck at a roundabout and I watched through my open window as car after car swept onto it from the right, blocking our path. There was no end to them, they just kept coming. Alice was screaming in the back about some vague injustice while Beth, twisted back in her seat, tried to placate her. Arthur started up too. Horns blared out behind me to get going, but there was no room for me to move. I sat there, helpless, as the traffic mounted behind. The kids' yells got worse and I felt Beth bristling next to me. Still the cars sped by, endless, a swollen sea of souls washing past the windscreen. I lost focus on the stream of traffic and let the sound of car horns, engines and screams merge until all around me was a smear of colour and noise. I closed my eyes and saw the earth from above, the biosphere stretched across its surface like cling film and the human race like mayonnaise trapped within. Bacteria, sludge; an ever-expanding mass with nowhere to go.

'ED! GO! GO NOW!'

'Mumeeeeeee!'

I pulled out, the car stalled, a BMW X5 screeched to a halt by our bonnet and the pinched-faced, platinum-blonde horror of a woman behind the wheel began shouting and banging her hands on the dashboard. Her husband wagged a loose, open fist at me, sneering with a mouth full of greasy dead animal matter. More car horns, more screams. I raised a hand in apology and pulled away.

The truth is I was tired of it all. I was tired of the clamour and the din of a world that made less sense by the day and a life that had me just where it wanted. The truth is that the end of the world, for me at least, came as a relief.

Perhaps that comes across as heartless or selfish. All those people, all that horror, all that death. But was it just me? Didn't you feel the same? Couldn't you almost hear that collective sigh, sense the world's shoulders loosen? Did you find no comfort in the knowledge that the show was over, that we didn't have to keep it going any more?

Maybe it really was just me, and I suppose it's fair to say I was in a bad place back then. I was struggling. But I kept going, didn't I? I kept stumbling on, putting one foot blindly in front of the other, watching it all, filling my fat face with it all, frowning at it all, wanting it all to just go away.

Which, of course, it did.

I can't tell you exactly what happened. It took a week. One week for the country to plunge from the blissful apathy of a heatwave, through detached concern, into that strange new territory of danger, threat, panic and, finally, oblivion. It doesn't add up when you think about it. I mean, somebody must have known well before then, *must* have. If we can watch stars dying on the other side of the universe and put a robot on Mars (one who's probably now wondering why everything's gone quiet), then surely we could see those things coming.

Maybe those German astrophysics students were right. What did they call themselves? The Watchmen, I think, something like that. I was never that much into social media (all those pleas to like this, share that, validate me, laugh at me, support me, update this or upgrade that – I just couldn't take it) so I'm sketchy on the details, but about a year before it happened The Watchmen announced on Twitter that they'd spotted something odd, something that shouldn't have been there. There was that famous picture they posted of Saturn with some blurry mark on its rings, then another one of a dark smudge across one of Jupiter's moons. The Internet pricked up its ears. NASA responded with just a few curt dismissals, but you could tell something wasn't right. Some celebrities got involved and they tried to get some scientific muscle behind them to corroborate what they'd found. Still nothing from NASA, and then they went quiet. And then there were conspiracy theories. And then they were forgotten about. Because there was a new series of *Big* fucking *Brother*, I expect.

Then a year went by and we were in a heatwave and that was all anyone had to talk about. And then everything happened very quickly. The survivors will always remember that week. In Scotland, any kind of appearance by the sun makes the front page, so that Monday – the one before it happened – the front pages were full of grins, short skirts and bikinis. The only real story was the happy threat of a hosepipe ban. Then an undercurrent appeared in the headlines around Wednesday: something odd, distant, unrelated to the heat. The news bulletins were so disjointed and confused that the mistakes were talked about more than the actual content of what they were trying to convey: that something very bad might be about to happen.

We laughed. Nobody really bought it. It was summer, it was hot; this had to be a joke, some kind of reality TV prank. That's what people said: 'It's a joke.' I think the supermarkets had a brief surge of cheery panic buyers, but hardly anyone really grasped what was happening. We're idiots. Creatures of denial who have learned not to be afraid of our closets. We need to see the monster in the room before we scream.

The monster burst in on Sunday. There was that final heart-stopping headline, there were those two blunt and terrifying words, capital letters, black on white. And *that's* when we finally got it, with no time left to prepare.

I'm not saying I thought it was a good thing and I'm not saying I thought it wasn't tragic. I'm just saying: I thought we had it coming. We'd had it coming for a long time.

I don't know what happened. Maybe the powers that be knew, maybe they didn't. Maybe they just didn't have the right telescope, maybe those things were just too small to see or track. Or maybe – just maybe – they realised we were fucked. Maybe they realised there was no way out and wanted us to enjoy the last few months we had of normality. That seems like a nice idea.

The plain fact is I don't know. All I know is that one minute you're watching your three-year-old daughter scrambling up a soft play fun-pipe, and the next you're hurling her into the cellar and slamming the hatch behind you.

All I know is that the end – in the end – came from the skies.

That Sunday I awoke from a long and difficult dream about cows. A small herd of them were stuck inside a pen, struggling to escape, their hooves sliding from each other's hides. Four or five bald men in white coats were standing around them with clipboards, watching them, prodding them, taking notes. The cows were getting more and more panicky, before one let out an almighty guttural *MEEEEEEEERRRR* and I almost fell out of bed. The sound still rang in my ears as I blinked in the low light and listened to my heart struggling for calm.

I looked at the clock. It was 5 a.m. and Arthur's cries were piercing the wall behind our bed. Beth groaned and elbowed my ribs. Arthur was still feeding through the night and waking early, so this was my shift, this was what I brought to the table. When his older sister, Alice, was born, I had made it very clear to Beth, very early in the proceedings, that *I* was the one who had to get up for work in the morning, that *I* was the one who needed my sleep, so no, *I* would most certainly not be helping with night feeds. I don't think I'm the first man to have ever pulled this one. It's a common enough shirk, one that conveniently ignores what *work* actually means for most men – i.e. comfy seats, tea and coffee, biscuits, nice food, adult conversation, the occasional pretty girl to ogle at, the Internet, sealed toilet cubicles where you can catch a few winks without anyone noticing. *Work*. Not like being at home breastfeeding a newborn and entertaining a two-year-old all day.

What work actually *meant* . . . *those* days. Careful with those tenses.

Anyway, yes, I hold my hand up, guilty again. I insisted on my right to sleep. Beth conceded, but only on the proviso that I took the early shift on Saturdays and Sundays. I couldn't really argue with her. There's only so much you can push it with a woman who's just given birth.

I grumbled something and pulled back the duvet, knocking the empty glass of water from my bedside table. Another groan from Beth. 'Sorry,' I muttered.

These early starts had been going on since Christmas. We had tried all the advice in the books, from friends and family.

'Let him cry it out', 'Change the bedtime routine', 'Put some water in his cot', 'Change his day-time naps', 'Fill him up with Weetabix before bedtime'. Or, from those who weren't parents: 'Can't you just ignore him?' Sure, ignore him. Ignore the thunderous screams of rage and the cot hammering against the wall as your wife's body stiffens with fury in the bed next to you, exhausted after another night of fragmented sleep.

We had called a midwife out in January. 'The main thing is not to worry,' she had said, one palm laid carefully on Beth's knee so as to avoid the various stains of sick, stewed apple and sour breast milk. 'It's just a phase, he'll grow out of it when he's good and ready.'

Beth had nodded back dutifully, sobbing quietly as Arthur drained her bruised, broken left nipple for the third time that morning. I'd been watching from the kitchen as I tried to cram cold porridge into Alice's bawling mouth. A metre of snow outside, still dark at 8.30 a.m., wondering again why we were living in fucking Scotland.

What if this all just went away? I had thought. *What if this all just blew away*?

I cringe when I remember how hard I thought life was back then. With no sleep, no sex, no time, no respite. Honestly, I thought having kids was hell. But Beth was the one who did it all. She was the one who took it all on, growing them, giving birth to them, changing more than her fair share of filthy nappies, never complaining when I snuck off to the pub or stayed up late watching telly, never complaining when I fell into bed beside her in the middle of the night, my breath heavy with wine. Beth didn't drink because of the breastfeeding, but I pretty much drank every night. I reasoned that it was my right as a tired parent, that I worked all week to provide for my family and that it helped me relax. I told myself that a glass or two on week nights and a bit more at the weekend was fine and perfectly healthy. In reality I was pushing at least a bottle a night and two on a Saturday, not to mention the pints after work on a Friday. And exercise – who had time for that with a nine-to-five and two children? The same tired, old excuses. The truth was that, aside from a minor decrease in sleep, my body had found a way of getting what it wanted: a sedentary life with plenty of carbohydrates and relaxants. And I gave in. I learned to avoid mirrors, learned to ignore the dull shock of seeing paunch, jowls and breasts growing day by day.

I made it easy on myself, *very* easy. And that made it hard on Beth.

I have to keep telling myself not to look back so much. I'll always regret not being a better father, a better husband, but I have to look forward or else I won't get to the place I'm going and I need beyond everything else to get there. The past is a foreign country, someone once said. They do things differently there. My past – everyone's past – is now a different planet. It's so different it almost makes no sense to remember it.

But still, everyone remembers that day.

'It's just a phase,' the midwife had said on that dark winter's day all those months before. 'He'll grow out of it when he's good and ready.'

Just a phase. A phase that saved our lives.

As I waited for the microwave to heat up Arthur's milk, I poured myself a glass of water, opened the back door and stepped out onto the deck. It was another sunny day and already warm. Arthur flinched at the low sun and snuggled into my neck, breathing little stuttering breaths in my ear as I closed my eyes and let the warm light flood over my face. I actually felt happy. I had another hangover, of course (wine and telly on my own the night before), but I didn't mind being up so early. Maybe it was the vitamin D, maybe I was still a little drunk from the night before, or maybe it was just holding my son in a warm sunrise when nobody else was around, I don't know. Cool, still air, warm sun, the distant roar of a road somewhere … I just felt happy. That's probably my last real memory of anything normal.

As I sat on the deck enjoying the warm sunshine and my son's quiet gurgles in my ear, a breeze suddenly whipped up around us. The plants gave a fierce rustle. The tree in the corner of the garden creaked and its branches twisted and bowed momentarily out of shape. The windows in the house rattled violently. The windows in the houses opposite rattled too. The kitchen door swung open and banged against the cupboards. It stopped. Behind the breeze came a very deep and distant rumble. A split second and then it was calm again.

Arthur gasped and looked about wide-eyed.

'What was that, Art?' I said, waggling his hand. 'What was that?'

He giggled.

What the fuck was *that?*

The microwave beeped inside.

Arthur gave a little shout and pulled his hand out of mine to thwack my nose. He grinned. I grinned back.

'Come on then, buddy,' I said, and we went inside.

On the sofa, I plugged the milk bottle into Arthur's mouth with one hand and found the remote with the other. I stopped.

My thumb hovered over the red button. Something jarred. Some flickering half-memory. I couldn't place it at the time, but I would soon enough.

Arthur sucked happily on his bottle and I pressed the 'on' button.

Nothing.

BBC2.

Nothing.

ITV, Channel 4, Sky. Nothing.

This wasn't unusual; our Sky box sometimes crashed and just needed a reboot. Still, a little red warning light flashed in my mind and gave me an uncomfortable feeling in my gut.

Arthur gurgled in dismay as the teat slipped from his mouth. I let the bottle drop to the floor and he squealed as I put him back on the sofa behind me. I scrabbled on the floor to the Sky box, took out the card and held the power button. Waited ten seconds, twenty seconds for the box to reboot. Arthur sounded a low warning note behind me, preparing for a full meltdown if I didn't return with his milk. The box finally came back to life and began its cosy introduction video. I grabbed the remote and sat back against the sofa, thumbing through the channels, trying each one in turn, moving through the international news stations: BBC World, CNN, Al Jazeera, the shopping channels, religious, music, adult ... all dead.

I told myself not to panic. All this meant was that Sky was out, maybe just in our area, maybe even just our dish. Still that half memory in the back of my mind, something I should remember ...

Arthur's warning note began to crescendo, so I lifted him down to the floor with me and reinserted his bottle. As he continued his disgruntled sucking, I took out my phone to see if I could get a connection on our Wi-Fi. Nothing. Broadband was out and I could never get a phone signal in the house anyway. I heard my son's last dry sucks as the bottle emptied.

'Come on, Artie,' I said, standing up. 'Let's take a stroll, mate.'

I slung Arthur in his backpack and hauled him onto my shoulders, stepped into my flip-flops and left through the back garden. We lived in Bonaly, a quiet scattering of small new-builds and gigantic mansions five miles south of Edinburgh at the foot of the Pentland Hills. Our house was a new-build, one of about twenty or so lined in terraces that faced each other across a small path. It was a nice area and they were nice enough houses, but cheap, so we didn't have a lot of space. *This is close living*, Beth's dad had grumbled when he first came to visit.

I walked down the main road trying to find a signal on my phone. It was a steep hill lined with huge houses set back behind long, gravel drives. Other roads fed off it: wide, tree-lined, well-paved cul-de-sacs with even grander properties spaced out along them. They had security gates, CCTV, triple garages, secluded gardens with ponds and trampolines. Some were styled with colonial wood, some like American bunkers. Beth was pregnant with Alice when we had first moved to Bonaly. We used to take walks around these roads, naming the most impressive one 'Ambition Drive'. We'd go arm-in-arm along it, seeing who could say the most offensive words the loudest as we passed by the gardens.

'Fanny batter.'

'Bub sucks.'

'Cunt bubbles.'

'Dick cheese.'

It was Ambition Drive I was walking along when I first truly started to feel that something was definitely wrong. I heard a motorised garage door open. It was still before six, usually too early for most people to be up. Then I heard a woman cry. It was a cry of fear. A child yelping, a man shouting. Then the door banging shut, then silence again.

I walked on slowly. I heard a glass break from an upstairs window. Loud, rattling footsteps on wooden stairs. Another bang, then silence again. A police siren whooped twice, far in the distance, possibly in Edinburgh itself.

There was something wrong with the silence, but I couldn't put my finger on it. Even though it was early on a Sunday, it was not usually this quiet. Something was missing.

Birdsong.

The birds. The birds were missing.

I looked up and scanned the tall trees for signs of life. The branches were perfectly still and empty. The bushes, usually trembling with tits and starlings at this time of year, were deathly quiet.

I heard gravel scrabbling and a dog's yelps behind me. I turned to see a golden retriever sprawled on a drive. It was looking over its shoulder at what I presumed was its owner, a large, bare-footed man in a crumpled shirt and no trousers who was hurrying back to the house. I had met him once at a neighbour's Hogmanay party when we first moved in. He had been guarded, predatory, scanning the room for opportunity. Some guests, mainly men (those in the larger houses, I imagined), he met with a single heavy tanned-palm slap to their shoulder and a loud boom of acceptance. When the circulation of the party threw the two of us into proximity, he met me with something halfway between revulsion and curiosity. I was not massively successful and therefore a strange thing, an alien. No shares, no property portfolio, no deals to close. What was there to talk about?

His wife had been stood in the corner, a small porcelain shadow of a woman sipping Bacardi in silence. They both had that strange, thick smell of wealth.

He caught my eye as he turned. He was snarling as he slammed the great oak door behind him. The dog whimpered and sat up, looking about in bewilderment. He saw me and gave a little wag of his tail, licking his chops. Arthur gave a gleeful hoot behind me. Why would he be putting a dog out at this time in the morning?

No room for a dog. Not any more.

That memory still flickered. That little red warning light in my cranium, that lurch in my belly.

At the bottom of the hill, I turned right onto the main road. There was no traffic, which wasn't unusual at that time of day. Suddenly a Range Rover tore out of nowhere and roared past me at sixty, maybe seventy miles an hour. I glanced four heads inside, a family. The father's fists were gripping the wheel and the mother had her head in her hands in the passenger seat. A discarded crisp packet was swept up in the tailwind as the car disappeared. It danced on the eddies for a few seconds before settling on the stone wall by the side of the road where it lay still, winking sunlight at me from its creases.

I couldn't find a signal. I followed the main road for a while and turned right, then right again onto the street back to our house.

It was after six o'clock by the time I reached the shop opposite our terrace. It was the only shop within a mile of the house. It should have been open at this time but the metal shutters were still down. I peered through the window to see if I could spot Jabbar, the owner, sorting through the morning papers, pushing the new milk to the back of the fridges so he could sell off the old stuff first. Jabbar was an overweight Pakistani who ran the shop with his brother. It was independent, not part of a chain, so it was filled with dusty cans and bottles already well past their sell-by dates and twice their RRP. Jabbar and his brother lived with their wives and kids in the house that joined onto the back. Close living.

There were no lights on, no sound. The door through to the house was shut.

'Jabbar,' I shouted through the shutter. 'Hey, Jabbar!'

I thought I saw some eyes dart at me through the glass panel of the door into the house, but when I looked again they were gone.

'Morning,' I heard somebody say behind me.

I turned around and saw Mark standing in shorts and sandals, carrying his daughter Mary in a backpack like Arthur's. She was about Arthur's age. Mark and I had met through the antenatal group that Beth had made me go to when she was pregnant with Alice. She'd made friends with three or four of the girls, her 'support network' as she liked to call them, who quickly huddled into regular Friday coffee mornings and unabashed texts about breast milk, cracked nipples and vaginal tearing. The husbands dutifully met on the fringes, nodding silently at each other at birthday parties, going for the occasional pint where we'd sit and discuss things like sport, work, news – trivial safe-houses, anything *but* the reason we were thrown together. Yes, there was the odd update on how the respective wives were doing, how the sons and daughters were growing every day, little bundles of joy that they were ... but we were each aware that we didn't want, didn't *need*, that level of discussion in our lives. We were really just a bunch of strangers sharing a pub table.

I had been the only English one there. 'We won't hold that against you!' boomed Mark one night in the pub, slapping me on the back and repeating the joke I'd heard a thousand times since moving north. Mark and I got on OK, despite the fact that he was a road-cyclist and therefore a bastard, being much fitter and healthier than me. He had always threatened to take me out cycling. I always made excuses. I sucked in my stomach when I saw him.

'Mark,' I said. 'Hey. Hi, Mary.'

I turned back to the shop and peered through the window. Mark joined me.

'What's going on?' he said.

'You tell me,' I said. 'Jabba the Hutt's hiding in there.'

Mark banged a fist on the shutters.

'Jabba! Come out of there you fat bastard!'

Nothing from inside. We stepped back.

'Weird,' said Mark.

'Aha,' I said.

Mark nodded up at the hills at the top of the road.

'I just passed a load of squaddies from the barracks running up to the Pentlands.'

'Training?'

'Didn't look like it. They were all over the place, no leader. Some had two guns.'

'Have you noticed the birds?' I said.

'Aye. Weird. Any signal?'

'No, you?'

'Nada.'

'Our telly's out as well.'

'Ours too; must be a problem with the cable, I guess.'

'We're on Sky.'

We looked at each other. It was still quiet, still warm. There are times when I wished I'd savoured that feeling more.

'Any newspapers?' said Mark.

'No, the van always drops them here before six though. Jabba's usually sorting through them by now.'

We looked around the pavement. There was nothing there so we walked round to the back door of the house. There on the ground was a fat stack of *Sunday Times* newspapers bound up with string.

Mark tore the invoice sheet – someone had incredibly still thought to include it, even with what lay within – and pulled out the first in the pile. It was thin. Only two sheets thick, not the usual hundred leaf wad you get on a Sunday. There was nothing on the front apart from the *Sunday Times* logo and a single headline taking up the entire page.

Two blunt and terrifying words.

STRIKE IMMINENT

Then I remembered. I remembered everything.

I remembered the night before, pushing myself up from the sofa and knocking the dregs from the second empty bottle of Shiraz onto the carpet. I remembered scrubbing the stain with a cloth. I remembered the light in the room suddenly changing as a giant BBC logo filled the television screen. I remembered the silence in the studio, the flustered looks on the newsreaders' faces. I remembered that the female presenter had no make-up on, that the male had his sleeves rolled up as he leafed through the stacks of A4 sheets on his desk. I remembered that he stammered, sweated, blurted out words like 'data', 'miscalculation', 'trajectory', then 'indoors' and 'vigilant'. I remembered him putting his head in his hands, his co-host covering her mouth, then a loud thumping sound and the camera seeming to wobble, footsteps running away on the studio floor. Then the picture flickered and a high-pitched tone sounded like a test card. I remembered words appearing on the screen, white letters on primary red:

STRIKE IMMINENT
STAY INDOORS

I remembered blundering up the stairs, blinking, trying to stop my head from swimming, wine and bile rising in my throat. I remembered calling Beth's name. I remembered falling through Arthur's door, falling against his cot, Beth's face full of recrimination as she looked up from the chair where she was sitting feeding him. I remember struggling for words, slurring, trying to explain something even I didn't understand. I remembered her disappointed eyes and her face flat as she told me to get out of the room. I remembered protesting, trying to explain. I remembered her shaking her head, telling me that I was drunk and she didn't want me near him. I remembered staggering through to our room, waiting for Beth to come through, trying to make sense of things, knowing that I should be doing something.

I remembered closing my eyes. I remembered waking up to Arthur's cries.

Strike imminent. A multiple asteroid strike on the United Kingdom is imminent.

Mark and I stared at the words for a few seconds before they made sense and I had processed my own dull memory of the night before.

'"Strike"?' said Mark. 'Does that mean what I think it does?'

I didn't answer. Simultaneously we ran back round to the front of the shop. We started banging on the shutters.

'Jabbar! Jabbar! Open up! Fucking open up!'

We kept hammering and shouting until we saw those eyes again behind the door. Jabbar hiding. We hammered louder.

Jabbar started waving us away. His eyes were set, determined, no longer the genial face of the local tradesman. We kept banging on the shutters and Arthur and Mary joined in the game with squeals and shouts behind us. Eventually the door behind the counter opened and Jabbar stormed up to the shutters.

'Go away!' he said, flicking his hand at us. He looked terrified. 'Go on! Clear off! I'm not open!'

'Look,' I said. I held up the paper and pointed at the headline.

'What's this? Are there any more papers?'

Jabbar stared at the words and then back at us. His fat cheeks were damp with sweat. Behind him I could see a woman looking at us, cowering in the doorway to the house.

She was holding a crying baby. Behind her were Jabbar's two brothers. *Close living.*

One of the brothers was holding a portable radio close to his ear, his fist pressed against his lips.

Jabbar shook his head violently,

'No,' he said. 'Nothing.'

I looked back at his brother.

'Mark,' I said. 'Look.'

He was looking down at his feet, the radio still pressed to his ear and his hand across his eyes.

'Jabbar,' growled Mark. 'What do you know?'

I stabbed the paper.

'What does "imminent" mean, Jabbar?'

Jabbar faltered, shaking, his eyes flicking between us both.

'It's already happened,' he hissed. 'They're already here.'

I remembered the sudden gust of wind on the deck, the bending branches, the rumble. *What was that?*

An aftershock. How far away? Glasgow? London?

'Now go away! Get ...'

But Mark and I had turned from the shutters. Jabbar peered up through the slats as well. Far away, we heard a low, nasal drone. It was an ancient sound, like a rusted handle turned on something that had not been used in a long time. A sound that was not supposed to be heard any more, a sound that belonged in a different century. It began to rise slowly in pitch till it reached and held its hideous, gut-wrenching howl.

An air-raid siren. A fucking air-raid siren.

Jabbar sprang back from the shutters and fled back through the shop. Mark and I shared one last look and then bolted in opposite directions.

'Beth!' I cried as I ran, Arthur laughing in blissful ignorance as he shoogled in his backpack.

'Get up! Get Alice up!'

I sped through the archway and onto the path. The siren was beginning its first awful dive back down. Where the hell did Bonaly have an air-raid siren? The barracks, I guessed. It echoed off the hills and howled through the empty streets; a demented, sickening sound that had only ever meant one thing and one thing only: Take cover, hell is coming, things are about to get VERY bad.

As I crossed the road, I heard the banished dog from down the road join in the howl. Some weeks later, I would suddenly remember this noise in the middle of the night and weep, actually weep, holding my hands to my face so I didn't wake and upset Beth and the kids.

'Beth!' I screamed.

I saw people at windows now, woken by the siren. Tangled dressing gowns, puffy, confused faces frowning in the light. The sun that had seemed so warm and welcoming before was now vivid and terrible.

'Get up! We're . . .'

The words actually caught in my throat. Ridiculous. I felt dizzy, the way you do when you're a child about to call out for your parents in the night.

'. . . going to be hit!'

My mind reeled. *Think. What do you do? What did those government broadcasts tell you to do? How do I arm myself? How do I survive?*

It occurred to me that I had subconsciously been preparing for this. Even in those last few strange and unfathomable days, a check-list had been forming in my mind, an old program from my youth kicking into life. In the 80s, nuclear war was absolutely, positively, 100 per cent how I was going to die. Not asteroids, and certainly none of this slow climate-change bollocks. The real deal. You were going to evaporate in an atomic blast: finished, done, end of. Then Aids came along and, if you were a teenager like me, your worries turned to the fact that death was now lurking within every pleated skirt and behind every cotton gusset. Now sex was going to kill you.

I could deal with AIDS. I knew I wasn't getting to have sex any time soon anyway, not with my face looking like an arse smeared with jam. But the nuclear threat was a different matter. That was real terror. And so began my first mini-obsession since my five-year-old self first heard that something called a Tyrannosaurus rex used to exist. I watched all the TV series, read all the books and kept all the survival pamphlets on how to make a home-made fallout shelter. I was fascinated and terrified. That bit in *When the Wind Blows* when the old couple walk out and think the smell of scorched human flesh is somebody cooking a Sunday roast gave me nightmares for a week.

Although I had long since stopped being hung up on the apocalypse, that part of my brain had started making a list as soon as the first reports of trouble came in. I think it always had done. Every major catastrophe, every natural disaster, every impending conflict gave me a little childish thrill. *This is it*, I would think with nothing short of glee. *This could be the one.* The Millennium Bug, 9/11, the London Bombings, Iraq, Afghanistan, the London Riots ...

There was no historical name for this one. This was just it. The End.

My apocalypse-obsessed teenager passed me up a list.

Water. Food. Medical Supplies. Light. Shelter. Protection.

Shelter. The cellar.

The houses on the terrace opposite ours had been built to a different design. They were wider and had five bedrooms rather than our two. The rooms were more spacious with higher ceilings and bigger windows; ours were just on the wrong side of poky and dark. There was a floored loft that you could stand up in. Some of the owners had built up into them to create a sixth room: the row of roofs now had dormer windows set into their tiles. Our loft was small and dark, enough for storage but nothing else. They were the posh houses. We were the cheap seats.

But what we did have – and what they didn't – was a cellar.

Our kitchen had a small walk-in pantry. For some strange reason – it probably appealed to her heightened nesting instinct – Beth thought that this was just about the best thing ever. It didn't have the same effect on me, of course, but in its floor was a hatch that led down some rough, pine steps into a space that was about the same size as the kitchen above it. It wasn't much, not very big. But it was underground.

'Uh-oh,' said Beth when the estate agent lifted the hatch. 'Man cave alert.'

Man caves. Sheds, garages, studies, attics, cellars. Places for 'men' – or at least their twenty-first century equivalents – to hide. To tinker, potter, be creative, build things, hammer bits of wood, listen to the music that their families hate.

Drink, smoke, look at pornography, masturbate.

The subtext of the man cave, of course, is that men don't want to spend any time with their families. For some reason this is perfectly acceptable; every man deserves his cave.

It is my right as a tired parent.

I'm fairly sure these two small, windowless symbols of domesticity – airy female bliss for Beth; dark male seclusion for me – were the real reasons we bought the house. But in the end the pantry was where we stored all the food we didn't eat and the cellar was where we kept the hoover and the empty wine bottles. I rarely went down there.

I leapt up the steps to the deck and burst through the back door, nearly tearing Arthur off my back in the process.

'Beth!' I bellowed up the stairs. 'Get up! Get Alice up!'

Arthur bawled, the game no longer fun. I swung him off my shoulders and propped him up, still in his backpack against the kitchen sink.

Thumping feet down the stairs.

'Beth! Oh, thank fuck, you're up.'

I'd never been more proud of her. She stood in the kitchen door, wide-eyed, pale, with Alice in her arms, dressed and still groggy from sleep.

'What's happening?' she said.

I started opening and closing cupboards.

Shelter. Water. Food. Medicine.

'Daddy,' said Alice, rubbing her eyes. 'Arthur's crying, Daddy.'

'I know, sweetheart,' I said. I picked up one of the recycling boxes by the door and started dragging tins and packets from the shelves into it. We were low on supplies; Sunday was our big shop day.

A bottle of balsamic vinegar landed on a tin of tomato soup. I picked it up and stared at it. It seemed poignant somehow, this totem of middle class, now a useless dark liquor: no good to drink, no nutritional value. I left it where it was and piled more things on top.

'What does that siren mean?' said Beth.

'Daddeee, Arthur's cryyyyiing.'

Rice, pasta, beans, tinned fruit, chocolate.

'Ed,' said Beth again. 'Please, I'm scared.'

I slid the box towards the pantry and started filling another.

'We need to get down in the cellar,' I said. 'Now. Get blankets, duvets, clothes for the kids.'

'What? But what . . .?'

I turned on her.

'NOW, Beth!'

Arthur stopped crying. It was all quiet apart from the wail of the siren outside. Then a door banging, a man shouting, a woman crying, a loud screech of car's tyres as it sped away.

'How . . . how long?' Beth said. She was making calculations. The same ones she used to pack up the mountain of kids' equipment into the car when we went away for the weekend.

I shook my head. *I don't know.*

Beth carefully placed Alice down and ran upstairs.

I pulled out the bottom drawer and emptied the lot into the second box. Bits of string, crumpled photographs, bulldog clips, screwdrivers, dead batteries, candles, takeaway menus, spare keys, cigarettes, lighters; all the detritus of kitchen life fell into the box.

Alice was now twirling with her hands in the air and singing.

'Look after your brother, sweetheart,' I said.

Alice sighed and slumped her shoulders, her 'teenager's sigh' we called it, though she was only three. She trudged over to Arthur as if I'd asked her to do her homework.

'Daddy, I want my milk,' she grumbled.

I found a first-aid kit and threw it in the box along with some plasters. I could hear Beth thumping about above me, pulling things out of drawers and cupboards. Two large boxes of nappies thumped at the bottom of the stairs.

'Daddeee . . .'

How much time do we have? Hours? Minutes?

I guessed minutes.

'Daddeeeeee . . .'

Think. What next?

Water.

I once saw a film about a girl who survives an apocalyptic event. It was some unnamed worldwide cataclysm; we weren't told the details. She lives on this farm in middle America and when it all starts happening the first thing her father does is turn on all the taps in the house. She says, 'What's happening Daddy? and he replies 'I don't know honey, I don't know,' and starts pelting round the rooms filling baths and sinks.

I shouted up the stairs.

'Fill the bath, Beth!'

'Znot basstime Daddeee!' shouted Alice, twirling in the sunlight that was still streaming through the kitchen window.

There were more thumps from above. Beth screamed something unintelligible.

'Keep the taps on!'

'Silleeee Daddeeeee woo woo wooo!'

I had a sudden vision of our house destroyed. Brown air, heavy cloud, nothing but dust, brick and bent iron. Perched on top of the rubble is our bath. It's a dry, scorched husk. The taps are stretched, black liquorish strings melting over the sides like a Salvador Dalí painting.

Water.

You want to know how long it takes for the fabric of society to break down? I'll tell you. The same time it takes to kick a door down. I once read a book about Japanese veterans remembering the darkness of the Second World War. They seemed like old men with happy families at peace with the world, but they could still recall the hunger that drove them to kill and eat Chinese women. More often than not they would rape them first. Ask anyone who has been in a crowd that becomes too strong, where bodies begin to crush you. Is your first instinct to lift others up, or to trample them down? That beast inside you, the one you think is tethered tightly to the post, the one you've tamed with art, love, prayer, meditation: it's barely muzzled. The knot is weak. The post is brittle. All it takes is two words and a siren to cut it loose.

'Stay here with Mummy, darling,' I said.

'Daddy, where are you going?'

I ran back to Jabbar's shop. There were people gathered there banging on the shutters and shouting for him to open up. Others were gathered around the stack of papers.

I stopped short of the pavement and ran around the back. A few from the front saw me and started to follow.

'Jabbar!' I shouted through the letterbox in the back door. 'All I need is some batteries and water! You've got more than enough in there!'

'Go! Away!' shouted Jabbar from inside.

There was another sudden great gust of wind. The tall trees down the hill creaked painfully as their branches crumpled. Then the short, deep rumble again. Everyone stopped. Then screams and renewed hammering on the shutters of the shop. Three cars sped past and down the hill. *Where the hell are they going?*

I was aware of people joining me at the door.

'Jabbar!' I shouted one last time. Hearing nothing, I stepped back.

Took a breath.

Kicked the door.

A shock of pain in my ankle made me howl. The door had not shifted. I tried again closer to the lock. This time the wood split and I heard footsteps running from inside. On the third kick, the door swung in and I followed it into Jabbar's hall, pushing his brother into a stack of boxes in the corner.

I couldn't remember the last time I had pushed or punched anyone. Primary school, maybe?

'Get the fuck out of here!' shouted Jabbar as I rounded the corner onto a corridor with a red, floral carpet and cheaply framed pictures. The place was hot, dark and stank of old curry and babies. Jabbar's wife was hiding in a doorway behind Jabbar, who was still sweating profusely.

'I just want batteries and water, Jabbar,' I said, storming up the corridor to the door into the shop. 'Not all of them, just enough for me and my family.'

'No!' said Jabbar, stepping out and squashing me against the wall with his shoulder. 'Get out of my house! Get out!'

His bulbous, wet stomach pressed into my chest as he tried to wrestle me back through the door. His breath was full of hot panic, his eyes wild. Jabbar's brother had picked himself up behind me and was trying to hold back the growing throng at the broken door.

Jabbar's hand was on my face now. I could taste the salt of his rough skin in my mouth. With a surge of effort, I managed to swing back my leg and kicked it hard against his knee. He cried out and fell like lead on the stained carpet, clutching his leg.

'Bastard!' he cried. 'Bastard! Get out! Get out!'

I ran past him and into the shop, grabbing packs of batteries from the shelves and picking up three crates of Highland Spring from a stack on the floor.

Jabbar was still curled up on the floor in the corridor and his brother was now being pushed back by the crowd of people. Our next-door neighbour Calum was the first through. He stared straight past me and elbowed me out of the way and into the shop. Behind him were an old couple I didn't recognise. They walked past me too, the woman flashing me a nervous smile as if we were passing in the street.

Jabbar's brother was on the floor now. Two of the crowd were kicking him and pushing him into one of the rooms. With the batteries balanced on the crates, I marched back down the corridor.

'Bloody bastard!' screamed Jabbar again as I stepped over his fat head. 'You bloody bastard!'

His wife was crouching next to him, holding his head and weeping.

At the end of the corridor I avoided eye contact with any member of what was now a mob. Most ignored me too, but as I got to the door, a man I recognised from one of the houses opposite ours fixed me with a sharp stare.

'Hey,' he said, blocking my path.

He was in his early sixties, perhaps. His daughter had recently given birth and we used to see the whole family quite often having barbecues in the back garden. Beth and I would wave and talk about inviting them over for a play date with Arthur. Frank. I think his name was Frank.

He nodded at the water.

'I need that.'

'There's more in the shop,' I said. I moved towards him, but he grabbed me by the shoulders and pushed me back. He made a lunge for the water but I threw my weight into him and crushed him against the door frame. He made a sound I hadn't heard before. It started with a '*Huhh-uhh-uhh* ...' as the air was pushed out of his lungs, but as I squeezed past him it turned into a comical childish squeal, his face crumpled as I pushed by. Perhaps, out of context, it would have sounded amusing. But this was a man I saw almost every day. I had never shaken his hand. The first and last time I ever had human contact with him, I squeezed his lungs until he made a sound like a child who had been denied chocolate.

Frank fell to the ground and held his chest. I crossed the road, trying to keep the stack of batteries balanced on the water and avoiding two more cars screaming down the hill going fuck knows where.

I had almost reached the path to our house when I saw Mike standing at the corner. Mike was an old widower who lived in a one-bed flat around the corner. He was seventy-three, bald with a white beard and a cheap blue jacket. He smiled and raised a hand.

'Hullo, Edgar,' he said.

'Mike,' I said. 'You need to get inside.'

He leaned forward on his walking stick and peered over my shoulder at the chaos breaking out at the shop.

'Can't you hear the siren, Mike? It's happening, you need to get inside.'

Mike puffed through his nose and flickered a half-smile as if I had just told him a joke he didn't quite get or approve of. He shook his head.

'You take good care now, Edgar,' he said. 'Look after your family.'

Then he took a long, quivering breath and turned his face up to the blue sky.

That long breath, the squeal, the dog's howl, the air-raid siren. These are the sounds that stayed with me, which will always stay with me.

The crates were slipping in my hands. I heard a shout.

'Hey!'

I looked behind. Frank had scrabbled to his knees and was standing in the middle of the road, staring straight at me.

'You!' he said. 'Cellars! You've got cellars!'

Shit.

A few of the other dressing gowns who were clamouring to get into Jabbar's house had turned as well. They were all now looking at me. Frank started to stride across the road. He was almost halfway across when another 4x4 came hurtling down the hill, hitting him square in the side and tossing him up like a rag doll. His broken body somersaulted over a hedge and landed against a dustbin while the car sped on. A few seconds later I heard a crunch of metal, and a chorus of car alarms joined the howls of the siren and the dog that still filled the air.

The others who were following Frank across the road stepped back momentarily. Then they continued across the road, glancing between me, each other and the road uphill.

I bolted up the path and into our garden and hurled the crates of water across the deck and through the kitchen door. I slammed the bolt down on our gate and sprinted up to the kitchen, scooping the batteries from the deck. As I closed the door I saw the others arrive at the gate. They were shaking it and screaming. More had joined them on the path and they were now trying all the gates along our terrace, streaming into the gardens and pummelling the back doors.

I locked ours.

Beth was standing at the open cellar door. She had thrown down the boxes and whatever else she had found and was now standing on the steps holding Arthur with her free arm stretched out to Alice. Alice was standing at the door of the pantry with her hands tucked under her chin, shaking her head.

'Come on, darling,' Beth whispered. 'Come down with Mummy.'

'Noooo,' said Alice.

Alice didn't like the cellar.

Beth was trying to smile.

'Come on,' she said. 'It's an adventure.'

'Nooooo Mummeeeee.'

I heard our bamboo fence start to break and turned to see two of the mob scrambling over it. One had caught his pyjamas on the top and they were torn from his legs as he fell face first into our raspberry bush. He shrieked as the thorns tore into his face, then into his bare legs and groin as he struggled to get to his feet. The woman behind landed on his head and made towards our door.

'Alice!' I shouted. 'Get down in the cellar, *NOW*!'

Alice began a low moan.

'*Ed!*' shouted Beth. 'Don't, you're upsetting her! Come on, darling, Daddy didn't mean it.'

'There's no time! There's no fucking time! Get down there *NOW*!'

Alice's moan rose up like the air-raid siren. The air was now a nightmare of wails and howls of different pitches and intensities. The woman's face was at the door, wild with terror and rage. Others had broken through our gate and were following up behind her. I ran to the cellar door and threw the crates of water down past Beth. I found our Maglite, grabbed it from one of the shelves and pushed it down the back of my shorts. Then I started pushing Alice towards the cellar hatch. She squealed and tried to wriggle away.

'Alice, you need . . .'

'NooooOOOO DADDEEEEE!!'

Bodies were now pressed against our kitchen door, hammering and kicking the glass from top to bottom.

No choice.

'Alice,' I said. 'I'm sorry, darling.'

Beth instinctively ran down the steps with Arthur.

I picked Alice up and dropped her down into the pit. She hit the stone floor with a thud and the air left her tiny lungs with a *huh*.

Silent, winded, she tried carefully to get to her feet, but slipped and fell on her face. As Beth helped her up and brushed her down, Alice whimpered in shock at the betrayal I had just dealt her.

I closed my eyes so I couldn't see the faces at our kitchen window. Then I followed Alice down and went to pull down the hatch.

'I want my bunnies,' she said quietly.

Fuck. The fucking, fucking bunnies.

'Tell me you got her bunnies,' I said to Beth.

'Oh, no, oh, shit,' said Beth. 'Oh, bollocks, they're upstairs in her bed.'

Alice's bunnies went everywhere with her. In bed, in the car, on the sofa, at the table, at nursery. Everywhere. When she had a fall or when she was tired or when she was scared, they were her only source of comfort.

When she was scared. I looked down into the gloom of the cellar.

How long ...?

'My bunnies,' Alice said again, deadpan, no emotion, hand held out, all business.

I weighed up the options. An unknown time spent in the cellar. An unknown time before fuck-knows-what happened to Edinburgh. Faces at the window trying to get in, trying to get to us. One of the square panes of glass in the door broke and a fist came through it.

Suddenly, the air-raid siren stopped. The air around us seemed to lurch in the silence as if we'd all just hurled ourselves over a cliff edge. We were free-falling now, free-falling into whatever came next.

I leapt up the steps and through the kitchen, up the stairs and into Alice's room. My heart thumped in my throat. Everything was eerily quiet after the noise. The dog had stopped. Alice had stopped. Even the mob outside had stopped in momentary confusion.

The bunnies were on Alice's pillow. I grabbed them and turned but stopped as I left for the door. Out of the window, on a branch in our tree, was a single small bird. It was a blue tit perhaps, chirping merrily away and flicking its head about like small birds do. Behind it, far away against the blue sky, I saw something else. A small dark shape that shouldn't be there. Not a plane but something like it. A tiny speck moving quickly, a dark trail behind it. Then more behind that.

I bolted down the stairs and threw Alice's bunnies down to her. She pulled them to her face and began furiously sucking her thumb, rubbing their soft ears against her cheek. I fell down the steps. As I did, I risked one last look at the door. The mob had renewed their attack on it. The first woman had her face and palms squashed against the glass. Fifteen or twenty others surrounded her, their pummelling fists sometimes connecting with the back of her skull.

By her side was a little girl not much older than Alice. She was wearing a nightie and holding onto the woman's leg – her mother, I supposed. She looked at me through one of the lower panes of glass, strange and calm amidst the rage and panic above her. A trickle of urine ran down her mother's thigh and over the girl's hand.

Silence again, the noise sucked from the air. A blinding white light blossomed in the sky behind the faces at the window.

I slammed the hatch shut.

Close Living

When I was a boy I had a favourite fantasy. It wasn't about sex – I was eight or nine and the world was an infinite green field; I had no inkling of the deep precipice of puberty that yawned ahead. My fantasy was of a world without people. I would wake up and open the curtains to a bright summer's day. Everything would seem normal. Cars lined the street, flies buzzed in the morning sun, starlings chirped in the tree on the street and a dog padded by our gate lolling its tongue. I would get dressed, walk downstairs and find breakfast laid out on the kitchen table. But no Mum and Dad, no sister, no brother. I would call for them through the house as if I didn't know what had happened. I always added this detail to the fantasy, pretending for as long as possible that I was finding myself in this world for the first time. There would be no reply. All the rooms would be empty, the beds made, the curtains drawn. My family had disappeared. I would eat breakfast – usually Sugar Puffs, as I was only allowed that on Saturdays, grab my BMX from the shed and head out into the village.

The streets would be empty and warm. I would call at friends' houses knowing that there would be nobody there, then try the newsagents and find an open, fully stocked shop with no one to serve. I would walk slowly between the shelves, helping myself to sweets and comics. Then I would ride around the village, swerving onto the wrong side of the road and back.

The primary school would be next. The gates would be open and I'd cycle around the playground, then into the building and through the dusty, cool rooms of the school itself, observing my own empty coat hook and desk, the walls still daubed with paintings and the blackboard rubbed clean. Then it was out through the back gates and down the lane past the big houses, shouting '*Hello!*' louder and louder, pumping my pedals faster and faster, filling with glee as I accepted the reality that I was alone in a world emptied of human life.

At the bottom of the lane I would stop at a curved row of mansions, the posh part of the village. I would step through the hedge and into one of the back gardens. It belonged to a woman I used to see walking her dogs down our street. She would have been in her thirties and her smiles gave me feelings I couldn't quite place, feelings that crept directly from that same yawning precipice ahead. Her garden had a pond with a willow tree and a swimming pool. In my fantasy I would jump into the pool, swim a length and then get out, dripping on the patio. The French windows that led into the kitchen would be open and I would walk through them, eating sweets from the newsagent's and letting myself drip on the black tiles and then onto the carpet as I walked upstairs.

It would usually end there or I would skip to another part of the village or get distracted by something else. Later, as puberty loomed larger, I modified the fantasy so that the world still contained people, but people who were frozen in time. I was the only one who could move about and I was able to do as I pleased without consequence. Generally this meant heading straight for the bedroom of Emily Turner from the year above me at school and finding her in various states of undress – the chemistry churning about inside me had easily turned the childish bliss of a playground planet into a base sex laboratory.

I suppose it was an unwritten rule of the fantasy that everything would return to normal once I had had my fun, that I could snap my fingers and everyone would return to their right places. I had no idea at the time that I was daydreaming something apocalyptic. Perhaps some part of me has always suspected, believed or hoped that I would end up here.

Well . . . here, but maybe not quite like this.

I woke with a shudder for the hundredth time that night. The twin howls of the air-raid siren and the banished dog silenced like the throats of ghosts slit as the dream snapped shut. The candle on the shelf had burned down to its last quarter and in its dim glow I saw Beth and the kids huddled in some restless breed of sleep. A day had passed. I sat back against the cellar wall and thought about what had happened.

After I had slammed the hatch shut, the cellar was lit up in bright, searing light. We could hear nothing, but not because it felt like there was no sound. It felt like the opposite: as if the air had been overpowered, like a loudspeaker bursting. One huge burst of almighty bass and white noise surrounded us and pressed down upon us.

The noise faded and the light left the cellar. I switched on the Maglite. Then came the blast and the heat and the sounds of the earth tearing apart.

The temperature in the cellar rocketed and I thought I had consigned us to cook in an underground oven. The sound above us was like an oak-sized blowtorch bearing down on the hatch. I grabbed Beth and the kids and we all fell to our knees in a huddle. I pressed my head against Beth's and let out some last strangled goodbye. The hot air caught in my throat. I looked down at Alice, who stared back at me in disbelief under the glow of the torch. She was still reeling from the fall down the stairs.

Was this you too, Daddy? Did you do this?

I prepared for the furnace to ignite us. *What would I see? The air quivering? Red skin peeling back on my daughter's reproachful face? My wife's hair smoking and catching aflame? The world itself smearing away as my eyeballs melted?* But the heat drew back and we remained squashed together breathing short breaths of baking air.

Arthur was crying, of course.

'Hot, Daddy! Too hot!' cried Alice, caught somewhere between terror and amusement.

I started to answer, to comfort her, but there was more disturbance above. It started like a distant subway train rattling up the tracks towards a platform. Very slowly it grew louder until it became a single whistling roar like a billion throats exhaling. Eventually all we could hear was a howling gale and the hatch rattled violently on its hinges. We huddled together as the sweltering air spiralled around us.

Beneath it all we heard distant, deep booms and crashes. It was too loud to hear our own voices, but I watched Arthur crying relentlessly before he finally gave up and settled into Beth's arms. Alice had clearly gone into some kind of shock. Beth lay back with her head against the wall. Her eyes were shut and her face was creased in what looked like prayer. I lost myself in the sound of the wind.

* * *

The noise settled down and we were left in numb silence with ringing ears. The hatch rattled occasionally and I wondered for the first time what was now above it. Had we been buried deep in rubble? Or were we exposed and vulnerable? My mind thought back to the nightmare nuclear scenarios I had imagined as a teenager: falling ash, levelled cities, burned corpses.

The silence continued. Beth looked at me expectantly and I saw her mouth move. I shuffled along the wall to where she was sitting.

'Is it over?' she whispered. Her voice was dry and cracked.

'I don't know,' I said. 'I think so.'

'Was it … was that …' she began, struggling to ask the obvious question and all the other terrible questions that it led to.

Was that an asteroid? Had Edinburgh just been hit by an asteroid? Had the United Kingdom just been hit by asteroids? Where else had been hit? What was left? Who was left? What about my parents, my family? Would we be hit again? What was outside now?

I nodded and put my arm around her shoulder. Arthur was, incredibly, asleep. Alice was curled up in a ball against her mother.

'It's OK,' I said. 'We're safe, we're safe here.'

Beth lay her head back against the wall and straightened her left arm. Alice flinched and let out a moan, thinking that she was losing her cuddle.

'Shh, it's OK, darling, Mummy's just stretching.'

Alice flashed me another look of distrust as she huddled back in. I stroked her brow.

'Those people,' said Beth after a long silence. 'Who were those people at our door?'

I shook my head. I didn't want to think about that last image of the world – a child looking back at me in the way only a child can: an open circle of curiosity, cold and untouched by everything around her.

'Don't think about them,' I said.

I was about to say *they're gone* when I heard a noise from above. We both turned our heads to the hatch. It was distant at first, very quiet, but undeniably human: a muffled sob. Beth stiffened and shot me a look of warning. Instinctively she raised her hand and gently covered Alice's exposed ear. Again, one single muffled sob in the far distance and then nothing.

Then, much louder, a shriek. Pain. Unmistakable pain. Beth brought up her knees and quickly handed me Arthur, bringing her free hand over to shield Alice further. Alice accepted the renewed embrace without question. She had heard the sound too.

The shriek was followed by a short, quivering wail and a low moan. Then several hacking, wet coughs. It was a woman's voice. She must have been about fifteen metres from the hatch. Another shriek, then something else. She was trying to say something. The voice strained and spluttered like a car starting on a cold day.

'*Hurrurr . . . urr . . .*'

Beth's breathing quickened. I gripped Arthur, still sleeping soundly, to my chest.

A third shriek and another attempt at speech.

'*Hurrurr . . . urr . . . urrr . . . urrr . . . urrrrr . . . eeee . . .*'

The hideous pattern repeated again and again: a single shrill shriek followed by a moment of quiet as whatever was making it pulled together the will to speak.

'Hurrurr … urr … urrr … urrr … urrrrreeee …'

'Hurrurr … urr … urrrpp … eeeee …'

'Hurrurrrp … eeee …'

'Huurrrpp eeee.'

Help. Help me.

'Oh, Jesus,' said Beth. 'Oh, no, oh, no, oh, please please no, oh, Christ.'

She started to cry. Alice stared straight ahead. I hoped Beth's hands were enough to stop her from hearing.

We tried to block out the noise in that strange and useless way you do by closing your eyes as tightly as you can and tensing every muscle in your body: the same way we had done that first night we had tried to break Alice of her night-time crying as a baby, smiling guiltily as we gripped each other in bed and buried ourselves into the pillows.

There were others too. A male voice began to howl. It was an inhuman, animal sound that seemed to be moving about. I heard the sound of brick moving against brick. I guessed this one was mobile.

Another male voice. This one was more of a wheezing growl that descended into coughing almost before it started. Then another female whimper that grew louder and louder until it was a single scream that wouldn't stop. Before long it was impossible to distinguish one from the next. The air above us became a choir of screams, howls, wails and moans. I heard a child crying, '*Want! Want! Want! No!*'

I don't know how long it went on but the cries seemed to drop off one by one until only a single voice remained. It belonged to a woman, quite close by. It wasn't a scream but an audible, intelligible, well-spoken whisper repeating the same phrase over and over.

'*Please ... help me ... please ... let me in ...*'

As she spoke, her words became closer until we could hear her outside the hatch. Then we heard a scrabbling sound on the wood. Beth shot me a look of warning.

'Ed?' she said.

'It's locked from inside,' I replied.

She must have heard us because she paused. We heard a croaking sound, as if she was thinking, then a slurp of saliva and a painful gulp. And then she began to thump, slow and feebly, on the hatch.

'*Please ... help me ... let me in ... kill me ... please ... I want to die ... please ... help me ... let me in ... kill me ... please ... I want to die ...*'

At no point did I consider opening the hatch. I sat down with Beth and we waited. After about an hour, when I felt sure that she would give up, we heard a sudden groaning sound – not human this time, but of concrete and metal. The woman stopped. I pictured her looking above her. Then there was a heavy, hollow crash. The hatch rattled and the ceiling shook and the woman was silent.

'What was that?' said Beth.

'Bricks,' I guessed. 'Concrete, the rest of our house.'

We said nothing to each other. Eventually Beth lifted her hands from Alice's head. Her palms were slick with sweat and Alice lay sleeping with her hair drenched and matted.

Arthur woke up and was beginning to make noises of hunger.

'Swap,' said Beth. She released Alice from her arms and lay her down against the damp pillow. We both stretched our numb legs as we stood up to change places. I passed Arthur across and Beth released her right breast for him to suckle.

There was no question of us talking about what we had just heard. We were learning quickly to bury what we couldn't deal with. It was a primal decision that seemed to come from somewhere far away from us: deep within us or deeply between us. Not quite fright, not quite flight; just a quiet and necessary abandonment of human thought, as if we had adopted some default state that had existed long before us.

I took out a bottle of water from the first crate. The riot at the shop was now a distant memory and I experienced another mini apocalypse as I imagined the building flattened. I opened the water and passed it silently to Beth. She began to gulp it greedily down – breastfeeding already made her thirsty at the best of times – but caught my warning look and stopped short.

'How long do you think we have to stay down here?' she whispered, replacing the cap on the bottle.

'I don't know,' I replied. 'I don't know what's up there.'

'Do you think ...' she began. 'Is it, like ... nuclear? Is there fallout?'

I shook my head. 'Dust and ash, probably,' I said. 'Can't imagine there's radiation.'

I suddenly felt claustrophobic. The baking air began to catch in my throat. I scrambled to my feet.

'Ed?' said Beth. 'What are you doing?'

'Opening the hatch,' I said.

'What? Don't be insane! You don't know what's outside!'

'I have to see,' I said. I clambered up the ladder and undid the lock on the hatch. Then I pushed. It didn't move. I pushed again: not an inch.

'What's wrong?' hissed Beth.

'It's stuck,' I said, hammering harder on the thick wood. 'Something's on top of it. Fuck. Shit. Shit.'

'That woman?' said Beth.

I stopped and looked down at her. 'No,' I said. 'Not unless she weighs thirty stone. It must be rubble. I need a lever.'

I jumped down from the steps and looked around the cellar. In the corner was a gleaming red toolbox. It was seriously underused, a hopeful gift from my father when we had moved in. I sorted through the shining tools and found a small crowbar in the bottom drawer which I took and rammed into the gap between the hatch and the ceiling. I pulled down as hard as I could but there was no movement. I put one foot against the wall and tried again with all my weight hanging from the crowbar. The surface began to splinter into a thin dent but the hatch gave no sign of moving. I gave one last heave and the iron came loose, sending me crashing down onto the stone floor in a shower of splinters. The crowbar clanged at my feet.

I sensed Beth's patience as she watched me fail at this simple task.

'The hinges are on the outside,' I said. 'I'll need to break through.'

I took a hammer and a screwdriver from the toolbox and began to chip away at the hatch near the lock. After some time the head of the screwdriver popped through the other side. I wiggled it about. It felt like it was stuck in something. I got another screwdriver and stuck it into the hole as well, moving both of them about until the hole widened. Finally, I got the crowbar and jammed it into the hole, tearing back a quarter of the hatch in one go.

I tumbled to the floor again, in a shower of dust and stone as the wood came away. Staring down at me from the hole was a woman's face, red and bulging, surrounded by charred hair. A single globule of blood fell down from the holes I had made in her cheek with my screwdrivers. Behind her was the dense pack of brick and stone that had fallen and crushed her against the hatch.

I jumped up, gibbering something to myself, and grabbed an old piece of sackcloth from the corner which I stuffed into the hole until it had covered the dead woman's head. Then I scrabbled back against the wall next to Beth.

Beth, who had fallen asleep again, roused.

'Did you manage it?' she breathed.

'No,' I said, staring madly at the sackcloth. 'We're stuck.'

I didn't tell Beth about the woman. Maybe she already suspected what I had seen by the horror on my face and the way I was squashing myself against the wall. Either way, she quite calmly accepted the fact that we were trapped underground, numbed again by the instinctive need to bury the unthinkable.

'There'll be rescue parties,' she said, staring straight ahead. 'We'll be rescued.'

Later, we shared some water. I had to fight back the urge to pour it down my throat. We had three crates of six two-litre bottles. Thirty-six litres. Two litres a day between the four of us? Probably not enough. Two weeks? Three before we ran out? Would there be rescue parties before then? All of these thoughts entered my brain in the same way: accompanied by a strange, nauseous pulse as if I had stepped too close to the edge of a cliff. My mind did not belong anywhere near these questions. They were off-limits. I had no map.

I sat down next to Alice and put my arm around her. She stirred and looked up at me. Her eyes focused in the dim light and she recoiled.

'I want Mummy,' she said.

This was a first. Alice had always been a daddy's girl, in spite of – or perhaps because of – my half-hearted efforts in that role. She usually called for me at night and was sometimes upset if Beth went through to her in the morning. It hurt Beth and flattered me. Now, at this sudden change in tide, I could feel Beth's heart rising as mine sank.

'Oh, darling,' Beth cooed. 'Mummy's just feeding Arthur right now. I won't be long.'

'I want Mummy,' Alice repeated, fiercer now and pulling away from me. I let her go and she stood up shakily and crept around to Beth's other side, snuggling under her arm again. I buried the urge to take this personally.

I decided to take an inventory, combining what we had taken into the cellar with what was already there. It didn't amount to much: some candles, an unopened tin of WD-40, a jar full of broken pencils, a stack of unopened bank statements addressed to the previous owners of the house, five paint colour testers, Allen keys, a screwdriver with a bent handle encrusted in paint, a half-empty pot of white emulsion, a sewing kit, a blunt bread knife, some superglue and two tea-towels with maps of Dorset stitched into them, thumb tacks, takeaway menus, power adaptors, batteries, bulldog clips, cling film, light bulbs, birthday candles, a first-aid kit, a Zippo lighter, a bottle of lighter fluid and a vase full of dried fucking flowers.

Tins – baked beans, minestrone soup, plum tomatoes, pineapple long past its sell-by date, peaches, pilchards and tuna. An entire bag of flour and half a bag of sugar. Three packets of dried, flavoured rice, one half-packet of pasta shells, a packet of digestive biscuits, a loaf of bread, cornflakes and Sugar Puffs.

And balsamic vinegar.

Beneath the shelves was a black bin bag. I stared at it for a while before remembering what it was. It had been sitting there since the previous spring. I dropped to my knees and tore the double knot I had made in the plastic opening. The smell of wood smoke and wet cloth burst out as I rummaged through it. Two scratched plastic plates, a rancid towel, an anorak and two white metal camping mugs stained with dried tea: the remains of our camping trip to Cornwall.

It had been my idea, an insane manoeuvre to get us out into the fresh air and put some distance between us and the house. Beth had been three months' pregnant with Arthur, Alice had just turned two, and Cornwall was a nine-hour drive. It rained most of the time and the tent had a hole that I couldn't mend. Instead I woke at hourly intervals to pour the water from the groundsheet. Beth hardly slept, the beaches were a washout and Alice got conjunctivitis. On the sixth evening, I crouched outside in the rain prodding three cheap sausages around a pan balanced on a wonky camping stove. Beth sat inside the tent glaring out at me with Alice. She pleaded with me to get a hotel. 'No,' I said. 'We're supposed to be camping, this is supposed to be fun.' I was trying to make a point, I suppose, something vague about the need for living more simply, but I wasn't even convincing myself. Then the stove caught fire and Beth grabbed a bag and took Alice to a bed and breakfast. I sat it out in the tent that night, hungry and wet and drunk on warm, flat cider I had bought from the shop in the campsite. I joined Beth and Alice in the morning and we drove home that day.

Sitting in the dried mud at the bottom of the bag were two Kendal mint cakes crushed into crumbs between flimsy plastic wrappers at perishing point. There was also a crumpled box of matches that had obviously dried from having been soaked. I took them and the cakes out and placed them grimly on the shelves with the rest of the useless stock.

Beth's box was more promising. Nappies, wipes, lotions, cloths, clean clothes, medicines … she had packed for the kids as thoroughly as if we had been taking a trip down to her parents' house. There were even books, including Alice's favourite one about a rabbit that wants to fly.

'Hey,' I whispered. Beth looked up and I threw her the rabbit book. Alice's brightening face flooded me with a mess of emotions. Hope, grief, pride and regret all fought for space in my heart. I turned away and gritted my teeth to stop myself from breaking down at the dreadful elasticity of my child's spirit. When do we lose that? When does that finally break?

Would it happen in the cellar? Would the darkness finally make that rabbit seem less magical?

'We can't read it, Ed,' Beth said.

I balanced one of the candles on the shelf and lit it with one of the matches from the camping bag. Beth started to read to Alice.

'Harvey Rabbit lived in a small burrow at the bottom of the lane …'

I noticed that the candle occasionally flickered towards the hatch. I looked about the cellar in the brighter light. A small panel had been built into the ceiling in one corner. In the centre of the panel was a circular arrangement of long slats. I stood underneath and held my hand up to it, instantly feeling a breath of cold air touch my fingers as a small whirring sound came from inside. I withdrew my hand instantly. This was a ventilation pipe.

I set my mind to work and tried to imagine where this led, tried to conjure up some kind of blueprint or anatomical understanding of how the hell our house fitted (or had fitted, there went another small apocalypse) together. These kind of exercises always filled me with a deep sense of failure. I was not a practical man. I didn't understand plumbing or wiring. The space between the boiler and the tap or the meter and the socket was a magical vacuum in my mind, something for small men in boiler suits to grapple with while I lurked in the background and quietly offered them tea.

Of course it didn't help that whenever I attempted something like this fathoming of the innards of my own house the imaginary figure of my father was always standing behind me: arms crossed, head shaking slowly from side to side.

Doesn't even know how his own house works . . .

I made a guess that the ventilation pipe fed out onto the deck in the back garden. How much was left of the pipe and the wall it fed through was another matter. Might there be some filtering mechanism inside? It could be an open pipe that was allowing the very dust we were trying to evade to flow directly into our shelter.

On the other hand, how else were we going to be able to breathe?

I glanced back at Beth and the kids.

'. . . I'll play on clouds and paint the sky, I'll find my wings and learn to fly!'

Then I looked back at the shaft. I pulled the Maglite from the shelf and switched it on, pointing it nervously up at the panel and peering inside. Strands of fluff waved from the slats in the light air current. I could see a gauze sheet about an inch up into the pipe that was smeared with grime. I imagined it was heavily blocked, but still there was air coming through. This was good, I thought. Wasn't it?

I scanned the rest of the cellar. Copper pipes ran along the floor and up the wall, disappearing into what was left of the pantry.

Gas? Or water? If they were water pipes, they might still contain enough to help us survive once we'd finished the water. If they were gas and I broke one of them, then I would be sentencing us to death.

I filed this thought in a very dark place.

I traced my hand along the top pipe for some reason, following it up past Beth and into the hole in the ceiling above. It felt cold. There were no taps, no labels, nothing. I tried to remember what the pantry looked like, where the pipe came out, whether it joined onto anything else that might give me a clue as to its purpose. Nothing. I remembered nothing of the pantry.

Doesn't even know how his own house works . . .

I sat back on the upturned box and switched off the torch. I watched the flame of the candle flicker in a breeze that could be either poisoning us or keeping us alive. I stared at a pipe that held either our salvation or our doom.

Life and death were taking bets on me.

The world had designed me to be something. I was supposed to be a survival mechanism, a series of devices and instincts built, tested and improved upon over billions of years. I was a sculpture of hydrogen, evolution's cutting edge, a vessel of will, a self-adjusting, self-aware machine of infinite resource and potential. That was what the world had designed me to be. A survivor. A human being. A man.

I sat still in the darkness of the cellar. Arranged on the shelves before me were objects I had not created and could not create; food I had not gathered crammed into cylinders of metal I had not mined; water I had not collected in containers made of chemical formulae beyond my intelligence. I was no hunter, no engineer, no fighter. I was nothing that the world needed me to be. Nothing that my family needed me to be. I did what my body wanted me to do: eat, sleep, stay still, fuck, eat, sleep.

Watch television. Drink. Smoke. Buy. Consume. Breed. Sleep. Die.

Whatever was happening above our heads, whatever our civilisation had become or was going to become, and whatever incredible new technologies it was going to come up with to pull itself out of this mess, I was not part of it. I never really had been. I was down here, biting my fingernails and scratching my stupid head about questions of basic plumbing.

I watched Beth reading to the kids, Arthur hitting the page with glee and Alice pointing and echoing her mother's words. I thought about a boy riding through the streets of an empty village on a summer's day.

More Than Enough on My Plate

The first few days in the cellar were better than they should have been. We spent them dealing with practicalities – food, water and a toilet Beth fashioned from a recycling bin, cling film and a camping holdall. It had made Alice nervous, so Beth had helped her by crouching in front of her, holding her hands as she balanced on the rim, stroking her hair and looking up at her face. Alice's legs shook as she concentrated. Then she looked up and smiled as the first squirt hit the plastic, both of them sharing a giggle just as they had done the first time she had used a proper toilet.

We arranged the few toys and books Beth had grabbed in the corner under the ventilation shaft. This was the only part of the cellar that received natural light: a thin glimmer from the open pipe above. Alice gravitated there quietly and without question to busy herself with her dolly. I envied her innocence in those first days.

We ate, we drank, we used the toilet. And, most surprising of all, we slept. We slept more soundly than I could ever remember. Even Arthur skipped his midnight feeds. Perhaps it was the shock. Perhaps it was closeness.

Whatever it was, it didn't last.

We had barely shut our eyes on that third night when Alice sat bolt upright and screamed. It was not her normal cry, not even her tantrum-powered shriek; this was something we had never heard before. Pure, unfettered, three-year-old terror. An ear-splitting whistle that she somehow managed to hold without breathing. Beth sprang up and I fumbled for the Maglite. I shone it towards Alice's face. Her pupils dilated in the sudden light; both eyes were wide open and staring at the hatch. At first I thought that someone might have come in; I jumped up to check, but it was still jammed shut. There was nobody there. The scream was at thin air. Alice's arms were stretched out in front of her, each tiny fist throttling the neck of a stringy, grey stuffed rabbit.

'Alice, Alice! It's OK, Mummy's here, Mummy's here.'

Beth's soothing voice was drowned in the scream. She wrapped her arms around Alice's chest and tried to bring her into her neck, but she remained rigid. Meanwhile Arthur had rolled out from the crook of Beth's arm and was now flailing in the blankets and crying in dismay. I dropped the torch and pulled him up in one hand. As Beth tried to coax Alice from her terror I hurried to the shelf to find a new candle. There were only two left now. Two candles and the wickless pile of wax next to them.

I wrestled with the matches with one hand wrapped around Arthur, who was now screaming and wriggling against me, pushing his hand into my eye socket. I broke one match and the second caught and went out. I managed to light the third and held it as carefully as I could to the fresh wick while trying to restrain Arthur, wondering at the perpetual struggle with other objects that existence sometimes seems to be.

Eventually the flame lit and I turned my attention to soothing Arthur. About an hour later, Beth and I sat in the dying glow of the candle, stunned, watching our sleeping daughter.

'Do you remember that first night with her, after she was born?' whispered Beth. 'She was so quiet.'

I did remember.

'We thought we'd hit the jackpot,' I said.

Like most prospective parents, the congratulations and smiles that followed our announcement of Beth's pregnancy had been tempered by low notes – smug warnings from the ones who had gone before us. For Beth it was the clucked tales of torn skin, colic and exhaustion from her mother and aunts. For me, it was the sneers of my colleagues.

I won't go into details about what I did for a living – 'in computers' just about covers it. I still remember the big, gloating red faces of my co-workers when I told them of my impending fatherhood.

'That's it for you then, pal!' they wheezed, slapping their clammy, blubbery palms on my back. 'Game over! Nae more nights oot! Nae more nooky! Nae more fuckin' nuttin! Game over! The end! Bye bye!'

We were terrified.

But then Alice was born, and the first night we took her home we rejoiced. She slept soundly. There was no stirring, no crying, just contented snuffled and snorts that we listened to as we drifted off into a sleep that lasted until morning. We thought we'd got lucky; that we had somehow sidestepped the fate that everyone thought lay ahead of us as parents. We would be free and well rested, with a happy, undemanding child. Those fat fucks at work were wrong.

A week in and that fantasy had flown, leaving in its place night feeds, floor-walking and perpetual fatigue. Beth laughed at me as I stumbled out of the door the morning after that first bad night. She pulled me back in and rubbed some of Alice's shit off my cuff with a kitchen cloth. 'Who were we kidding,' she said, before sending me off to spend the day staring at the mess of pixels and wondering what I was supposed to be doing.

It wasn't long after that I imposed my *he-who-works-sleeps* rule.

I turned to Beth. She was watching Alice with that look she had. Nervous determination. Fearful volition.

'I should have helped more in those first few weeks,' I said. 'I should have done more.'

She turned to me. I imagined the words before they came out of her mouth. *That's OK, you did plenty. It was hard for both of us. You were under pressure.*

But that wasn't what she said. Instead, she looked at me curiously and then turned away.

'How long, Ed? How long will we be down here?'

We had been avoiding the question. We had talked about what might have happened, piecing together what little we had absorbed from the news in the days before; what had hit us, where else had been hit, whether people we knew were safe, what state the country was in, what state the *world* was in. Speculating made it seem safer, separate, as if the hatch was protecting us rather than trapping us. But we had not yet spoken about what was to come.

I shook my head and folded my thumb over her long fingers. I had been trying to remember the government broadcasts and whether or not there had been any mention of rescue parties or time limits.

'I don't think there is a set time,' I said. 'It all depends on how much … how big … I think they sound an "all-clear" siren. That's what they'd do after a nuke anyway.'

'And what does that sound like?'

'Like the one before?' I shrugged. 'How should I know?'

'What if there is no siren?' she said. 'What if there's nobody to sound it? What if there's nothing up there at all? What if …'

'Jesus, Beth, I'm not a fucking expert,' I hissed.

'But we need …'

'And it's not like I had a lot of time to prepare for it.'

I stopped short at the sound of my own lie. I clearly could have prepared for it. I could have had at least four more hours to pull together supplies if I hadn't been drunk. We might have had hundreds of candles, basins and buckets full of water, more food, more batteries, more blankets.

Beth looked up at the meagre supplies on the shelves.

'I'm not letting my children die down here, Ed. We need a plan.'

'The plan is to ration food and water. That's all we can do.'

Life became a cycle of triggers, tasks and responsibilities. Every event developed a protocol that generally led to another, and another after that, each one designed to keep Alice away from her own terror. We spent the days and nights waltzing endlessly around each other. We walked a hairline between control and panic, and at any moment the quiet darkness might suddenly fill with Alice's piercing screams.

I tried my best to occupy Alice, but she still didn't trust me. In fact it was as if she had removed me from her view of reality altogether. I had been her world before. Now the world had become cold, frightening and claustrophobic, and it was all down to me. I knew Beth was secretly and guiltily enjoying her renewed companionship with Alice. This was touching, of course, but, like most things that happen to you when you're stuck underground, also unbearably crushing.

After a week – three nights of relative peace, four of madness – Alice stopped screaming. Very soon afterwards she stopped speaking as well. She spent most of her time tight-lipped with her dolly clasped to her chest in her corner or staring at the opposite wall with her thumb firmly planted between her lips and a bunny's ear pressed against her nostrils. She was emotionless. Unresponsive unless she needed food, water or the toilet, in which case she would simply move towards whichever one was required and stand waiting until it was organised for her. We panicked, immediately craving her screams. Beth tried to coax her back with the usual bait of cuddles, stories and songs. But a wall had come down. A door had slammed shut. Her brain had moved to its next level of defence: complete lockdown. Nothing goes in, nothing goes out; sit tight and wait for this all to disappear. Her trust belonged to no one else but her.

One night, we were eating the final two cans of beans for dinner. I passed a crust of bread smeared with the last of juice to Beth. She looked at it uncertainly.

'You have it,' she said.

'No, you're breastfeeding. You take it.'

'Eat it,' she said. 'I'm fine. You always eat more than me anyway.'

It was just a little glimpse in the dark. Her eyes dropped too low, landing on my midriff for a split second before returning to Arthur.

'What was that?' I said.

'What was what?'

'You know very well what. *You always eat more than me anyway.* Are you saying I eat too much?'

Her 'no' came a second too late.

'You think I'm fat,' I said, placing the empty can as noisily as I could on top of the other one.

'Ed, no, you're not fat, not at all . . .'

There it was again. The eyes dropped straight to my belly.

'You did it again!'

'Och, Ed, you're not fat, but . . .' she sighed, 'you know, maybe some exercise wouldn't hurt once in a while.'

She was right. Of course she was right. I had swollen slowly with the blubber of wasted calories. My plates had been piled high with squashy carbohydrates, fatty protein and refined sugar that masqueraded as a balanced, nutritional, middle-class diet. Large, expensive cuts of meat and home-cooked chips hid behind slivers of baby broccoli like fat thieves behind a twig. Lean fish drowned in cream and packed with double helpings of pasta. Bowls of rich ice cream, 'hand-made' crisps, rustic dips . . . with the wine, I was probably topping over 4,000 calories a day. On the rare days when I watched what disappeared down my gullet, my brain stepped in and rounded down, compressing the total to the magic 2,500 figure you're led to believe is what an average male should be living on, what the average male *needs* to live on. The problem with this, of course, is that the *average male* is not a good target to shoot for. The average is very low.

Beth began trying to feed Alice water. Alice kept her eyes away as she accepted small sips.

'Oh, Alice, sweetheart, I wish you'd look at me,' said Beth.

'Exercise,' I grumbled, banging the two cans together.

The nearest thing I got to exercise was sitting in the park at lunchtime with some meaty, cream-smothered sandwich, baulking at the runners strutting past in Lycra, spitting my crisps at their sizzling earbuds, knocking back disgusted gulps of fizzy chemicals at their leers of determination. Why did they bother? Why did they struggle?

To me, running was just showing off, a way for self-obsessed pricks to show how much more focused, disciplined and healthy they were than you. How much more *average* they were than you, the sub-average gibbon who watched from a park bench with its pre-packed lunch. Gyms were just as bad, except in gyms you had it coming at you from all angles: weight lifters out-lifting each other, cross-trainers quietly tapping up their speeds to match their neighbour's, treadmillers pounding their feet to some nauseating soundtrack of their own puffed-up lives. Entire, windowless rooms crammed full of sweaty, unashamed, Lycra-clad peacockery.

And I didn't have the time. I was a dad, I had responsibilities. I had more than enough on my plate.

'I don't have time for exercise,' I said.

'What about that charity run your work's doing?' said Beth, unscrewing another bottle and trying to coax Alice with it. 'You could do that. What is it, 5K or something? Come on, sweetheart, drink this for me.'

I laughed.

'Running,' I said. 'That's not really my thing, Beth, is it?'

Once more: I hated runners. I hated running.

'It could be,' said Beth, turning to me. Her face was serious, resolute. 'If you wanted it to be.'

I snorted, but her face didn't falter.

'Yeah, well,' I said, glancing up at the hatch. 'I'm pretty sure the entries are closed now, don't you think? Besides, I couldn't run 5K.'

Then she turned so that she was facing me entirely.

'Edgar, I believe that you could do anything you wanted to. If you only put your mind to it.'

We stayed like this for a few moments – her noble and honest, me idly turning the cans and unable to meet her eyes. Then she turned back to Alice.

'Here you go, sweetheart, have some more water. That's a good girl.'

Alice stared at the dim shaft of light. Beth slumped against the wall.

'Ed, why won't she talk?'

'I don't know,' I said. I was grateful for the change in conversation. 'It's like she's too far away.'

Then I had an idea. I picked up the empty bean tins and reached for the bent screwdriver and string from the shelf. It was starting to get dark, so I prepared the last candle and took a match from the box so it was as easy to light as possible later on. Then I took the cans, string and screwdriver back to my place by the wall.

'What are you doing?' said Beth.

'Not sure yet,' I said.

I upended the first can and held it between my feet. Then I started working the head of the screwdriver into the centre of its base. The metal scraped loudly on the floor and I glanced up to see if Alice had become interested. Her eyes were lost in the light that was creeping up the wall from the ventilation shaft, the last faint rays of sunlight leaving the cellar for the day. Eventually the screwdriver burst through the can with a loud pop. I yanked it out and began work on the second, watching Alice gaze silently at the wall. When I had finished I cut a long piece of string and threaded it through the two holes, knotting it inside both cans. Beth, realising what I was trying to do, took one of the cans from me and walked it over to Alice.

'Here, Alice,' said Beth. 'Hold this up to your ear.'

Alice ignored her.

'Here you go, darling. Take it.'

Alice breathed a long, tired sigh, still lost on the dying light that was seeping from the wall.

Beth pulled the string tight and crouched down next to Alice. She held the tin up to her ear.

'*Boo*,' I whispered into my can.

Alice's eyes flickered and she flinched from the can as if it were a fly buzzing at her head. She glanced at it, then at me, then her eyes fell back to the light on the wall.

'*Hello Alice*,' I tried.

This time there was no reaction at all. Instead she pulled one of the blankets over her and closed her eyes, resting her head against the wall.

Beth placed the can next to her. Then she came over and placed a long, soft kiss on my head before taking a blanket herself and lying down next to Arthur. I sat turning my can in my hands. That was the first night that sleep became something different for me, something less than what it used to be; a thin, watery version of itself. I don't know whether it was a feeling of giving up, or a feeling that some part of me was no longer of any use, or whether the sight of my three-year-old daughter resigning herself to something like an old woman to a disease was too much to bear, but I was never fully unconscious for a long time after that evening.

Things began to deteriorate quickly. One by one we got sick, and used up all the painkillers within a couple of days. Our water supplies were now very low. Food too. The candles had all gone and the torch's batteries were running out. Alice wouldn't eat. She began crying quietly in her sleep, still the only noise she made. The toilet box was starting to reach its limit. I tried double sealing it but in my haste I spilled some of the vile liquid onto the floor. I covered it with an anorak, but it did no good. The close air in the room was now thick with the smell of shit.

I spent long periods staring at the hatch, yearning to be outside in whatever hell now lay above. I imagined fluttering ash and molten rock, a heat haze on the rubble, a poisonous breeze. And yet how cool and fresh the air would feel against my face compared with the fetid atmosphere of the cellar.

Then I would stare at the pipe. The more I stared, the more I convinced myself that it was full of water. I could break it, drain it, prolong our survival, perhaps enough for ... for what? A rescue party?

Or it could be a gas pipe. I could break it in the middle of the night and kill us all. Beth, Alice and Arthur would not know what had happened.

One evening, shivering in a blanket by the wall, I fell into a dream in which I was the glass within the kitchen door of our house. A hundred faces were pressed up against me, saliva drooling from their mouths and spluttering from their noses as they heaved and panicked to push through me. I stood, unable to move, my glass arms and legs stretched out as if I was on a rack. I felt my glass face bake in the sun. Then the sun became bright, overexposed light that seared and finally exploded everything around me. The faces burst and sizzled against me. Their cheeks charred and crumbled into dust, their eyeballs boiled and melted down my neck like marshmallows.

I woke up gasping, fumbling for the water bottle. I almost had it to my lips when I paused. It was our last one, less than half full. I tightened the lid and put it back. As I sat back against the wall and caught my breath in my dry throat, I saw Alice's face in the single shaft of evening light. She was looking at me. I watched her for a while, trying to work out what she was doing. He lips were moving. She had the can in front of her mouth.

Very slowly I picked up my can and pulled it to my ear. All I could hear was Alice whispering in the corner, but then I shuffled along the wall so that the string was taut.

'Just a dream, Daddy,' she said. 'Just a dream.'

My heart buckled. I put the can to my mouth and motioned for her to swap hers to her ear.

'Just a dream,' I said. 'Are you thirsty?'

'Daddy?'

'Yes?'

'The lady, Daddy. The lady was sad. She was crying.'

I picked up the water bottle and crawled across the floor to Alice. She sat up with the can between her knees and I flung my arm around her neck and kissed her cheek. She buried her face into my neck and grasped my ear tightly and we both sobbed into one another as Beth and Arthur snored in the corner.

Eventually I clambered around so that I was sat next to her and looked up at the ventilation shaft. There was still some light.

'Have some water,' I said. 'Here.'

I opened the bottle and raised it to her lips. She brought her hands up to meet it, but in doing so she dropped the can to the floor. The loud noise made her jump and she flinched, knocking the bottle from my hands. I struggled to catch it but it flew out of my reach.

'Sorry, Daddy,' Alice cried in alarm. 'Sorry! Sorry, Daddy! Sorry!'

Beth roused in her bed.

'What's going on?' she murmured.

Arthur started to wake as well. Both still feverish. Both still thirsty.

I leaped to rescue the bottle but it was too late. Most of the water had flooded onto the floor. I stood in the middle of the cellar with my hands to my head.

'Fuck!' I screamed.

'What's happening?' said Beth again. 'It's OK, Alice, Mummy's here ... oh, Christ, Ed ... what's going on?'

'Fuck!'

Arthur was whining now, wide awake, and Alice was huddled with her knees to her chest still crying out her panicked apologies.

'Fuck!'

Everything seemed to become a dense tornado of sound. Alice's desperate cries, Arthur's bawling, Beth's slow, croaky groans and my own growls and shouts of frustration.

Time slowed down. I looked down at the pipe, barely visible now in the dark. It held water or gas, life or death.

I strode towards it and fell down upon the floor. I began to wrench at it, pulling it back and forwards from the wall, trying to tear it from its brackets, bend it break it, burst it, furious at my own weakness, furious at my own ignorance. Eventually it tore away from the wall, but it didn't break so easily. Alice was now squealing, Arthur wailing, Beth trying to get to her feet. I got my left arm behind the pipe and prised it away from the concrete, then pulled with my knees against the wall. Something shuddered, then another bracket burst, and then finally came the sound of pressure releasing from a point beneath the ventilation shaft. I felt a spray of cool liquid on my face. It was water.

I put my mouth around the torn metal. I tasted my own blood mixed with the cold water in my mouth. Then I filled the bottle and passed it to Beth. Then I filled another, and another before finally the flow began to stop and I fell to my knees, sobbing in either relief or grief. I don't know to this day which. There's a fair chance I had been hoping for gas.

I filled three bottles; barely enough for another two days.

The kids stopped crying momentarily while Beth gave them the water. Then Alice started whimpering again.

'It's dark,' she said, trembling. 'I want the candle ... where's the candle.'

We had been underground for barely two weeks. We had no light, no food, only a few gulps of water left. We were out of choices.

Arthur started up again, a loud, rasping cry that drowned out everything around it. I stood and stormed over to the hatch. I couldn't breathe, couldn't see, couldn't hear, couldn't think. I shouted up into the darkness. No words, just noise from my throat, a growl and a roar.

Then I heard another noise. It was coming from outside – something fast and repetitive. *Thud-thud-thud … thwup-thwup-thwup-thwup-thwup.*

A bright light suddenly flashed down the ventilation shaft.

'Quiet!' I shouted. Alice, Beth and Arthur carried on, but the noise beneath them got louder. Another flash of bright light came down the shaft.

The distant thudding suddenly opened up into the roar of rotor blades directly above us. A helicopter. Search lights now swept around us, illuminating the room through all of the hidden cracks and holes. Thin white shafts moved around the room like light from a glitter ball as the chopper hovered above. Then voices, shouts, a megaphone.

'DO NOT MOVE. STAY WHERE YOU ARE. DO NOT COME OUTSIDE UNTIL WE TELL YOU. DO NOT MOVE. STAY WHERE YOU ARE.'

I fell back against the wall and pulled Alice close to me. She had stopped crying and was shivering with her arms over her head.

'It's OK,' I said. 'It's OK, we're safe.'

I rested my head on the wall and closed my eyes against the light.

Pot Noodle

THREE MONTHS LATER

Bryce grunted.

'I could take one out. Two. Right now. Easy. Bam bam.'

We were crouched below a high dormer window looking south. It was one of a handful of lookout points we had managed to find along Lawnmarket, the medieval street that led down from Edinburgh Castle. We called it Pot Noodle because of the single, unaccountably intact, empty plastic cup of the same name that we had found perched on the window ledge. The room had once been somebody's bedroom, probably a student's; the scorched walls still had a few remnant shreds of film and band posters, flyers, pictures of Che Guevara. Shreds of burned carpet clung limply to what was left of the floor. The boards were scattered with broken objects: a cracked mug, a bent fork, a lamp twisted by heat; nothing we could use. A charred metal bed frame stood in the corner, ready to disintegrate at a single touch like a used matchstick. On the wall beside it I had briefly registered the black outline of a human shape. We saw these a lot. Bryce called them man-stains: shadows of the dead scorched onto walls, steps, pavements, each a perfect imprint of the person in their last position as whatever blast of superheated sub-space rock had incinerated them.

Everything in the room was covered in a dusting of snow. There was no roof and no back wall. Half the room was empty space and there was a six-storey drop beneath it.

Behind us were the remains of the city centre. Princes Street, Rose Street, George Street, Thistle Street, Queen Street: all now just black stumps and rubble. Cathedrals, churches, tenements and houses: all gone. The roads were strips of chaos dotted with lumps of upturned concrete that made them, for the most part, impassable. The long, wide hill of Leith Walk, that had once stretched down to the Shore, was now scrubbed down to a black skid mark. Dundas Street, once a long, straight thoroughfare through the wealthy streets of New Town, was now a deep gash piled with the shells of cars and bricks. The New Town itself was reduced to ash. All that was left was the bare outline of the streets; a flat grid of dust.

Beyond, everything had once been views out to the north: ocean, sky and mountain. Now all you could see was grey murk with the occasional glimpse of the dark waters of the Forth. On clearer days you could just make out the mangled wreck of the suspension bridge upended in the water like two metallic claws.

There was little sign of life. The dead outweighed the living. The dead *far* outweighed the living.

If you're reading this then you're probably in a better time and place than the one I'm in right now. You probably didn't witness the extent of the devastation. You probably don't know how it feels to see that everything in your world has suddenly stopped, died or vanished.

I can only do so much to help. Writing is just a trick after all; you turn images into words that you hope will trigger similar images that already exist in the reader's head. Your images are built from films and books, perhaps even stock footage of Hiroshima, Nagasaki, Chernobyl, the grainy documentaries at which my nuke-obsessed fifteen-year-old self used to thrill. Those images – the empty streets, rubble, dust, corpses, burnt-out buildings, broken bicycles, blackened tree stumps, dark skies, charred teddy bears – they only go so far. They lack scale and time. They have boundaries: a street, a city, a country, an era, a film reel. They start and they end.

My own boundary was the size and shape of a small, stinking cellar for a little over two weeks after the strike. On 26 August, when soldiers from Castlelaw Barracks tore back the cellar hatch and hauled us out, my boundary expanded to the size of a city. It's been expanding ever since.

The remnants of some of Edinburgh's buildings still stood. The Old Town had fared better than most, its chaotic jungle of cobbled streets perhaps confusing the blasts just enough to prevent them from achieving the same annihilation as the younger streets. The long rear wall of tenements that stretched down from the castle high above Princes Street Gardens (now a black swamp of filth) had been torn away, exposing a cutaway of homes and offices, their insides torched. If you clambered up the scree beneath them you could just about manage to climb up through the rooms and half-demolished staircases to reach the top, now the highest point in the city, and where we were hunched down.

'Two bullets, two heads,' said Bryce, peering through the sight on his rifle. 'Bam. Bam. Nighty night.'

'Great idea,' I said. 'Kill two, let the rest know where we are. Go for it, let's see how far we get before they catch up.'

Bryce pulled his head back from the lens to look at me, the barrel still pointing down onto the street.

'Be good though,' he said, his gigantic, hairy cheeks twisted into a grin. 'Eh?'

It would not have been good. Apart from anything else, I doubted Bryce's aim from that range. He shouldn't have even been carrying a gun. It was only after weeks of pestering that Yuill had finally given in. Watching him now, grinning down the barrel of a standard issue SA80, made me nervous; picking off rabbits from your bedroom window as a teenager does not make you a sniper.

'We're here to watch them,' I said, squinting down at the base of the building where Bryce had trained his rifle, halfway along the crumbling remains of South Bridge. I blew into my hands.

'How many?'

Bryce fixed his eye against the sight once more. He rested the barrel on the wool of his gloves, his one bare index finger poking out from a hole he had cut in them, twitching on the trigger.

'Five,' he said. 'No, six ... seven. Seven of the little fuckers. They're moving something, looks like ...'

'Let me see,' I said, moving over to take over the sight.

'Wait, fuck off!' Bryce elbowed me away and I slammed into the window frame.

'Give it here ...'

As I scrambled back to grab the rifle, my hand slipped on the wood and knocked a slate free from its place on the roof.

'Shit.'

'Edgar . . .' Bryce growled.

The slate slid down and caught on the edge of the drainpipe beneath, tumbling down and shattering on the slick cobbles below. The quiet street suddenly echoed with noise.

'We're done,' said Bryce.

There was a shout from the bridge, some movement.

'They've seen us,' said Bryce. 'Run.'

I saw three small figures in the distance, running towards us.

'*RUN!*' Bryce shouted, grabbing my shoulder and pulling me away from the window. I staggered and fell, my legs numb from two hours of crouching. As I sprawled on the bare floorboards I heard voices, angry shouts, coming nearer. Bryce yanked me upright and shoved me towards the gaping hole where the rest of the room should have been. Beneath and beyond us, stretching out as far as we could see in the late winter afternoon was a sheer drop into dark chaos.

We leaped into it.

I landed first. The remains of the flat below stretched further than the one we had been in. We knew this because we knew this entire stretch of rubble; every hole, every walkway, every ladder, drop and climb. The voices were closing in. I heard shouts and footsteps begin to echo up one of the ancient stone staircases that spiralled up into the building.

Bryce landed like a sack of bricks behind me. We both scrambled to our feet and made our way to the edge of the room. The floor stopped here. There was no wall between this one and the next, only two oak beams that stretched across a thirty-foot drop. We took a beam each and high-wired across them. Light was fading and I concentrated on my footing, trying to ignore the shouts getting louder behind me. Above us, under the low sky, the brittle, broken remains of Edinburgh Castle rose up on their plinth of volcanic rock. Snow fell on my outstretched arms and my face.

Bryce faltered near the end of the beam but corrected himself and jumped over into the last room, a bare floorboard that we sprinted across as seven figures spilled out of the stairwell and gave chase. As we reached the edge of the floor I heard two shots fire and a bullet whistle past my ear. I jumped the final few metres and fell over the edge onto the muddy slope beneath the castle. This had once been a steep, green bank that swept up from Princes Street Gardens to the Royal Mile. A few winding paths had led tourists up from the town to the castle on sunny days. Fireworks had exploded above it and showered down onto throngs of heaving Hogmanay crowds. Now it was dirt and glass and gravel. Nothing grew there.

Bryce was already ahead of me and running down towards the tracks. The old railway line from Waverley was still our quickest route back out of the town. The tunnel to Haymarket station had held, despite the fires that had raged within it. A single burned-out shell of a train sat halfway along, but aside from that it was a clear run.

Another shot rang out behind us as we both hit the tracks and started picking up the pace. I followed the dark outline of Bryce as we neared the tunnel, his rifle slung over his shoulder, his long coat flapping behind him like a tent. Not for the first time I marvelled at his speed.

Our pursuers had hit the slope and slowed down as they picked their way gingerly down it. A few wild shots flew harmlessly above us and we made up some distance. I caught up with Bryce as we hit the tunnel. The sound of our feet slamming against the ground closed in around us like the darkness. There was no light. Bryce flicked on his head torch and I followed the beam as it swept around the crumbling brick, catching the shadows of rats scurrying into the walls. We reached the first bend where the train wreck was lodged and I heard footsteps on the track behind us, voices close by and rattling off the walls.

Now it was just a matter of speed.

We knew the geography of the train well: the blockages, the angle of each carriage, the width of each door and how it led to the next, the position of each blackened husk sitting in its seat. There had been only a few passengers that early on a Sunday morning. The train would have stopped in the tunnel as the warnings came, an apology from the driver over the tannoy, a few tuts and papers shaken, then the very faintest sound of the sirens, not enough time to panic before the first one hit, flooding the tunnel with liquid fire.

I followed Bryce's route through the train and out into blackness. We lost our pursuers for a moment, but as we saw the dim light of the tunnel's exit at Haymarket we heard them gaining on us once again. They were quick.

A shot rang out and another bullet flew past my head, a little too close for comfort this time. I pushed down my head and lengthened my stride, putting some faith in my feet. I could feel them now closing in now. They were no longer shouting, just running; using all of their energy to catch us.

Bryce reached the end of the tunnel and immediately launched his huge bulk onto the platform on the left. He hit the stone wall with his chest, with his arms scrabbling on the concrete and his legs kicking the thin air beneath. His buttocks heaved in great circles as he struggled like a water buffalo in a rising river, unable to pull himself up.

'What are you doing?' I shouted as I reached the end of the tunnel. 'Keep running!'

'Get me up! Get me up!'

'They're almost on us!'

'Just get me fuckin' up!'

I stumbled on the gravel as I ran into the grey light and heaved Bryce's legs onto the platform. He grabbed my arm and hauled me effortlessly alongside him. I followed as he sprinted up the remains of a metal staircase. At the top, Bryce crouched and swung his rifle round. I fell down behind him, wheezing, gasping.

'Bryce,' I spluttered. 'What the hell are you doing? Let's keep moving!'

Echoes of footsteps clattered off the walls of the tunnel, louder and louder.

'I'm buying us some time,' said Bryce calmly. His own breathing had already slowed and I could tell his heart rate was doing the same. Mine was still hammering, trying to escape from my ribcage.

Bryce was a freak. From what I knew of him, his life before the strike had had a single purpose: pleasure. Food, drink, drugs and sex. He had never lifted a weight, never cycled a bike, would have hurled you across a room if you had suggested that he take a jog. You would never have seen a man with a build like his on a track, but Bryce could run five miles flat out without breaking a sweat. Against all evidence to the contrary, he was a natural runner with the heart of an Olympian. I could never keep up with him.

'There are at least seven of them, you idiot!' I said, trying to pull back his shoulder. 'Come on!'

'They're pussies,' said Bryce, shrugging me off and adjusting his sight. 'A couple of shots and they'll run home to mummy.'

'No no no, Bryce, come on, think. They've usually given up by now, but they're still running. They're fed and they're armed and they're pissed off. They'll kill us. Now for fuck's sake let's keep running, they're almost on us!'

'Toooo late,' sang Bryce, his finger wrapping itself around the trigger of his rifle.

The front runner hurtled out of the tunnel and skidded to a halt on the tracks. He was tall and lean, with a thick black hooded top pulled down over his gaunt face. He pulled a pistol from his green combat trousers and held it out in both hands, scanning the station. I ducked behind Bryce. Another two arrived from the tunnel and almost tumbled into each other. They were both shorter than the other, but just as skinny, hoods up as well. They were all young, probably still teenagers. The leader held out a hand towards them and they spread out on the tracks, pulling out their guns and looking warily around the station.

'Bryce,' I hissed. 'This is not a good idea.'

'It's a fuckin' great idea,' he said, and let off a shot.

The bullet hit the wall of the tunnel and a cloud of dust and rock exploded around the three young men. They instinct-ively fell to the tracks and started scrambling back towards the safety of the tunnel. Bryce fired a couple more rounds and the leader returned fire in our direction before disappearing into the darkness.

I fell back against the rear wall of the steps, my ears ringing from the shots, my heart still pounding from the run and now from the gunfire. Until a few months before I had never even seen a gun in real life, let alone one spitting bullets at me.

'Shit,' said Bryce. He checked the indicator on his magazine. 'Shit,' he said again, training the gun back onto the exit of the tunnel.

'Great,' I said. 'That's just great, Bryce. Now they know where we are.'

We heard the other four runners catch up and stop before the end of the tunnel. Some muffled voices and shouts came from the darkness.

'You've had your fun,' I said. 'Now will you *please* stop fucking about and COME ON!'

'You go if you like,' said Bryce. 'I'm finishing what I started.'

Suddenly a pistol appeared from the tunnel and shot three times up at the stair. Two bullets flew by above us, but the third ricocheted off the metal girder beneath my leg. I sprang up the stair and huddled into a ball.

'Jesus Christ, Bryce! You're going to get us fucking killed!'

'Run on,' he said. He hadn't moved a muscle. 'I'll catch you up.'

The pistol appeared again, this time farther out into the light. I could see a pale and hollow face looking up at us from the end of the outstretched arm.

This time Bryce fired first, a single shot that slammed straight into the gunner's shoulder.

'Fucking up ya!' shouted Bryce. 'Right fuckin' up ya!'

He let out a deep laugh as shouts and howls echoed from the tunnel.

'Did you hit him?' I said.

'Aye,' said Bryce, still chuckling to himself. 'Oh, aye.'

He rested his rifle down on the step as if he had just hit a deer on a hunt. He turned to me, grinning. I stared back, not quite believing what had just happened.

Bryce smacked his lips.

'OK,' he said. 'Time to go.'

We clattered down the steps and sprinted across the platform onto the opposite tracks. Bryce sped away laughing. I followed with my head swimming, trying to keep pace. We were clear of the station and on our way south-west by the time we heard them following again. Bryce's stunt had managed to give us a rest; it had slowed one of them up and put an extra few hundred metres between them and us.

After about a mile on the tracks, the runners seemed to be closing in again. We came to the bridge at Slateford and Bryce swung left, climbing the steps onto the main road that crossed the railway.

'Where are you going?' I yelled.

'Canal,' Bryce called back.

As we hit the road, Bryce tripped on the kerb and fell, letting out a great *oof* as he hit the torn, blackened tarmac. He flinched as I helped him up and I noticed a dark patch on the left arm of his coat.

'What's that?' I said.

Bryce inspected it gingerly.

'Must've hit me too,' he said. 'I'm alright.'

He looked pale, not the same laughing maniac that had sped out of the station.

I peered over the wall at our pursuers, who were almost at the bridge. Farther back, I could see the one that Bryce had hit crouching down on the tracks, clutching his shoulder, another one of them stopped next to him. Five now almost on us.

The canal was the quickest way home. It ran parallel to the tracks, but the road that ran towards it was long and wide with no cover. We would be sitting ducks.

Bryce gulped and took a few trembling breaths.

'Come on,' I said. 'This way.'

I led us across the main road and up a cobbled side street that had once been lined with Victorian tenements. It was the last in a row of eight similar streets, all of which had blown backwards and were now leaning against each other like gigantic dominoes. Being the last, it had suffered the least. One end of the street had collapsed in a flattened sandwich of charred stone, metal and furniture. Home upon home upon home. The rest of the street still stood upright, a husk of brick with holes where the windows and doors had been. A wind had picked up and was starting to whistle through the empty rooms.

I pulled Bryce into one doorway and around a corner, into the remains of a ground floor flat where we crouched against the wall.

There was silence for a while, just the sounds of our breathing and Bryce's occasional grunts of pain. I guessed that a family had lived here. The shell of an upright piano stood against one wall. A gust of wind sent a blackened pile of sheet music rustling across the floor beneath it. A black crust of a satchel hung from one corner, thrown there the evening before the strike, one small shoe poking out of it.

Bryce was beginning to bleed heavily now. I glanced back around the corner, crossed to the piano and grabbed the satchel. The strap was still in one piece. I took it off and tied it around the top of Bryce's arm, above where I guessed the wound to be. He winced a little as I pulled it tight.

'Thanks,' he said.

I held a finger to my lips. I had heard something outside, a bang, something kicked.

'Ho!'

We both froze.

I tapped the magazine in Bryce's gun. *How many rounds?*

Bryce slowly held up a single finger.

I sank down to the ground.

'Ho there ya fucks!'

They sounded like they were two doors down, banging walls, kicking things over. Their voices echoed off the ancient tiles in the stairwell as they clattered up and down, checking the flats. One of them was making sucky kissing noises and whining in a fake, nasal American accent.

'Here kitty kitty ... here kitty kitty kitty ...'

Bryce bristled and fidgeted. He tapped his magazine again and jabbed his thumb back at the door, miming a quick shot to the head. I held my palms down at him and shook my head slowly. Bryce gripped his gun to his chest and glared back at me.

''Mon cunts!'

The voices reappeared on the street and then disappeared again into the stair next door. Hoots and shouts and screams like kids trying to scare other kids.

Bryce was sucking long streams of air in and out of his nostrils. He was going to go for them as soon as they found us, if not before. I looked around the flat. We only had one choice.

'Come on,' I said. 'Quick. Up.'

I pulled Bryce to his feet and led him through to a living room that was now just a dirty, frozen cave. Amongst the junk and clutter was a long sofa, charred like everything else but still with its cushions intact. I pulled them away and took a knife from my belt. This was my one weapon. I didn't share Bryce's need for a gun. I ran it around the fabric underneath and tore it away.

Voices and footsteps were out on the street again. I looked up at Bryce, who frowned.

'Ladies first,' I whispered, directing him to the exposed cavity.

Bryce went to protest, but I could hear them coming into the stair now. I pulled Bryce forward and bundled him into the sofa. He fought a yelp as he landed heavily on his arm and I jumped in behind him, pulling the cushions on top of us.

I didn't know if we were fully covered and had no time to check.

''Mon ya cunts,' said a voice quietly as one of them entered the room. I could hear the others running up the stairwell. Bryce's giant, wet face was pressed up against mine, breathing heavy, hot, stinking breaths across my mouth. I fought to control myself, not to move. I was sure we would be heard.

'... gonnae fuckin' kill ye when ah find ye ...'

He was moving slowly around the flat, inspecting the debris. A sudden discordant clang rang out as he kicked the piano. He kicked it three more times in quick succession, laughing wildly in the half-broken voice of an adolescent.

'Haw haw haw haw ...'

A death chord rang out on the piano strings. He came into the living room and shuffled around, picking up objects and dropping them or throwing them against the walls. I could smell him. Even through the wet, mouldy fabric of the cushion and Bryce's stale breath, I could smell him. The smell of sweat, smoke, piss, grease and old wet dust.

Suddenly the cushion pressed hard against my face. I gulped back a cry of protest as my cheek squashed harder against Bryce's. He was sitting right on top of us.

I heard the metallic chink and scratch of a Zippo. There was a crackle and a long suck, then the smell of marijuana.

Then a loud, deep fart pushed its way through the cushion above us.

He sat there above us, smoking his joint and farting into my face until I thought we would have to take our chances with him, push the cushion up and overpower him before he could call the others down from the stairs. I was edging my hand down towards my knife, ready to make a move, when we heard the others descending the stairs.

'Anyhn?' shouted our boy.

'Nah,' came the reply. ''Mon.'

He took one last suck of his joint and then bounced up from the sofa. 'Where now?' he said.

'Back 'n' report a couple of soldiers shot Danny,' said the voice from the corridor.

'Soldiers?' said ours.

'Aye. Tellin ya, that was a squaddie gun, definitely. Not like these fuckin' polis pea-shooters.'

I heard two harsh metallic taps against a wall.

'Aye, fuckin' barrack boys alright,' he said. 'I reckon it's time we paid a trip up to the hills likesay?'

They haw-hawed out of the block with the rest of their pack. When we were sure they had gone, I pushed up the cushions and we both scrambled out, spluttering, pushing away from each other. We stood in the centre of the room, bent over double and catching our breaths. Bryce still looked white, but the makeshift tourniquet had stopped the bleeding.

'Fuck,' I said. 'Now they know where we live.'

'Come on,' said Bryce, 'Let's get back before they find us.' Then he smiled as something caught his eye on the floor.

'Wee fucker left half his joint,' he said.

We followed the canal out of town and turned onto the Water of Leith, where it slunk beneath the bouldered rubble of the A70. The river had once joined the Pentland Hills to the Shore. Dirt tracks, iron railings and asphalt paths had lined its banks as it meandered and frothed and waterfalled beneath stone bridges and tree canopies. It had been a quiet place. The water had allowed nature to flow through the city. Now it was a dry ditch. Weed, metal and rotten matter sprung from the mud. It had always smelled wet and pungent, the cycle of life and death in constant motion. Now it just smelled of death.

It began to rain as we reached Colinton Dell, rounding the corner onto the hill that led up to Bonaly. This had once been my home. Now it was just a dangerous mound of loose mud and mortar. Every few steps we would sink or stumble. Fallen trees made climbing even more difficult. Roots, stumps and trunks stacked across each other like giant matchsticks. Occasionally we would see human remains. Blackened skulls, torsos smeared against concrete, the occasional tiny clawed hand. We had learned to let our eyes slide away from these horrors, swallowing the sickness fast and moving on. Even Bryce now quickened his pace when he saw them. We knew the best routes. We knew the places to avoid.

We reached the top and the ground flattened out. Bryce stopped at a set of rusted swings, the remains of a playground I had once taken Alice to. He sat on the swing and lit the remains of the joint he had found, watching me struggle through the last few metres of mud with thin lines of smoke trailing from his nose and through his thick hair. The brittle chain squeaked as he rocked slowly back and forth on the swing. I caught him up and bent over double, spitting.

'You need to get more exercise,' he said, handing me the wet stub. I puffed the last few hot drags and squashed it into the earth. I hadn't smoked cannabis since university. Now any chance of escape was welcome. Something hard scraped beneath my boot. I cleared the mud and dug out a piece of metal – half a sign, white with black letters.

aly Store

Bonaly Store.

'This was near our house,' I said.

Bryce nodded and looked around. The black wreckage of the bypass lay ahead of us, dotted with the crumbling remains of burned cars. Behind and beneath us lay Edinburgh.

'Nice neighbourhood,' he said. 'Lovely outlook.'

He seemed to remember something and gave me a sly look.

'How *are* things at home, by the way?' he said.

'What do you mean?'

He shrugged.

'Thought I heard raised voices from your room last night. Trouble in paradise?'

'None of your business.'

I saw movement behind Bryce. He turned his head back across his shoulder.

'Oh, well, here come the boys,' he said, getting to his feet. Yuill, Henderson and Richard were walking down from the bypass to meet us. They stopped and we exchanged nods. Bryce coughed. I could see he was struggling, but he kept his eyes fixed on Yuill.

Yuill was expressionless, hands behind his back. He eyed Bryce's shoulder.

'Well,' he said. 'What happened?'

What Happened

Castlelaw was a mess, but not as much of a mess as Redford or Dreghorn, the other two military barracks in the south of Edinburgh. I had seen them from the rescue helicopter moments after we had been pulled from the cellar – flat sprays of brick and bent metal like everything else. I had looked down upon the levelled city with my head against the window. Streets had been wiped from the surface. There were countless craters. The castle was in ruins. Every road was now an impassable hell of rubble. I saw two plane wrecks. One had crashed into the Newhaven docks with its nose sunk deep into the harbour wall. The sea was awash with debris and brown foam. The second plane lay in two pieces, snapped against the summit of Arthur's Seat, which was itself now just a black stump.

I don't remember much after that, only finding myself standing between Beth and Alice in a makeshift medical ward full of nervous soldiers and wounded civilians. Alice was crying for the toilet. I saw an old man in a bed. His wide, brown face broke into a smile as he caught my eye.

'Different rays, mate,' he said in a cracked, Australian drawl. I frowned and felt myself losing consciousness. 'Different rays.'

Nobody knew what was happening in those first few weeks. We were given a room to live in and a number. Ours was eighteen. Groups of us were called out every day for food; five or six families or individuals at a time traipsing up to the canteen and eating in silence. We were well stocked. Meals were good and served three times a day.

We saw little of the soldiers. They seemed organised and moved quickly from room to room, avoiding eye contact. Answers to questions were short.

Power came from a generator. The noise woke us when it started in the morning and stayed with us until the lights went off in the early evening. There was little daylight in the barracks and the frosted glass of the windows showed us nothing of what was outside. We lived beneath low ceilings and between close walls reverberating with the deep thrum of an engine. It was as if we were on a cargo ship creeping through a calm sea.

Fuel ran low. Every morning of the first week I heard a helicopter leave and return some hours later. A few more people were brought in from these rescue missions. Then the sound of the chopper was replaced with the crunch of boots on gravel. Troops left on foot and returned late.

Then our meals began to be served only twice a day. Portions became smaller.

One day we were called for a briefing in the mess hall. Lines of red and blue plastic chairs faced the front. A television stood unplugged in one corner. Photo collages lined the walls: group hugs, rock horns, beers held aloft and simulated sex positions between troops, most of whom were now dead.

Arthur and I were the first ones to arrive. Alice was helping Beth wash clothes in the laundry. We sat in the corner, making a tower of empty plastic bottles.

'This your boy?' came a deep croak behind us. Arthur looked up and squealed, pointing over my shoulder. I turned. The old Australian man from the ward stood with his legs apart, leaning forward with his hands on his knees. He was big and barrel-chested, strong-looking. His hair was thick and tufted with grey, his eyes still white and vital. His brown, weathered cheeks pulled into a beam and he gave Arthur a slow wave.

'Yes,' I said, standing. 'Arthur.'

'Hello, Arthur. That's a good name. I'm Harvey.'

He extended a shovel-like hand. The shake was firm and well-practised.

'Harvey Payne.'

'Edgar.'

'Nice to meet you, Ed.'

He turned back to Arthur and gave another wave. Arthur released a tremendous cry, his face creased with delight.

'Good lungs, too,' said Harvey. 'That's a good scream there, sonny. Don't you muffle it.' He coughed and wagged a finger. 'Don't you let 'em muffle it now, will ya?' He dragged a chair over and sat down, leaning forward with both giant hands clasped together like tree roots. Then he picked up a bottle and offered it to Arthur.

I stepped back and let the old man play with my son. People were filling the room and soldiers took seats along the front wall. Stuck to a whiteboard was a large map of the United Kingdom. An officer called Yuill stood before it. He must have been in his twenties. He had fair, cropped hair and nervous eyes that flicked around the room. Next to him stood Private Grimes. She was small and serious. I recognised her from the rescue helicopter.

Men and women moved their children cautiously through the room, picking chairs. I recognised a man near the front who I had seen in the canteen. His name was Richard. It was just him and his son.

Alice and Beth arrived and we took seats along the back row with Harvey. Just when it seemed that everybody had arrived and the low murmur dropped, the doors suddenly burst open and a mountain of hair and leather walked in.

Alice ducked behind my shoulder. She tapped my hand and passed me one of the two cans I had strung together for her in the cellar. She called it her 'stringyphone'. It went everywhere with her. I put it against my ear as she held the other end to her mouth.

'Daddy,' she whispered, voice fluttering with fear. 'It's the bear.'

Alice and I had seen him a few days after we had arrived at the barracks. A nurse in military fatigues had been wheeling him down the corridor on a stretcher that strained under his weight. His bloodied right arm had been clutched to his great bare chest, the barrel of his belly spilling out over his leather biker trousers. He had winked at Alice, shot me a menacing grin as he passed. 'Lovely day, eh pal?'

'Bear, Daddy,' Alice had said once he'd disappeared around a corner. 'Bear.'

Alice was right: he did seem to have more in common with a bear than with a man. Even his shoulders looked like they began halfway up the back of his head.

He paused as the doors swung shut behind him and scanned the room. His eyes twinkled like diamonds from a deep coal pit. His hair was black and long and a beard covered half of his face, all of his neck and what appeared to be a permanent grin. His long coat fell open, revealing his right arm supported in a sling across his gigantic chest. He strode up to the front row and fell heavily on the last seat, looking up at Yuill as if we were all about to watch a cheap strip show.

His name was Bryce.

Yuill took one last look about. He was fit and lean with pale-blue eyes. 'Good morning,' he said. His voice fluttered. There were some mumbled greetings back. Bryce boomed back a pleasant 'Morning!'

'My name is Second Lieutenant James Yuill. I am the … I am now the ranking officer here at Castlelaw Barracks.'

I scanned the quiet room. People were craning their necks to see the map. '*Ranking officer?*' I heard someone whisper.

'Welcome,' said Yuill.

Silence, apart from a single loud laugh from Bryce, which Yuill ignored.

'I need hardly remind you that this situation is …' He opened his palms to the room. 'Well, it goes well beyond anything any of us have had to deal with before. We're all in shock. We're all injured, tired and grieving. All of us have lost friends and family. Most of the people we know and love are unaccounted for. We have survived the ruin of a devastating …'

A man in the third row raised a tentative hand. Yuill raised his own against it.

'There will be time for questions later. But in the meantime I have some good news. Er …'

He ushered the soldier to his right forward. He was stronger built than Yuill.

'Private Guthrie, please.'

Guthrie took Yuill's place at the front.

'Yes, sir. In the weeks since the event, we have been attempting to make radio contact with the outside world. We set up a distress beacon holding information about our whereabouts and status.'

He held up a piece of paper.

'Two days ago, we picked up a signal. It was very faint and very distorted. At first we couldn't hear what it was saying, but we managed to decipher what we believe to be the following fragments of information.'

He cleared his throat and began to read from the paper.

'The United Kingdom is being evacuated. All functioning planes are grounded due to the ash cloud. Ships are to depart from Falmouth Harbour in Cornwall at the end of the year. Country-wide sweeps will be made over the coming months to pick up as many survivors as possible.'

Guthrie looked up. 'That's all we have.'

He eyed Yuill and stepped back. Murmurs broke out around the room. Yuill held up his hands.

'Please, please, there will be time for questions, please ...'

The noise gradually abated.

'These are the facts: we have shelter, a generator, medicine. We're safe. All we need to do is—'

'What about food?' asked a voice.

'All we need to do,' continued Yuill, 'is—'

'Water?' said another.

'is—'

'Why did the helicopters stop? How much fuel do we have?'

Yuill stammered, holding up his hands again as if he was trying to quell an angry dog. He looked back at Grimes for support. Suddenly, out of the mass of questions being thrown at him, one rang out.

'What happened?'

The room hushed. People turned to see who had spoken. Richard was standing, his son looking up at him.

'What happened?' he repeated. 'I mean … evacuation? The entire country? What … what the hell happened?'

Yuill's hands fell as he realised. We were ignorant. We had been awoken a few weeks ago to bedlam and had spent every minute since then underground. No television, no radio, no Internet, no news. We had no idea what had happened to the world.

Yuill took a breath.

'Private Grimes,' he said. He offered her his place at the front. 'If you please.'

Grimes stepped forward and glanced around the room. She held a pointer in her hand which she touched against the map. Her hand was shaking.

'We don't know the full extent of the damage, but we do know that we were hit hard up and down the length of the country.' She moved the pointer from south to north. 'London, Birmingham, Liverpool, Manchester, Sheffield, Leeds, Newcastle, Glasgow, even towns and cities as far north as Aberdeen saw strikes.'

She circled back south over the North Sea.

'Edinburgh itself was devastated. Four or five strikes wiped out most of the buildings. As far as we know, the fires burned for at least two weeks. There was no access for emergency services …'

She faltered.

'In actual fact … no emergency services were left to provide help.'

Gasps and cries. A woman in front of me held her hand over her mouth. Richard's hand shot up again and the noise died away.

'Excuse me,' he said. 'Strikes? What actually hit us?'

Grimes stood still. I could feel her backtracking even further, finding words to describe the things she had assumed we already knew. She blinked and began again.

'In the early hours of the morning of August third, we received news that a large number of ...' – she faltered a little at the word – '... objects ... were following a trajectory that would place them on course for a direct hit with the planet, landing mostly in the northern hemisphere, including a great many across the United Kingdom. Along with ...'

Richard's hand again. 'How many?' he said.

Grimes paused again. 'We don't know for sure, but best guesses were that around thirty to fifty thousand individual projectiles were on course.'

She let the gasps and mutterings subside again.

'Asteroids?' asked Richard, still standing. Grimes returned him the barest of nods.

'Asteroids, meteoroids, we don't really know. At the time we had no idea how big they were, where and when they would land, or what damage they would do if they did. Every military base in the country was mobilised, including Castlelaw, Redford and Dreghorn barracks. Troops were sent into the city to keep control, to prevent panic, stop people from clogging the roads, help people if anything ... if anything happened. They were sent out to Midlothian, Perth, Glasgow, the Borders, too.'

Grimes looked back at the slim ranks of soldiers behind her.

'The soldiers you see here are some of those who were asked to remain. Our orders were to maintain contact with other bases and provide strategic support to those on the ground. We waited to hear news.'

She looked back at the map.

'At 0500 hours, we got news from the United States that a rural area in Oklahoma was seeing small hits. As far as we know, they were the first. They weren't doing much damage and for a while we thought that most of them might be burning up on entry. Very soon afterwards, more sightings were reported on the east coast of America. Then New York suffered a massive strike. Reports came in across the US, from cities and rural areas alike. They were landing everywhere: every city, every town, every state.'

Grimes cleared her throat and edged closer to the map.

'Just before 0600 hours, we received news that London had been hit.' She touched her pointer against the dense coil of roads and words in the south-east corner of the map, the thick muscle of the capital exploding with arteries out across the country.

'It was big. It wiped out most of the East End. We were still in contact with London then. There was panic, obviously, and most of the military down there was deployed to cope with the aftermath. Then there were two more strikes, much larger this time.'

Grimes withdrew the pointer.

'After that, we lost contact.'

'How many hit London?' said Bryce.

'We don't know. A base on the south coast reported something like twenty or thirty independent sightings within the M25 corridor, more outside of it.'

Sighs and gasps fluttered from the floor.

'Then,' Grimes continued, 'reports came in from the RAF of eight extremely large clouds of smoke over Birmingham.

A flyover confirmed that the Midlands had suffered countless massive strikes.'

She looked around the room. I could see she was trying to choose her words carefully. Every new piece of information could spawn another funeral for someone in the room, another nightmare for a child. But there was no other way, no other words for what she was about to say. She took a breath before continuing.

'These wiped out most of central England. Fires were reported in Wales, Yorkshire, Cambridgeshire ...'

She began to raise her voice above the noise that was now filling the room.

'It happened very quickly after that. Manchester, Birmingham, Cardiff, Liverpool, Leeds, all reporting single strikes followed by many more. Before we lost contact completely, we were hearing about strikes across the Lake District, in the Irish Sea, in the North Sea. One huge cloud was reported over Northumberland.'

The room was hushed again.

'Then we heard that Glasgow had been hit. Then Redford sounded the air-raid siren. Pretty soon after we felt the strikes here.'

'How many?' I said.

Grimes shook her head.

'We don't know. Enough to take out most of Edinburgh. We believe the entire Central Belt was hit very badly.'

Grimes stopped talking and stood holding her pointer behind her back. For a while nobody moved or made a sound. Eventually, Beth broke the silence. Alice cuddled into her arm as she spoke.

'In total . . .' she said '. . . across the UK . . . how many?'

Grimes paused. 'We estimate somewhere between two or three thousand.'

The room seemed to release a single shuddering breath at this before returning to silence.

Like everybody else, my brain attempted to process the impossible. I thought back to the pamphlets and books I had hoarded as a teenager, the 1980s government service broadcasts they would use in the event of a nuclear war, all grainy, the announcer's voice urgent and well spoken. BBC English from another time and way of life.

'. . . *in the event of a strike . . . stay indoors . . . get underground if you can . . .*'

In the event of *a strike*; singular.

Global atomic war was always depicted by some cheap animation of a globe, a few oversized mushroom clouds sprouting from its wobbling, crayoned surface like stalks of broccoli.

The advice was always to remain indoors, to wait.

'. . . *remember . . . remain in your inner refuge . . . listen to your radio . . . wait for advice . . .*'

There was always a radio, there was always a radio station. There was always a place where the strike had not happened, there was always a time when things got back to normal. There was always a boundary to the devastation.

'So, what's left?' somebody asked.

Grimes shook her head. 'We don't know. Aside from the signal we picked up two days ago, we've had no contact with anyone. We don't know anything beyond what we've seen in Edinburgh. Luckily one of our helicopters survived the fires. We used that to search for survivors at first, but fuel is scarce.'

I tried various ways of fitting the information in my brain. I imagined myself flying over a life-size relief map of the UK, place names etched on the landscape, a wide grid superimposed over its contours. I tried to imagine a thousand asteroids slowly making impact as I passed each city, but your brain is smaller than you think, as it turns out. Try to imagine a thousand of anything, let alone a thousand spinning asteroids. I had barely counted ten explosions before the map began to fold and distort and lose its scale.

I tried to focus on a single city. I imagined a face-down view of London from the air, thirty bright pulses erupting around the curled blue snake of the Thames. I tried to imagine 60 million people swept up in a thousand firestorms, attempted a dreadful calculation that divided lives equally between eruptions, applying some cold and bizarre weighting algorithm between cities and guessing at the space between them.

However I tried it, the result was the same. Instead of accepting, my brain rejected. Instead of an emotional response, I became detached. The event was intangible; a cold, numb thing that barely made sense. It was only later, when I saw it all for myself, that I was able to absorb the extent of it. For now, all I had was numbers.

After more silence, Richard raised his hand.

'Yes,' said Grimes.

'We have fuel and a helicopter. There must be cars. Why don't we leave? Why don't we go somewhere safe?'

Grimes stepped forward. She traced the pointer down through the hills beneath Edinburgh and Glasgow. 'We have flown reconnaissance missions across Midlothian and as far south as the border with England.' She tapped the A74, A76,

A7, the A1, every line that ran south from Scotland. 'These roads have been brought to a standstill by traffic.'

'What do you mean?' said a small man on the second row. 'A traffic jam? It's been weeks, surely they must have been able to move it by now? Redirect it or something?'

Grimes looked back at him.

'The traffic is no longer moving,' she said.

'But . . .' said the voice. 'But surely . . .'

'They're all fuckin' dead, y'eejit,' said Bryce, still facing forward.

The room was silent.

'But . . . but . . .'

Grimes touched the pointer back at the map. 'There was massive damage to this part of the country. Like I said, the impacts were everywhere, not just in the cities. Basically we're cut off from the south.'

A hand shot up from the back row.

'Yes,' said Grimes.

'What about Glasgow?' said a trembling voice.

'As I say, we have had no radio contact with any other base. Reports from our trips across to the west coast suggest that Glasgow was hit even harder than us. We believe that a large Atlantic tsunami spread across most of the city. The roads are crippled, the buildings . . . the buildings all but demolished, everything flooded.'

More cries, more gasps and urgent conversations. A woman began to weep '. . . My sister . . . oh, God, my sister . . .'

'Come on,' roared Bryce. 'Weegies'll be alright. They already live in a shithole, a couple of deep impacts won't make a difference.' He turned and grinned at the now-silent crowd.

'They probably woke up and thought someone had redecorated,' he continued.

There were tuts of disapproval, heads shaken.

'Just trying to see the bright side,' he said, turning back. 'Christ.'

Harvey chuckled and leaned towards me.

'Different rays, mate,' he whispered. 'Different rays.'

For the short period I knew Harvey I didn't really understood much of what he said. Most of his words were caught somewhere between a riddle and a rant. But I would understand them later. 'Different rays' was his way of saying that everyone was different: horses for courses, live and let live, that kind of thing. 'We're all born under the same sun,' he told me once, as we pawed through the wreckage of a National Express coach somewhere near Lancaster, 'just different rays.'

But I'm getting ahead of myself. Striding on, as Harvey would say.

'So what's our plan, then?' said the small man, now panicking near the front. 'What the hell are we going to do?'

Grimes stepped back and turned to the other soldier standing behind Yuill.

'Lance Corporal Henderson?'

The soldier stood forward. He was well over six foot tall, square-soldiered, iron-jawed, chest like a truck. He kept his hands behind his back as he spoke. His accent was London English; the West Indian street twang barely restrained behind his clipped, military bark.

'Short term: we source supplies. Long term, we maintain our distress beacon and wait for the evac rescue teams.'

Henderson stepped back and Yuill took his place at the front.

'To do this,' said Yuill, 'we need to make salvage missions into the city. We believe there are a number of locations where fuel and food can be found. These missions will be made on foot.'

'What about the air?' somebody said. 'Is it safe outside?'

'We've conducted a few tests,' said Yuill. 'We believe the air is safe to breathe, but we're taking precautions with biosuits and masks all the same.'

'You said that the soldiers in this room were *some* of the ones who were left behind,' said Richard. He was still standing up, one hand resting on his son's shoulder.

'Yes,' said Grimes.

'Then where are the rest?'

Yuill stepped forward and nodded at Grimes.

'As Private Grimes mentioned,' he said, 'Edinburgh was hit very hard. The blasts and shockwaves caused damage far into the Central Belt. Redford and Dreghorn were destroyed. Castlelaw sits behind a hill, so we had some protection … but we were severely damaged just like everything else. Many of the soldiers in the barracks died either in the blasts themselves or putting out the fires that had started. Only a fraction of the buildings are still standing. We managed to secure the east wing and a couple of the store houses. These are our living quarters now. This is where we live.'

Yuill flicked his eyes between us.

'Because our numbers are somewhat …' he glanced behind him '… depleted.'

A snort from Bryce. Yuill kept his eyes straight ahead.

'Because of this, we need to ensure that we maximise our human resources . . .'

'Human resources?' said Bryce 'What is this, *The* fuckin' *Apprentice*?'

Yuill turned to him.

'Because of this,' he repeated, holding Bryce's stare, 'we need to ensure that every one of you is trained. That every one of you is fit, healthy and able to defend yourself.'

Unrest rippled across the room.

'Defend ourselves?' someone shouted. 'Defend ourselves against what? I thought we were stuck here alone?'

'Training starts tomorrow,' Yuill continued over the shouts of concern.

'Men and boys over fourteen and women over the age of sixteen who are not nursing will begin basic military training under the supervision of Corporal Henderson, Private Guthrie and Private Grimes.'

Bryce threw back his head and began laughing as shouts of disapproval broke out.

'Tomorrow morning. 0600 hours in the gym,' said Yuill. He snatched his papers and walked out.

Most people were off their seats, trying to follow Yuill and being placated by Grimes. I sat in my seat and watched Bryce's huge, hairy head roar with laughter. Beth laid a hand on mine and squeezed it.

'Different rays, mate,' said Harvey in my ear. 'Different rays.'

We were separated into groups. They made no bones about how they split us up; Guthrie took those who were already fit. Grimes took the women and boys. The rest – my group, the overweight and undertrained – got Corporal Henderson. At 6 a.m., just after the sound of boots on gravel had disappeared from outside, there was a light knock on our door. I slipped out and followed the rest of the group through to a small gymnasium cleared of equipment.

Training did not have the effect you might have expected. This was no cinematic montage; we weren't transformed from soft civilians into hardened soldiers overnight, or even after the weeks that we spent trying to follow Henderson's increasingly disgusted orders. There were no moments of triumph, no tears, no hidden wells of determination suddenly plunged. There was no electricity to waste on treadmills or exercise bikes, so our workouts involved push-ups, star-jumps, sit-ups and short sprints between lines. We performed badly. It was dark, hot and uncomfortable; the room was too small, the ceiling too low. Nobody spoke and we all left in silence for breakfast.

Just like any form of exercise I had encountered before, there seemed little point to what we were doing. The world was in smithereens and we were spluttering beneath the ground like fat moles. I hated every moment of it, but I wasn't the worst in my group. One morning in the second week, a doughy man named Alan failed a fifth attempt at a sit-up and rolled onto his side, curled his legs up and wept as an outraged Henderson screamed obscenities down at him.

The average is low. Very low.

I had been a squat, overweight child until the age of fifteen, when a sudden growth spurt had stretched out my body to average height and created an illusion of leanness. My face, once round, now appeared gaunt. My limbs, once plump with puppy fat, now appeared lithe. You may have been forgiven for believing that my torso, beneath clothes, was taut and muscled. Lift the shirt, though, remove the trousers, put me by the swimming pool and my hunched shoulders and folded arms hid a very different story. My body had stretched, but there was no definition. I had a concave chest upon which sat two soft, pudding-like breasts with pale nipples. Beneath them was a shapeless stomach surrounded by doughy flanks that spilled out over my trunks. Wide, freckled mounds of flesh clung to my lower back, hovering above my buttocks like unhappy clouds.

In the years since puberty, my body had eventually settled for a slightly more ordered version of this strange shape. Excess had added a pot belly, some lines and wrinkles, more hair, tougher skin. The training sessions didn't transform the soft body I had abused and ignored into a hardened slab. What I did see was a rough shaving of its outer fat, like a tree stump run once beneath a blunt lathe: not exactly sculpted, just less than what it had been. I also found it harder to sit still. My legs were uncomfortable when I lay down. I felt unused muscles ache. I discovered that I could climb stairs with ease.

I began to fidget more and more. Arthur had started teething, wailing late into the night. I took to walking the corridors with him, stretching my shoulders and thighs, pulling my neck. I felt the need to twitch my muscles as strongly as I felt the need to stop Arthur's cries. Frustration in my head, frustration in my body; the need to explode from all corners of your being – a feeling I was already used to.

It was one of these evenings, just after midnight, and a wild storm had flared up outside that battered the windows of the barracks. I had just settled Arthur and was about to return to our room when I heard a gruff cackle and the sound of glass from somewhere above. I climbed the darkened stairwell to the canteen with Arthur asleep and burrowed into my neck. The canteen was also in darkness, but I could see a small light coming from the kitchen. I opened the door to see Harvey and Richard sat around a wooden table, a bottle and three glasses surrounding a single candle. Bryce was there, too. He and Richard were in Guthrie's group and Harvey was spared the training on account of his age. I hadn't spoken to any of them in the weeks since our sessions had begun.

Bryce looked up as I opened the door. He was leaning on the table, still chuckling and cradling a glass in one hand. Richard was leaning back in his chair, one long leg crossed casually across the other. He looked back over his shoulder while Harvey refilled his glass.

'Hello,' whispered Harvey. His eyes twinkled in the candle-light as he looked at Arthur sleeping on my shoulder.

'Wee man asleep?' said Bryce out loud.

I nodded. 'Yes, finally.'

'What's his name?'

'Arthur,' whispered Harvey loudly. 'His name's Arthur.'

Bryce laughed and offered his glass for Harvey to refill.

'A king no less,' he said. 'An *English* king,' the word deliberately stressed for my benefit. He drained his glass and I resisted the urge to reward his joke with an unconvincing laugh. Beth had always said that Arthur's name might be difficult for him in Scotland.

Harvey had produced another glass. He unfolded a chair and motioned for me to sit. 'Ignore him,' he said. 'Come and have a drink.'

I sat down.

'And you,' said Bryce, 'what do we call you?'

'Edgar,' I said. I offered him a hand. He looked at it and raised an eyebrow.

Harvey shook his head. 'Ignore him,' he said. 'This is Richard.'

Bryce released a long, guttural belch.

'Or "Dick",' he said.

Richard leaned forward and shook my hand. 'Pleasure,' he said.

I immediately thought of a remote Scottish boarding school, wooden trunks, golf clubs and cheques from Mother. He had the easy-going grace and manner of some officer from a different time. If he had been smoking a pipe I wouldn't have blinked.

'What's that you're drinking?' I said.

Harvey raised his eyebrows. 'Whisky,' he said, filling my glass with deep, amber fluid. He looked up at me and grinned. 'Single malt.'

I raised it to my nose and took a sniff. The three men watched me enjoy the rush of sharp fumes filling my sinuses. I had had nothing to drink since the early morning of the strike. I raised my glass to them and took a long, slow gulp. I kept my eyes closed for as long as possible as heat spread into my torso. When I opened them again, Harvey, Bryce and Richard were each still watching me in silence. I turned the glass in my hand.

'Where did you find this?' I said.

Bryce nudged his glass towards Harvey, who obliged and then saw to my own half-empty tumbler. Harvey hooked a thumb at Richard.

'This man here,' said Harvey, 'is what you might call a *forward thinker*.'

'The man knows how to pack,' said Bryce.

Richard uncrossed his arms and reached out a long arm for his glass. He sat back and shrugged.

'My cellar was well stocked,' he said.

I nodded, fighting back a rush of guilt as I thought of the pit I had put my family in for that fortnight. 'You planned ahead?' I said hopefully. Richard looked into his glass.

'The same as everyone else, I expect,' he said. 'We – Gabriella, my wife, and I – we didn't think anything was really going to happen. Nobody really did, did they? We boxed up some supplies anyway: water, pasta, medicine ...'

He looked up at me, father to father. 'You know what I mean?'

I kept quiet, nodded, remembering the panic, the largely useless box I had packed before hurling Alice down into the cellar.

'Just in case.' He laughed to himself. 'My son, Josh, called it the 'apocabox'. He was just as sceptical as us. Anyway, we went to bed the night before thinking nothing more about it. Then I woke up to the sirens. Gaby was gone, up early, out for her morning run. She was training for a marathon and Sunday was the day she took her hill session ...' He stopped and swirled the liquid in his glass. 'Which meant that she was on her way up Arthur's Seat.'

Harvey and Bryce looked patiently into their glasses. They had obviously heard Richard's story already.

'I tried calling her – she always took her phone with her on her runs – but she didn't answer. We have that GPS thing on our phones that lets you see where the other one is. I checked that and, sure enough, she was almost at the top of the hill. I called her again, but that's when I lost the signal. I tried the television, the Internet, nothing. Then there was shouting outside, glass breaking, cars speeding away. I woke Josh, explained what was happening and took him out to the car. I was going to drive out to collect her. I had the engine started and was halfway down the drive when Josh pointed up into the sky. "Dad," he said, "Dad, what's that?" I barely had time to answer before we heard the first explosion, then fire and smoke in the distance. Arthur's Seat raged like a volcano.'

'Christ,' I said. 'I'm so …'

'Then there was no time to do anything. Two more landed a little further away. I swear I could hear the screams. It was like some terrible choir. I froze; couldn't decide what to do.'

Richard cleared his throat and lined it with another drink from his glass.

'Eventually I realised that Josh was shaking me and shouting at me to move. He said, "Dad! Dad! Come on, Dad! Look!" The sky was filling up with streak after streak of light. I snapped to and we left the car, ran back into the house and down into our wine cellar with the apocabox and water tanks.'

'Where did you live?' I asked.

'The Grange,' he said. This explained the wine cellar; the Grange was a moneyed area – wide Georgian avenues lined with mansions protected by high trees and fences.

'There's still a chance …' I started. 'I mean, maybe she got down before it hit.'

Richard frowned, pushed out his lips and shook his head. 'Our cellar was deep and we were well protected, but we could hear the fires burning above us, the sound of buildings collapsing, voices sometimes, too.'

He sneered at this, turning the whisky in his glass as if he'd found something unpalatable floating in it. I remembered our own first night, the sound of the woman's pleas against the hatch and her silence as the rubble fell.

'It was dark once things had settled down outside. Unsurprisingly, we didn't sleep that first night,' said Richard, glancing up at us. 'I don't expect many did. Josh wanted to get out and search for his mum. I had to virtually pin him down to stop him from getting out. I knew it wasn't safe out there. And I knew . . . I . . . well, I *calculated* . . .'

Again, that sneer as he rolled his drink around the glass. He seemed to shake away the thought.

'It didn't matter what I thought, though, Josh believed his mum was still alive. The next morning we could still hear the fires but they seemed less fierce, so I told Josh to stay put while I took a look upstairs. When I got out I was amazed to find our kitchen still standing, but it was the only part of the house that was. I could barely see with all the ash falling everywhere. I couldn't even make out where the floor was. I wrapped a scarf around my face and walked out onto the street, but I'd barely made it past where our gate had been before I had to turn back. The air was like fire and I couldn't breathe for the smoke. When I got back inside, Josh ran at me, screaming at me to get back out. I tried telling him, but he pushed me aside and went outside himself. I ran after him, found him halfway up the street on his knees, almost passed out. I managed to drag him back and get him cleaned up. He wouldn't talk to me for a couple of days, but he didn't go outside again. Neither of us did until we heard the helicopters a week later.'

We allowed the loose ends of his story to dangle in silence for a while.

'He's only fourteen,' said Richard.

A sudden blast of storm wind hammered the windows of the canteen and howled off into the night. I jumped a little and Arthur began to stir against my neck. He let out a croak, then a long wail as consciousness resurrected the pain in his mouth. I patted his back and shushed him.

'Teething?' said Richard.

'Yup,' I nodded.

'Poor little mite,' said Harvey.

Bryce jabbed his index finger into his glass and began twirling it around.

'Only one thing for that,' he said, and held it up.

I watched it for a while, that grubby stump dripping with whisky in the candlelight. Arthur's wail became a scream in my ear. I turned to Harvey and Richard, who both shrugged. Then I took Arthur from my shoulder and gently lay him back over the table. The sudden change of position and light surprised him and he stared up frantically at the three new faces looking down at him, mouth wide open, hands clawing for purchase on something.

'Which side?' said Bryce.

'Upper left,' I replied. 'Be careful.'

Bryce gently slid his finger into my son's mouth and rubbed it against his gums. Arthur squealed as if to scream again, but began suckling on Bryce's finger instead.

'That's not a tit, son,' said Bryce, removing his finger. He doused it in more whisky and gave it back to Arthur, who chewed it hungrily, wide-eyed. Richard and Harvey laughed at the horrible sight until eventually Bryce took out his finger again and wiped it on his jeans.

'Mum always said that worked for me,' he said, picking up his glass.

Arthur smacked his lips and lay silent, looking around at the flickering walls, the shadows, the world's strange illusions that he would soon take for granted. His eyelids began to droop and I placed him on my shoulder, expecting him to start up at any moment. But he nuzzled in, lay still, fell asleep. Harvey and Richard smiled in wonder. Bryce raised his glass to his lips, but paused halfway.

'You were right not to go outside again,' he said, glancing at Richard. 'I'm sorry, but there's no way anything on Arthur's Seat would have survived what hit it.'

'You saw it?' I said.

'Aha,' said Bryce. 'I was halfway along the coast to Portobello, got a clear view. I stopped my bike when I saw the first one flying overhead, watched that hill burst apart like a watermelon.' He went to mime an exploding hill, but thought better of it when he saw Richard's face.

'Bike?' I said. 'You cycled out of town?'

Bryce puffed and snorted. 'Did I fuck,' he said. '*Motorbike,* man. Christ, do I look like I ride a fuckin' push bike?'

'Well, you're in the top group at school,' I said, referring to the training sessions.

Bryce turned to face me. 'And?' he said.

'I mean, you don't exactly look . . .'

Bryce laid down his glass and turned to face me.

'Oh, I get it. I'm a big man, so I must be unfit?'

'No, wait, that's not what I ...'

He prodded one of his immense fingers in my direction. 'I *walk* everywhere, sunshine. *And* I do a lot of shaggin'. What about you?' I followed his eyes down to my gut, visibly bulging beneath my T-shirt. 'What's your excuse?'

'Ease up there, Bryce,' said Harvey, giving me a look that got stuck somewhere between kindness and pity. 'Give the man a break, he's got kids.'

'Wait a minute ...' I began. Bryce swivelled to Harvey and frowned.

'So?' he said.

'Well,' said Harvey, struggling. He looked me up and down, gesturing half-heartedly as he looked for the right words. 'It's, y'know, hard, I imagine. To keep in shape, I mean.'

'What? Hold on,' I said.

Bryce had turned back to me, lip and eyebrow pulled into identical curls.

'Knew it. Parents, you're all the same. You're all "I can't do this, I can't do that or I can't get my arse off the sofa, I'm tired or my kids are so fuckin' demanding, I don't have time for anything else." Fuckin' pathetic, the lot of youse. You chose to have the wee bastards.' He jabbed another finger at me and sat back in his seat. 'You take your medicine!'

Bryce and I had a shaky start to our relationship. Everything I did or said seemed to piss him off at first. He had marked me as weak and conforming, a middle-class English misery with no balls who secretly wanted to be liked by people like him. I dismissed him as a loud-mouthed boor, all mouth and swagger that concealed a deep-seated nervousness about his intelligence. We both bristled with tired quarrels born in grey playgrounds.

One evening I had been sat with Alice at the corner table, waiting for Beth and Arthur to come up from our room. Alice had been especially quiet that week and we were worried that she was going to revert to that state of shock she had fallen into during our time in the cellar. I had passed her the stringyphone and whispered something into my can that had made her smile. Seeing my chance, I jammed a finger into her ribs and tickled her until she was lost in her giggles and leaning helplessly into my side. Out of the corner of my eye I had spotted Bryce watching us. He was in line for food, midway through spooning a pile of tinned peas onto his plate. There was no menace in his face, no mockery, just appreciation. He gave a quick smile when I saw him, then looked away. Things seemed to get better between us after that, although Bryce was not the kind of person I could easily describe as a friend. And certainly not when I first met him.

'Come on, Bryce,' said Richard, folding his long, lean arms across his fatless torso. 'It's hard, isn't it, Ed?'

All three men were now facing me, regarding me impassively like scientists at some watery specimen they would soon discard.

'Bollocks,' muttered Bryce across the lip of his glass.

I said nothing, looked down at my son's peaceful face. Arthur released a long, thoughtful fart that trailed off into something wet.

'Smartest thing I've heard so far this evening,' said Harvey. We laughed. It's hard not to when a baby farts and an old man smiles.

Rabbits

The next morning, at breakfast, Grimes stood and announced that they were looking for volunteers to join the salvage missions into the city. It had been another night of broken sleep and the whisky had given me a hangover. Arthur was sat on my knee, screaming again, one fist jammed between his sore red gums as I struggled to force porridge past it. Alice was crying too, tired, clinging to her mother like a limpet and clawing at her clothes. Beth sat trembling and sniffing with her head in her hands. Her nose and eyes were wet with tears.

Grimes looked around the room as some of the men raised their hands tentatively. I saw Bryce and Richard raise their hands. Arthur flailed in my arms and threw his other fist at me, slamming a chunk of porridge into my eye. He laughed and then hurled the bowl to the floor.

I wasn't a completely bad father or husband. But I wasn't a good one either.

I wiped the goo from my eye and raised a hand.

My first run was a couple of weeks later. Beth wasn't happy about it.

'I'm just doing what I can,' I said before we left.

'You're just doing what you want,' she replied, not looking up from the bed.

Four of us joined the soldiers: Bryce, Richard, his son and me. We wore heavy coats, a pair of thick trousers, boots, a helmet and a gas mask. We were each given a large empty pack to carry and marched behind and within the six armed troops. We were mules.

At dawn we stood sweating behind the main doors like deep space astronauts preparing to set foot on an alien shore. Through the condensation in my mask I watched Richard lean in and say something in his son's ear. The boy nodded and Richard reached his hand around and gripped his shoulder, pulling him into his chest. Bryce stood beside me staring straight ahead, fists clenched at his sides, fuming after his first request for a gun had been denied.

Corporal Henderson was leading the run. I saw him raise a hand and the plastic sheets that surrounded the main doors were pulled back for us to walk through. We followed the soldiers into the early light.

Despite the confines of our kit and masks, there was a sense of a weight being lifted, of tension relieved, like removing a hat that you've been wearing too long. Cold air hit my face and the world opened up around us. The sun was not yet up, but it was still brighter than inside the barracks. The sky was heavy with thick, low cloud, but still higher than any ceiling.

It could have been any other dark winter's morning in Edinburgh. The fog and low cloud stretched from the Pentland Hills towards the Forth and beyond, obscuring the view north into Fife. Even as we hiked the long track down towards the foot of the hills, we couldn't see any detail of the wreckage we knew to be ahead. That day we were spared the full view of something that would soon become familiar, the one I had seen glimpses of from the helicopter: an ancient city blown away like dust.

We made our way into the centre, learning very quickly to avoid looking at anything for too long. I saw the charred figure of a man halfway through the windscreen of a Volvo. It looked as if he had been crawling, with one hand outstretched and the other beneath him. He was on his knees with his buttocks raised the way babies sometimes sleep. His head was turned to face us with his cheek against the metal of the car bonnet. There were no features, just gaping black holes of ash.

We reached our destination, a small café off Lothian Road next to an office block that had been torn apart. They signalled the all-clear and then the remaining troops followed them in, leaving the four of us outside in the still, grey morning.

Bryce lifted his mask and lit a cigarette. Richard sat down on a wall with his son, who was holding his head between his hands and shaking. I lifted my own mask and looked around. The air was not fresh. It was cold but not fresh. It was like … it *was* … a fridge full of rancid meat.

About a mile away I could make out the dim outline of Edinburgh Castle rising up behind the fog. The shape was all wrong. Chimneys were gone, turrets were cracked, the whole thing seemed to have heaved to one side.

Bryce offered me his cigarette. I shook my head and he turned to lean against a broken pillar.

Then I saw a glint of light and froze. Somewhere to my left, deep within the iron girders of the office block, there had been movement. I peered in. Nothing. Then a shape, a shadow flitting between other shadows.

'Bryce,' I croaked. 'Bryce, I . . .'

At that moment, Henderson and the troops emerged from the café. They carried crates of water, cans, packets, coffee, tea. Henderson was grinning.

'Good haul,' he said. 'Let's load these boys up and head home.'

They made three trips in and out of the café until all our packs were filled. Then we marched home. As we left, I looked over my shoulder, feeling eyes watching me from the darkness of a ruined building.

We made more runs after that. Sometimes we returned with full packs and other times we returned empty-handed. Occasionally I saw the shadows move. I was sure Bryce and Richard did too, although we never spoke of it.

The runs became more regular. By the middle of November we were going every other day. That's when we met them face to face.

It's quite possible that there were many more survivors in Edinburgh than we had first thought, perhaps clinging for life in the maze of Old Town tenements or the protection of New Town basement flats. We didn't know much about them. If they were there then we couldn't reach them. The ones we found first were those who had laid claim to the streets. They were lean and hungry, organised, armed and aggressive. Bryce called them 'Rabbits', basically because they lived underground and he wanted to shoot them. The name stuck.

We had no idea who they were or where they came from, although Bryce had a theory. It seemed fair to assume that the only people who survived the strike were those who were underground and awake at the time. The impacts would have swept away the wide streets of mansions in the New Town, but it would have made a natural warren in depths of the Old Town, upon whose medieval squalor the backs of those mansions were firmly turned.

Early morning on a Sunday in the Old Town, this meant people in lock-ins and clubs – the rough and dirty ones, places to be avoided. Bryce reasoned that the Rabbits were pill-heads, stoners and kids on acid; thieves, criminals and neds. They were used to running, used to surviving in shitholes. Those who survived the wreckage would find filthy, safe holes to shelter in, routes in and out of abandoned underground shops and plenty of storerooms to plunder.

It was ridiculous, of course. It spoke more about Bryce's views on society than anything else. But nobody had a better theory.

The Rabbits were quick and understood the new layout of the crippled streets left over from the strike. Wherever the patrols found sources of food or fuel, they found Rabbits. Wherever they widened their search area, they found Rabbits. They were everywhere and they didn't like other people taking their haul. They didn't like us.

One day we heard boots running on the gravel outside the barracks. That day's salvage party had returned early. I was in the corridor outside our room when the doors burst open and two soldiers came through, supporting a third between them. He was young, possibly not even twenty. He looked up at me as they barged past. His face was pale and gaunt and he clutched both hands to his belly. They were slick with blood. The two soldiers dragged him through to the medical ward. I don't know his name and we never saw him again. He was the first.

Two others were killed as well. I don't know their names either.

The Rabbits were now a threat. The salvage missions stopped. Smaller patrols – armed soldiers only – were sent out in their place to monitor the Rabbits' activity: where they were hiding, what they were doing, how many there were of them. These didn't last long. Each party was met with an ambush or an unseen hit from a sniper. Within weeks the Rabbits had picked off over thirty soldiers.

We had one thing in our favour. The Rabbits had a territory that they didn't seem to like leaving. They must have guessed that the soldiers they met and ambushed came from one of the barracks to the south, but they had no idea which one and no idea how many soldiers were there or what kind of supplies they had. There was no suggestion that we were in trouble; for all they knew there was an entire army waiting for them in the hills. The last thing we wanted to do was to let them know otherwise.

Things became desperate. We were low on food, water and fuel. The temperature was dropping. Our numbers had diminished and chronic flu had broken out around the barracks. Many of the soldiers who were left were confined to their beds.

Our only hope was to keep our heads down and hope that the rescue party reached us soon.

It was decided that the salvage parties would start again, this time concentrating away from the Cowgate. In addition, further patrols would be made to watch the Rabbits' activities from a distance. Because there were now so few soldiers, Yuill asked again for volunteers to make these runs into the city. Anyone signing up would be given a gun. Bryce put his name down immediately. Beth watched me as I put my name next to his.

'It's insane,' she said, as we argued later. She was holding Arthur, bouncing him as he screamed from the pain in his teeth. 'It's not safe. Apart from those bloody ... *Rabbits* ...' the name stuck in her throat '... those buildings could collapse at any moment.'

'I have to go,' I said. 'I have to help.'

She laughed at me.

'Help? How can you help, Ed? What are you going to do if you get caught? Fight? Run? You've barely done enough training to run a mile without collapsing.'

I looked away, stung. She sighed and closed her eyes. Arthur continued to scream, oblivious.

'I'm sorry,' she said through gritted teeth. 'I just ... I just don't know how I'm supposed to do this without you.' She looked up at me, her face suddenly open. 'Remember you said that you could have done more in those first weeks with Alice? Well, you could do more now.'

I blinked.

'What?'

'You heard me.'

'But ... but ... I am doing more! I'm going out there, just like I did before. I went out every day to work and ...'

Beth rolled her eyes.

'Aye, aye, you went out every day. Hunter-gatherer, bringing in the kill, supporting your family, big man that you are.'

'Well ... yes, if you put it like ...'

'Do you want to know—'

'Shhh, keep your voice d—'

She didn't.

'Do you want to know how many times I used to fantasise about going to work? Just once, to leave the house and get on a bus and drift off for half-an-hour, get a coffee, sit at my desk, make some phone calls and put my brain to work on something that doesn't involve me pretending to smile at some stupid little game or getting shit all over me? Do you want to know, Ed? Do you?'

She glared at me. I had nothing. She turned away.

'I'm trying to save us,' I said. 'I know I'm not everything I could be, but I'm trying. And you told me once that you thought I could anything if I put my mind to it,' I said.

She shook her head with a bitter smile.

'If I believed that's what this was about, then I'd say go. Go, go, get out there and prove yourself, my husband. But it's not, is it? So stop lying to us both. I know the truth.'

'What?' I said, though I knew it too.

Her smile was hopeless. She turned her back.

'You'd rather be out there than in here. You always have done.'

Bryce and I became partners. Our orders were to watch the Rabbits from a distance. Just to watch. Never to make our position known. Never to fire unless fired upon …

Stop me.

I'm talking as if we were soldiers. We weren't soldiers. The fact was we were twenty scared and unfit civilians pretending to be soldiers. The fact was we were fucked.

And yet Yuill kept his uniform pressed and clean. Yuill barked orders at us as if we would snap our heels at the sound of his voice. Yuill demanded explanations.

'Well?' he said.

Ranking Officer

'Well?' said Yuill. 'What happened?'

A cool breeze whipped around our boots and blew up some ash from the surface of what had once been my street. Yuill glared at me as he waited for my explanation. His hands were on his hips, his head was leaned towards me, his lips were tight and he was frowning; doing everything possible to show enraged authority. Yuill still considered himself to be ranking officer in charge of a functioning squadron of troops, but beneath every command and reprisal lay a quivering undercurrent of fear. He was not a leader; he was a young man in a situation he didn't want to be in, trying too hard to be something he didn't want to be.

'Bryce was hit,' I said.

Yuill frowned and nodded slowly. He glared at the dark-red stain on Bryce's coat as if he were speaking only to the wound and not to us. A breeze picked up and set one of the broken swings creaking behind him.

'I can see that,' he said. 'But why?'

Bryce sneered.

'Because one of the little bastards fired a gun at me,' he said, spelling it out.

Yuill nodded again.

'And why would they have done that, I wonder,' he said.

Bryce grimaced and drew himself up. Yuill was getting to him. He always did.

'Ach,' he said. 'My finger slipped, alright?'

Yuill turned his eyes up to Bryce's face. He looked him over for a while like a farmer assessing the worth of a wounded bull. Then he turned to me.

'They followed you?' he said.

'Yes. But we lost them at Shandon.'

'Good. No reason to expect that they know where you came from.'

'Well,' I said. 'About that . . .'

He turned back to Bryce.

'You may have just narrowly missed starting a war,' he said.

Bryce was just about to launch a retort when we heard a sound: a sound we weren't expecting to hear. At first I thought it was an engine, a car; perhaps the Rabbits had found some working vehicle with which to renew their chase. But the sound got louder and more defined. It was coming from above. A low drone sliced into fast, dull segments. Blades chopping the air many times a second.

We looked up to the south. In the distance, beyond the flattened streets of Colinton, high above the torn forest of Allermuir Hill, a large yellow helicopter appeared. It hovered for a few seconds, then turned and tipped forwards, disappearing down behind the summit.

Nobody spoke. We all stared at the space where the chopper had been.

'Who the fuck was that?' said Bryce at last.

Then, from nowhere, we heard more of them. To the west we saw one, then two, both yellow. Then one suddenly burst out over our heads and roared towards the hills.

'Rescue choppers,' shouted Henderson. 'One's at the barracks. Follow me.'

Henderson turned and began running. Yuill and Richard followed, leaving Bryce and me standing in the mud.

'Can you run?' I said.

Bryce looked down at me as if I'd asked him if he wanted to hold hands.

''Course I can fuckin' run,' he said.

He sprinted after the others, clutching his shoulder. I followed behind as always.

We made it across the bypass and began the climb up Allermuir. Halfway up we turned left onto a track that took us across its face, offering us a view of the skyline behind us, at least as far as the perpetual murk would allow. There were many more helicopters. Some seemed to be returning from across the Forth, others from further inland. All of them were flying south.

The track was now at its steepest. Even Bryce had to slow down at this section. Yuill and Henderson were still marching ahead but Richard had fallen back.

'What do you think, Dick?' said Bryce as we caught him up.

'I don't know,' said Richard. 'RAF? Yuill's trying to radio the barracks, see what's what. Are you alright, Ed?'

Richard and Bryce had stopped and were looking back at me. Bryce was grinning, still holding his shoulder but standing straight. Richard had his foot up on a rock, looking for all the world like a man enjoying the view on his morning stroll.

I puffed and wheezed behind them, tripping on my feet and scrabbling on the rocks with my hands.

'Fine,' I managed as I caught them up.

Suddenly we heard the drone again. Above us, just beyond the summit, we saw a long yellow tail rise up and turn.

'Is that ours?' said Richard.

'Aye,' said Bryce. 'That's us.'

'Wait!' I shouted, waving my arms. 'Wait for us.'

Bryce turned to me in disdain.

'Aye, that'll do it, Eddie.'

Yuill and Henderson had already started running. Bryce and Richard followed with me at the back, my lungs heaving like dry furnaces and my eyes bulging with the strain.

I fell far behind. By the time I reached the barracks Bryce and Richard had already caught their breath and were standing by the gates. Yuill and Henderson were talking with Grimes in the main doorway, with Harvey loitering behind them. Bryce was smoking. He gave a slow handclap as I collapsed onto the tarmac, pulling off my pack and screaming for breath.

Richard helped me to my feet. He seemed uncomfortable, worried.

'Keep moving,' he said through gritted teeth. 'Keep moving.'

'What ... what ...?' I spluttered.

Bryce exhaled smoke and pointed a gloved finger southward. The helicopter was long gone. It was getting dark, but I could just make it out, now just a speck on the horizon.

'We missed the bus,' said Bryce, taking another drag.

I watched it disappear into the black smear. There were no others now, nothing else in the sky but cloud and the approaching night. I looked at Richard, his jaw set, arms folded, feet pacing the tarmac.

'What's wrong?' I said, as I finally found my breath. 'Who were they?'

Bryce flicked his cigarette into the dirt.

'Why don't you ask her?' he said.

Grimes was walking across, Harvey behind her.

'You need to come inside,' she said. 'All of you, now.'

'What just happened?' I said. 'Where is everyone? Where's Beth?'

'Come inside, mate,' said Harvey, giving a weak smile. 'Everything's going to be alright.'

We went to the medical ward to get Bryce patched up. Even as we passed through the main doors, I felt a dreadful emptiness in the place. My insides began to churn.

'What's going on?' I said. 'Where is everyone?'

Grimes wrestled Bryce's great trench coat from him and inspected the wound to his shoulder.

'Bullet passed straight through,' she said. 'Just needs cleaning and bandaging.'

'Bastards fucked up my coat, though,' said Bryce.

I sat on a bed opposite them. Harvey stood next to me and Richard leaned against the wall with his arms still folded. Yuill and Henderson came in and sat down. And that was it. Seven of us.

I caught Richard's eye. He was coming to the same conclusions as me.

'Where is everyone?' I repeated, warbling now. 'Where's my family?'

Harvey laid a hand on my shoulder.

Flight

'Don't worry, Ed,' said Harvey. 'Your family's fine.'

I shook off his hand and he drew back.

'Where are they?' I shouted.

Grimes had finished Bryce's bandage and was wiping her hands on a towel.

'Harvey's right,' said Grimes. 'Don't panic, your family is safe. They've been rescued.'

'Rescued? Rescued where? By whom?'

'They're new,' said Grimes.

'New?'

'Not British, not NATO, not United Nations. We don't think any of those exist any more. They called themselves *Sauver*. They're helping to evacuate Europe.'

We let this sink in for a little while. All I could think of was Beth, Alice and Arthur disappearing on the horizon. I realised I had never been farther than a few miles from them in my life. Eventually Harvey broke the silence.

'The girl I spoke to was a Kiwi,' he said. 'Pretty sure she was. Or maybe South African. Always get them mixed up.'

We all looked at Harvey. He tried a smile.

'Somewhere below the equator anyway,' he said. 'She seemed real nice, very efficient. Their uniforms were yellow, just like the choppers. All clean too.' He looked at Grimes for support. 'Looked like they'd eaten well too, didn't they?'

'Where are they evacuating from?' I said.

'Cornwall,' said Grimes. 'There are ships taking passengers south. It seems the northern hemisphere was the most badly affected.'

Richard nudged himself from the wall with his shoulder.

'And they took everyone?' he said. There was aggression in his voice. Grimes took a step back.

'You let them take everyone?'

He strode over to Grimes and shouted into her face.

'You let them take my son? Without me?'

Yuill and Henderson leaped forward to restrain him.

'Easy,' said Yuill. 'Let her finish.'

Richard backed off, still staring furiously at Grimes. She met his fierce eyes without flinching. I sensed that she had faced up to male anger before, either in or out of the army.

'We told them you were out on a salvage mission,' she continued. 'But they said they couldn't wait, that if anyone was going with them, they had to go now . . .'

'And you let them go,' Richard broke in. He was shaking. 'You let my son go.'

Grimes held up her palms.

'But we managed to persuade them to send another chopper,' she finished. 'There are a few more still in the north. They radioed for one to change its route to pick us up.'

Richard seemed to relax a little. I was still wound up tight, a coil of fear in my belly.

'When?' said Richard.

'They said within two days.'

There was silence in the room for a while. Even Bryce seemed lost for words.

'Private Grimes made the right call,' said Yuill. 'Our main objective was to make contact with the outside world and get the survivors to safety, and that's exactly what we're doing.'

'Thank you, sir,' said Grimes, looking down at the floor.

'What are you still doing here, Harvey?' I said. 'Why didn't you go?'

'Figured I'd stay and make sure you blokes were alright,' he said.

Yuill crossed his arms and looked between me and Richard, who had positioned himself back against the wall. 'Your families are safe,' he said. 'They'll have food, shelter and medical supplies.' He scanned our worried faces, his full of relief. 'So we wait it out. One or two days and we'll be on our way back to civilisation. We'll stay out of the city and when the help arrives we'll tell them about the other survivors too.'

'Rabbits?' said Bryce.

'Yes, the Rabbits,' said Yuill. 'Presuming they want rescuing. Now I suggest this evening you get some rest and—'

'About that . . .' I said.

'Yes?' said Yuill. 'About what?'

'About the Rabbits,' I said. 'There's a problem.'

We crammed as much as we could into the back of the Land Rover. We shut off the generator and emptied as much of the remaining fuel as we could into tanks. We filled jerry cans with water and packed plastic boxes with dried food. We took two portable stoves and two large gas canisters, radios, batteries and blankets from the store, clothes, possessions. We hadn't planned on going any great distance – only far enough away from the barracks to be safe until the chopper arrived – but we didn't want to have to risk returning to the barracks. If the rescue didn't come as expected, then we were going to push south.

The news that we were under threat rocked Yuill visibly, his face flickering with fear as I told him that the Rabbits knew our location. It became very clear to me then how desperate he was to find civilisation.

We considered the possibilities: stay and fight or leave and risk being abandoned. Fight or flight. We opted for the latter, to drive south and find somewhere safe to camp where we could spot our rescue helicopter coming.

It would only be for a couple of days.

It was almost dark and freezing cold by the time we were ready to leave. I ran down the main corridor, heading for the stairs with the last pile of blankets. I stopped when I reached the end, then walked back to our room and looked inside. The light was low, but I could make out clothes and bedsheets strewn around the place, imagining Beth hastily pulling together the stuff she might need for the trip. Had she paused, I wondered? Had she considered staying and waiting for me? Had she been given a choice? Had Alice cried for me?

Had Beth even thought about staying?

I slumped down onto the bed.

After our argument the night before I had been lying on the floor in the dark. Arthur and Alice were asleep. I heard their covers move and Beth's feet on the floor. She padded over and slid quietly underneath my blanket, pressing her warm body on top of mine. She kissed me, moved her hand down and pushed me gently inside of her. I was surprised at how wet she was and how much I could smell her, surprised at suddenly realising how much I missed that smell. We both stifled a noise as she began to move gently against me, pushing me deeper and deeper inside of her until her pelvis ground against mine. I stroked my hand down her back and over her buttocks, slipping my finger between them. Beth usually hated this, but she gripped my hair and pushed her face against mine, sliding her tongue into my mouth as we both came. She lay on top of me for a while, then stroked my brow and kissed me. I could feel her watching me, although I couldn't see her. She kissed me again, then rolled off me and got back into her bed without saying a word.

She was trying to talk to me. She was trying to tell me, one last time, not to do it, to stay with my family. But I had ignored her, and now they were gone.

Grimes called down from the main doors. I went to leave, but saw something else in the darkness. Alice's stringyphone was tangled in a heap on the pillow. I lifted it gently and slipped it inside my coat, then closed the door and went upstairs.

Carlops

Henderson drove. Yuill and Grimes sat up front. The rest of us sat in the back.

We crawled into the Pentland Hills and away from the city, aiming for the road that went south to Carlisle. The hills were no longer green and rolling. They were a mess of dried scrub and churned up, stagnant mud pits. Tracks no longer existed. The headlights passed over the bones of sheep and dogs. Everything was covered in dull, grey snow.

We became stuck in a ditch and spent an hour pushing ourselves out. Richard and I sat shivering with freezing mud sprayed across our bodies. We hit the road after midnight. It was potholed and strewn with fallen trees and dirt. After another hour of cautious driving we reached a village called Carlops, where we stopped.

Henderson turned off the engine and let the headlights die. It was utterly dark and utterly still. No life, no sound, apart from Bryce's deep snores from the back and the slow sloshing of fuel and water coming to rest in their tanks. I was cold and tired. I missed warmth and sleep. I missed Beth.

Yuill and Henderson got out, leaving Grimes asleep in the front. I watched their torch lights bobbing along the ground towards the village. Carlops had been a single cottage-lined street, but in the sweep of Henderson's beam I could see an unnatural bulge in one side of it. Bricks were scattered across the pavement. Branches had burst through windows and doors.

I heard Yuill's voice.

'Grimes!'

Grimes woke with a start, unbuckled herself and slid out the passenger door. Her flashlight quickly joined the other two scanning the wreckage.

'A fallen tree?' I ventured to Harvey and Richard.

'I'm going to take a look,' said Richard. 'Coming?'

I turned to Harvey.

'That's alright, Ed,' he said. He nodded back at Bryce, still asleep. 'Reckon I'll stay here and look after Cujo. You go ahead.'

I took my Maglite and followed Richard. Dark tufts of snow floated through my beam and joined the hard-packed ice on the road. The air was frozen but not fresh. It was dusty and sharp and the taste caught in my throat. To be inside with the warm smell of my family, even on a stone floor, was suddenly all that I wanted. Not to be standing with strangers outside in the fetid frost, far from anything that might be called home, trying to work out what had caused a street to burst open.

'Not a tree,' said Richard as we reached the others. We trained our beams on the buckled brick. 'A hill.'

Every house was filled with dirt. Splintered furniture lay on the pavement, some reaching the other side of the street. The houses on that side were crushed under car-sized chunks of mud and rock. Every roof was demolished, every wall cracked or smashed apart. One house was buried entirely in a brown boulder of earth. Another one had a bath hanging from its window. Everything was shattered and covered in mud.

Looming behind the street lay the cause of the destruction: an immense tower of brown earth stretching higher than our beams could reach.

'A landslide?' I said.

'Something like that,' murmured Yuill.

A wind picked up. We heard creaks and flutters as it disturbed the bloated innards of the ruined buildings. Yuill scanned further up the street.

'We can investigate in the morning. Right now we need ...'

He stopped as the light picked out other objects. Bodies; half out of windows, slumped against walls, buried in rubble.

What used to be a woman hung upside down from a telegraph wire by one foot. Her tattered nightgown had fallen down over her head. Most of her grey corpse had been picked clean. I covered my mouth. I had already seen plenty of corpses on the salvage runs, but death was still a shock. Yuill spun his torch away and we did the same.

'We need to find shelter,' he went on. 'Henderson, Grimes, follow me. You two, back to the car. We'll come for you when we've found somewhere suitable.'

We got back in next to Harvey. Bryce was still out for the count.

'Fellas,' said the old man happily. 'So what caused all the mess?'

'We don't know,' said Richard. 'But it was big enough to move a mountain.'

We found a building at the end of the street that had not been damaged as badly as the rest. It had been a small hotel and the front door opened into a bar. We stood there shivering by flashlight.

'Henderson and I will keep watch outside for the rescue helicopters,' said Yuill. 'You can all sleep here.'

We set up camp with blankets from the Land Rover. I zipped up the hood of my jacket and lay down on a bench. My eyelids were heavy. I watched Henderson crouching on the floor, cleaning his gun. His sweeps were short and fast.

'It's alright,' he said, one gold tooth glinting from his grin. 'It's not loaded.'

I opened my eyes to dull light. I heard voices from outside: Yuill and Henderson arguing. I could only hear the odd word hissed or growled.

'... won't come ...'

'... will ... patient ...'

'... kidding ourselves ...'

'... calm down ...'

'... old man ... us down ...'

'... me remind you ...'

'... never supposed ...'

'... ranking officer!'

There was a pause, then the sound of one set of boots marching away. I got up. Richard and Harvey were still asleep and Grimes was at the stove, trying to fill a pan with water. She was balancing one of the containers on her knee, one elbow stuck up awkwardly. I thought of Alice trying to help Beth pour flour into a mixing bowl when they were baking. I went over to help her.

'I can manage,' she warned. She nodded over to a plastic box of food. 'Get me some tea bags.'

I did what she asked. Harvey flinched as I passed him. He frowned, smacked his lips and let out a low, rumbling sigh as he fell back to sleep.

'Think he's OK?' I said.

'Harvey?' said Grimes. She puffed through her nose. 'Harvey's as strong as an ox. It's the rest of you I'm worried about.'

'And those two?' I motioned outside.

She shot me a look that told me I was on dangerous territory. Perhaps she was considering how much she should tell me, how much she still valued that necessary border between soldier and civilian.

'Men being men,' she said.

'I thought they were supposed to be soldiers.'

She ignored me and stirred the water. Then she seemed to soften.

'Don't worry about them,' she said. 'We'll get you to your family, I promise.'

'You don't think they're coming.'

'What?'

'*Sauver.*'

She sealed the water container and dropped it to the floor.

'I said we'll get you to your family.'

'And what about you?' I said.

'What about me?'

'Don't you have family too? Don't you want to find them?'

She frowned.

'I mean nobody would blame—'

'That's not what I signed up for,' she said. 'Besides, I'm from Glasgow. I don't think there's much hope for them.'

'I'm sorry.'

'Don't be. My mum was an alcoholic and my dad . . .'

Her face wrinkled and she stared into the steam rising from the pot.

'What?' I said.

'Let's just say I don't send a lot of Father's Day cards.'

There wasn't much I could do with that.

'Where's Bryce?' I said.

She nodded at the door and I walked outside. The snow had stopped, but it had been heavy through the night. Everything was covered, including the bodies. The telegraph lady had picked up a drift and her nightgown was now frozen into a stiff triangle.

'Morning!' came a voice from above.

I looked up. Bryce was crouching far above the rooftops on the mound behind the street. He looked like a fat wizard, with wisps of brown mist snaking around him. He grinned and waved.

'Want to see something?' he called down. His words found a dull echo in the silence of the snow-covered street. I looked up and down the hill, not fancying my chances on the loose earth.

'Walk farther along,' he shouted. 'There's a wood about half a mile out of the village where it's not so steep.'

I peered into the dense fog beyond the hotel.

'See you soon!' he called. His cackle disappeared behind me as I set off up the road.

After a while I found the wood and left the road, picking my way up the hill. I was scrabbling when I met Bryce, now sitting on a rock and smoking a roll-up. I looked down on the village below and saw Grimes and Richard – now awake – outside holding steaming cups. We must have been a hundred metres above them.

Beyond them, behind the pulverised houses on the other side of the road, the gentle incline that had once risen up to the Pentlands was now pockmarked with craters. Huge ditches ran down like scars. What looked like boulders were embedded in the earth as far as I could see, as if the whole hillside was a nest of alien eggs.

'How's your shoulder?' I said to Bryce.

He scowled at me.

'Lovely,' he said, eyes like slits. 'Thanks for asking. I'm touched.'

I made a mental note to never ask him anything like that again. He jabbed a thumb to his left, away from the road.

'Now check this shit out.'

I turned to look and nearly fell down the slope. It was the clearest day I had seen for a long time. The sun was not exactly visible – no bright disc cutting through the thick cloud – but the light that made it through gave us miles of illumination. Before us was a deep crater that stretched out towards the horizon. This landscape had once been full of forests, farms and small villages. Now it was a canyon, miles wide and hundreds of metres deep. We were sitting on its outer ridge.

I steadied myself.

'Pretty fuckin' cool, eh?' said Bryce.

'I guess ...' I stammered. 'I guess that's one word for it. Jesus. Was that an ... an ...'

'An asteroid?' said Bryce. He cast a hand theatrically at the sky. 'You mean one of those streaks of light that started falling from the heavens? The ones that knocked the shit out of us for a couple of days?'

He flicked his cigarette over the ridge and spat after it.

'Aye,' he said. 'Probably.'

I slumped to the ground and sat with my arms around my knees, looking out at the bizarre scenery. I had only seen the destruction of Edinburgh and I was strangely used to it. The idea of a city being levelled, even the one I lived in, was somehow easier to accept than a landscape I barely knew.

Bryce rolled two cigarettes, lit them and passed me one. We smoked in silence, transfixed.

When I had finished, I stood up. I was about to suggest that we head back down to the village when a deep groan sounded in the distance, rising up and stopping suddenly. We said nothing. The groan sounded again, higher now, like mournful whale song. It stopped. Then sharp cracks and twangs reverberated around the crater walls.

'Fuck me,' said Bryce. 'Look at that.'

He pointed at the wall opposite ours. The southern end of the ridge was crumbling into the pit. A huge wedge of earth came away and slid down in slow motion. We felt the ground rumbling beneath us, dirt dancing around our boots. We exchanged a glance. Bryce sprang to his feet and we both jumped down the steepest part of the slope. I fell through thin air for longer than I was comfortable with, then hit the earth on my back. The impact knocked the wind from my lungs and I gasped for breath as I slid down the hill. My coat had ridden up and was half-covering my face. I couldn't see but I heard Bryce rocketing past me, whooping like a child.

I was picking up speed. I yanked down my hood with one hand and dug into the earth with the other. I saw Bryce nearing the buildings below, digging in his heels and tumbling into a heap by the hotel. Soon I was next to him, spluttering into the snow while he lay on his back laughing.

'Again, Daddy, again!' he said, getting to his feet and patting his bad shoulder. It now seemed nothing more than a nuisance to him. He grabbed me around the chest and hauled me to my feet as the others came running to meet us.

'What was that noise?' said Yuill.

'That?' said Bryce, brushing himself down. 'That would be a landslide.'

He squashed a finger over one nostril and blew a round out into the dirt, then did the same with the other.

'Now,' he said, clapping his hands together. 'Did I hear somebody put the kettle on?'

We drank strong black tea in the bar. It made me think of Cornwall and the dismal camping trip I had forced Beth to go on. I thought of her – pregnant and patient as I fumbled for matches in the rain, then packing the tent in the dark, her laughing as I slid in the mud. It was my childish insistence that we went, to prove a point, stamp my foot, make some idiotic rebellion against the world I thought was dragging me down into its mire. I saw camping as a way of removing us from modern life and all the things I thought we didn't need. I had no idea what that actually meant until then, in that devastated village, when modern life had – along with my family – been removed from me instead. Perhaps there was a reason why we had filled our world with distraction after all. Perhaps there was a reason why we surrounded ourselves with plastic and light and excess. Perhaps our collective consciousness remembered all too well what it was like in darkness, surrounded by wet, rotten wood, mud, and nothing good to eat.

Yuill walked in and filled his cup from the stove. His hand shook as he poured. He turned to face us, cup against his lips, fist on his hip. Richard broke the silence.

'We should move on.'

'We're staying here,' said Yuill. 'We'll keep watch for the chopper.'

Richard frowned.

'What about that thing?' he said, pointing at the hill outside. 'It's clearly unstable. It could fall on top of us at any moment.'

Yuill stared at nothing. His cup hovered before his lips.

'We'll take precautions,' he said.

'Precautions?' said Richard. 'What precautions can you take against a mountain that's going to fall apart at any moment?'

Henderson walked in and stood by the door.

'It's worth the risk,' said Yuill. 'The ridge is a good vantage point. It's high up. We can keep a fire going up there, make sure they see us. We'll take watches. There's a flare gun in the Land Rover.'

Richard got to his feet. He was taller than Yuill by a foot.

'A fire on the ridge?' he said. 'Watches? Are you *barking* mad?'

Yuill flinched, suddenly looking like a foot soldier being scolded by a senior officer. Something of Richard's background had left him with a natural sense of authority. Far more than Yuill, at least.

But he had no gun.

Henderson stepped out of the shadows and stood behind Yuill. For a moment, nobody spoke. Then there was a loud slurping noise from the corner as Bryce drained his tea. He tossed the cup over his shoulder and it clattered against the wall.

'Right,' he said, lying back on his bench. 'Wake me up when you boys have finished . . .'

'Hey!'

Henderson was upon him, looming over the bench.

'Get up!' he shouted.

Bryce puffed out a laugh of surprise. He didn't shift.

'Well . . . hello to you too,' he said.

Henderson bent slowly down so his face was in Bryce's.

'Get up, you lazy cunt. Get up and find some wood. We have a fire to make.'

I thought for sure that Bryce would swing for him, but he seemed to think better of it. He lay there for a moment, then eased himself up from the bench.

'Alright, sweetheart,' he said. 'I'll light your fire.'

He brushed past Henderson and filled a fresh cup with tea, which he drank slowly.

'But I hope you're not expecting a cuddle as well.'

He turned round to face Henderson, but he had already left the room.

Articles

We built a fire and kept watch on the ridge for three days and nights. We changed every four hours, as Yuill had suggested. We saw nothing.

On the afternoon of the third day we sat in the hotel, each quietly acknowledging the fact that the rescue was officially late. Yuill got up to relieve Grimes of her watch. He stopped at the door, staring outside.

'The snow is clearing,' he said. 'There are some … articles appearing. Perhaps you could do something about them.'

He looked around the room, then left.

'Articles?' I said after the door had closed.

'Aye,' said Bryce, getting up. 'Dead ones.'

He sniffed and pulled on his gloves.

'Better than sitting around in here, eh?'

Richard and I followed him out. We started with the bodies slumped against walls and sprawled in the street. These were easy and we were grateful for the freezing temperature. Then we took the ones from the windows. These were more difficult as they required manipulation. All wore shreds of nightclothes or less; there would have been no sirens this far from Edinburgh.

Our thick army-surplus gloves protected us from feeling too much, and the snow and ice hid much of what would have been visible. But we could not escape the sound. We spoke loudly about anything until we had dragged them to the ditch and rolled them in.

There was a small body lying curled around the base of a post box which we all avoided. Bryce eventually picked it up, wordlessly, and wrapped it in a tattered sheet he had found in the back of a car. He carried it across and bent down over the ditch, lying it carefully on top of the others. Richard and I watched from a distance, wondering at this unusual act of care as much as at the horror of the whole afternoon.

When he had finished, we brushed earth and snow over them all with our boots. Then we looked up at the telegraph woman.

She was no longer dangling. The temperature had frozen her into a stiff flag of bone and fabric. Her free leg stuck out in grisly semaphore. Both arms reached for the ground, her inverted nightgown covering everything but the bones of her hands. One of them was gnarled into a fist. The other seemed to be pointing.

'How do you think she got up there?' I said.

Richard scanned the houses behind.

'From that one probably,' he said, pointing up at a large window that had been burst apart. Behind the window and in front of the earth, which packed the room like every other along the street, was an upended metal bed frame.

'Flew through the window, caught her foot, hit the brick on the way,' he said. 'Probably unconscious or dead by the time she hit the wire.'

He stepped up to the telegraph pole and looked it up and down. He placed a hand against the wood and tried it. It rocked a little but it was still firm. He stood back and assessed the house next door.

'We could try climbing that wall,' he said. 'Loop a rope around the pole, shimmy across and . . .'

A large rock sailed across the top of the wire and landed in a gutter.

'Oof ya . . .' said Bryce. I turned in time to see him launching a second. This one hit the wire near the woman's foot and span to the ground. 'Go on, ya bastard . . .' he said.

Richard raised his eyebrows. 'Or that,' he said.

We went to work in the rubble. Richard favoured smaller, sharper bricks which he threw with speed and spin – I imagined he was no stranger to fast-bowling. Bryce stuck with the larger bricks that he hurled at the wire like a shot-putter. My approach evolved into a basketball-style upwards push, my plan being for the bricks to drop down upon the wire, dislodging the woman's foot from above. Most of them fell short; Bryce's crashed into the rooftops and Richard's whistled by like bullets. We cheered whenever there was a direct hit. We were like boys doing something they shouldn't in a place they shouldn't be.

Eventually Bryce gave up with his method and copied mine. He chose larger chunks of masonry, at last finding a ten-brick slab in the wreckage and dragging it to the road.

'Watch out, boys,' he said.

We both stood back as Bryce hauled the brickwork onto his chest. He stood for a second like a weight-lifter preparing for a jerk, but instead he took two steps back, then three forwards, ending in an almighty thrust that sent the bricks spinning in a slow, steep arc. They landed directly on the wire, which bent down and snapped, releasing the woman to the ground.

We instinctively raised our hands in a cheer, but stopped as the woman's body rolled over. Her head was exposed now. The bottom part of her face was gone, now just tooth and jawbone, but the top was still covered in grey flesh. Long strands of silver hair had come loose from a tight bun and now trailed across her furrowed brow. Her eyelids were open. What was left of one eye looked up at us from the ground. The wire shook back to position above us, sending soft flakes of snow down upon the woman's broken body. A silver cross lay in the snow in front of her, hanging from a chain around her neck.

Henderson and Yuill took the watch that night. Sleep was difficult. Ghoulish faces danced in front of my eyes. I wandered empty streets. Dread lay around every corner, jerking me awake with some nameless panic and filling my head with strange, tangled thoughts that made no sense. My chest felt heavy. I clenched my teeth. I wanted to move.

But I must have slept because I woke up. I woke up to the sound of wood scraping on the floor. And shouts, and the sound of an engine roaring.

Gone

I blinked in the daylight. Bryce was standing over me and Richard was out the door. Grimes was trying to sit up on her bench.

'Up!' roared Bryce. 'Get up!'

I murmured something and struggled to my feet. Grimes was already outside.

'What's going on?' said Harvey.

Bryce thundered through the door and I followed him out into the freezing morning. It was snowing again. The Land Rover was gone, speeding south over rocks and clods of earth. Richard was halfway down the road behind it and was now slowing down, his arms and legs cartwheeling. He came to a halt and stood, panting clouds of steam with his hands on his head. The Land Rover disappeared in the dawn mist. Richard shouted something that was lost in the wind.

'Fucking great,' said Bryce. He jumped three times, grunting as he landed and finally falling into a crouch with his mass of tangled hair in his fists.

'Who were they?' I said, still coming to my senses. 'Did you see them? Where's Yuill? Henderson?'

Bryce turned on his heels and looked at me as if I was an idiot.

'That fuckin' *was* fuckin' Yuill and fuckin' Henderson!' he said, pointing at the now-empty road. He slammed one hand against his head. 'Ya fuckin' idiot!'

He howled some other obscenity at me and then ran across the street to a small Toyota that had been crushed by a boulder, kicking it, hammering its hood with his fists, punching its doors and what was left of its windows.

My gut felt like it had taken a swing from a crowbar, quivering and tightening as I stood breathless in the snow. Wave after wave of blood filled my head and rocked me back and forth. I tried to form words, questions. But nothing came. My mouth fluttered and twitched in the freezing air as if muttering some silent incantation or unintelligible equation.

We had been abandoned.

I heard Grimes behind me breathing short breaths full of whistles and squeaks like a child trying not to cry. She was standing still, rooted to the spot in her torn, stained uniform. Her hair was pasted across her brow collecting flakes of snow. She wore the beginnings of a snarl, clenching and unclenching her fists by her side as she ground her teeth.

Richard marched past me.

'We need to check the cars again,' he said. 'We need a car. We need to go!'

'They're all fucked!' shouted Bryce, still hammering on the Toyota.

'Check them again!' said Richard.

'They're all FUCKED!' repeated Bryce.

'We'll wait,' muttered Grimes. 'Wait for the rescue chopper.'

Richard swung round and faced her with his arms outstretched. 'There is no rescue chopper!' he bellowed. 'They're not coming. They knew that, that's why they left us. It's just us!' He stopped, seeming to flinch from his own anger. 'Just us,' he repeated. Grimes turned her face away. Her mouth hardened into a thin line.

Richard turned and ran madly up and down the street, checking the engine and fuel tank of every mangled, rusted, broken and crushed vehicle he could find. Bryce followed. They slammed door after door with yells of frustration. Grimes blinked, aware that I was still looking at her.

'They didn't tell you?' I said.

She shook her head once, almost imperceptibly. I turned back and looked up the road, now empty and smeared with mist. I could just make out the fresh tracks of the Land Rover in the snow. Bryce and Richard returned.

'Nothing,' said Bryce. 'Like I said, they're all—'

'Yes, *fucked*!' shouted Richard. 'I know.'

Richard began pacing frantically, long arms bent above him with his hands over his head. Grimes walked back to the hotel.

'We'll go back,' said Bryce. 'Back to the barracks, back to Edinburgh.'

'And do what?' said Richard. 'Start a fight with an army of hooligans? Steal some petrol from them?'

Harvey appeared at the door.

'They've left us food,' he said.

'And a stove,' said Grimes from within the hotel. 'And water.'

'Oh, give them a fuckin' medal,' said Bryce. 'Give them the fuckin' Victoria Cross!'

'We should stay put,' said Grimes. 'Keep the fire going, wait for the rescue—'

'There's NO RESCUE!' bellowed Bryce, arms wide, beating his chest with every word. 'Why can't you see that? THEY'RE NOT COMING!'

Richard gave one last yell that echoed from the burned brick on either side of the street. He took a long, shuddering breath and was quiet.

'Come on,' he said, walking towards the hotel. 'Let's see what they left us, work out what we're going to do.'

Grimes had opened the box of food that Yuill and Henderson had left. Harvey made some tea on the stove and passed us cups while we pulled out packets of noodles, rice, pasta and beans and stacked them in piles.

Bryce broke the silence at last.

'Well, I can't think of a better idea,' he said, throwing his empty cup on the table.

Richard was sat forward in his chair, long arms folded on his knees, staring solemnly at the dried food on the table in front of him. One of his legs was bouncing up and down on the floor. He glanced at Bryce and sat up straight, folded his arms and shrugged, leg still tapping.

'We can't go back, can't stay here. There are no cars. We have no other option.'

Grimes stood up.

'We move on then,' she said. 'We pack all the food and carry as much water as possible. We move as fast as we can, keeping to the road until we find a vehicle.'

She looked around.

'Agreed?'

Bryce and Richard nodded and got up from their seats. Bryce picked up an empty pack and threw it at me. I caught it with one hand, spilling tea on myself with the other.

'Here,' he said. 'Fill that.'

We packed the dried food into our rucksacks as tightly as possible and then put blankets on top. Each pack came with a four-litre hydration bladder. We filled them to the brim and then put as much water as we could into empty plastic bottles that we found in a bin behind the bar. We put as many of these as we could into the space remaining in our bags and tightened the rest to the outside of the packs using the loose straps.

When we had finished, we zipped up our coats and slung on the packs. Bryce threw his on as if it was filled with feathers. I tried to hide the fact that I was almost toppling backwards under the weight of mine. When we were all set we stood around in a circle, waiting for something. But there was nothing left to do but walk.

Gloria

I knew this road well. It was the one Beth and I had always taken when we drove south from Edinburgh. Many miles of long, straight tarmac drew a line roughly straight down through the Scottish Borders, banked on each side by gentle hills and long plains of farmland and forest. There was the occasional bend or hill and every so often you might pass one or two houses. There were only a handful of villages and only one example of what you might call a town. Otherwise it was sparsely populated and the lack of buildings and any real terrain meant that, on a good day, the sky opened up into a huge blue canopy. This, combined with a road that disappeared into the horizon, always made me think of driving through the mid-western states of America, despite the fact that I had never been.

After about thirty miles, the road joined a motorway that soared in great long bends through a series of hills, bridging rivers and cutting through rust-coloured moors and pine woods before widening again and crossing the border into England.

We walked out of Carlops sometime in the mid-morning. The road stretched out ahead of us, long and straight as it always had been, becoming a dull white under the dirty snow. There was no huge sky – just a very low, dark mass of cloud. Mist pressed down upon everything, cocooning us even further from the world. Visibility was no more than fifty metres at best. We had no idea what lay beyond us or on either side of us. We were walking within a dense, oppressive bubble.

We passed the end of the crater's mound. After that we were in unknown territory, following the faint and disappearing tyre tracks that Yuill and Henderson had left behind as they fled.

Richard checked his watch.

'West Linton is about a mile away,' he said. 'It's bigger than Carlops, probably more chance of a vehicle there.'

Grimes and I walked with Harvey. We trudged with our heads down, feeling the brittle snow break beneath our boots. After a while I could feel Grimes watching me.

'You were trapped in that cellar, weren't you?' she said. 'Underneath all that rubble. We'd almost given up for the day, did you know that? The pilot didn't want to land, but I made him.'

Harvey looked up with interest.

'How did you know they were there?' he said.

'Thermal imaging binoculars,' said Grimes. 'They were almost out of charge, but I had one last scan out of the window and I was sure I saw something flicker.' She turned to me. 'We wouldn't have gone back to that area for another week at least.'

I allowed the silent questions hang unanswered. I knew that we wouldn't have made it another week in the cellar, probably not even another day, and that would have been my fault. Grimes was only stating simple facts, but they threatened to reveal the bigger truths I was already trying to hide.

I was drunk. I fell asleep before I could warn my wife. My son woke me up, otherwise we'd all be dead. Among the supplies I hastily crammed into a box was a half-full bottle of balsamic vinegar. I found some pipes in the cellar and I didn't know what was in them because I didn't know how my own house worked. I thought it might be easier if the pipes were full of gas ...

'We were lucky you found us,' I said. 'Thank you.'

I turned to Harvey, looking for a route out of the conversation.

'What about you, Harvey? What were you doing in Edinburgh?'

He smiled and pointed at his mouth.

'Don't let the accent fool you. I've lived here most of my life. Moved here to marry.'

'What about your wife?' I said.

'Died a few years back,' said Harvey.

'I'm sorry,' I said, with that useless spasm we give to another's grief.

'Nah, don't be,' he said. 'It's a good thing really; Mary would've hated all this.'

'You were waiting for us when we found you, weren't you, Harvey?' said Grimes, smiling. 'Outside with your bag packed, clean clothes, hair combed, like you were going on a bus tour.'

'I could hear you coming a mile off,' chuckled Harvey. 'Besides, when you get to my age, you like to get ready well in advance.'

'How did you survive?' I asked.

He wagged a finger.

'Old widowers always rise early,' he said. 'And we eat a lot of canned goods.'

He chuckled and shouted behind him.

'What about you, Bryce? What's your story?'

A groan from Richard. He had heard this before.

Bryce's story, so he told it, was that he was still awake when the early warning alarms sounded. He had owned a tattoo shop on Cockburn Street. The evening before it happened, he had closed the shop early and headed to the local, where he had knocked back several pints of Caledonian 80 before wandering down to the pubs at the Grassmarket. After four or five more rounds, he'd taken in a few private shows at one of the three lap-dancing clubs that made up the Pubic Triangle. Then he'd bought two kebabs and eaten them, one in each ring-encrusted fist, while making his way across town to a pub on Thistle Street. There was a lock-in and Bryce had helped two or three other regulars finish off a couple of grams of cocaine before picking up a straggler from a hen party and taking her back to his flat in the New Town.

According to Bryce, the sirens had started mid-coitus. After the same process of realisation that everyone else was making around that time – the time that I was kicking down the door of our local store – the girl had bolted, screaming, from Bryce's house, pulling on her jeans, stilettos and pink T-shirt emblazoned with the words 'Three-pinter' across its chest. Bryce had scoured his flat for a few supplies and crammed them into a backpack before spinning away on his motorbike. After seeing Arthur's Seat cleaved in two and realising he wasn't going to make it, he had swung the bike into a school playground, crashed through the front doors and thrown himself down into the store cellar. The rescue chopper had found him two weeks later surrounded by filth, empty crisp packets and tins of pop. Those two weeks and the following months did little to trim Bryce down to anything approximating the size of a human being. He was still huge.

'Any family?' said Harvey, when he had finished.

Bryce began walking faster, catching us up. He had his eyes on Grimes.

'I have a brother. Don't see him much, he works on the rigs. Can't imagine there's much hope for anyone stuck out in the North Sea. Dad left us when we were little. Mum popped her clogs a few years back. So no, no family.'

His voice changed.

'And you.'

Grimes looked over her shoulder.

'What's keeping *you* here?' he said.

'Pardon?' said Grimes.

'Or did those fannies just beat you to it? Are you waiting for your chance to fuck off as well, is that it?'

'Bryce,' warned Richard.

Grimes stopped and turned on her heels. She glared up at him.

'It's not my job to *fuck off*,' said Grimes.

'Your *job*? And what's your job then, darlin'? Eh?'

She took a step towards him. Her neck bent back as she held his stare.

'My job is to protect you,' she said. 'All of you.'

Bryce laughed.

'Protect me? Oh, that's nice, sweetheart but, you know . . .'

He brought his face down to hers.

'. . . I don't fuckin' need protecting.'

She looked into his face for a few seconds.

'We'll see about that,' she said, and turned. Bryce watched her walk away.

'And what about you?' he called after her.

'Bryce, stop it,' I said.

'Who protects Private Grimes? Eh?'

She stopped and looked back at him.

'I don't need protecting either,' she said.

Bryce gave a nasty smile.

'Really?'

He walked slowly towards her.

'Not even just a bit? Just a wee bit of protecting, just you and me? We could protect each other, darlin', eh? Would you like that?'

He towered before her, grinning. She took a breath and looked him up and down. Her shoulders fell as she breathed out.

'You don't know what protection means,' she said. 'You don't know what *not* having protection means. You don't know how important that is. That simple thing: to look after someone. To put yourself in front of someone. To say you'll die for them and mean it. You don't know what that means because all you do is look after yourself.'

She looked at Richard and me.

'You don't know what these men are feeling right now. And you never will. You'll never be the father of a child. So, aye – maybe you're right, maybe you don't need protecting. Maybe you're not worth the effort.'

She turned and continued up the road. We followed, leaving Bryce standing like a tree stump, grinless.

We walked some more in silence. The tarmac and the Land Rover tracks had now disappeared completely under the snow. The sides of the road seemed to be changing as well. Gaps appeared in the hedgerows. Then they became lower and clustered, before disappearing altogether and leaving a thin line of scrub in their place. I saw a cluster of trees far away in a field, branchless and black. The dirt beneath them was black too. There was a faint smell of smoke.

On the other side of the road I saw some dark outlines halfway up a hill. As we got closer I saw that they were cars, five or six of them, upended and burned down to their chassis. Dark fragments of metal and rubber lined the slope beneath them like the innards of flies smeared beneath a fist.

After another mile we saw dark shapes looming in the mist ahead – buildings. As we drew nearer we saw that the road turned right onto a street of houses running down a hill.

'This is it,' said Richard. 'West Linton.'

Bryce tutted. 'Aye,' he said. 'The big smoke. Stick together and watch out for pickpockets.'

'Let's just find a car and get going,' muttered Richard.

'I wouldnae put money on that,' said Bryce as we turned the corner.

The houses became clearer through the mist. These had once been tall, grand mansions set back from the road on steep drives. The hedgerows and trees that had provided privacy had been burned down to their roots and the houses stood naked for all to see. Each one was the same: a black, windowless shell, barely standing. No roof, most of the walls completely gone, the innards of the house exposed and still filled with broken, burned objects. All that was left was a brittle framework of charred struts dripping with meltwater.

Every drive had a car or two, all in the same state as the houses.

We walked slowly down into the village, picking our way carefully through street after street of scorched, empty buildings. We saw no bodies, or so it seemed. Almost everything we saw had disintegrated so much that it was impossible to recognise. We passed a post office. The pillar box in front of it was now a sharp-edged, rusted stump. Its top had been blown clean away and inside was a pile of ash – the mail that had roasted inside of its red oven. The remains of a single envelope offered its corner up through the snow as if still expecting its collection.

'This entire road must have been on fire,' said Grimes. 'All the way from Carlops. It might have been burning for days, weeks even.'

'So much for a car then,' said Harvey. 'How far do you think this goes?'

'We know there was the big impact in Northumberland,' said Grimes. 'Possibly there were other smaller ones around it. If the firestorm reached this then it could have affected everything south of here as far as Carlisle.'

Richard stopped walking. 'That's almost a hundred miles from here,' he said.

Grimes turned and nodded. 'More like eighty,' she said.

'Wait,' I said. 'Are you saying there might be nothing ahead of us for eighty miles? How far have we walked today so far?'

'Three,' said Richard, chewing his lip. He looked at his watch. 'And it's already past midday.'

'That's over a week's trek,' I said.

'We don't know how far this goes,' said Grimes. 'We don't know anything about what the country is like further south of this point. It might be alright.'

'Well, we know what it's like back that way,' said Bryce, pulling out his tobacco and papers.

Grimes looked around at each of us. 'Anyone who wants to go back,' she said, 'now's your chance.'

Bryce lit his cigarette. 'Back to what?' he said, squinting as the smoke hit his eyes. He looked ahead and jabbed a finger south, then walked on.

'Let's push on then,' said Grimes.

We left the village and picked up our pace. I tried not to think about the time and the distance, about how far I was from Beth and the kids, about whether or not they were safe, still in the country or already powering away from it on a ship. I tried not to think about finding a car that had petrol, or about how to start it, or about what we would do when the petrol ran out. I tried not to think about the knot of panic and hopelessness that tightened in my gut with every step. I tried not to think about the cold, or our food, or our water, or about how much I wanted this not to be how life currently was. I tried not to think about anything.

We walked for two hours and then stopped to eat biscuits next to a dried stream. There were no other villages and every farm or lonely cottage we came across was the same burnt-out husk as the last. The mist had lifted and we could see further than before. The landscape on either side of us was the same: every tree and hedgerow, every blade of grass, was gone, leaving an undulating, lifeless plain of discoloured snow with nothing taller than a stump to punctuate it. The road was damaged too. Occasionally one of us would stumble into a deep pothole in the hidden tarmac beneath our feet.

As the light faded it began to snow. Before long we were walking in a blizzard and we tumbled into a three-walled cattle shed in a nearby field for shelter. We managed to get a fire going and cooked some pasta as flurries of sleet blew in from outside. We spent the night huddled together in a corner with our hoods pulled tight.

The snow had stopped by morning and we continued down the road. We walked all day without speaking much. Sometime in the late afternoon we turned a corner onto a long stretch of road. About a mile or two ahead of us was a hill. We could just make out a wooded area near the top where the trees didn't seem so badly damaged.

'It'll be dark soon,' said Grimes. 'We're going to need to think about shelter.'

'Those trees,' said Richard. 'Could we try there?'

'Better than nothing,' said Grimes. 'There might be some wood dry enough to make a fire ...'

We stopped in our tracks. As if on cue, a thin trail of smoke had begun to rise from behind the trees.

'Is that a camp fire?' I said.

'Has to be,' said Richard. 'Let's take a closer look.'

We made our way towards the trees. It was almost dark by the time we had reached them, and we could see flames flickering high on the ridge above us.

We waited by the ditch and watched.

'Yuill and Henderson?' breathed Bryce.

Grimes shook her head.

'They would have made it a lot further already,' she said. 'Besides, I don't see their Land Rover and there are no tyre tracks up the hill.'

'All the same,' said Harvey. 'Could be them. Who else have we seen along this road?'

The smell of the smoke reached us and we heard the distant cracks and pops of the fire. There was no other sound, no voices from the hill, no movement but the flicker of orange flame against the barely visible twilight.

We picked our way gingerly through the ditch and over the razed hedgerow. We kept close to the tree line as we walked up the hill, avoiding the deep snow and the exposed space of the field. I felt the warmth of the fire growing stronger and we instinctively stopped before we reached the top, moving back into the shadows. I crouched next to Grimes. There was still no sign of life. Grimes patted me on the shoulder and pointed at something beyond the trees. I peered up through the smoke at the remains of a building. The shadows of stone walls flickered in the light of the flame. Rubble and slate lay on the ground. We edged closer up the hill until we were almost next to the fire. The heat on my face and hands suddenly made me want to crawl closer and sleep by the flames; I hadn't realised how tired I was.

We looked at each other, all asking the same silent question: *Is it safe?* Nobody had the answer, but the heat of the fire was hard to ignore. Richard moved first. He stood and walked out into the open, through the remaining expanse of ankle-deep snow and up as far as the edge of the circle of orange light. Bryce and Grimes followed, then Harvey and I, until all five of us were standing on the perimeter. The fire was small and spitting sparks from thin logs. On the other side of the fire was a single, white, plastic, garden chair. One arm was blackened and warped. Behind that, farther into the darkness, we could see the stone walls of the building more clearly. It had been a small farm cottage. Like every other building it was badly burned and one half of it had crumbled into ruin. The other half, however, still seemed intact and sheltered by the remains of a roof. One window clung to its frame.

We stood warming ourselves for five minutes, maybe more, each of us aware of the stone building beyond, the single chair and the fact that the fire had been recently tended. I have no idea why we stood there for so long. Or why she let us.

I heard a click. At first I thought it was the snap of the fire, but it had come from further away. The sound was more metal than wood. Grimes had already held out her arms as if to signal us to move back from the fire, but it was too late.

'Stay where you are,' said a voice from the darkness on the other side of the fire. It was young and female, but low, with no hint of fear. A long barrel appeared from the shadows pointing straight at us.

'Don't shoot,' said Grimes. 'We're not armed.'

'I know,' said the voice. She had hidden herself perfectly in the shadows so that the only thing we could see was the solid and unwavering tip of her gun. It was clear that she had done this before.

'Hands above your head,' said the voice, pointlessly, since we had already complied. 'And move into the light.'

We each stepped into the firelight.

'Stop,' she said. 'Now, one by one, drop those packs. You.' The barrel swung to Bryce. 'You first. Easy does it.'

Bryce hesitated, bristled.

'Come on, big man,' said the voice, quietly and slowly like a come-on.

Bryce eventually let his pack fall from his shoulders onto the ground in front of him.

'Well done,' she said. 'Now kick it forwards and kneel down. Put your hands behind your head. Good, now the rest of you ...'

'Please,' said Grimes, taking a step forward as the rest of us slowly released our packs. 'We don't want any trouble.'

The barrel swung towards Grimes and into the firelight came a small, strange figure. She was dressed in a thick, black woollen coat that hung almost to her feet. The sleeves were rolled up tightly, freeing the tiny, gloved hands beneath them. Inside the coat was padded with blankets and jumpers that escaped from every opening. She wore a coarse woollen hat that would have been more at home on a workman and the bottom half of her face was covered in a red scarf. The only part of her that we could see was her eyes, which were dark brown and already seemed older than their years.

'Too late for that,' she said, training the gun further on Grimes. 'Now be quiet and do what I say.'

Grimes stepped back and dropped her pack, kicking it forwards with the rest of them.

'Knees,' said the figure, jabbing the barrel down at Grimes's feet. Grimes slowly knelt and put her hands on her head. The figure edged carefully around the fire towards where Bryce was kneeling. She kicked her boot against his pack.

'Going somewhere?' she said.

'Aye,' said Bryce. 'Wee spot of camping now the weather's good.'

'Huh, funny.' She kicked the pack towards Bryce. 'Open it. Slowly.'

Bryce released the hood of the pack and undid the drawstring. A few packs of dried noodles fell out.

'Good,' she said. 'What else is in there?'

'More of the same,' said Richard.

'I wasn't asking you,' she said, swinging the barrel to Richard, then quickly back to Bryce.

'What else?'

Bryce smiled up at her.

'More of the same,' he said.

'Pull it out,' she said.

'Darling, we just met,' said Bryce, still smiling with his hands held out.

She turned the gun and cracked Bryce in the forehead with the butt. Bryce collapsed silently onto his back. I heard him grunt and struggle in the snow, saw his legs kicking in the firelight.

'F-fuck me!' he said finally as he clambered back to his knees. He was holding a hand over his forehead, blood dripping from his glove down one side of his face.

The figure stepped towards Bryce and retrained the barrel on his head.

'One more joke and you're dead,' she said. 'Now empty the pack.'

Bryce said nothing, just stared up at the barrel clutching his head and breathing through his teeth. She moved the barrel even closer to his head.

'Slowly,' she said.

Bryce began pulling out water, tins and packets from the pack with his free hand. The figure stepped back, satisfied.

'Those look like army packs,' she said. 'You don't look like army though.' She scanned our faces. 'Not all o' youse anyway.'

'We're not,' I said. 'We're just ...'

'Wasn't a question,' she said, looking sideways at me, the gun still trained on Bryce. Bryce pulled the last of the supplies from his pack and sat back on his heels, inspecting his bloodied hand.

'Farther back,' the figure said, motioning to Bryce, who edged farther away from the fire. The girl pulled the scarf down from her mouth. She was not even as old as I had thought, probably not even into her twenties. The skin of her face was pale, drawn and hollow but she still had the full, flush lips and round eyes of an attractive young girl. Blonde curls of hair fell from the worker's hat down below her chin and around the skin of her long neck. Youth was still trying its best, despite everything.

She looked at us all in turn, then knelt with her gun pointing up into the sky, sorting through the contents of Bryce's pack. Her eyes flicked between the food and us, making sure we were still in our places.

'Some camping trip,' she said. 'Where were you going?'

Were. Past tense. I felt Grimes and Richard's discomfort at this too.

'South,' said Richard. 'To Cornwall.'

The girl puffed through her nose as she inspected a packet of dried milk.

'The boats?' she said.

'Yes,' said Grimes. 'You know about them?'

The girl spread her lips into something far from a smile. Large white teeth shone back through the paired red flesh.

'Aye,' she said, tossing the packet back on the pile. 'I know.'

'What do you know?' said Richard. 'Please, tell us. I have a son.'

Her face flickered at Richard as he said this, some emotion caught between recognition and agitation. He seemed to catch it and glanced at me.

'My family,' I said. 'They're in Cornwall too. My daughter, my son … please, we need to get down there. We're searching for a car, take the food, but …'

'I will, thank you,' she said, standing up again and aiming the gun once again at Bryce.

'Please let us go,' said Richard.

'Right,' said the girl, ignoring him. 'All of you, turn around, stay on your knees.'

'No,' said Richard. I felt my stomach flip. I think I fell forwards, I must have made a noise too. I could see Bryce glaring up at her, shaking his massive head in the darkness.

'No,' said Richard again, struggling to his feet. 'You don't have to do this, let us—'

'Down!' said the girl. Richard fell back to his knees.

'Please,' said Grimes. 'Put down the gun, we just want to be on our way.'

'All of you, down!' she shouted.

She stepped further towards us and swung the gun in an arc between our faces. I flinched as it met mine. I went to speak, heard Richard make another attempt as well, then heard something else, another voice coming from within the cottage. The girl froze and glanced over her shoulder, then turned back on us. Her eyes flashed in the firelight. Fear.

'Down!' she said. 'Turn around! Stay on your—'

The sound again. Human. No words, just a high, quiet, trembling warble.

The girl stopped and looked back again, for longer this time. Whatever the noise was, she couldn't ignore it. It was calling her, calling something deep within her. When she turned back her face was no longer calm and no longer in control. She was almost on her haunches, jabbing the gun at us and breathing quick sharp breaths.

'Turn around!' she said. 'Now!' She looked back over her shoulder again.

I caught Bryce's eye.

'What was that noise?' he said quietly to her.

'What?' she said.

'That noise,' he said. 'What was it?'

We heard it again, longer and louder and now unmistakable; a piercing squeal followed by a mournful wail and babble. A baby's cry.

'Or maybe who?' said Bryce, looking the girl up and down as she paced up and down in front of us. Bryce seemed to brace himself. I saw Richard do the same, ever so slightly lowering his hands from his head. I guessed their plan and prepared to follow.

Suddenly the cry erupted into a full-blown scream. The girl's legs buckled a little and the barrel of her gun dropped as she turned. This time, Bryce pounced.

'No!' screamed the girl as she turned back to us, raising the gun at the dark mass of hair and flesh approaching her. Bryce just had time to slam his hand up against the barrel and the shot exploded off into the sky as he landed heavily on top of her. Richard, Grimes and I followed until we had her screaming and kicking beneath us.

The gunshot echoed around the dark hilltop as we wrestled to free the gun from the girl's wiry hands. She gripped it to her chest, the tip of the barrel rubbing dangerously against her skull. I felt sure the gun would go off and send the contents of her small head shooting into the flames next to us. Richard and Grimes struggled to stop her legs from kicking, while Bryce pushed down on her shoulders and Harvey tried to calm her down.

'That's alright girl, that's alright, slow down there, we're not going to hurt you.'

I tried to prise her fingers away from the metal. At some stage my hand became trapped between the barrel and her body. Beneath the layers of clothing I could feel the heat of a swollen breast pressing against my wrist, the fabric damp with leaking milk.

All the while, the baby's cries still bawled from within the cold and dark of the stone cottage.

'Please,' sobbed the girl. Her eyes were shut tight. 'Let me go, my baby, my baby, she's sick, my baby ...'

I wrenched my hand free and the gun came with it. I fell back in the snow and the girl wriggled free of the others, stumbling back around the fire and into the cottage. Grimes quickly took the gun from me and aimed it in the direction that the girl had run. She stepped away from the fire.

'Get out of the light,' she said. 'She might have another gun.'

We each stepped back into the darkness and waited. From the cottage we heard the baby's cries subdue and stop, then soft footsteps in the snow. The girl reappeared by the fire with the baby slung around her neck in a brown shawl, suckling on one of her breasts. The girl looked for us, blinking in the dark. She looked mortified, furious, afraid. She spotted Grimes holding the gun and her face softened into a look of resignation. She turned her eyes down to her daughter, a child once more.

'That's my only gun,' she said quietly. 'I'm not armed. I promise.'

'I promise.' A child's words. Grimes stepped back into the light and lowered the barrel.

'We're not here to hurt you,' she said.

'I know,' said the girl, still gazing down at the baby on her breast. 'I know that.' She began singing a quiet series of tuneless, wavering notes.

'I'm putting down the gun,' said Grimes, carefully pulling one of the packs away from the fire and propping the barrel against it. 'There.'

Grimes looked back at us and waved us in. We walked slowly into the light and stood facing her over the fire. Harvey walked further around and stopped a safe distance from her.

'I'm Harvey,' he said.

The girl looked up at the old man.

'What's your name, sweetheart?'

'Gloria,' said the girl.

Harvey nodded and smiled at her, eyes twinkling, then looked down on the baby who was falling asleep on the nipple.

'Beautiful,' he whispered. 'Do you mind?' He carefully reached out a hand. The girl stepped back warily, but when she saw Harvey do the same, she took a breath and stepped closer again, offering the child's head. Harvey carefully stroked it twice.

'And this is Sofia,' said the girl.

'I hate to be rude,' said Bryce from the shadows, 'but my head's pissing blood here.'

The Cold Voice

Richard and I bandaged Bryce's head up as best we could. It almost certainly needed stitches but we had nothing to stitch it with. When we were done, Bryce sat back on his pack and smoked in silence, staring into the flames. He wasn't used to having his head split open by a teenage single mother.

While we were seeing to Bryce, Harvey and Grimes had taken Gloria back into the cottage. I guessed they were trying to assure her that we were no threat. This was the truth, of course, but I was fairly sure that Gloria already believed this. I was more concerned about what would happen if she ever managed to get her gun back.

Grimes led Gloria back to the fire by her arm. She had given her the detachable fur-lined hood from her jacket and the baby was still sleeping in the shawl, now wrapped up tightly in a clean blanket. Harvey followed behind carrying two pots and a grill pan from the kitchen. There was water in the pots and he set them on the grill pan over the fire. He busied himself with packets from Bryce's pack as the water slowly boiled.

'Sure you don't need protecting?' said Grimes, as she walked behind Bryce and took her seat at the fire. Bryce ignored her and blew a long flume of cigarette smoke up into the sparks.

'Did anyone else survive here?' I said.

'Here?' she said, then shook her head slowly. 'No,' she said.

'I'm sorry,' I said.

'Why?' she said, looking at me sideways.

'Your parents, your family ...' I stammered.

She slowly rolled her eyes with a glimmer of a smile and puffed through her nose.

'I'm not from here,' she said. She moved her face closer to her daughter's. 'We're no' country girls, are we darling?'

'So where *are* you from?' said Richard.

'Glasgow,' said Gloria. 'Council block in Easterhouse.'

'How did you get here?' said Grimes. 'Where's Sofia's dad?'

Gloria's eyes glazed a little as if she was only just considering this. Then she suddenly seemed to remember something and frowned at Richard.

'I walked,' she said. 'You lost your boy?'

'Not lost,' said Richard. 'He's already gone south, to Cornwall.'

'Did he go on his own?' said Gloria.

'No. He was rescued. A helicopter took him.'

Gloria slowly nodded her head.

'Aye,' she said. 'Aye, I saw them. So why didn't you go with him?'

'I wasn't there when he was rescued.'

Gloria made a face, as if what Richard had said made no sense.

'Weren't there? What do you mean? Where were you?'

'I was ...' he stopped and looked at me, correcting himself. 'We were in the city, looking for ...'

'But why would you leave him? Why would you leave him on his own? He's your son.' She turned to me. 'And you. Your family. Why weren't you with them?'

She looked between Richard and me as if we were dirt.

'We were . . .' I began. 'I mean, it's not as if we . . .'

She breathed out in disgust through her nose and turned back to the child.

'I'm never leaving Sofia,' she said. 'We're sticking together. I'm never taking my eyes off her. You're meant to look after your babies. That's what my mum and dad did. I'd be dead without them.'

'You must have been pregnant when it happened,' said Grimes.

Gloria nodded. 'Six months,' she said.

'And you walked all this way? On your own?'

The girl darted around, searching for something.

'I didn't know where I was heading. I just started walking away from the water. I tried to follow the roads, but it was difficult to see.'

'Water?' said Grimes. She had suggested that a tsunami might have hit the west coast during her briefing at the barracks.

'It was everywhere,' said Gloria. 'Even when I made it out of Glasgow, it was like a swamp, but with nothing growing, no grass, just mud and rocks. I made it to some hills and took a rest at the top of one to see how far I'd come. The ground was wet as far as I could see, but it was drier on the other side of the hill. It was darker too, and I remembered what my dad had taught me about the sun rising and setting. It rises in the east because *rise* ends in an 'e'. It sets in the west because 'west' sounds a bit like 'sets'. So I knew that the darker bit was east, and that's where I was heading.'

Gloria gave a glimmer of a smile, pleased with herself, like a child getting a question right at school.

'And where's your dad now?' ventured Grimes.

Gloria blinked. 'The bin shed. That's where Dad took me and Mum the day it happened. Clever man, my dad. Everyone else had run off screaming, but he found us shelter. I had to leave because of the smell. I don't think they would have minded.'

The baby suddenly jerked and made a whimper. Gloria hunched instinctively over her child and hushed her back to sleep. She looked around at us.

'I wasn't sure if she was OK at first,' she said. 'I thought she might be ... I couldn't feel anything, you know? I walked around the city trying to find someone I knew, but I got lost. Everything was different. Most of the buildings were gone so there was more sky, but it was full of black clouds. I was glad it was dark. There were lots of things floating around in the water that I knew I shouldn't look at. Then I found a street that still had some flats on it, tenements, you know, with stairs? One of them looked OK, safe enough, even though the top half wasn't there any more. I found a room with most of a ceiling but no front wall, so I could see out onto the city. I found an old curtain and wrapped myself up in it on the sofa. Then I just lay there and looked outside till I fell asleep. It was weird, all that water everywhere instead of roads, no buildings, just piles of stone, and all these wee orange fires burning. I don't know if they were people or what.'

'Grub's up,' said Harvey. He ladled some noodles into bowls and handed them out. Gloria snatched hers and poured it into her mouth with her free hand. We stared as she slurped at the hot broth and gulped down mouthfuls without chewing. When she was done she picked at all the noodles she had spilled on her face, neck and hair, cramming them in her mouth. Then she licked her bowl and threw it in front of her.

'You want some more, sweetheart?' said Harvey, taking the bowl. Gloria nodded and he refilled it. She ate slower this time.

'Did you meet anyone?' said Grimes.

Gloria's face darkened and her mouth shut. She put the bowl at her feet.

'Someone. He tried to get me in a supermarket.'

'Tried?' said Bryce.

'I'd almost given up, still hadn't felt anything in my tummy. He had me against a shelf, put his hand in my knickers. I felt dizzy, like I was drifting away somewhere. He stank of dogs.'

Gloria wrinkled her nose.

'What happened?' I said.

Her face suddenly filled with joy.

'I felt a kick,' she said, beaming. 'A big fat kick. It was like someone had thrown a bucket of cold water over me. My eyes opened and suddenly I was angry. Awake and angry. They say you see red when you're really angry and it's true, I saw red in the dark, like blood pouring down over everything. I could see clearer somehow, too, like everything had just come into focus. I looked above me and saw a stack of those big metal pans they have in restaurants. I pulled one arm free and grabbed one. He grunted and looked up just as I brought it down on his head. Then I threw myself forward and made a noise I didn't know I could make, like a wolf or something. I jumped on him, hammered my fists on the pan until he fell over in the water with me on top of him. He was struggling, trying to get the pan off and stand up, but I rammed it down so that it was over his face, then knelt on it so that the rim was squashing his neck. I felt amazing, like my blood was on fire. I screamed down at him and put all my weight on the pan. He started thrashing around with his legs, trying to claw at me with his hands, his belly flopping in and out of the water. And all the time this gurgling sound was coming from inside the pan, getting higher and higher till it was just a squeak. I didn't know a man's voice could get that high. Then I felt something snap under the pan and he just stopped.

'I knelt there for a while, still screaming and spitting at him, even though he wasn't moving. Then I got off him and stood up. I realised that Sofia was still kicking me, again and again as if she was joining in too. That made me laugh. I actually stood there and laughed, holding my tummy as the pan floated away down the aisle.'

I looked at the others. Each face shadowed with a gawp of disbelief in the firelight.

'Fuck me,' said Bryce quietly. He tapped his head. 'Now I don't feel so bad about this.' He got up.

'Where are you going?' said Gloria.

'Taking a piss,' he grunted, making off for the cottage.

'Don't go back behind the house,' said Gloria. 'It's not safe.'

Bryce stopped, grunted again and changed direction. We heard a zip and then a long stream of fluid hitting a tree.

'I realised two things then,' said Gloria. 'The first was that I could survive. I could look after myself and look after Sofia, so long as we were together. The second was that I couldn't stay in Glasgow. I had to find somewhere safe. I found two backpacks on one of the supermarket shelves and filled them with as much food as I could. Then I left. I don't know how many days I walked, but one afternoon I found this place. There were some dead sheep in the field, just bones. The door was wide open and I called in but nobody answered, so I went inside. There was nobody about. One of the doors was off its hinges and the rest were wide open. There was stuff everywhere; clothes, objects all over the place. I found a bed at the back of the house with its covers all thrown back. I was tired and it smelled a bit like my mum, so I crawled in and fell asleep. I don't know how long I slept for, might have been a day or two.

'When I woke up I was starving. I still had some food left from the supermarket, but I had a look in the kitchen and found a larder that had a few packets and tins. When I was full I looked outside. The barn door had fallen off. There were two bodies underneath it, a man and a woman, I think. I guessed they were quite old, but I don't really know, it had been too long. Their heads and shoulders were sticking out of the door and they were face down in the dirt, but they were looking at each other. The man had a shotgun in his hand.' She nodded over at Grimes. 'That one,' she said. 'I didn't want to look at them too long because they reminded me of Mum and Dad, so I took the gun, found a spade and threw dirt over them until they were buried.'

She kissed the baby's head and stroked it. Bryce returned with some wood, which he threw on the fire. He sat down and started smoking.

'I decided to stay,' said Gloria. 'I knew that it would start to get cold soon and I was going to need a safe place to have Sofia. You can see quite a long way from up here, and there isn't much else for miles. I had shelter, food, and I found a stream running through the woods. That's where I get my water. I boil it up in case it's dirty.'

'So what's with the fire?' said Bryce.

Gloria looked up at him. There was a sudden darkness to her, not quite the child any more.

'Food ran out,' she said. 'Nothing left from the supermarket, nothing left in the larder. I was pregnant and I had nothing to eat. I started to eat bark, wood, pine cones, mud ... I got sick a lot, spent most of the time in bed. Then I was outside one afternoon dragging water back from the stream, feeling like I was going to die, when I saw something far away down on the road. I saw this man walking. I hadn't seen anyone alive since the supermarket, I was all ready to start waving my arms and shouting, but something stopped me. It felt like something spoke to me, something inside me that wasn't me. I sometimes think it was Sofia. I can't really explain it, but it just said, *No, don't wave. Start a fire.*

'I didn't know whether or not the man was friendly, or whether or not he had food. But I had nothing to lose. The voice in my head said, *Light a fire.* So that's what I did. I lit a fire where he could see it and I waited, and he came.'

She looked up at each of us, that darkness in her face again.

'Just like you did,' she said.

'He wasn't friendly,' she said after a pause. 'But he did have food. I ate for two weeks on what he had. After that, I spent my days preparing fires and watching the road. Every so often, I'd get a visitor. Sometimes they were friendly and sometimes they weren't, but they always had something useful.'

We sat in silence for a while. I didn't want to ask any questions. I was just glad the gun was where it was.

'And Sofia,' said Grimes. 'When was she born?'

'Three weeks ago,' said Gloria. She looked into the flames and little snarl of resentment curled her lip. 'This was my first fire since.'

'How do you know about the boats?' said Richard.

'Some visitors told me,' said Gloria. She spoke as if her 'visitors' were friendly travellers looking for rest, which I imagine some of them probably had been.

She glanced up at us again, eyes still full of disdain.

'Must hurt,' she said. 'Does it?'

'What do you mean?' said Richard.

'Them not being near you.' She spoke impatiently, nodding each word as if she was explaining something to a child. 'It must hurt.'

Richard and I shared an uncomfortable look, not sure how far we should take this. Gloria was already agitated enough.

'Yes,' I said. 'Of course. That's why we're trying to get to them.'

Gloria gave a purposeful sniff, as if at least that had satisfied her.

'Your daughter will be upset,' she said, looking right at me. 'She'll be crying, unhappy, wondering why her daddy's not there.'

I winced. The words felt like needles.

'What did the … visitors say?' Grimes broke in.

'What?' said Gloria.

'The people who told you about the boat. What did they say? Who were they?'

'A couple. They were married, I think. They said there were boats taking people away to another country where it wasn't so bad. They told me that they were going to find civilisation and that I should go with them so I could have Sofia somewhere safe, where there was medicine.' She puffed through her nose. 'What do I want with civilisation? We've got everything we need here, haven't we, darling?'

She cooed into her daughter's sleeping face.

'What else did they tell you?' said Richard, who had sat up and was leaning towards the fire.

Gloria shrugged. 'Not much. Except that they leave on Christmas Day.'

'Christmas Day?' said Richard. He looked around at us. 'That's just three weeks away.'

'Gloria?' said Grimes.

'Mm-hm?' sang Gloria, the darkness gone from her face once again.

'We need to get to those boats. We're going to stay here tonight and then we're leaving tomorrow morning. We need a vehicle. Is there one on the farm? Do you know anywhere around here that might have one?'

'A vehicle?' said Gloria. 'You mean like a car?'

'Yes,' said Grimes. 'A car, truck, anything with an engine.'

'Ummmm ...' Gloria looked up at the sky as if thinking over a problem. 'There might be one,' she said. 'There's another place near here, down the other side of the hill.'

'Does anyone live there?' said Grimes.

'Aye, a family. I've seen a truck down there. I don't know if it works though, I've never seen them drive it.'

She yawned.

'I'm sleepy,' she said. 'Think we'll head to bed.'

'Gloria,' said Richard. 'This is important. How do you know them?'

'The Hamiltons?' she said, stifling another yawn. 'The Hamiltons and I have an agreement. We stay out of each other's way.'

'Well, we need to talk to them,' said Richard. 'See if they'll let us use their truck. Are they friendly?'

'Friendly?' said Gloria, getting up from the fire. She seemed to consider the word as if it had some strange meaning.

'Do you think they would consider a trade?' said Richard.

'I don't know,' said Gloria, turning for the cottage. 'You'll have to take your chances.' Then she disappeared with her daughter into the darkness.

We kept watch that night, mostly in case Gloria came back out for her gun. We found some more logs in the wood to keep the fire going. I took the first turn. I stared into the flames and thought about Beth's pregnancies with Alice and Arthur, then the births and the difficult months afterwards. Nothing came close to what Gloria had been through, so why had we found them so hard? Why was the process of bringing life into the world, even in a bubble of middle-class comfort, medicine and relative safety, so fraught? Why did it take so much emotion? Why did this process keep perpetuating itself, generation after generation going through the same thing, time after time? Why did life bother?

Gloria had talked about the thing inside of her, the cold voice of something that wasn't her taking over and giving her strength and will when she had none of her own. I had read once that we were just vehicles for our genes to propagate, nothing more than hosts for a parasite with a much bigger plan than any of our own. Maybe that was true.

In the morning Richard shook me awake and put a cup of black tea on the ground next to me.

'We're heading off soon,' he said, then knelt to pack his bag.

Harvey was cleaning dishes in the snow. He saw me and nodded, then went back to smearing a cloth around the corners of a blackened saucepan. I sat up and shook off my blanket, stretched my back. Bryce was towering above the embers of the fire in front of me, smoking. The bandage around his head was tattered and dark red.

'Sweet dreams?' He grinned.

'Where's Grimes?' I said, rubbing my face.

'Inside with Goldilocks,' said Bryce. 'Checking her over.'

'And the gun?' I said.

Richard held it up for me to see, then got back to packing his bag. I stood up, stretched some more and looked around. Gloria had been right: there was nothing for miles.

'Three weeks,' I said. 'Five hundred miles in three weeks, and we don't know what's out there.'

Bryce squeezed his face into a smile and nodded, bouncing on his toes and blowing smoke through his nostrils. I turned to Richard.

'How are we going to get that truck?' I said. 'What can we possibly trade?'

'If they haven't used it for four months, then they're not likely to use it now, are they?' he said. 'We have food. Perhaps they'll take that. Otherwise …'

He glanced at Bryce.

'Otherwise what?' I said.

'We take it,' said Bryce. 'Like Dick says, it doesn't seem like they're using it anyway.'

'Maybe they just don't have any fuel,' I said. 'What then?'

'Then we're back to where we were,' shrugged Richard.

'Fucked again, you mean,' I said.

Richard stared at me as he stuffed the last of his belongings into his bag and pulled it shut.

'I need a piss,' I said. I threw my tea on the embers and walked off towards the cottage. I heard Grimes and Gloria talking inside and walked around the back to where the farm buildings were. In the yard I stopped and saw the burned-out barn and its fallen door next to a mound of dirt. I walked past it, around the back of another stone building that seemed to be suspended in a state of permanent semi-collapse. I followed its wall through the mud until I reached the end, where I stopped and unzipped my trousers.

As I relieved myself, I caught something out of the corner of my eye. The hill to my left ran down to another road parallel to the one we had been on the day before. The hill was steep and covered in snow, with the occasional patch of mud showing through, but a little way down I saw something else poking through. It looked like a stick or a branch. I zipped myself up and edged carefully down the slope towards it. As I got nearer, I saw more of the branches sticking up through the snow. Some seemed to be broken, their thin ends pointing at right angles.

Little thoughts arrived in my head as I made my way down the slope. My brain didn't quite allow them to register, but they were there all the same.

What happened to Gloria's visitors? What did she do?

I stumbled to a halt. I was close enough to see now. They weren't branches; they were limbs. Human limbs sticking up from a pile of bodies buried beneath the snow and the dirt. For a few moments I was frozen to the spot, wanting to turn back but unable to move as those terrible thoughts made themselves clear in my head.

Here they are. Gloria's visitors. This is what she did. This is what life made Gloria do.

Finally I turned and made my way up the hill. As I got to the top I rounded the corner and came face to face with Gloria in the yard. Sofia was awake and upright, strapped to her front and looking around with wide eyes. Gloria shook her head at me.

'I told you it wasn't safe back there,' she said, her face dark and serious.

I faced her for a while, readying myself, convinced she had some weapon concealed in her jacket that she would use to cut me up and send me down into the pit behind me with the rest. But then her face softened and she looked at her feet. She took a step to her left and let me past.

'We need to go,' I said when I got back to the fire. I picked up my bag and strapped it on my back. 'We need to go now.'

Pigs

We knew that Gloria's gun would have been useful to us but, despite everything, it still felt wrong to take it. We might have felt otherwise had it not been for Sofia. She needed protection, and the only thing she had was her mother, and the only thing her mother had was a gun. It did no good to think too deeply about this, about what sort of world we were allowing Sofia to be raised in. This question is already the burden of every parent, no matter when or where they live.

Gloria showed us where the Hamiltons' house was, but she wouldn't walk there with us. Staying out of each other's way was part of the 'agreement' she had with them. This should have concerned us, but with all the strangeness of the previous evening it didn't seem out of place.

We made a deal with Gloria. We would take the gun with us on the way to the house. When we reached the road, we'd leave it next to the ditch for her to collect, along with some food for her in return for our safe passage. Again, it seemed wrong to leave Sofia with nothing.

We walked carefully down the hill, avoiding Gloria's burial ground, and dropped the gun at the bottom. We looked back at Gloria's silhouette against the bleak, burned farm. She raised an arm and dropped it. Then we walked for a mile or two in the direction she had pointed us in. The road followed sharp bends down a hill. The trees from the wood next to

Gloria's cottage ran down the hill beside us and another steep hill to the right made a natural, deep valley that seemed to have formed a protection from the fires. I could even see grass sprouting through the snow and a small stream ripened with meltwater ran alongside us. It was the first normal and natural thing I had seen in a while; it felt like we were somewhere that hadn't been touched by the destruction.

Eventually the road flattened out and we came to an old white house set back into the trees. Smoke rose from a chimney and one window was lit up with a dim, flickering light. In front of it was a yard and some small, single-storey outhouses. Parked in the yard, facing the gate, was a well-used orange jeep. Nothing – neither the buildings nor the truck – seemed to bear any marks of damage.

We stopped at the gate and Bryce leaned over.

'Be careful,' whispered Harvey. 'We don't know who they are.'

'Can't be worse than Bo Peep, can they?' said Bryce, jabbing his thumb back along the road. 'Ho!' he shouted.

Richard pulled him back. 'Just let me do the talking,' he said.

Bryce stepped back. He raised his hands. 'Alright, Dick,' he said. 'Go for your life.'

Richard stepped forward.

'Hello?' he called. 'Anyone there?'

We heard a rattle and a wooden door slam shut in the yard. A man appeared from one of the outhouses and stopped, facing us, open-mouthed. He looked in his sixties, well fed, with a round face and bald scalp. Thick tufts of white hair sprouted from the sides of his head. He was wearing wellington boots, beige work trousers and a heavy, plaid shirt underneath a tank top. The shirt was untucked and his sleeves were rolled up exposing strong, thick forearms. In one big hand he carried a bucket.

'Sorry to startle you,' said Richard.

'Huh,' he said, looking at each of us in turn. Then he suddenly shook his head and smiled, striding towards us.

'Not at all,' he said, laughing. His accent was full of Yorkshire warmth. 'My apologies!'

He laid a hand on the gate and tapped his nose twice.

'Not that used to visitors,' he whispered, then grinned. 'Now, how can I help?'

It felt as if we were ramblers asking for directions. The white of the house behind even gave the impression of sunlight.

'We were wondering if we might talk to you?' said Richard. 'We need some help.'

The man looked us over quietly with a quizzical half-smirk, taking in our bags and clothing. Then he looked at Richard and nodded.

''Course,' he said. 'Come in.'

He held the gate open as we walked through.

'Go up to the house,' he said. 'We'll have tea.'

We walked to the side of the house and he let us in through a tall oak door. A blast of warmth hit us as we went in.

'Ellie!' he shouted. 'Visitors! Put tea on! I'll just let the boys know,' he said, running around the side of the house. We stood in the hallway and waited. In a minute or two he was back, ushering us through a low archway and into a kitchen, the source of the light and warmth. A single lantern was hanging from an electric light fitting and a wood-burning stove roared in one corner. Next to the stove stood a small woman, who looked back at us with the same expression of shock as the man had worn in the yard. She was younger than him, maybe by twenty years.

'My wife,' he said.

She said nothing.

'Alright, alright,' said the man. 'Close your gob, girl, you'll draw flies.'

The woman looked at her husband, shut her mouth and then looked back at us.

'Well, don't just stand there!' snapped the man. 'Put the kettle on!'

She jumped, then shook her head and began busying herself with iron kettle, which she began to fill from a spout in the wall. She pulled on what looked like a beer pump to force water through it.

'Like I say,' said the man quietly, flicking a thumb at his wife and widening his eyes. 'We're not used to visitors. Sit down, sit down.' He pulled some chairs out from the table and motioned to them. We smiled nervously and dropped our packs, took a seat each. The man remained standing by the stove. I felt warmth begin to seep up my feet and legs from the fire, into my fingers and face.

'I'm Hugh,' said the man, suddenly thrusting a hand in our direction. Harvey took it first.

'Harvey,' said Harvey. 'Much obliged, mate.'

'Bryce.'

'Richard.'

'Ed. Edgar.'

'Laura,' said Grimes.

We each looked at her in surprise. It was the first time she'd told us her first name.

'And this is Ellie,' said the man.

The woman nodded and smiled nervously as she heaved the iron kettle onto the stove. A slow, tidal roar began to build inside it. She pressed herself back against the sink with her hands behind her back.

'We have two sons as well,' said Hugh. He took a seat for himself and leaned his thick forearms on the table. He shot a dark glance at his wife. I remember this unnerved me, but I shelved the feeling. 'They're out with the pigs, should be back soon.'

'Pigs?' I said. 'You have pigs?'

He raised his eyebrows and gave a pleased grin.

'Oh, aye,' he said. 'Pigs, some hens. Nothing like we had before, but some survived the worst of it.' He smoothed his fingers over the wood of the table and sat back in his chair, hands behind his back.

'We do quite well here,' he said with a wink. 'Not too badly at all.'

The kettle started to whistle and he glanced at his wife, who sprang into action again, filling a pot and placing cups in front of us.

'No milk, 'course,' he said. 'Hope you don't mind.'

I leaned forward to pour the tea. He swatted my hand briskly away from the pot.

'Time,' he said. 'Needs time to brew.'

Teapots had always made me nervous. I understand how ridiculous that sounds, but it's the truth. They seemed to represent something that I was somehow not allowed to attain. There was a ritual to tea-making – the warming, the temperature of the water, the settling, the brewing, the stains maintained within the pot – all part of a delicate care that had just never made it into my life. I made tea by throwing a tea bag into a cup and covering it with water, not leaving it long enough, pouring the milk before removing the bag, then squeezing the bag against the side of the cup with a spoon. The dark tendrils that emerged provided the only flavour in the otherwise pale, tepid mixture. I knew all this was wrong, I knew tea should and could easily be made in a far better way, and every time I was a guest in a place like this I was reminded of this fact. But teapots did not belong in my life. I know, it's ridiculous, but the truth is sometimes that way. The act for which I had just been admonished – pouring the tea too early – caught me out. It marked me, branded me, weakened me. In that moment, there were two kinds of people: those who knew how to make tea and those who did not. It was clear which side I stood on.

I sat back in my chair.

'Now then,' said Hugh. 'What's all this about help?'

Richard cleared his throat.

'We're headed south,' he said. 'To Cornwall.'

Hugh raised his eyebrows and gave a single laugh that was more like a cough.

'Cornwall?' he said, looking at his wife and then back at Richard. He brought his hands down from his head and folded them across his chest.

'Why?'

'There are boats leaving,' said Richard. 'I don't know if you . . .'

Hugh waved a hand at him.

'I know, I know,' he said. 'Big fuss if you ask me. You want to get on them?'

'Yes,' said Richard. He nodded to me. 'We have family. The thing is, there's no way we can get down to Cornwall in time. Gloria told us that ...'

Hugh sprang forward in his seat. I saw his wife shuffle uncomfortably.

'Gloria?' said Hugh.

Richard paused. We hadn't yet said anything about our stay at the farm.

'Yes,' he said. 'We came from Gloria's ... I mean ... from where Gloria was staying.'

'You stayed with Gloria?' said Hugh. He looked around the table, giving each of us the same serious look. 'You met her?'

'Yes,' said Grimes. 'We met her last night. We asked her if she knew anyone with a vehicle and she said that we might try here.'

Hugh sat slowly back in his chair and folded his arms again. He nodded lightly, appraising something.

'It's been very hard for her,' he said. 'Very hard. We've tried to, er, speak to her, you know, make sure she's alright up there on her own, what with her condition and all. I've been up a few times myself, but we've not always ...' He broke off. 'Let's just say she doesn't like company.'

'We got that,' said Bryce, tapping his bandage.

'She told us you had an agreement,' said Richard.

A smile twitched on Hugh's face. 'Agreement,' he said, clearing his throat. 'Aye, could call it that.'

'Did you know that she'd given birth?' said Grimes.

Hugh suddenly gave a frown of concern. 'No, no, we didn't, did we, love?' he said, looking back at his wife, who shook her head and smoothed her apron. 'Is she alright?'

'She seems to be, given the circumstances.'

'Good,' he said. 'That's good.' He looked at his watch. 'Where are them boys?' he grumbled. He leaned forward and poured the tea, allowing me a small look of superiority which I met with a thin smile.

'So, er,' said Richard, 'we were wondering . . .'

'You want my truck,' said Hugh. He kept his eyes on the cups as he pushed them towards us.

'We know it's a lot to ask,' said Richard. 'And we don't have a lot to give you in return, some food and blankets perhaps . . .'

Hugh nodded and tipped his chair back on its legs. He sipped hot tea from his mug and seemed to bask in the warmth from the stove behind him. He glanced at his watch again.

Richard went on. 'It's just that . . .' He slumped his shoulders a little, shook his head, shrugged. He searched Hugh's face. 'I'm sorry to ask, but we have no other choice.'

Hugh frowned and nodded slowly, running a hand around his stubbled chin.

'Like I say,' he said. 'We do alright here. We live on what we have, just like we did before, you know? We don't go anywhere, don't have much need to travel, certainly got no need for *boats*.' He spat the last word. Then he looked at his watch again.

'I just want to find my son,' said Richard.

'I have family too,' I said. 'My wife, a daughter and a son.'

Hugh looked me up and down.

'Family's important,' he said. Suddenly there was a click behind us and the creak of a door opening. Hugh looked over our heads.

'Ah,' he said, grinning. 'Speak of the devil.'

I spun round. Standing behind us were two identical young men, eighteen at most, wearing farm overalls and long boots covered in manure. They had wide faces with small, glittering eyes and cropped brown hair. They were tall and broad with thick arms, like their father, in which they held two shotguns pointing directly at us. The stench of animal shit filled the kitchen. We each reeled back in our chairs, Bryce nearly taking out the table with his weight. My cup shattered on the tiles and I stumbled back, slipping in the hot tea. Hugh was on his feet, laughing. He grabbed me and gave me an almighty shove that sent me sprawling on the floor at the feet of his sons. The one I was closest to moved his boot and I fell face-first in the stain of excrement it had left on the floor.

'What the fuck is this now?' I heard Bryce say, as I struggled to my feet, wiping my cheek.

'Boys!' shouted Hugh. 'Take our guests here outside. Give 'em a tour.'

'Wait a minute!' said Richard, standing forward. 'What—'

The son farthest from me swung his gun around and caught Richard in the chin with its butt. Richard's head snapped back and he staggered back into Bryce, who caught him and held him upright. Harvey stepped forwards to speak, but was held back by Grimes. Richard touched a finger to his bleeding mouth and looked back at Hugh.

'Want my fucking truck, do you?' His laughter boomed around the room. 'Come on,' said Hugh. 'Out.'

The son nearest me grabbed my collar and hurled me effortlessly through the archway into the hall. My legs spun in a cartoon cartwheel behind me but I managed to stay upright before crashing into the front door. He opened it and pushed me outside. The rest fell out behind me and we stood in a huddle, the two teenagers bearing down on us silently from the steps. Their father stood between them on the step above. Ellie appeared at his shoulder and looked around at us like a child from the safety of its parent's leg.

'Put the guns down,' said Grimes. 'You don't need to do this, we'll leave now, be on our way.'

'Huh?' said Hugh. 'You've only just arrived. How very rude.'

He slapped one of his sons roughly on the shoulder.

'Show them the pigs,' he said.

'Hands on your heads,' mumbled one of the twins. His voice had barely broken. 'Now,' he said. He jabbed the end of his gun at us. 'Turn around. Move.'

It had started to snow again. Soft flakes fell slowly around us as we were bundled across the yard, past the truck, stumbling in the drifts as we approached the main outbuilding.

'Stop,' said the talking twin in a rehearsed monotone. 'Face the doors. Keep your hands on your head.'

The other twin pulled the doors open and the air was suddenly filled with squeals. Inside the building was a bare enclosure separated from the main doors by a metal railing and a strip of chicken wire. Four large pigs waddled frantically across the muddy floor and began snuffling at the air and rubbing their glistening snouts up and down the sharp wire. Hugh strolled up to the gate and leaned across it. He dangled one hand down and clicked his teeth. The smallest pig ran up to meet him.

'Aye,' he said, casually, as if he was leading a tour for a school trip. He scratched the pig's ear. 'Of course we had a lot more. We were more protected down here when it happened. I don't think we got it anywhere near as bad as some other places we heard about.' He looked over his shoulder at his sons, who were now standing on either side of us. 'Still scared the shit out of us though, didn't it?' he said. He winked at them. One of them smirked. Hugh looked back at the pigs. 'We did get a few fires, lost a few of these buggers.'

He gave the young pig an affectionate slap around its chops and turned around to face us with his arms along the rail behind him.

'The strong survive though,' he said. He turned to his sons. 'Don't they? Eh?' The twins murmured a response as their mother walked quietly around them and stood next to her husband. Hugh put an arm around her shoulder. 'Like Gloria,' he said, and spat in the dirt. 'Maybe it's time to pay her another visit, Ellie, see how she's doing with the baby, eh? I've heard it's quite hard in the first weeks, leaves you quite weak.' He narrowed his eyes. 'Maybe that's how you got past her.' He nodded to himself. 'Aye, maybe time for another visit. Maybe time to teach her a lesson for this.' He hissed and pointed to the scar on his face.

After a moment, he laughed and relaxed back against the railing.

'Strong always survive,' he said. He cocked his head and watched us for a while, looking between our faces and chewing his cheek. The pigs squealed and snuffled hungrily behind him.

'Pigs need fed though,' he said at last. 'To keep 'em strong.'

Something bounced in my stomach. I felt panic rise up in the other four too. Bryce shifted his weight anxiously between his boots. Grimes and Richard exchanged looks. Harvey suddenly dropped his hands and stepped forward, holding out his palms to Hugh.

'Now look,' he said, his voice cracked and wavering. 'Just hold on a—'

Hugh glanced at one of his sons, who drove the butt of his gun hard into Harvey's belly. Harvey's lungs emptied themselves with a high, '*Guuuuh*,' and he fell to his knees in the muddy snow. I went to help him up, but was dragged back to my place by the other twin. Harvey knelt with his hands in the snow before him, gasping.

Hugh pushed himself up from the rail and walked towards Harvey. He held out a hand to him. Harvey grimaced up at it, then knocked it away. He fixed Hugh in the eye and got himself to his feet, spat in the snow to his side. Hugh rolled his eyes and motioned to his sons, twirling his finger around in the air.

'Turn around,' one of them said. 'Move along from the shed.'

They ushered us around so that we were standing in a line facing back towards the road. I was at the end, the other four to my left. My heart, which had been racing since we had been in the kitchen, picked up the pace. The pigs were next to us, still squealing urgently and straining against the clattering chicken wire. The family stood before us, the sons on either side of the parents. Hugh's left hand curled around the small shoulders of his wife and his other was a tight fist against his hip. Smoke trailed from the chimney of the white house behind them and up into the snow-heavy pines.

One of the twins turned to his father, who nodded. The two boys raised the butts of their shotguns against their shoulders.

I felt my knees weaken, my bladder too, felt the uncontrollable and ridiculous urge to turn my head from the blast. My heart was now struggling against my chest like a crow trapped in a bucket. I felt like my neck and eyes might burst with blood, had a last hopeful thought that there might be some chance of me passing out before the end.

I heard Bryce groan, looked sideways and saw Richard staring straight ahead, trembling. Grimes dropped her hands and lifted her chin. Her lip flickered once and tightened. Next to her, Harvey dropped his hands and looked down at the floor, shaking his head.

Different rays … he seemed to say. *Different rays* …

I have no idea if there are common human responses to circumstances like this. Perhaps it is predictable, perhaps everyone facing sudden death like this – particularly execution – goes through the same mundane series of states as their brain searches in vain for the right tools to counter the inevitable. Perhaps it is all logged somewhere in a psychiatric journal, I don't know. All I can say is that, in my case, it was not quite what I might have hoped for: strength, peace, dignity, that kind of thing. I think I wet myself a bit. Then I lost control of my facial muscles. My mouth seemed to spasm and gurn as if it was chewing something too big for it. My eyes lost the ability to focus. Strange things happened around my knee area. My throat dried up completely so that a huge portion of what was set to be the last few moments of my life was dedicated to trying different methods of swallowing. While all this was going on, some frantic part of my cranium was having a last-ditch attempt to find some meaning to a life that was about to end, flitting through ideas and abandoning half-finished philosophies like an accountant shredding incriminating paperwork to the sound of police sirens. Nothing flashed before my eyes. I had no sudden feeling of inner calm, no feeling that I was going to be OK, that everything was for the best. I just felt the same mixture of confusion and inability to cope as I always had done, only this time compressed into microseconds. I thought about Beth and Alice and Arthur, wondered if there was any possible way they would find out that this had happened, felt dutifully bad that I would not see them grow up, then pitiful about the fact that I might not want to know what the world had left for them anyway. Then I felt disappointment. Then I probably wet myself again. Then I heard two loud shots.

I opened my eyes to see the two twins lying face down in the dirt. Hugh was kneeling in the snow, looking at them. His face was confused, as if he was searching for a word. Blood appeared at his shoulder. He looked down and watched it spread through his shirt. Behind him stood Ellie. Her eyes were wide and her mouth was clamped shut. There was a fine spray of blood across her pale face. She held her arms diagonally out from her sides, her fingers stiff and open so that the skin stretched tight around their bones. She stared down at her sons and her husband and breathed a few shuddering breaths. Then, with her arms still held out, she spun around on her heels and faced Gloria, who was stood by the house, looking back at her down the barrel of her still-smoking gun. Sofia was upright in the sling around her mother's chest with her arms and legs sticking out in a star. She was looking at the pigs, still squealing and snuffling in their pen. I swear she gave a chuckle.

Ellie seemed to tense up even more so that she was nothing but a taut string of bone and muscle. A low noise rumbled in her throat and she began to run across the yard towards Gloria, arms outstretched into pincers. The noise rose into a piercing howl of rage that was silenced instantly by a third blast from Gloria's gun. Ellie's head snapped back, as if by some invisible leash around her throat that had reached its limit. She lay still as the snow grew red around her. The pigs seemed to quieten at this. Hugh had held his hand to his wound. He turned, still wobbling in confusion on his knees, squinting as he looked back over his shoulder. Gloria walked past Ellie and stood over him.

'Hello, Gloria,' he said. Sofia gurgled at the snowflakes gently parachuting around her. 'And hello—'

'Don't look at her,' said Gloria. She planted a boot in Hugh's side, knocking him to the ground.

'Easy there,' he laughed. He reeled on his back, then steadily pushed himself up to a sitting position. He sighed and smiled. She raised the gun and looked back at him down the barrel. Hugh looked across at us, still standing dumbly in our line.

'Made a friend, did you?' he said. 'That's interesting.' He coughed and gripped his shoulder tighter. Blood was streaming faster through his fingers and making a red river of his forearm. 'Very interesting.' He looked back at us as if he'd suddenly thought of a joke. 'Strong survive, eh?' he said, nodding at Gloria. He laughed again, then coughed again, then became quiet.

'So what now,' he said. 'What now, Gloria? Shoot me and take my truck?'

'I don't need your truck,' said Gloria.

'Let them have it then?' he said. He looked back at us. 'You really did make friends, didn't you?' This seemed to amuse him and he started to chuckle. Gloria put her boot on his shoulder and pushed him back into the snow. His laughter became a coughing fit as he struggled against her weight. She pressed her heel down on him until he gave up, rested back, looked up at her with cold eyes. He began to sing softly.

I saw three ships come sailing in
on Christmas Day
on Christmas Day
I saw three ships come sailing in
on Christmas Day in the morning.

Gloria raised the gun to his head.

'Careful girl,' he breathed. 'Don't want to give her nightmares.'

'Too late for that,' said Gloria. She squeezed the trigger and I looked away as Hugh's head became a stain in the snow. The blast echoed around the pine trees above. Gloria stepped back and we faced each other. None of us said a word. I had the urge to bolt. We had no idea what she intended to do next.

At last she lowered her gun. 'It's OK,' she said gently. She looked around at the yard with a peaceful look on her face. 'I'm not here for you.'

The truck had two rows of seats and a flatbed at the back. It started first time, to a roar of delight from Bryce. We found a barrel of red diesel in a shed and strapped it into the back.

Then we got ready to leave. Bryce was in the driving seat, the engine rumbling, with Richard next to him.

'Thanks,' I said to Gloria as I threw my pack in the back. 'Why did you come back?'

Gloria held her arms around Sofia and swung gently on her hips. She frowned a little as if I had misunderstood something.

'You need to find your daughter,' she said. She looked down at Sofia, who was starting to gurgle.

'You hungry, poppet?' she said, turning away and walking across the yard, around the four bodies. 'You want fed? Think these piggies want fed too.'

Grimes and Harvey climbed in the back, leaving the door open for me. Bryce stuck his head out of the driver's window.

'I'd like to get the fuck out of here now, please,' he said.

Return

We drove fast. We joined the main road again and began to head south. The thrill of sudden speed, of seeing the road rushing to meet the tyres and the landscape circle by outside the window, mixed with the adrenaline of having just escaped death, filled me with a rush of hope. I felt that we might have a chance of making it to Cornwall, that seeing Beth, Alice and Arthur again was a real possibility. The presence of this feeling in itself was enough to make me realise that it hadn't existed until now. I had been travelling without any belief that I could get to where I needed to be.

The last time I had driven this road we'd been on our way to see Beth's brother, Simon, and his family, who had moved up to Wales from London the year before. He had previously worked for a large corporation in a tall building, doing something intangible with money that had made a lot of it come his way, but had decided to pack in the stress and long hours of City life and head out to the country, trading in their Hampstead townhouse for a steading with substantial acreage, stables, horses and a sea view.

We spent a weekend strolling around warm meadows and along impossibly long, empty beaches. On the first evening we sat outside at a distressed oak table and watched their three blonde, curly-haired daughters take Alice running through the long grass of their garden as the sun set. We ate salad from the vegetable patch and locally caught fish from cracked plates, drinking cold, expensive wine from Simon's collection. I sat and felt the warmth and effortless peace of their home, allowing my glass to be refilled and becoming drunk with love and envy. Beth was pregnant with Arthur at the time and Alice was two. I had no idea how to achieve a life like this.

'We just wanted to return to the basics,' said Simon's wife, a tanned, blonde Norwegian, impossibly attractive and witty. I felt guilty just sitting next to her. 'You know, feel nature again. London's so full on and, well, with the girls getting a bit older we thought, you know, let's downsize.'

I think a fair few people had thought that they'd wanted this: a return to something quieter and simpler than the life they had found themselves in. They had watched the television and seen the property and cookery shows. They had wanted the grass, the tall trees, the stone, the wood, the wool, the bulbous tomatoes picked from their own greenhouses, the candlelit parties in local barns with cups of home-made cider from old casks, the fiddler in the corner, the old clothes and muddy boots. Against the muddled pallor of their own existences, they had seen these things and wanted out. They actually thought of it as being *out*. An escape from the machine.

But it wasn't an escape. It wasn't a return to a *simpler life*; it was a version of a simpler life. A version that replaced cholera, dysentery, freezing winters, lost harvests, frequent stillbirths, domestic violence and incest with underfloor heating, Sky Plus, solar panels and plump trust funds. It was just another decoration: wallpaper, not a return.

Perhaps I'm being unkind or just jealous. But seriously, how many people could ever have afforded to live like that?

I thought of Gloria, wide-eyed with love for her daughter, gazing around the yard of her new home as if she was being given a tour by an estate agent, feeding the bodies of its owners to their pigs. She had returned to something, and it wasn't wallpaper. I thought of Cornwall, of the hoards of survivors for whom escape to the simple life seemed like the brightest outcome. I thought of them trickling out of the country, escaping back to civilisation. The place we came from, the place many had yearned to return to, was not a place we really wanted to be.

Around midday we joined the motorway. I watched the landscape spin past as we drove. The changes to it were dramatic and everywhere. Hills were flattened, imploded, fields and forests corrupted and burned. As we got nearer to Carlisle, the road showed more and more signs of damage, and we had to slow down in places to negotiate potholes and bulges in the tarmac. The few cars we saw had been either tossed into fields or stopped eerily in their tracks.

As I looked out of the window, I suddenly became aware of Grimes next to me. She was looking across my line of sight. I followed her gaze to Richard in the front seat. When I looked back at her she caught my eye and looked quickly away.

Just then, Bryce slammed on the brakes and the truck came to a shuddering halt.

'What's happened?' I said. 'Why have we stopped?'

'Up ahead,' said Bryce. 'Look.'

'Christ,' said Richard.

Harvey, Grimes and I leaned forward and peered through the windscreen. We were on a shallow uphill climb. About a quarter-of-a-mile ahead of us, parked at the summit, was a black Land Rover.

'Do you think it's them?' I said

'Yes,' said Grimes. 'That's them.'

'Why have they stopped?' said Harvey. 'They were a day's drive ahead of us at least.'

'Fuel, perhaps?' said Richard.

Grimes shook her head. 'They had plenty in the tank to take them past this point, and plenty more in reserve.'

'So what, then?' said Richard. 'Breakdown?'

Bryce turned around to Grimes. 'What do you think . . .' he said, pausing. 'Laura?'

'Possibly,' she said, ignoring the jibe. 'Or someone found them.'

'Which means they could find us,' I said. 'Which means they could be watching us now.'

We looked ahead, waiting for something to happen, for the car to start, lights to come on, a door to open or a movement of any kind. Nothing happened. Bryce shifted the gear lever into first.

'I'm going up,' he said. Nobody argued as he pulled away.

The hill flattened about fifty metres from the Land Rover, allowing us to see beyond it. The reason why it had stopped became clear. For about half-a-mile in front of it lay hundreds of abandoned cars. Some had stopped, others were overturned or piled into each other, those furthest away were black, burned shells. The road was impassable. Even if it were, there would have been little point in driving the short distance. Beyond the burnt-out cars, the road rose vertically into the air. A torn lip of tarmac hung above the cars with broken pipes and twisted girders sticking up from it like veins and tendons from a severed limb.

'The road . . .' said Richard in astonishment. 'It's been blown apart.'

We stopped the truck next to the Land Rover and inspected it. It was empty. No food, water, guns or ammunition.

'They've taken everything,' said Grimes, slamming the boot shut. 'Let's take a look up ahead.'

We took our packs from the truck and walked. Bryce reached the broken piece of road first and climbed up to its edge. When he got there he stumbled back a few paces, then steadied himself on a pipe. As I climbed up to him he turned and, for the first time since I had met him, I saw an expression of genuine surprise on his face. He blinked.

'I think we're back to our feet,' he said. 'Take a look.'

I held onto the pipe and looked over the lip of road. Behind it was a gigantic pothole, at least ten metres across and spanning the entire width of both carriageways. The ground on either side of the road was thick with mud, littered with cars that had tried to pass around it. The road beyond the hole was in an even worse state than the side on which we stood. It had shattered. Whole cars had disappeared into the gaps between its fragments. It stretched on as far as we could see. There was no possible way of driving onto it.

Richard reached us, took one look around the edge and jumped back, throwing up his hands in frustration.

'Fuck!' He paced up and down, rubbing his hands on his head, then took another look.

'Fuck! Fuck!' he said again.

'What is it?' said Grimes as she and Harvey caught up.

'We're fucked,' said Richard. 'Take a look.'

Grimes and Harvey peered over.

'Oh,' said Harvey. 'Oh, crikey.'

'There's no way we'll be able to drive through,' said Grimes. 'We should go back, find another road.'

Richard stopped pacing and surveyed the destroyed road before us. He put his hands on his hips and blew a sharp puff of air through his nose.

'There's no other road,' he said quietly. 'We'd have to go miles back to find another route, and even then there's no guarantee we can rejoin the road south, or that it won't end in something like this.'

He tightened the straps on his pack.

'The only way is forward,' he said. 'The road might be less damaged further on. We walk until we find another vehicle.'

We followed Richard across the pothole and picked our way along the road on the other side. After a couple of miles, as Richard had predicted, the road became less damaged. But it was still filled with cars. The entire road was a string of abandoned, crashed or burnt-out vehicles, a ghostly traffic jam that stretched endlessly into the mist. I pictured the morning of the strike, the road quickly filling with cars, people trying to escape mindlessly from the cities, not even registering that the damage would be unprejudiced. A bright and boiling morning, the air suddenly alive with car horns, the sound of screeching tyres, crying children, metal upon metal, people standing on roofs trying to see into the distance, pointing at something, shouts of rage from drivers trying to manoeuvre around wreckage, their wild eyes suddenly distracted by something above them, smoking lights streaming across the brilliant blue sky.

We spent the afternoon checking the cars with the least damage and avoiding those which had been involved in collisions and contained bodies. We targeted the ones with open doors, their drivers gone to face whatever life or death awaited them in the wake of the strike. We found some with batteries still working, but their tanks drained of petrol. Others had petrol, but no battery. We tried moving working batteries into fuelled cars and managed to start them, only to find we could drive them for just a short time before we hit another obstacle, had to walk some more and start again. We found a 4x4 that worked, managed to get it off the road and drove it for half a mile before the ground fell into a sharp drop. Our only choice would have been to drive it down into the valley. But there were no other roads there and the tank was almost empty. We abandoned it and started back along the road.

A strong, foul-smelling wind had started early in the afternoon. By sundown it had become a gale. We were tired and frustrated. The hope and elation I had felt as we had sped away in the Jeep earlier now lay in pieces at the foot of a brick wall. We were making hardly any progress. Each time we found a car that worked, we could only drive it so far before our path was blocked by a pile-up or a hole in the road. Then we'd get out and start searching for another car. Even as it got dark, I was sure I could still look behind us and make out the pothole where we had originally stopped.

There was a friction between Bryce and Richard, worsened by the fact that they couldn't hear each other over the wind. I think I knew that Grimes had something to do with it, although I didn't consciously register it. When it became too dark to continue, we took shelter in two empty cars. We didn't eat. The gale howled through the night, shaking the chassis and sending debris clattering along the road like hoards of metallic rats. None of us slept.

In the morning, the wind was still gusting angrily. We lit a stove inside one of the cars, drank tea and ate undercooked, sauceless pasta. Then we continued along the road, trying car after car like the day before.

Sometime in the late afternoon, we trundled to a halt in a red Vauxhall and stared at the pile of metal that spanned the road in front of us. Cars, trucks and at least one motorbike lay heaped on top of each other or had spun off the road. In front of them were four articulated lorries, bent and twisted, their necks twisting around each other like broken swans. Grimes had been driving. She switched off the engine and we sat listening to dregs of fuel swilling in the tank and the wind outside.

'We can't keep this up,' said Richard. 'It's almost dark and we've only managed five miles. What date is it?'

'December fifth,' replied Grimes.

'It's about four hundred and fifty miles to the south coast,' said Richard. 'Which means we have to average over twenty miles a day.' He opened the passenger door and swung out his legs. 'At this rate, we'll barely make Manchester by Christmas.'

Richard slammed the door and walked towards the wreckage. He stood with his hands on his hips, head pushed forward, surveying the scene as if it was something to be set straight, taught a lesson. He began pacing up and down the gigantic pile-up. He shouted something that was lost in the wind, then crouched on his haunches and rested his forehead on his long arms. Grimes left the car and went over to him. Harvey followed. Eventually Bryce began fidgeting in his seat, then kicked his door open and strode across too. He swung his boot at a hubcap. It frisbeed in a fine arc across both carriageways and bounced off a signpost. Whatever place or directions had been written on it had been burned away. It was just a single, thick arrow pointing south. The sign clanged loudly and decayed into a whistling hum. Bryce watched it wobble and become still, then sat against the boot of a crumpled Ford. He took out his tobacco and began to roll.

I stayed in the car, in the middle of the back seat, my seat belt still strapping me in, staring through the dirty window. I felt sick. Everything inside me was draining away. The invisible cord in my chest seemed to be pulling so hard that my ribs might explode at any moment, pulling out my shaking heart and yanking it from the car. I reached down and unclipped my seat belt, then slid slowly out of the open door, taking my pack with me.

Harvey had sat down next to Bryce. Grimes was with Richard, one hand on his shoulder, trying to reason with him.

'We're just approaching Carlisle,' I heard her say. 'If we head back a few miles, we might be able to find an exit that takes us through the city. The roads might be easier to pass.'

'And then what?' he said. 'We rejoin this? Take the scenic route? What?'

'I don't know,' she said. 'But we're on the motorway now. It's not going to get any less busy.'

I looked down at my boots. My left lace was undone, coiled in a broken figure-of-eight. I stared at it for a while, then bent down and picked it up.

'I can't go backwards,' said Richard, rubbing his brow. He stood up.

'We need to,' said Grimes. 'We have to try.'

'My son's at the other end of this country!' screamed Richard.

Nobody spoke. I looked up from where I was crouching. His arm was extended high above me, one long skeletal finger black against the sky, pointing south down the splintered road.

Things became dream-like, I suppose, although I have never had a dream so clear. Every thought and every action was slow and separate from the last, like the world had gently untangled itself for me, just for a few moments, to show me how it all worked. *This happens, see? Then this, and then this, and then you do this . . .*

I allowed my gaze to follow the direction of Richard's gnarled finger, then saw the wordless signpost again, pointing the same way. Then I looked down at the lace in my hands. I slowly began working its frayed ends through the top hoops of my boot.

I looped the laces around my ankles once and tied them in a double knot. I undid my right lace and did the same with that. Then I stood up. I tightened my pack, tightened the zip on my jacket, felt the steel can against my chest.

I walked past Richard and Grimes. Bryce and Harvey looked at me curiously. The wind began to blow furiously around me, as if it had realised what I was about to do, even though I had not.

You have to understand, you see, this wasn't a choice. I hadn't weighed up the options, I hadn't considered the practicalities, I hadn't reached a logical conclusion. What happened next was not because of my own volition, not because I had found some hidden well of courage and determination.

It happened because ... well, I can't tell you exactly why it happened. Perhaps it happened only because I let it happen.

I shall say this again: I hated running.

I picked my way through the wreckage. Then I began to run.

Some memories of my childhood.

I had a collection of *Star Wars* figures which I played with endlessly. My parents couldn't afford to buy me as many as some of the other boys in the village, so when I was treated to a new one, I spent a long time deciding which one to choose from the display in the toy shop. Lacking the appropriate vehicles and combinations of characters to recreate scenes from the films, I created an entirely new universe in which Yoda was a vengeful dictator, Stormtroopers defected regularly and Darth Vader helped Han Solo overcome his terrible disfigurement at the hands of his deranged Wookie and joined him in his ceaseless fight against plasticine Kraken in giant seas.

My favourite figure was the Gamorrean guard. He was a green, hog-like creature with large upward-pointing tusks, steel armour, animal-hide clothing and a thick, heavy axe. In my universe, he was vastly more intelligent than his clansmen and questioned the system to which he belonged. His disillusionment forced him one night to abandon his sentry and head off for the sand hills of Tatooine, where he lived his life as a recluse. He was my friend and I took him everywhere with me.

One Saturday morning, I was halfway on my way home for lunch when I realised he had fallen from my pocket while playing at the stream that ran through the village. I ran back in panic and began wading up and down in my wellies, searching through the rocks and small rapids where I had been crouched. I became more and more frantic, this being the worst thing in the world my eight-year-old self could imagine happening at the time. I stumbled about, letting water into my boots as I trawled the cold water and scrabbled about in the stones beneath the surface. I couldn't find him. He had been swept away.

Deep, deep loss. I ran home crying and fell into my mother's arms with bubbles of snot popping from my nostrils as I wailed at her, explaining what had happened.

I was inconsolable for the rest of the day and most of the next. But, on Sunday evening, after my bath, I found a paper bag wrapped up in my pyjamas. Inside was a brand-new Gamorrean guard figure with a little note from my father saying, 'Shhhhh! Dad.'

There was a tree in the village – a gnarled, ancient yew that stood on a small green by the school. It was easily climbable with a natural, deep seat where the trunk split into its two main branches. One day two other boys and I found a pornographic magazine hidden in the seat. As young boys, there was no other option available to us but to read it. We were just reaching the end of a spread featuring a couple having intercourse with their vests on when we heard a noise from the road below. We looked down to see a girl called Amy looking up at us. Amy was fifteen and deaf. She had a small white dog on a lead. I don't know how she knew what we were doing, but she was clearly wise to us. She started making angry noises, the half-strangled moans and growls of profoundly deaf speech for which we all made fun of her. Then she started throwing her hands up, shouting and gesturing for us to get down. Her dog barked up at us. One of us started laughing and I joined in, then we jumped down from the tree and threw the magazine at her feet. We ran off whooping as she yelled behind us. I remember looking back and seeing her looking sadly down at the tattered, grubby pages, her dog sniffing them.

I remember kicking a tennis ball against the wall of my house and building up complicated rules and scores based upon the number of volleys and half-volleys I could manage in a single rally, where I could place the ball on the wall, how high I could bounce it, which objects I could hit with it and in which order. The end result saw me running wildly along the wall of the house, positioning myself in stranger and stranger positions to achieve the most complex shots with the greatest rewards. Occasionally, without warning, certain points became special in that they led magically to some real-world reward. *If you get more than five volleys and manage to hit the sixth of the gutter and catch it in your left hand, Emily Turner will fall in love with you.* The rules evolved over an entire summer and only I knew them.

I remember running downstairs to the smell of mince and the sound of pips on the radio.

I remember sprinting upstairs to the toilet when the adverts came on during *The A-Team*, flushing the chain halfway through and racing it to the end, then leaping down the stairs again, running across the living room floor and diving over the top of the sofa. I had to be sat down before the last beat of the music to the first advert or something bad would happen.

I remember walking our dog one November morning before school and hearing my sister's voice calling me back across the field, then running back with the dog through the frozen mist because Adam Ant was playing on the radio.

I remember my ninth birthday, being told to go to the garden shed, then running down to find a BMX shining against the back wall.

These things are all gone now. Not just in my time, but in possibility too. But I remember them, I remember running, running everywhere without thought. And yet I don't remember actually running. Not the effort of it. I remember lightness, I remember speed, I remember the earth seeming to bounce beneath me as if it were a giant balloon that I could push away from me with my bare feet. I don't remember stiff, slow limbs or tight lungs or the feeling of concrete pounding through my bones.

Somewhere along the line, gravity had overtaken me.

Less than a minute after I had begun to run, I heard shouts from behind. I couldn't make out the words but they came from Bryce first, with some cold laughter, then Richard and Grimes together. Then, when I failed to respond, silence followed by worried murmurs. The road I was on was long and straight. Snow was drifting at its sides and coating the devastation caused by whatever had happened on either side of it. I could still see the ridges and potholes of the shattered tarmac but, other than that, I was running south on an empty highway.

Pain arrived instantly. Whatever had pushed me – or pulled me – to start running, whether it was instinct, desperation or spirit, I was still a physical thing; I was my body. And my body didn't want this. My body wanted nothing to do with this. By the time I could no longer hear the shouts behind me, my chest had started to squeeze in on itself. My fists tightened, my arms drew in and I found that I was looking across my brow to see the road ahead.

My legs started to ache. I felt as if I was being pulled down under the earth, as if I would buckle at any moment like a plastic bottle crushed under the weight of an ocean, and disappear beneath the snow like dust.

I kept running. There was still nothing that you might call thought going on in my head, just two wordless drives spinning in each other's orbits like opposite particles.

Go. Stop. Go. Stop.

I had time to register this on some level, and then realise that the road on which I was running seemed to be changing, before I heard something behind me. Footsteps. Too light to be Bryce's, too short to be Richard's. Grimes?

I heard a voice in my right ear, warm and cracked like a tin plate.

'That's not the way.'

I glanced over my shoulder. Harvey was behind me, padding softly through the snow. He smiled at me.

'What?' I said between breaths.

'I said, that's not the way.' He spoke naturally, without breath or effort, as if he were taking a stroll. He ran up beside me.

'What do you mean?' I said, trying to swallow, get some spit in my dry throat. 'I'm not going back. Like Richard said, my family are this way.'

'I mean that's not the way to run,' said Harvey. He pointed down at my feet. 'Striding like that, trying to anyway. Your feet are landing too far in front of you.'

'What?' I spluttered.

'Look at them,' he said. 'Go on. Look at them and feel what they're doing.'

I looked down. I saw and felt what I always saw and felt when I tried to run: one leg stretched out and landed with a thud as far as it could ahead of me. While the impact travelled painfully up my shin, thigh and spine, the other one trailed behind loosely, curled up beneath my body and then took over by stretching ahead again, repeating the process.

'Striding on,' he said. 'You're trying to pull the road under you, trying to turn the earth with your heels.'

I turned my head to look at him. He had his pack on like me. His wide face was clear of pain. He smiled back at me.

'The planet's much bigger than you, son,' he said. 'It's not going to work.'

I stared back at him, unable to think or say anything useful.

'Look,' he said. 'Think of it this way: you're turning a flat road into an uphill climb. You should be turning it into a descent. Look at my feet. They never go past my waist. They only take little steps. It's like I'm falling – see, that's all running is, controlled falling.'

He nodded to himself contentedly as if he'd just come to some satisfying conclusion. Then he took a deep breath through his nose. He bounced along next to me in the mist, his footsteps like feathers against my clumsy, pounding hammers. His smile never left his face.

'What ...' I said, still struggling for breath, still feeling gravity haul me into the ground. 'How do you know so much about running?'

Harvey ignored me and nodded down the road.

'Long way to Cornwall,' he said. 'What did Richard say? Four hundred miles? Five?'

The numbers hit me hard. Not because I had not considered how far it would be to travel the length of the country on foot – as I said, I had not considered or decided anything – but because of how far Beth, Arthur and Alice were away from me. I felt the cord tighten again and I stumbled to a halt, bent over double.

'I'm not going back,' I said. 'There's nothing ... back there.' I was struggling to speak.

'Slow down, mate,' said Harvey. 'Easy, take your time.'

'There is no time,' I said. 'There is *no time.* We're probably already too late.'

'Then why did you start running?'

Just then I heard more footsteps behind us. I looked around to see Bryce, Richard and Grimes running towards us. As they drew near I saw the looks of concern on their faces. Concern tempered by just the tiniest trace of something else: interest, or maybe a kind of appalled respect.

Suddenly Bryce released an almighty roar as he fell to the ground.

'Ow! Fuck! Ow!' he yelled, clutching his leg. Grimes and Richard caught up and stopped.

'What happened?' said Richard, kneeling down next to him. Grimes took off her pack and started rummaging around inside.

'My ankle,' he said. 'I didn't see a pothole. Went over on it.' He straightened up to a sitting position and stretched out his leg. Grimes pulled out a torch and shone it down on Bryce's boot. Flakes of snow danced in its beam.

'Broken?' she said.

'Nah ...' said Bryce. He loosened the lace and put an exploratory hand down inside. 'Don't think so.'

Grimes reached out a hand and helped Bryce to his feet. He winced as he put weight on foot, then wiggled it and tried again.

'It's OK,' he said. 'I'm alright, just twisted it.'

He turned to look at me. 'Are you fuckin' *serious*?'

'I'm sorry,' I said. 'I wasn't thinking . . . I . . .'

'Bloody right,' said Harvey quietly, just to me. 'Not thinking. Maybe you should do some more of that.'

'Ed's right,' said Richard.

'No, I'm not,' I said. 'I'm not right, like I say, I wasn't thinking. I just panicked.'

'No, you didn't,' said Richard. 'You just did what the rest of us were thinking. This is the only way we'll make it to Cornwall.'

'Speak for yourself!' spluttered Bryce. 'Running? Are you out of your fuckin' *minds*?'

Grimes worked her jaw, thinking. 'We can't walk safely on these roads at night, we've already seen what happens.' She motioned to Bryce's ankle. 'Even when the sun rises, the cloud cover's too thick. It's mid-morning by the time you can see anything properly.'

'And it's dark before sunset as well,' said Richard.

'So we get about five or six hours of light to move by,' said Grimes.

'To do twenty miles in five hours, we need to do more than just walk.'

'So we alternate,' said Richard. 'We run a few miles, then walk a few.'

Grimes nodded. 'That'll work.'

'Are you serious?' I said.

'Makes sense on paper,' said Grimes.

'Twenty miles, every day, for three weeks,' I said to myself.

'There or thereabouts,' said Richard. 'Now let's get through this shit heap and find shelter. Get some sleep. We need to rest if we're going to . . .'

'Run to Cornwall?' Bryce boomed. 'Is that what we're doing now?' He looked around at us, open handed, awaiting a response. 'Just so I know. Anybody?'

Richard stared at him for a while.

'That's right,' he said. 'But right now, we walk.'

He pulled on his pack and headed south.

We hit another pile-up soon afterwards. It took us an hour to clamber through the jumble of mud, stone and metal and find the tarmac again. By that time it was fully dark, so we walked a little in the light of Grimes' torch until we found an overturned lorry. The red canopy of its trailer was half torn away and some of its cargo had spilled out onto the road. We pulled open some of the boxes, disappointed to find them filled with stationery.

'This will have to do us,' said Grimes. 'We can make a fire from the paper. How's everyone doing for water?'

'I'm pretty much out,' I said.

'Me too,' said Bryce.

'Right,' said Grimes. 'There was a sign back there for services about a mile ahead. I'm going to go and see what's what. There might still be some supplies there, water in the pipes at least.'

'I'll come with you,' said Richard.

Grimes paused. 'OK,' she said. 'You three can stay here and get the fire going.'

'Sir, yes sir,' said Bryce, flipping a salute and sitting down on a crate of ballpoint pens.

Richard and Grimes left. Harvey and I searched the depths of the trailer for the driest paper and brought it out to the entrance. I kicked at the wooden floor until a piece broke away, then I prised it back. A rat shot out from beneath, squeaking and running over my arm. I yelled and fell back on the floor as it scuttled out of the trailer.

'You alright?' called Harvey from outside. 'Oh, hello little fella.'

'Yep,' I said. 'Just a rat.'

'A rat?' said Bryce. He frowned and ran a hand down his beard. I could tell what he was thinking; I was hungry too. He stood up and walked past me, disappearing into the darkness of the overturned trailer.

I got to my feet and tugged at the wood until it broke off, then lugged it out to the fire that Harvey had started with the paper and Bryce's lighter. There was a lot of smoke, but it was warm. Harvey and I sat close to it as Bryce hammered and stomped about inside.

'Reckon they'll find anything?' said Harvey. 'Richard and Grimes?'

I shook my head. 'Doubt it,' I said. 'We passed a service station two miles back with a van sticking out of its roof. I could see inside. It was empty, stripped clean.'

We heard some shouts from Bryce, things falling, then a pause, silence, some loud banging and a whoop of victory. Seconds later he appeared with a proud grin and two fat rats hanging by their tails from his fist. He dropped them by the fire and lit a cigarette.

'Dinner,' he said.

We ate the rats. They weren't good. When we'd finished, Harvey got up and went into the trailer for more paper. When he was out of earshot, I turned to Bryce.

'Do you think we can do this?' I said. 'With Harvey, I mean. Do you think he'll be able to manage it?'

'You saw him today,' said Bryce. 'He was barely out of breath.' He looked me up and down in the same way he had done when we had met over whisky. 'What about you?' he said. 'Will you manage it?'

Harvey appeared, smiling, carrying a few packets of A4 paper. 'I can hear you, you know,' he said, tapping his ear. 'I'm not deaf.' He tossed a stack of paper onto the fire and his eyes began to twinkle in the growing flames.

'Did I ever tell you I used to be a postie?' he said.

We shook our heads. He looked between us, searching for recognition. He mimed posting a letter.

'A postman, you know? Delivering letters and parcels?'

Bryce frowned. 'Aye, we've . . . we've heard of them, Harvey; go on.'

'This was when I was a young man, back in Australia, back in the sixties. I come from New South Wales originally, lived out in the country, north side of Sydney. It wasn't like in the cities, you know with a van. The country was spread out, miles between houses sometimes.'

He stood up and walked to the side of the road. When he returned he was carrying a short stick. He sat down and held it to the light, smoothing it over in his hands. Then he used it to poke the fire, pushing back the blackening sheets of printer paper that were slipping from the pack.

'I had two dogs that came with me. We were up at 5 a.m., out the door into the sunshine, spent the day racing around the bush and back home by the afternoon. Great life, always on the move. Me and the other fellas had dirt bikes to get around and my dogs would jump on the back. A lot of the time, though, if I knew I was going up a road I was going to come back down again, I'd just leave the bike and run with the dogs at my side. I started doing it more and more, probably clocked up around twenty miles a day most days. Got really fit. Great life.'

He smiled, then his face darkened and he scratched the road at his feet with the stick.

'Anyway, if you live out in the bush then you're pretty much a member of the bush fire brigade as well. Some years are better than others. One summer it was sweltering hot, a real bad one. Then the sheep on a farm close to us got sick and started dying. The farmers didn't know what to do with all the corpses; couldn't burn them, see, in case they started a fire. Then, there were fires anyway, bad ones that spread and took out some houses. We spent two or three weeks trying to put them out, ambulances all over the place taking injured people back to Sydney. I didn't sleep much. My dogs came everywhere with me, of course; I couldn't keep them at home. Then everyone started to get sick, other animals too. Agnes and Annie, well, they got sick too. Real sick. I couldn't do anything for them.'

Bryce nodded slowly, the corners off his mouth turned down. 'Losing dogs,' he said. 'Hardest fuckin' thing. My grandad died when I was twelve. I remember Mum telling me when I got in from school and she might as well have been telling me what was for dinner. I didn't give a shit, fuckin' alcoholic old prick. Our dog died a year later and I cried for a week. It's hard.' He punched his chest. 'Harder than losing a person.'

'Well,' said Harvey. Bryce seemed to have knocked him off course. 'I don't really know about that. All I can say was that after that I didn't cope too good. The fires stopped eventually but a lot of people had lost their homes.' He cleared his throat. 'And more than that in some cases. Everyone was exhausted and nobody was particularly happy but, like I say, I'm ashamed to say I was doing worse than most, so I suppose what I did next had something to do with that.'

'What did you do?' I said.

'Well, one day, after everything had died down, I got up at 5 a.m. as usual and went outside to start work. I rode my dirt bike a few miles down the track, turned left at the creek and stopped at the top of the hill. The sun was coming up and I could see the light spreading west over the plains. The hill had cast a shadow on the plain beneath me. There was still smoke coming off the burned scrub and I could see the places where houses used to be, little black squares full of rubble, nobody there any more. It was all in this dark shadow. It felt like the end of the world.'

He looked up suddenly and laughed.

'Yeah.' He gestured at the darkness. 'Not much compared with this, I guess, but that's what it felt like at the time. Anyway, between all the burnt-out houses and black scrub-land, there was this long, straight road running south-east out of the shadow. No bends or hills, just this sharp line running through all the shit and leading out towards the horizon. As the sun rose, I could see the line extending further and further, as if it was a drawing for me on a map. Such a simple picture.'

He stamped one foot on the ground.

'Everything *here* was dark and dead.'

Then he pointed his stick out across the fire.

'Everything out *there* was bright and living.'

He looked at us nervously, as though seeking acknowledgement for something he'd only just tried the very first time.

'There was no path down to the road,' he continued. 'I dropped the bike and picked my way down the slope to it, fell a few times, skidded down most of it on my arse and fell in a heap of dust at the bottom. Then I stood up and looked down the road. And then . . .' He shifted a little on his seat and shrugged. 'Then I just started running.'

He looked into the fire for a long time, then up at us as if he had just remembered we were there.

'I know,' he said. 'Stupid, really.' He tapped his stick on the ground and laughed through his nose, then stared into the flames once again and was quiet.

Bryce raised his hands and looked between us.

'That it?' he said. 'That's the story? You went for a run?'

'Ah, yeah,' said Harvey. 'Yeah, that's about it, I guess. Went for a run. Pretty big one, mind.'

'How far did you run, Harvey?' I said.

'Oh, well,' said Harvey, scratching his chin. 'Hard to say, really; I didn't have a map and I wasn't following a route. I met a few people on the way, you know, other folk on the road. I remember one pair of blokes in a truck who spent their time driving around the country, following the coast, just looping and looping around. I met them five or six times, I think, coming in the opposite direction. I slept wherever I could, ate and drank whatever I could find. Eventually I reached a bay and saw an ocean I hadn't seen before. I stopped and sat on a rock and looked out at the sea crashing against these huge rocks. I could smell the salt, feel it getting on my skin and in my air, tasted it on my lips. It felt good, I felt like I'd reached where the road was taking me, felt like I'd found my coast.'

'Where were you?' said Bryce.

'WA, mate,' said Harvey. 'Western Australia, place called Kalbarri.'

Bryce thrust his head forward and gawped.

'Western Australia?' he said. 'That's on the other side of the country.'

'That's right,' said Harvey. 'Beautiful place, too. I slept rough on the beach for a few weeks before one of the locals took pity on me and let me stay for a while. I found a job cooking fish.'

Bryce's mouth was still agape, a cavern of flickering shadow in the firelight.

'And you ran all that way?' said Bryce.

Harvey scratched his head, rocking it this way and that.

'Hard to say exactly how I got there,' he said. 'A while later, some university people got wind of what I'd done and wanted to talk to me about it. They wrote about me in some journal or other. I told them what I knew, the places I'd seen, and they tried to piece together my route.'

He began to trace lines in the dirt with his stick.

'Near as they could place it, I ran south, meandered around Victoria for a while, found my way up into South Australia where I got lost in the lakes, circled back a few times, eventually hit the south coast and then joined Route 1, straight across the Nullabor Plain before gravitating north and getting lost again before Kalbarri. They told me I should have died a few times. Truth is, I don't really remember many of the details, and some of the people I met might not really have been there; hallucinations, you know? Dangerous thing to do, stupid like I say.'

He paused and drew a single line through the others he had made at his feet.

'I didn't choose it, though,' he said, meeting my eyes and narrowing his. 'That road. I didn't decide to run that far on it. It chose me.'

Bryce stared across the fire at Harvey. Eventually he snapped his mouth shut and shook his head.

'Fuck me,' he said, getting to his feet. 'Just fuck me sideways. *Ow.*'

'Take it easy there, big fella,' said Harvey, getting up to help him. Bryce waved him away.

'I'm alright, just going for a piss.'

Bryce hobbled around to the back of the truck. Harvey held my gaze for a while, then let it drop back to the flames.

'So what *do* you remember?' I said.

Harvey reached across and pulled another two packs of A4 from the pile and threw them onto the fire.

'Well,' he said, 'bearing in mind this was almost fifty years ago, Ed, and I don't remember much about anything back then … I remember … I remember the feeling of becoming lighter somehow. Not physically, although I lost a lot of weight. Mentally, maybe. I felt like things became a lot simpler when I ran.'

'What things?' I said.

'Ah, you know, things. Life.'

He tapped his foot nervously a few times.

'Ed, I didn't have any reason to do what I did. It just happened, and I saw it happen to you today. When you ran off like that, you didn't really decide to, right?'

I nodded slowly, chewed my lip. 'I suppose so.'

'Well, that's how I felt too. When I left. I remember that. There was no decision made, and no reason. The big difference is that you have a reason. Your family.'

He threw a hand out at the darkness.

'Look at all this shit,' he said angrily. 'There's no way we can keep going searching for cars every day. They're all fucked, the roads are fucked and if we keep crawling along then we'll be fucked too. There's not enough time. What you started today, that's the only way through, I'm certain of it.'

I shook my head.

'Harvey,' I said. 'We can't run that far in that time, or I can't at any rate. I'm just not capable.'

He fixed me with his bright blue eyes.

'Ed,' he said. 'You have no idea what you're capable of.

Bryce returned and sat down.

'So,' he said. 'You ran across Australia and got a job in a chipper at the seaside.

'It wasn't a fish and chip shop,' said Harvey. 'More of an outdoor BBQ really.'

'Aha, sounds lovely,' said Bryce. 'So what the fuck made you come to Scotland?'

'Ahh, well, see Kalbarri's a nice place, great beaches. Over the years it became a bit of a tourist trap. We'd get visitors from all over the world, especially in the summer. Anyway, one night, about five years after I arrived, a girl came to the BBQ and caught my eye. I used to cook the fish up front, you see, so the customers could watch. She was called Mary, on holiday from Edinburgh. We became, you know, friendly ...'

Bryce grinned. 'I bet you did, you dirty bastard,' he murmured.

'... but she was only there for two weeks and then she had to go home. We wrote to each other, this was all before email and Facebook and all that crap. We had to actually write the letters and post them, you know?'

'Yes, yes, Harvey, we've established that we know about letters,' said Bryce. 'What happened next?'

'The next year she came back. And the year after that. The third year, I decided to go back with her. We got married and I stayed.'

'Just like that?' said Bryce.

'Just like that,' said Harvey, smacking his palms together.

Bryce shook his head in disbelief again.

There were footsteps on the road and Richard and Grimes appeared in the glow of the fire. They both dumped a box each on the road.

'Everything alright?' asked Richard.

'Oh, aye,' said Bryce. 'Everything's hunky-dory.' He gestured at Harvey. 'We just ate some rats and Forrest Gump here told us his life story. What have you got?'

'Water,' said Grimes, pulling open a box and handing out bottles. 'Not much, but it should see us through most of tomorrow.'

I broke the seal on mine and poured it down my throat. It was freezing cold and I spluttered a mouthful out down my front.

'Take it easy,' said Grimes. 'It has to last us.'

Bryce took a sip from his. 'And what else,' he said.

Richard opened his box and a pile of brightly coloured plastic-coated slabs fell out.

'Noodles,' he said. 'Lots and lots of noodles.'

We laughed, all of us, and I felt something like warmth rippling around the fire.

That night I dreamed about cattle again. They were stuck in a pen inside a burning barn, mad with fear. I was looking down on them from a great height, watching them clamber over each other, panicking, their wide snouts wavering about, slick with mucus. The sound became louder and more frantic until a single cry rang out above the rest: a high-pitched, canine howl. I awoke.

I was lying on my side inside the truck, facing the opening in the roof that led onto the road. It was light and I could see the fire's loose ashes fluttering in a breeze. Beyond the fire was broken road and burned metal. I sat up and looked around the truck, heard Richard's snores. Grimes and Harvey were nowhere to be seen. I heard a noise from outside, then Bryce's voice.

'Yes! You beauty!'

I shook off my blanket and walked out. The lorry's cab was not quite horizontal, propped up against the side of another. The passenger door opened and Bryce jumped down onto the road. He walked towards me, grinning, only slightly limping. In his outstretched hand he held a bottle.

'Shame we didn't check it last night, eh?' he said.

'What is it?'

'Vodka!' he said. 'Half bottle. Didn't think the driver would mind.' He threw a thumb back to the cab.

'Anything else?' I said.

Bryce reached in his pocket and showed me a thick grey roll of duct tape.

'For my ankle,' he said. He opened the bottle and took a long drink, five gulps, eyes to the sky, then exhaled loudly and passed it to me. I took a pull, felt my chest sear, took another and handed it back. Bryce belched and Richard appeared, his hair stuck out in owl-like tufts. He rubbed his face and frowned up at the sky with one hand against his forehead.

'Is it brighter today or am I imagining it?' he said.

'Dick,' said Bryce, handing him the vodka.

'What's this?' said Richard squinting at the label. Bryce sat down and began undoing his boot laces. We looked down as he first eased off the boot and then the sock beneath it.

'Doesn't look like there's any swelling,' said Richard, taking a swig from the bottle. 'Or bruising.'

Bryce rubbed the thick, hairy flesh of his ankle between his hands and rotated his foot back and forth.

'I told you,' he said. 'It's fine. Just went over on it.'

He took out the tape and made four strips that he placed vertically on each side, then wound the tape around a few times and tore it off. Then he put his sock and boot back on and stood up.

'Brand new,' he said, then reached his hand out to Richard. 'Don't be shy, Dick.'

Richard passed him the bottle.

'Did either of you hear that sound?' I said.

'What sound?' said Richard.

'Like an animal. A howling sound,' I said.

'Aye,' said Bryce. He passed me the bottle. 'I did. Dogs, maybe.'

'I didn't hear anything,' mumbled Richard. 'Sound asleep. Where's Harvey?'

'No,' I said. 'It didn't sound like a dog. There was something else to it, something a bit more, I dunno, human?'

'Fox then,' said Bryce.

'Do you think there are foxes out here?' I said.

'Expect so,' said Richard. He rubbed the light stubble on his cheeks. 'Scavengers. They'll be aggressive too; we should keep an eye out for them. Make sure we keep our food wrapped up at night.'

He looked up at something behind me. I turned to see Grimes walking back towards us. Her hair was damp, pulled back under a black woollen hat. She carried some clothes and a towel which she stuffed inside her pack.

'Good morning, Laura,' said Bryce. 'I see you've washed. Are you sure we have enough water for that kind of luxury?'

'Had to be done,' said Grimes. 'Besides, I didn't use much.'

'These gentlemen and I were just having a spot of breakfast,' he said. Whenever he spoke to her it was like this: pretending to be a station above himself, purely to draw attention to the fact that he wasn't. It seems obvious now why he was doing it, though it wasn't at the time.

'Would you care to join us?' he offered her the bottle. Only a few dregs remained.

'No, thanks,' she said. She looked down at his ankle.

'Suit yourself,' he said, finishing it.

'Can you walk?' she said. 'Run?'

'It's fine,' said Bryce. 'No problem.'

'Good,' she nodded. 'All the same, we need to take better care. We can't afford injury if we're going to … if we're …'

'Run to Cornwall?' said Bryce once again. He tossed the empty bottle into the embers of the fire. 'This is *definitely* what we're doing, is it?'

Grimes squared to face him.

'If you have any better ideas, just shout,' she said.

Just then I heard Harvey's voice.

'Fellas!' he shouted from around the other side of the trailer. 'Come here, quick! Take a look!'

We went around and saw Harvey standing on the side of yet another overturned juggernaut that had sprawled into the crash barrier.

'Come up!' he said. 'You won't believe it.'

We each climbed up and followed Harvey's finger, pointing at the horizon. We were on top of what had been a bridge, the beginning of an interchange into the town. Beneath us the streets were bleak ruins, the occasional pillar or crumbling tower block still standing alone, three-dimensional anomalies in an otherwise flat world. But Richard was right. It was brighter that morning. There, just above the Earth's natural horizon and unobscured by any man-made structure, a faint disc of light floated behind the thick black clouds.

For the first time since the strike, we could see the sun.

'Now if that's not a good sign, I don't know what is,' said Harvey.

London's Shored

We stuffed the noodles in our packs and refilled our rehydration bladders with the water that Grimes and Richard had found. After Bryce's find earlier, we decided to take a look inside the cabs of the other lorries in the pile-up. We found a first-aid kit, another torch (empty of batteries), a bar of chocolate, a lighter, a map of the UK and a cricket bat. Bryce claimed the last of these and stuffed it in the webbing of his pack.

'Foxes,' he said.

There may have been more to take, but nobody wanted to spend too much time inside the cabs.

We shared the chocolate and left, clambering through the wreckage until we found the road. Then we began our first twenty-mile stretch. We walked for an hour, then began to run. I knew I had to keep my eyes on the treacherous road in front of me, but they kept drifting upwards, hypnotised by the sun, still visible and peering glumly through the clouds at the bare earth beneath, stripped of the life it had once ignited from dust.

Eventually it disappeared again, but my eyes still sought it out in the dark sky.

We were now running through Carlisle on what had once been the M6 motorway. The 'backbone of Britain' as my father would have said, chin raised proudly as if he were talking about a war hero and not a bleak strip of pollution-carrying tarmac. This backbone – broken now – would be our trail south until we hit the Midlands. We planned a rough route using the map from the lorry, our first aim to hit Penrith before nightfall. Penrith was twenty-one miles away. I had never run more than three in my life.

Harvey ran at the front, with Richard and Grimes behind and Bryce and me at the rear. My pack felt heavy, even though it only contained noodles and water. My legs strained too, my boots like lead. A few steps in and my body began to tell me how little it wanted to do with this. Whatever this was I thought I was doing, I should stop right now – give up while I had the chance.

I didn't give up; something kept me going, but whatever watery breed of will it was that got me through those first steps, those first miles, I knew then it wasn't going to be enough. It already seemed hopeless to continue, and yet I had barely broken my stride.

A strange, broken rhythm appeared between my breathing, my heartbeat and my boots on the tarmac. This seemed to occupy me for a while, before Bryce interrupted my painful trance. I became aware of his great head leaning towards mine.

'You don't believe that shite, do you?' he said.

'What shite?' I breathed.

He nodded at Harvey. 'That shite. Running across Australia.'

I looked up at Harvey, springing on his heels ahead of us.

'Old man's lost a few up here, don't you think?' said Bryce, tapping his temple.

'I don't know ...' I said. Every word was a gulp. 'He seems pretty good ... at running.'

'Not denying that,' said Bryce. 'But there's nothing unusual about an old man who runs.' He leaned in again. 'They're always out there, aren't they? Skinny bastards hobbling about in mangy shorts with their wee cocks flapping about inside.' He mimed a few flaps with his hand and grimaced. 'Big difference between that and running thousands of miles across a desert, though, isn't there? I'm telling you, he's not right.'

Bryce suddenly looked over my head at something.

'Service station,' he shouted to the others. 'On the right. Worth a shot?'

'How long have we been going?' said Grimes

Richard checked his watch. 'A little over two hours,' he said.

'OK,' said Grimes. 'We can take five minutes.'

We crossed the barrier and found the service station. It was empty. We rested and moved on.

The road and the landscape changed again. We saw craters on our left, small at first, then large. One huge canyon loomed to the right. The ground around us seemed to become even more absent of anything man-made than before. There was nothing, not even the memory of buildings remained, and no trees, of course. The road itself became more cracked, the spaces between potholes ever shorter. More of the cars appeared to have been burned until every one was a black husk, some still with bodies at their wheels like used matchsticks that might turn to ash in the next strong wind. Then, fewer and fewer cars were even there at all. Eventually the road disappeared completely until we were running on nothing but rock-strewn dirt covered by a layer of frost. The landscape was flat, colourless, scrubbed clean of life. It was as if the world had disintegrated into two dull halves: brown earth and grey sky.

We could still see the faint marks where the road had been, so we kept within their boundaries. The ground began to fall away beneath us and we began to walk downhill into a wide and shallow bowl of barren dirt. A bank of brown mist loomed in front of us, as if the ground itself was evaporating, mud ghosts rising into the gloom above them and obscuring everything around us. I felt some relief in my legs, then we were within the mist, running blind on flat, dry ground.

'I feel like I'm inside a fart,' said Bryce.

I could barely see Harvey now; he was just an outline in the mist ahead. The sound of our boots in the dirt and our packs shuffling on our backs became amplified, as if somebody had closed a door on the world. I felt an odd respite, cocooned from the road ahead, as if there was no more distance to go, that the journey itself was just in this small bubble. There was no longer any great expanse to endure.

Harvey's shape became dimmer as he pulled away from us. Then I heard a noise, very distant, a dull plucking sound and a soft, high voice. It grew louder until I could hear that it was music: a man's voice singing softly over a guitar. The strings sounded metallic, like steel, but dampened by the air around them; a low scale played slowly with mournful chords springing above it. Notes that didn't belong to the chords beneath them snapped and twanged in the upper registers like wild birds trapped against a ceiling. The melody was lost and I couldn't make out what he was singing, but every word was a breath, growing warily in his throat and dying with a warble, so that every note sounded like a hand stretching up out of a pit for something just out of reach, trembling and falling back.

I looked at Bryce.

'Do you hear that?' I said.

'Aha,' said Bryce.

Harvey was out of sight. Then I heard his boots scrabble on the ground and stop ahead. Almost immediately, we saw him again, stone still, rooted to the spot, looking ahead. Grimes had side-stepped him and had turned to look at his face. She followed his gaze up above us.

'Christ,' she said.

'Watch out!' said Richard, as I stumbled into his back.

'Shit, Harvey!' shouted Bryce as he hopped around him. 'What ...' Bryce's mouth clamped shut as he too saw what Harvey was looking at in the dying brown haze. I straightened up, caught my breath and saw it too: an aeroplane, crumpled and twisted and sprawled on its front, its wings stuck up in the air like those of a maimed gull.

The music stopped short. A loud belch sounded deep in the mist.

'Holy fuck,' said Bryce.

'Planes,' said Richard. 'There must have been ...' he turned to Grimes. 'How many do you think were in the sky when it happened?'

'In the UK?' said Grimes. 'Four, five hundred maybe. Maybe fewer. The warning would probably have grounded the domestic flights. All the others would have been international.'

'The big ones,' I said.

We started to walk towards the wreckage. More detail emerged from the mist as we moved. The cockpit was scorched and tarry streaks ran back along its fuselage towards a tattered slit halfway along. Innards of seats and shredded metal spilled out of the hole. We kept our eyes up, aware of but ignoring the disintegrating corpses that we had started to make out around us. Most of them had already been half-claimed by the hungry, dry ground on which they lay prostrate.

'And in the world?' said Richard.

Grimes shook her head. We looked up at the mess of metal. 'Thousands.'

We stopped. Next to the opening, sat on a box, was a man. He was peering back through the mist at us, trying to make us out, frowning, mouth open and top lip curled in a faint snarl. His beard was thick and brown and high on his cheeks. He wore a stained, red baseball cap and a silver cross dangled from his left ear. He held a battered guitar in his hands, his left hand still gnarled into chord around its fretboard, right fingers stroking the string they had just been about to play. In front of him was a small, steaming pot sitting on a pile of ash.

'*London's shored, the coast is clawed, Birmingham's a hole in the ground*,' he sang. His accent was southern English, but with a drawl that made me think he'd been somewhere else. The vowels rolled like smoke in his mouth. He watched us for a moment, index finger still slowly stroking the string beneath it. A loon-like Popeye grin suddenly sprang across his face. Two front teeth hung down like a cartoon rabbit's.

'Hello,' he said. He pointed a finger at the pot and raised his eyebrows. 'Sausage?' We kept our distance from him. When we failed to answer his question, he turned his attention back to playing his guitar, the same song again. The words were those he had just said.

'*London's shored, the coast is clawed, Birmingham's a hole in the ground...*'

Every time he reached the last word, he stopped and retraced the scale back down, then searched the fretboard with his hand as if making some minor adjustment. Then he started again, slower or faster, quieter or louder, higher or louder, different each time.

Eventually Grimes spoke to him.

'Are you alone?' she said.

The man looked up, smiling serenely at her, still crooning until he reached the end of the lyric.

'... *Birmingham's a hole in the ground* ...' He let the smile suddenly fall from his face and threw his guitar into the dirt and picked up a skewer.

'Yeah,' he said. 'Just me. Why don't you sit down?' He coughed and spat. 'Sorry.' He pointed at the pot again, wincing as he swallowed. 'Have a sausage?' He began to stir and scrape at the pot. 'I *think* they're sausages,' he said, peeping over the brim.

Grimes turned to us.

'I'll check the plane,' she said.

'Me too,' said Bryce, dropping his pack. 'Have fun.'

Richard, Harvey and I threw our packs down and sat down while Grimes and Bryce climbed up through the mess of broken plane into the fuselage.

'I found them in there,' said the man. He frowned as he stabbed something with his skewer. 'In those foil containers.' He pulled out the skewer and held it tentatively in front of him, turning it in the light. He peered suspiciously at the bulbous, fatty blob steaming before him.

'Pretty sure they're sausages ...'

He looked at each of us, pointed the thing in our direction. We shook our heads, so he shrugged and took a large bite.

'How long have you been here?' I said.

'Me?' he said, frowning as he turned the gristle in one side of his mouth. He watched the remaining meat quivering on the skewer as if it might try to escape at any moment. 'Just passing through. Arrived this morning, thought I'd see if I could get some breakfast.' He nodded back at the plane. 'I've been through it already, there's nothing there.'

He reached a finger back into his mouth and picked something from his molar. He inspected it for a moment.

'Nothing but these ... sausages,' he said, popping whatever he had found back into his mouth. He swallowed the rest of the meat in one bite and picked up his guitar again.

'*London's shored, the coast is clawed, Birmingham's a hole in the ground ...*'

'Are you singing from experience, mate?' said Harvey.

The man raised his eyebrows and adjusted his cap. 'Yes, as it happens,' he said. 'Pretty much, but d'you know the funny thing?' He sat back and lifted the toes of his boots off the ground, stretching his back. He pointed at his guitar.

'I wrote these words before it all happened,' he said. He beamed proudly back at us. 'They were about something different back then, had a different tune and all. Now it's a whole new song.'

He sat forward again, swallowed and belched. He blew out, looking glumly at the pot.

'I don't think they were sausages,' he said.

'You don't sound like you're from Penrith,' said Richard.

The man took his eyes from the pot and flipped his cap again, shuffling in his seat. He moved with a nervous quickness like a character in a silent film, as if his life was playing too fast and he had to slow himself down to stay on the same timescale as the world around him.

'Nah,' he said. 'Nah, I'm from down south. South coast.'

'How did you get up here?' I said.

'I walked,' he said. He sniffed and wiped his nose with a finger 'Had to after it happened. Everyone did. Everyone who was left. Most people started heading for London though, didn't they? Why? I told them not to, what's the point? What were they going to find there?'

He looked at us, the question clearly not as rhetorical as it sounded. We heard some bangs and clattering noises from the plane as Bryce and Grimes worked their way along the fuselage. The man glanced back, then placed his hands back on the fretboard and looked down at it sadly.

'Stupid. Why does everyone always head for London? What are they looking for? What are they going to find? I went the other way.' He pointed a flat palm to his left. 'I went east along the coast ... well, what the coast is now anyway.'

'Where were you going?' I said.

'Cornwall,' he said, picking out a few notes on the strings. 'I had family there. I made it across in a week. It was OK, better than where I'd come from, but it was still a mess. Fires everywhere, holes in the ground, everything different. I couldn't find anyone where I thought they'd be, so I found a safe place and holed up for a bit.'

He stopped and held his fist in front of his mouth, blowing a gust of intestinal gas through it.

'Yeah ... definitely not sausages,' he said.

'That was, what, three, four months ago?' said Richard.

He nodded, still holding his hand to his mouth.

'Why are you up here, then?'

He released another belch and took a breath.

'That's better, yuck, sorry.' He waved his hand in the air in front of him. 'Why am I here? I had to move on again. It got crowded, dangerous. People started coming from all over the place, then there were people with guns in uniforms trying to sort everything out, trying to divide everyone up.'

'Army?' said Harvey.

'Dunno, don't think so. They looked foreign, wore yellow. They started building this big fence.'

'A fence?' said Richard. 'What kind of fence?'

'Don't know, I couldn't work out what was happening. I asked but nobody would tell me. I saw somebody get shot. This girl. She was trying to find out too, but they wouldn't listen so she grabbed one of them and he turned and shot her in the chest.' He slammed his chest with one hand. 'Right through the heart. She just fell like a doll, dead.' He sniffed, spat, shook his head. 'I got my stuff and left, started walking back across the country.'

'To London?' I said.

'Yeah,' he said. 'Big smoke. Huh. That's all there is there now: smoke.'

He looked up at us.

'I'm not kidding either,' he said. 'Literally. Nothing. There. No buildings, no roads, no people. After four days' walking I thought I'd taken a wrong turn, you know? Thought I'd gone too far north. Then I found this hole and I looked inside and there were all these dead people, families all sitting cuddled up together against walls. On one of the walls I saw this metal sign and I realised it was a tube station and I was already halfway across London. Seriously, nothing but smoke and ruin. Then I saw water everywhere and I heard an explosion, so I thought I'd better head off again.'

He looked across at me, then at Harvey and Richard, eyes scanning all over our clothes and packs. Suddenly he stood up and thrust a hand across the pot.

'I'm Jacob, by the way,' he said. We shook his hand and he jumped spasmodically back to his seat and took up his guitar.

'What are you guys doing, then?' he said.

Richard raised his eyebrows and puffed through his nose.

'We're going to Cornwall,' he said.

'Shit,' said Jacob. He gurned and scratched his cheek hard. 'Why?'

'Have you heard about the ships?' said Richard.

'Ships? Yeah, someone I met in Sheffield said something about that. Are they real then? I thought they were made up.'

We told him about the barracks, the helicopters, about Yuill and Henderson, about our families. Grimes and Bryce jumped down from the plane.

'Nothing,' said Grimes.

'Not even booze,' said Bryce.

'Sorry man,' said Jacob. 'This is all that was left.' He pointed down at the pot. 'Help yourself... although I wouldn't...'

Bryce had already speared a lump of bubbling matter and was chewing it down. 'Mmph,' he said, releasing a squirt of grease through his lips that dribbled down through his black beard. Jacob looked up at him, a smirk of disbelief on his open mouth.

'So,' he said at last, fidgeting with his cap. 'If you want to get to Cornwall, keep east, but not too far east. Anything west of the Pennines is dangerous; too unstable. There's nothing there but holes and crags. The water's inland as far as Manchester, which means you have to go through it. There are still buildings there, shelter, water and some food. But there are people as well.' He winced a little. 'So go as quickly as you can. You'll have to leave this road after the Lakes and head inland; approach Manchester from the north, unless you want a swim.'

'What are the roads like after Manchester?' said Grimes.

'Better. You can walk them OK, but you're pretty exposed.'

'Exposed?' I said. 'Exposed to what?'

'What about cars?' said Grimes.

Jacob blew a puff of disbelief.

'There are no cars,' he said. 'None that works.'

Richard looked at his watch.

'We should get going if we want to reach Penrith before sundown,' he said.

'Penrith's OK,' said Jacob. 'I stayed in the train station last night. There's a ticket office that still has a roof there.'

We picked up our packs to leave.

'Where are you headed, Jake?' said Harvey.

'Dunno,' said Jacob. 'Not back to Manchester. They don't like me there. Thought I'd maybe try and find a boat and see what's what.'

'What about your family?' said Harvey. 'Friends? What happened to them?'

Jacob smiled up and nodded, as if Harvey had told him something instead of asking a question. He turned back to his guitar.

'London's shored, the coast is clawed, Birmingham's a hole in the ground ...'

We found our way around the front of the plane and started off again into the mist. I heaved my legs back into action. My body protested like an old man being disturbed in his sleep.

'Keep east,' Jacob shouted behind us. 'And sorry about the sausages!'

On Our Feet

I began to fade after we left Jacob. We had made it only two miles from the plane before I called the others to stop. They stood around me, sipping water and mumbling words of encouragement as I gasped for breath on my knees. I said nothing back, because I knew that all I wanted to say was that I couldn't go on, that I had never felt this bad, that the road ahead would defeat me without even noticing I had trodden on it with my weak and trembling feet, that I had made a mistake, that I was cold and hungry, that I was fantasising about what giving up would feel like, that there would probably be other ships, that I was already dealing with the shame of accepting that my family was gone so that I could return to the relative comfort of not walking. That I did not like running or walking or any kind of exercise. That I despised it. That I would never ever get used to it.

I said nothing. Caught my breath. Carried on.

From then on the stops became more and more frequent until, as we reached Penrith, I was barely walking and stopped every hundred yards.

'We'll go on ahead,' said Richard. Then it was only Bryce who stopped with me, silently, until I found the will to move. I barely remember making it to the ticket office Jacob had suggested, and I must have fallen asleep pretty soon after.

When I woke, I saw Grimes looking intently down at me, cold yet caring, like a nurse over a patient. She knelt beside me.

'Ready?' she said quietly. I hadn't moved yet, but I could feel my muscles hanging on some strange precipice, as if they themselves knew better than me what would happen when they stretched or compressed. I tried a leg. Sure enough, pain arrived somewhere in my ankle and travelled quickly up through my calves, knees, thighs and hips. I winced and felt the drone of my own detached consciousness start up again.

You can't do this.

Your body wants nothing to do with this.

Your mind wants nothing to do with this.

'I can't . . .' I began, closing my eyes. 'I can't . . .'

'Come on,' she said, lifting me by the arm. 'Get up.'

'But . . .'

'Don't talk. Here.' She handed me a mug of black tea. 'Move your legs slowly,' she said. 'Like this.' She lifted her legs up and down, marching gently on the spot without lifting her feet from the ground.

I kept my eyes closed as I drank sips of tea, moving my legs a little and feeling some life and warmth come back to them. I felt as if gravity had doubled overnight. The prospect of using my feet to move both myself and my pack even a single step was horrific.

I opened my eyes and saw Harvey walk over the debris of the ticket office. He looked me in the eyes.

'Horrible feeling after the first day, isn't it?' he said. He took a sip from an almost-empty water bottle. I looked back at him with barely open eyes.

I cannot . . .

'Worse than a hangover, I'd say,' he said. 'Worse than the worst hangover.'

I cannot do . . .

'You know what the worst thing is about hangovers?' he said. He tapped his head. 'This. All this shit up here. Sore head, sore stomach, pah . . .' He waved a hand. 'Nothing. It's all this nonsense going around your noggin. All the doom and the gloom and the guilt and woe. All the stuff that doesn't really exist. That's what brings you down.'

Harvey made me run up front with him that second day. We began again with an hour of walking, then transitioned to running. Bryce, Richard and Grimes kept their distance behind us. Perhaps it was only because I felt so bad, but they seemed to have been unaffected by the day before, moving with apparent ease as I wheezed and plodded next to Harvey. I knew now that I was their weakest link and I wondered how long it would be before they decided my fate for me, before I became the only thing holding them back from reaching Cornwall in time.

Harvey tried to keep me talking. Whenever I let a conversation run dry, he started up another, asking me about Beth, or the kids, or my life before. I felt him looking at me as we neared the top of a hill. I had been staring at the ground and daydreaming about the things I wanted to say to Beth, editing arguments, deleting things I had said to her.

'I know what it's like to miss someone, mate,' he said. 'Burns you up inside, makes you think bad things, feel bad things – guilt, fear, despair – like you could have done more or shouldn't have done anything.'

I kept staring at the road ahead.

'I spoke to your Beth a few times,' he said. 'She loves you, Ed. And she's a strong woman. She'll protect those little babies of yours, mark my words she will.'

I felt his hand brush my back.

'You're not to blame for this, you know that, don't you?'

'Yes,' I said.

'Huh?'

'Yes, I just ...'

'Hey?'

'I just wish I'd ...'

'S'that, mate?'

Harvey had a tick. Whenever he asked me a question, he would cut off my answer after one or two words with a sharp 'Hey?' or 'Huh?' or 'What's that?' Occasionally, in the weirder moments when I felt myself falling into a trance, I heard these loud, questioning barks of his over and over again without, it seemed, any question to precede them. They replayed in my mind, sometimes backwards, sometimes delayed and repeated very quickly like a dance-music sample. Then they would silence and I would be running normally with Harvey quiet by my side. At other times, I wiled away minutes of brain activity imagining the same conversation with him: me telling him exactly how wrong it was for him to ask someone to repeat themselves when they had barely started talking, that you could work out missing words in sentences by the context provided by the others. He was unfair to demand perfect diction from somebody who was under such physical pressure. Unfair and unkind. This was something he should be aware of and change in himself to make others around him more comfortable.

I sometimes lost myself in the detail of this fantasy argument.

It didn't even occur to me that he himself might be finding it as hard to run as I was, that this annoying affliction might simply be because he was a tired old man moving a long distance over a destroyed country. Such was my preoccupation with my own condition.

'I need to stop,' I said.

Harvey ignored me.

'Keep talking,' he said, winking. 'And keep running. Keeps the mind away from the dark places. I used to sing to myself on my run. This was before Walkmans and iPods and the like, you know. I used to sing anything; made-up songs, made-up words, just sounds really. Sometimes I'd listen to the noise my feet made on the road and the noise my breathing made on top of it and I'd make a word out of it, sing it all day. Becomes a bit like a mantra, very soothing, hypnotic. Listen, I'll try and get one for you. *Shhheee . . . shee . . . wah . . . buh . . .*'

'Harvey, I need to stop.'

He put his head down and started making noises.

'*Shee . . . wa . . . buh . . . heh . . . duppa . . . shef . . .* yeah, that's it. Here's one: *Sheewabuh Hehduppa Shef . . . Sheewabuh Hehduppa Shef . . . Sheewabuh Hehduppa Shef . . .*'

He said the words in triplets, like a train on a track

'Come on,' he said 'Try it with me.'

'*Sheewabuh . . . Heh . . . Hehbuff . . .*'

'*Sheewabuh Hehduppa Shef . . . Sheewabuh Hehduppa Shef*,' he corrected.

'*Sheewabuh . . . Hehduppa Shef . . . Sheewabuh Hehduppa Shef.*'

'That's it!' he laughed. 'Good one, that'll keep you going all day, that will. *Sheewabuh Hehduppa Shef . . . Sheewabuh Hehduppa Shef.*'

'Who had her head up a chef?' shouted Bryce from behind. 'Filthy old bastard.'

'*Sheewabuh hehduppa shef* ... *sheewabuh hehduppa shef*.'

I shook my head. 'Where do you find the energy?' I said.

'*Sheewabuh hehduppa shef* ... energy?' said Harvey. '*Sheewabuh hehduppa shef* ... energy, well, I dunno, we're made of energy, Ed. Everything is. You're just kind of ... energy ... *sheewabuh hehduppa shef* ... moving through other energy ... *sheewabuh hehduppa shef* ... aren't you?'

'But, I mean real energy, energy to run, to walk, to exercise. Calories in your blood, glucose, that kind of thing.'

'Oh, well, that's important you know, of course. If you don't eat you die, that sort of thing, yeah, but ... well, when you're talking about going a long way like I did, let's just say once you get past a certain point it doesn't matter so much what's in here.' He patted his belly. 'More about what's up here,' he said, touching his head. He let his hand fall down the side of his head as if he'd touched something he didn't want to abandon so quickly. 'Clear your mind and things start working out for you,' he said.

'You can't run five hundred miles just by clearing your mind,' I spat.

Harvey shrugged. 'You can't do it without it either.'

I plodded on for a short time.

'Harvey, did you really run across Australia?'

'Ah,' he said with a grin. 'You been talking to Hagrid back there, have you?' He nodded back to Bryce.

'I don't think he believes you,' I said. 'And, to be honest, it's a pretty tall story.'

'I know,' he said. 'I know. But don't get into the habit of letting people tell you what to believe son. That'll get you into all sorts of strife. Hey, Ed?'

'What?'

'Still want to stop?' he said. 'Only it's been half an hour since you told me you did. Can you believe that?'

We stayed on our feet.

I stayed on my feet.

Every day, we woke and left and walked. Then we ran for a while, and then we walked, and then we ran again. I ran beside Harvey each day and barely registered the others or how they were coping. He kept me talking, although most of the noises I made were just grunts or a 'yes' or 'no'. Running became the most familiar and unfamiliar of movements for me. Physical pain and mental torment swirled around me as I dragged leg after leg, willed every step into being. Everything I did met with resistance. This wasn't just gravity and the tightness of my muscles, but something that seemed very real; an aggressive entity that had lain hidden and dormant for decades of physical inactivity, but which had now shaken itself up, like a ray shakes itself from the seabed, and risen above and around me, repulsed, indignant and furious at this sudden decision of its host to move.

The body wants nothing to do with this.

The mind wants nothing to do with this.

The resistance wants nothing to do with this.

And yet . . . you're running. Who are you?

Every twitch of my torn and quivering muscles seemed to meet an opposite force much stronger than its own.

And yet, still, I stayed on my feet.

This didn't occur to me at the time. I didn't feel like I was winning and couldn't imagine a time when I might overcome these physical and mental obstacles standing in my way. Every second was a breath away from screaming out *stop* and falling to the ground. At times it felt like I was so close to doing so that I actually felt my legs slowing down, my head bowing and my hands falling to my knees, actually felt the sickening combination of shame and relief as I gave up. But then I would realise that I had not slowed down, that my head was still facing up, that my arms were still swinging weakly by my sides, and I would be back to feeling torment, mixed, for the briefest of moments, with a kind of proud surprise.

At these times, I felt as if I had just split away from a version of my life that had taken another direction, another universe where I'd actually given up and would have to face a different future. In this one, the walk, the moving landscape, the noise of my breathing and of Harvey's footsteps, the pain and the hunger and the tiredness carried on, relentlessly.

I had no control over anything any more.

Harvey told me that the resistance I faced wasn't something I could ever beat. The best I could hope for was to learn how to fight it daily, to parry and lunge and keep it at bay by learning about how it worked. Some days it would win, others it would lose. He told me he learned this for himself while running through the Nullabor Plain. He had spent countless days beneath the sun, watching his shadow move around him as the sun arced across the sky, losing his mind with the heat and the unchanging landscape and fighting his own resistance. He realised that this resistance was like a shadow, and that the darker the shadow was, the brighter the light that shone. It was a part of me and it would always be with me. When it was at its strongest, when things seemed to be at their worst, that's when the brightest hope could be found.

I should learn not just how to fight it, he told me, but, like every enemy, how to love it.

The Struggle

We made our way along the shredded remains of the M6 motorway for five days. We slept in blown-out cars and gutted service stations and beneath smashed flyovers. Every morning I woke from the same dream. Every morning I woke thinking that I had heard a howl. Every morning we drank hot black tea and ate noodles, packed up and left. We found cars that still had water and filled our hydration bladders with it. Some even had fuel in their tanks and working batteries, but we knew enough not to waste our time taking them. We found some mountain bikes in a van and rode them for a while, but negotiating the mud and deep gouges in the road proved impossible. We stayed on our feet.

I stayed on my feet.

I got blisters. Sharp, stinging pain blossomed around my heels and toes, distracting me from the aches in my bones and muscles. I inspected my feet in the evenings, marking the progress of each bulging sack and wondering when they would burst.

My lips cracked, my head thumped, my back tightened. Everything screamed at me to stop.

But every day we woke and left and ran.

Somehow we managed to make close to one hundred miles in five days. We met nobody and the landscape changed little – hills and moors swathed in thick mist and potholed with craters that had long lost their spectacle. We saw two more plane crashes: one far away into the crags of a cliff, another just next to the road. We found water in the second. The food was ruined, but Bryce filled every space he could with miniature bottles of spirits he found and spent the rest of the day grinning like a maniac.

Each day was harder than the last. On the fifth night we found shelter in the carriage of a train that had buckled from the track and was now being slowly reclaimed by a hedgerow. Thankfully it was largely empty, apart from a few bodies, which we removed. I took a seat, fell asleep and woke up sometime later, thirsty and frozen. It was still dark. I could see the shapes of the others sleeping in their seats. Shadows flickered and I heard a noise from the front. Richard was sitting at a table seat with a plastic tumbler and a bottle in front of him. He was staring into a short candle flame. I got up and walked over. Bryce snorted and heaved himself onto his side as I passed.

Richard silently offered his hand to the seat opposite. I sat down and inspected the bottle. It was sticky and old.

'Bacardi?' I said.

'All I could find in the buffet carriage. It was either that or Chardonnay.' He wrinkled his face. 'Here.'

He pulled out another tumbler and filled it. Richard raised his and we both drank. I took a slug and felt warmer. We both watched the flame for a while.

'I used to be a salvage diver,' he said after some time. 'Before I was married. I used to travel quite a bit – Indonesia, Singapore, Australia, South Africa – anywhere there was work. Shallow-water stuff mainly, not always that interesting. Sometimes I just had to help remove the working parts from boats that were slowly sinking, other times it was valuable cargo from something that had already sunk.'

I replenished our glasses. He flicked the plastic rim of his with his thumbnail.

'I used to enjoy it,' he said. 'Not just the diving itself but the feeling of being somewhere … somewhere that I shouldn't really … be. You know? Somewhere that should be somewhere else.'

He glanced up at me.

'You get a strange sense of perspective when you see an alarm clock under water.'

He looked back at his glass and shrugged.

'Like I say, most of it wasn't very interesting, but occasionally you'd get something special.'

He drained his glass and slid it towards me.

'Once I was asked to dive a plane wreck in the Philippines. A Second World War Japanese fighter that some magazine had been given permission to photograph. It had taken a nose dive.' He traced the arc of a crashing plane with his hand, whistling. 'Sploosh … landed about thirty metres down, nose buried in a sand trench. One of the wings was torn off and there was a hole in the fuselage. I was just there as a guide and to provide safety instruction, nothing else.'

He looked up.

'You're really not supposed to do anything else with these kind of wrecks,' he said.

'Sea graves?' I said.

He nodded. 'Quite right. Outside only. But sometimes … well, the photographer was taking too long and there was nobody else with us. I got bored.'

Richard took the bottle and filled our glasses again. I was no longer cold. The sweet rum had even helped with my thirst.

'So you went inside?' I said.

'Yes. I swam in, took a look around.'

'What did you find?'

'Not much in the back. Some bottles, boxes and ammunition; nothing interesting, so I went up front. To the cockpit.'

He paused and took a sip.

'I swam up beside him, my head right next to his. He was sitting back in his seat, still in his uniform, still buckled in. His head was forward, chin on his chest. His hands were on his knees, both palms up. Like he was meditating.'

Richard turned to the window and looked out into the darkness, still thumbing his glass. The light made sharp shadows of his hawk-like features and dark pools in his eyes.

'I felt strange,' he said, and paused, frowning. '*Vertiginous.*' He seemed to roll the word around in his mouth as if tasting it for the first time. 'I think that's the word. Like a climber suddenly finding himself on ledge, staring down into a deep canyon. I was looking at sixty years of stillness, a violent scene from before my birth that had persisted out of sight throughout my entire life and would no doubt continue to do so after my death.'

'Maybe not any more,' I said. He ignored this.

'He had a locket around his neck that I didn't want to open, but in his shirt pocket was a pair of sunglasses. I took them. I don't know why, I wish I hadn't; I knew I'd never wear them. A souvenir of the moment, I suppose, like those photographs everyone takes but never looks at afterwards.'

He smiled, sat forward and leaned on the table, staring into his glass.

'You see,' he said, 'I used to like diving because it was a way to escape the small stuff for a little while – girls, money, life ... none of that existed under water. But when I met my friend there in that plane ... that was something else, something permanent. Suddenly nothing mattered at all. I saw my future, everyone's future ...'

He reached up to the cracked window next to him. A thick weed was creeping through a hole in the corner. He rubbed it between his finger and thumb, releasing a spray of dry vegetation onto the table.

'Entropy,' he said. 'Entropy and decay. Everything turns to dust. Everything is constantly trying to return to the dust from which it came.'

He frowned and picked up his tumbler. His face twisted into an attempt at a smile.

'So why all the struggle?' he said.

He drained his drink, sat back and ran a hand through his hair. Light was beginning to show through the window pane.

'Morning soon,' he said. 'Expect we should sleep.'

He licked his fingers and pressed them around the candle flame. Then he took his blanket over to a seat and lay down, immediately still. I sat watching the blue trails of smoke weave up into the dusty light. I realised that my left hand was numb from clutching the tin can of Alice's stringyphone beneath my jacket. I pulled it closer, thinking about the creaking of timber and the slow crumble of concrete in deep saltwater, until I too was asleep.

Bartonmouth Hall

The next day was darker. The clouds were getting heavier. We only made it fifteen miles before the light was too low to see by. That night we slept beneath a bridge and woke up before dawn in a river of rain. Our kit was soaked and we stumbled around each other as we packed. We left without eating and ran out into a storm that continued all day, washing the snow into sludge and drenching our boots. Sometime in the afternoon I called for a stop, fell down and found I couldn't get up again. I had gone into cramp. I spent an hour trying to pull myself up while the others waited. Harvey and Grimes took turns pushing and pulling on my legs, trying to stretch them out of their spasm. I stared up at them, their faces hidden in black hoods haloed with rain, dimly aware that their attempts were being foiled not just by my knotted muscles but by my own pleasure in lying down. Eventually I managed to sit up and Richard helped me to my feet.

'Let's call it a day,' he said, above the din of the rain. 'Ed, do you think you can walk far enough for us to find shelter?'

'I think so,' I said. 'I'm sorry.'

'Don't worry. We've only a couple of hours of daylight left anyway.' He shook the water from his face. 'Now let's get out of this *fucking* rain.'

Bryce was by the side of the road, looking down into a valley.

'Think I've found just the place,' he said, pointing down to a large clearing surrounded by trees. 'There, how does that look?'

In the middle of the clearing was a large stately home. It didn't appear to be badly damaged; the red brick walls were upright, the roof was still intact and I could even make out the busts of lions still sitting on the pillars at the top of the stone steps that, I imagined, had once led down into the gardens.

'That'll do nicely,' said Richard. 'Let's go.'

The slope down from the road was steep and boggy. After a few steps, Bryce slipped and fell on his back. Richard reached to help him up and slipped too. Before we knew it, we were all on our backs, beginning a long descent through slick mud. I struggled for a few seconds and then stopped, looked up into the rain and let gravity take me where it wanted.

Where gravity wanted to take me was a bare and stubby bush that lined a deep ditch. I sat up and began removing the thorns from my trousers, heard a scrambling, grunting noise behind me and turned in time to see Bryce crashing into my back. The impact sent us both bouldering through the bush and we landed in a heap on the other side, my face in the mud under the full weight of Bryce's torso.

'*Gmmt mmmmfff!*' I said. I felt Bryce floundering above me, then the weight lifted and he pulled me to my feet. I cleared the clods from my eyes and wiped my face, feeling fresh cuts where the thorns had torn at my cheeks. Bryce stood before me like a mountain of dirt, laughing. His teeth flashed beneath the mud.

The other three arrived in a similar way. I helped Grimes through the bush and Bryce and Richard pulled Harvey from the ditch. Then we cleaned ourselves up and looked around.

We had arrived in the gardens of the house. We were standing on a long slope of brown scrub dotted with patches of moss and grey grass. There was a gravel clearing in the centre where a cracked and stained fountain stood overflowing. Four stone lion heads surrounded it, spewing brown rain onto the ground. Beyond this was more earth leading up to a wide flight of steps that ran up to the house itself, which was long and bleak. The main door was closed. Tall windows lined the two storeys surrounding it, most of them smashed. The flat roof was decorated with blackened turrets.

I imagined what we might have seen before: rich, cropped turf and colourful beds surrounded by clipped green hedgerows; a grand fountain trickling clear water, white steps and shining red walls.

'Do you think it's empty?' said Harvey.

'Only one way to find out,' said Bryce. He took a step forward. There was a crack in the distance and a clod of mud exploded by his feet.

'Christ!' shouted Bryce, dancing away from the spray of dirt. 'What the fuck was that?'

'There,' said Grimes, pointing up at the house. 'Third window from the left, top floor.'

I looked up. There was some movement behind the dirty glass.

'Is that a gun?' said Richard.

Bryce held up his hands. 'Hey!' he shouted. 'Don't shoot! We're not . . .'

A barrel appeared through a hole in the window. Another crack and another thump in the ground by Bryce's feet, this time closer.

'Jesus Christ!' yelled Bryce. 'Run!'

We ran. The hedge behind us provided no cover, so we made for the fountain. More shots rang out as we stumbled towards it, showering us with mounds of mud – like blasts from a mine field. We fell with our backs to the stone, still cowering from the shots. One hit a lion's head and it exploded into dust. Then it was quiet, apart from the sound of the rain and our own frantic breathing.

'Has it stopped?' said Harvey. 'Have they stopped shooting us?'

I craned my neck and peered back over the lip of the fountain. A figure was standing at the window, peering around.

'I think so,' I said. 'For now at least.'

Richard carefully turned around into a crouch and raised his hands.

'Hello?' he said. I saw the figure behind the window duck and raise his gun again.

'No!' shouted Richard. 'Please don't. Please stop shooting at us. We're not dangerous.'

The figure paused and straightened a little, then seemed to reconsider and take aim again. Richard ducked, but there was no shot. When we turned again, the figure had disappeared.

'Bastards,' said Bryce. He stood up slowly. 'Where are they?'

Harvey reached up and gripped the hem of Bryce's coat. 'Careful!' he said. 'Maybe they're reloading.'

'Ach, I've had enough,' said Bryce, shaking Harvey off and raising his arms. 'Hoy!' he shouted. 'Youse in there! Come out and say hello!'

'Bryce!' I hissed. Bryce grunted and kicked the gravel at his feet.

Nothing happened. Bryce stood impatiently with rain dripping from his face and the rest of us hid behind the fountain, expecting him to be shot at any moment. Suddenly Bryce twitched and sprang back a little. I heard a long creaking noise from the house followed by a dull thud. Bryce seemed to relax and raised himself to his full height. I looked back and saw that the door to the house had opened. On the steps stood a tall, thin man in tweeds, wellingtons and a green wax jacket. Wisps of grey hair fell from beneath a cap and what appeared to be a black patch covered his left eye. His other eye glared down at us along the barrel of his shotgun.

The rest of us stood up slowly and raised our hands.

'We don't want any trouble,' said Richard.

'Quiet,' said the man. 'Stay there.' His words wobbled with age and he cleared his throat. 'Stay where I can see you now.' He trod sideways down the steps, still keeping the gun trained on us, then walked across to a few metres away from us.

'What do you want?' he said. His voice was dry and rich like sediment in a glass.

Grimes took a step forward and pulled back her hood. Rain began streaming down her face, drawing pale rivulets through the dirt on her skin.

'Just shelter,' she said, blowing water from her lips. 'We're very wet.'

The man's eye flickered a little. He seemed to be scanning us, looking up and down at our torn, muddy clothes and soaking packs.

'Not armed?' said the man. 'Up to no good?'

'No,' said Grimes. We each shook our heads.

The man tipped the gun in Bryce's direction.

'And what about this one?' he said. 'You going to be trouble, young man?'

Bryce pulled some more mud from his face and wiped it on his coat.

'Good as gold,' he said.

The old man's eye narrowed. 'Your word,' he growled.

Bryce flicked three fingers from his forehead. 'Scout's honour,' he said.

The man paused and made a little noise in his throat. He lowered the gun to his side.

'Well, then,' he said. He gave a brisk nod. 'Name's Bartonmouth. Welcome to Bartonmouth Hall.'

The End of the World Running Club

'Trying to keep fires to a minimum these days,' said Bartonmouth. He was at the far end of a kitchen, wrestling with the door handle of a large black stove that took up most of one wall. 'Firewood ran out couple of months back. All bloody wet outside. Furniture's running low. Not much left to burn ... since we have guests though ... *come* on, you bloody ...'

With a scratch and a clang the door opened and he fell back against the long oak table behind him. 'Got you! There. Right now.' He brushed his palms together and stood with his hands on his hips, looking down at the open door. 'Wood,' he said. 'Wood wood wood wood wood ...'

He turned to a door on his left and disappeared through it.

We were standing at the opposite end of the kitchen, dripping and shivering on the worn, red tiles. The rain swept by in dizzy squalls outside, hammering against the windows and making them rattle in their tall frames. It felt good to be out of it, although it somehow felt colder inside. The kitchen was like every other room and corridor Bartonmouth had led us through: long floor, high ceiling and virtually bare of decoration. There were light, square patches on the walls where pictures had once been. Beneath each one were the pictures themselves; deep, dark-lined portraits and landscapes now lying frameless and curling on the cold floor.

There was a crash in the distance and the sound of stamping. A moment later Bartonmouth returned carrying a blue, canvas-covered book and a pile of splintered wood. Odd shreds of patterned fabric hung from it like seaweed. He tossed most of the timber into the stove and put the rest of it in a pile. He took the book and tore pages from it, throwing them in as well. Then he patted in his pockets, muttering, until he found what he was looking for. There was a chink and a glint and a small *whumf* of flame. He knelt down, lit the stove and closed the door, standing back.

'There,' he said, clicking his lighter shut and turning to face us. 'Usually heats up pretty quickly. Should be some hot water soon as well. Expect you'll want baths? Installed some grey-water collectors before … you know … the *thing*, so all our water comes in from the rain. Good for the environment and all that. Bloody good thing for us now too. Not supposed to drink it mind, but not much choice any more. Don't mind a bit of rainwater, do you? Good, good.'

He stood, hands behind his back, wobbling back and forwards on his tiptoes. Eventually he looked up from the floor and jumped.

'Well, sit down,' he said. 'Sit down.' He pulled out a few chairs near to the stove. 'Put your jackets over here if you don't mind. Boots, too; they'll soon warm up.' We hung our filthy coats on a rack by the stove and dropped our boots beneath them, then took our seats in silence. I was still dripping on the floor. The glass panel in the stove began to glow orange and a low roar travelled up the flue that led away through the ceiling. I felt warmth creeping up my legs and smelled wood smoke on the cold, musty air. Bartonmouth took the chair at the top, laying his hands on the worn oak of the table. He was old, maybe in his eighties, his skin lined with deep folds and blue veins. His mouth hung open in a quivering, pink arc as his one good eye darted about our faces. His brow flickered with question.

'So,' he said. 'Who's going to start?'

Richard told him about the barracks and the boats and then each of us told our own account of what had happened to us before. He listened intently, his face twitching with emotion, saying nothing but 'Heavens', 'Good gracious', 'Well I never' or 'Dear, oh, dear' at the right moments. When we had finished, he turned and replenished the stove with more wood, still shaking his head and chuckling quietly at something Bryce had said.

'Did you know about the boats?' said Grimes.

'Boats?' said Bartonmouth, taking his seat. 'Yes, yes, heard all about the boats.' He waved a hand in dismissal. 'Not much point for someone like me. Besides, couldn't leave the old place. Not after everything.' He sat back and crossed his arms, looking around the walls. 'Family's been here from the beginning. Hundreds of years. Not many left like it . . . not many at all now, I expect. Opened up to the public a few years back of course, had to; the old girl wasn't too keen but I made her see sense. No money you see, all bloody gone . . .'

'Old girl?' said Harvey. 'Is that your missus?'

'Yes,' said Bartonmouth, smiling. 'The *missus*, yes. Gone now, of course, sad to say. Couple of years ago.' He tapped a long thumb on the wood. 'Just me left now.'

'I'm sorry to hear that, mate,' said Harvey. 'Know just how you feel.'

'Just you?' said Richard. 'All on your own in this house?'

'I know,' said Bartonmouth. 'Bloody silly. Ridiculous. Far too big. But got no choice, you see? Too much history. Too much . . .' He flapped a hand over his shoulder. 'Too much behind.'

'What about staff?' said Richard. 'Didn't you have cooks? Servants?'

'Pah!' said Bartonmouth. He laughed and waved a hand at Richard. 'Very good, very good. Couldn't afford all that. Used to have a cook but he left. Gardener, too; no idea where he's gone.' He rubbed his chin and looked uncertainly out the window, craning his skinny neck to see through the sheets of rain. 'Keep meaning to go out and see if I can tidy up those beds, get the lawn ship-shape and what not. Maybe try in the spring. Anyway, staff. Rest of them weren't real. Actors. Put on by the company running the tours, you see. Maids, butlers, all that. All for the public. Lived somewhere else. Never saw 'em again after, you know, the *thing*. All gone. Vanished. Poof. Would you like a drink?'

'Yes,' said Bryce. 'Yes, please.'

'Good man.' Bartonmouth smiled and pushed himself up from the table. 'Back in a jiffy.'

He left through the same door he had gone through to get the wood. We heard his footsteps disappear down a creaking corridor. Bryce cocked his thumb back at the door.

'Does he even know what's happened?' he said.

'You mean the "*thing*"?' I said. 'He has to. There's no way he can't know.'

'Maybe he doesn't know the full extent,' said Grimes. 'If he's been on his own here, without a telephone, Internet. He's an old man.'

'He's a nice sort,' said Harvey. 'I like him. We don't want to upset him.'

'All the same,' said Richard. 'He might have family elsewhere. We should make sure he knows.'

We heard Bartonmouth's slow footsteps out in the corridor and the sound of glasses rattling. When he returned he was carrying a silver tray of tumblers and a brown, thick-glassed bottle with a fraying label. His arms were shaking and he was frowning in concentration. Bryce jumped up.

'Let me help you there, buddy,' he said, carefully guiding the tray down onto the table and inspecting the label on the bottle sideways as he did so.

'Wizzo, much obliged,' said Bartonmouth. He sat down and lifted the bottle to his eye, peering at the scrawled writing on the side. 'Never was much one for Scotch. More of a brandy man myself. But thought, present company and all that.' He looked between Bryce, Richard and Grimes. Then he tilted the bottle at Harvey and me. 'You, er ... mind, gentlemen?'

I shook my head.

'Brandy, whisky; anything's good,' said Harvey.

'Excellent,' said Bartonmouth. 'Then I'll be mother.' He poured good measures and handed them round. 'Good health,' he said, raising his glass. We raised our own back and drank. I took a particularly large mouthful. It was glorious, nothing short of it. The way I was feeling – bone soaked and frozen – a capful of cheap supermarket rum would have done the job, but this was something special. I could taste it immediately, as if a door I'd never seen had been flung open onto a long, wide landscape of forest, earth and ocean, tall stone pillars clawed with brine and weed, cold starry skies, ancient, candlelit rooms, deep eyes, short lives and whispered promises. I felt as if somebody had filled my head with a thousand years of secret, guarded memories.

'Well,' said Bartonmouth. 'Well, this is actually rather good.'

'What *is* this?' I said.

'Let's see now.' Bartonmouth peered at the label again. 'Mor … Mort … Mortlach, think it says. Nineteen … can you read that old man?' He passed the bottle to Richard. Richard blinked. His mouth fell slowly open.

'Nineteen thirty-eight,' he said. 'That's over seventy-five years old.'

'Hmm, almost as old as me,' said Bartonmouth. He took another drink. 'Well, what do you know? Looks like I'm a whisky man after all!'

We continued to drink in silence. Bryce in particular seemed genuinely moved. At last, Grimes leaned forward on the table.

'Lord Bartonmouth,' she said.

'Rupert, please.'

'Rupert,' she said. 'You … you do know what happened, don't you?'

The old man gave a frustrated wince, as old men do at questions with no clear beginnings or endings. 'What's that?' he said.

'I mean, you know what happened back in summer? To the country? To the planet?'

Bartonmouth looked back at Grimes for a moment. A small frown of understanding crept up on his brow and he sat back in his chair.

'Bartonmouth Hall was built in a valley,' he said. 'First Lord Bartonmouth, my great-great … whatever he was … had it built for his wife. She liked rivers, you see, so he built it next to one, deep in the valley. Hills to the south, hills to the north. Protected, see? Not much reached us here. I heard it all, of course; saw things, knew there were fires. But Bartonmouth . . .' He stamped his boot on the stone floor. 'Solid. Firm. Protected.'

He picked up the bottle and raised an eyebrow at me. I offered my glass and he filled it, then did the same for the others.

'Knew something was up when the radio stopped working. Electricity next and no telephone – not that I used it much before anyway. Then all those clouds and storms after all that glorious weather we'd been having. I stayed inside just in case, didn't go out. Locked the door. Nothing for weeks, no one around. I thought I might take a drive. There's a village about fifteen miles west, thought I might try there, see what's what. But then . . . then I had some visitors.'

He swallowed his drink and put down his glass, crossed his arms.

'Who were they?' said Harvey.

Rupert turned down the corners of his mouth. 'Nasty sorts,' he said. 'Ruffians, youngsters, men mostly but a few women too. Certainly not ladies, that's for damn certain. Came down the front drive as I was getting ready to leave, about twenty of them, striding up large as life without so much as a how-do-you-do. Most rude. One came up to me, foul man he was, grotty and rude, said they were going to stay. In my house. In Bartonmouth.'

'What did you do?' I said

'Told them to clear off, didn't I? "Go on," I said, "get away with you, the lot of you." Then this one just started laughing at me, calling me names, and then the others started laughing. Didn't like that much, I can tell you. "Now look here young man," I said, "if you don't bloody get off my property I'll set the dogs on you." Course, hadn't seen the hounds for a while, no idea where they went, but I wasn't going to tell *him* that. Hooligan just laughed harder, called me more names. "I'll call the police!" I said.'

The old man frowned a little and shuffled in his chair.

'Got a bit rough after that, 'fraid to say. Not much I could do. Tried my best, got a few in, couple of left hooks and that but, well, too many of them. Far too many. Knocked me around a bit, gave me this.' He tapped his eye-patch. 'Then they dragged me inside, started making themselves at home. Terrible mess they made, terrible. Started going through all the cupboards and drawers, drinking all my booze, raking through the food, breaking things, using the bedrooms for God knows what.'

'How long did they stay for?' said Grimes.

'Best part of a week. Most unpleasant time. They made me do things ...' He looked up at us and leaned forward suddenly. 'Not like that, you understand; a man has his limits.' Then he settled back. 'Just, you know, serving them, making them food, cleaning up their filth, doing their bidding. I played along, thinking if I could just hold out they'd eventually get bored and leave me in peace.'

'And did they?' said Grimes.

Rupert sighed.

'One day they're all lying around in the drawing room, drinking some of my Pétrus, and then one of them picks up this vase and holds it out at me. "Dance," he says. "What?" I say. "Dance," he says. "Or I'll drop this vase." I say, "That's my mother you're holding. Put her down this instant." Bastard just starts leering at me. "Dance or I drop her," he says. "Dance. Dance." Then the rest of them start saying it too, chanting it, clapping their hands, "Dance dance dance," those horrid women too, all cackling and sneering like some bloody football crowd or something.'

'Hooligans,' said Harvey softly. 'What did you do, mate?'

'Stood my ground, that's what I did. Had enough, hadn't I? Fixed him in the eye and said, "Put my mother down right now or you'll regret it." Said it in my strongest voice, as loud as I could. That shut 'em up. They all stop chanting and the room goes quiet. Then the bugger drops it. Drops my mother. Right on the floor in front of me. She went everywhere, of course; all over the floorboards, all over the rug.'

'Christ,' said Harvey. 'I'd have swung for him.'

'Almost did myself, Harvey, almost did myself. Stopped myself though, knew that wasn't the best thing to do in the situation. Only get myself hurt.'

'So what did you do?' said Richard.

'Well, the room's dead quiet, all the rest of his little group can't believe what's just happened. A girl in the corner, horror of a woman, she starts tittering. Then this chap looks down at the floor at the mess he's made and takes a step forward so he's standing in it, standing in *my mother*. He stamps up and down a few times, Mother puffing up the sides of his dirty great boots, and says, "You'd better clean this mess up, hadn't you old man?" Then he waves his hand at me and says, "Off you pop, get a dustpan" or something equally vulgar.'

Rupert leaned forward and poured the rest of the bottle into our glasses.

'You didn't,' said Harvey. 'They didn't make you clean up your own mum's ashes in front of them, did they?'

Rupert stood up and opened the stove. A wave of fierce heat blew into the room as he threw the rest of the wood on the fire.

'I turned on my heels and left the drawing room. They all burst out laughing. I could hear them still hooting and caterwauling as I walked down the corridor, past the main hall, past the paintings of my mother and father hanging by the dining room, even as I crossed the kitchen and got out back. First day they arrived a few of them had found the hunting room, taken all the guns and shells for themselves. Expect they thought they'd need them for wherever they decided to go next. Thing is, they didn't know about *Daddy's* gun. That's the one I use.'

'The one you shot at us with,' said Bryce.

'Yes. Yes, sorry about that,' said Rupert. Bryce waved away the apology.

'Anyway,' Rupert went on. 'I'd left Daddy's gun down by the river in the boathouse, last time I'd been out shooting. Those buggers never went down there, just stayed inside all the bloody time. So down I went to get it, picked up a couple of shells and pumped them in on the way back. They were still laughing when I got back to the drawing room. Stopped dead when they saw me though. Silence. Nothing. Not a peep. I raised the gun and pointed it straight at the brute who's still standing in my mother. He looked back at me, not so happy any more. Think he went to say something but I couldn't hear what it was. Pulled the trigger. Boom. Just like that.'

'Christ almighty!' said Harvey, eyes wide. 'Did you kill him?'

'Not much hope with a shotgun at that range, I'm afraid. Flew back against the wall and dropped like a stone. Sprayed a bit of lead into a few of the scoundrels behind him as well.'

'What did they do?' said Richard.

'Panicked. Absolute pandemonium. They all start rushing around. One of the women runs over to the body and starts shouting at me saying, "You killed him, you old bastard," and I say, "I'll kill you too if you don't clear out now, the lot of you, get out!" 'Course I was worried they might fight back, get their own guns and shoot me. Not much I could have done in that situation with only one shell left, but they didn't. Suppose they were too shocked. Besides, they'd probably never fired a gun before in their lives.'

'Did they leave?' said Grimes.

'Damn bloody right they left,' said Rupert. 'Cleared off sharpish. Watched them running up the drive, most of them still crying or screaming or pulling on their clothes. Never saw them again. After that I was a bit more careful, kept a closer eye on things. But I've not left and nobody's been back.' He looked up at us. 'Not till you chaps, of course.'

'How did you know?' said Bryce. 'How did you know that we weren't dangerous too?'

Rupert fixed him with his one bright eye. 'Gave me your word, didn't you?' he said.

'Aye, but . . .'

'Moment you can't take somebody on their word, might as well give up. Not worth it any more. Civilisation's *dead*.' He banged a fist on the table and grunted to himself in satisfaction. 'Besides, I know trouble when I see it. And you're not trouble.'

He turned to Grimes.

'I know what happened, my dear. I may be an old man but I'm not senile.' He looked around at us. 'We live on a rock. A rock that's flying through a place filled with other rocks. It was only a matter of time, wasn't it? We spent all those years worrying about what we were doing to it, scrubbing our tin cans for recycling and installing things to catch rainwater ...' He turned to the window again. The blocks of grey light were fading to darkness, but the rain still pounded the glass. 'Seems to me we should have been spending less time worrying about the garden. More time trying to find the gate.'

'Amen to that,' said Bryce, raising his glass.

The old man took a long, wavering breath through his nose and smiled at us.

'So,' he said, frowning. 'Cornwall, then, is it? Long way from here. How are you planning on getting there?'

'We're running,' said Richard. Rupert spluttered.

'Come again?' he said.

'We're running,' repeated Richard.

'Pah!' said Rupert, his face beaming. 'I like that! Running indeed!' He threw back his head and laughed a long, wheezy laugh. There was no trace of mockery in it. It just tickled him. When he had finished, he looked around at us nodding.

'So the world ends, and you lot start a running club. I'll drink to that.'

Bryce raised his glass and we followed. 'To the end of the world,' he said.

'To the end of the world running club,' said Lord Bartonmouth.

Broken Telescopes

Rupert ran us two baths in separate bathrooms, one at each end of the corridor at the back of the house. One was for Grimes, the other for the men. There wasn't enough hot water to replenish after each turn, so we drew straws on order and I came last. Bryce had winked at me as we crossed paths at the doorway. I now lay in the long ivory tub of rain, grateful for the fact that only a single candle dappled the water with light in an otherwise dark room.

The rest of the room was bare and grand. The bath stood next to a pair of long, blue curtains hanging open on the far wall. The window shook and rattled in the wind still circling the house and the rain made tortured patterns on the black glass, twisting rivulets endlessly seeking each other out, joining, breaking, shifting and shattering in some frantic, hopeless romance. There was nothing behind them – no lights, no shapes to make out in the darkness. I felt a sense of being under protection, but by something that might buckle and break at any moment. What was outside – the cold storm, the distance, the remains of a country that was no longer held together, perhaps whatever was making the animal howl I still heard every morning – was too large and too strong to be kept at bay. The water was hot and deep and I felt it go to work on my muscles. It would be good to take shelter in this old house, drinking an old lord's whisky and warming ourselves on his burning furniture, but I knew we would have to leave in the morning.

I closed my eyes and let my thoughts run off, making shapes of Beth. Beth making eyes at me, in the kitchen, the morning after I'd asked her to marry me. Beth hanging out baby clothes in the sun. Beth plonking herself down on the toilet as I showered, pulling a face at me as she emptied her bladder. Beth lost in one of her own jokes, things that she thought would only made her laugh and so kept to herself, despite my protestations. Beth slipping naked into the bath with me one evening, the bump that was Alice now starting to show, reaching forward and holding my head in her hands, drawing her lips to mine …

I must have fallen asleep because I suddenly found myself looking up through the water. I sat up, spluttering and grasping for the sides of the bath. The water was now cool and the candle had spread into a buttery cloud of melted wax by the taps. I wiped my face and looked down at my right foot. Slowly, I lifted it out of the water and turned it in the dying light. One huge blister dominated the instep. I touched it and felt the water move beneath the hard callous. I knew it wouldn't be long before the skin ruptured, baring the raw flesh beneath and bringing a new type of pain to add to the rest.

I pushed myself up and onto my feet, steadying my weak legs, then got out of the bath and stood dripping on the cold tiles.

Rupert had found us some clothes to wear while ours dried by his stove. He had given us a small candlelit tour of the house as he searched for them (avoiding one closed door without comment, which I assumed must lead to the drawing room where he had shot his unwanted guest). I have no idea how many lives had passed through this house over the centuries, but many of them seemed to have been remembered by their wardrobes, most of which were still filled with ancient dresses, suits, robes, uniforms and shoes. In one small cupboard was a line of green school uniforms, identical apart from their size, which grew from left to right along the rail.

My outfit was found in a small bedroom at the end of the upstairs corridor littered with books and papers. He'd selected a pair of thick woollen trousers, a matching jacket and an off-white shirt with cuffs that were still crumpled from having been rolled up to the elbows. He had also very carefully chosen a pair of brown Y-fronts and long tennis socks from a drawer next to the cupboard, and a pair of brown brogues from the beneath the bed.

I got dressed in the near dark. The difference between my age and that of the clothes could have been described in wars and funerals, not just decades, but the fabric felt strong and somehow luxurious, despite its fraying edges and fusty smell. When I had finished lacing the shoes, I took the remains of the candle and found my way out along the corridor, navigating towards the sound of low voices coming from a large room near the kitchen.

The room was filled with heat. Broken strips of delicately carved wood crackled and spat in a gigantic hearth – more of Rupert's furniture being burned. Candles surrounded the fire and lined the mantelpiece above it. Harvey and Richard were sitting next to it on a long sofa. They each held a glass of wine. Richard lay stretched out with his legs crossed and one long arm along the back cushion. Rupert had found him some hunting tweeds, which he was now wearing as comfortably as if they had been from his own wardrobe. Harvey was in a thick sailing jumper and red corduroys, sitting forward with his elbows on his knees and cradling his glass between them as he stared into the flames.

Bryce was sitting with one leg crossed beneath the other in an armchair opposite. His hair hung down in wet, black ringlets and his beard glistened in the orange light. His size had made Rupert's selection of clothing for him difficult. After some thought, Rupert had decided that there was only one wardrobe which might contain something large enough to fit him. This had belonged to his wife's sister, a very large woman who had lived with them in her dying years. Bryce was, therefore, now wearing a voluminous, pink night robe decorated with black Chinese lettering and pictures of swallows. Beneath, he appeared to be wearing two pairs of long walking socks that disappeared up over his knees. What lay beyond that was anybody's guess. The three raised their glasses when they saw me.

'Very smart,' said Harvey. He patted the seat next to him. 'Come and sit down son.'

I took a seat and Richard poured me a glass from a bottle that had been warming by the fire.

'Took your time,' said Bryce. He wobbled his eyebrows at me, grinning. 'Not easy is it, in another man's bath. Can take a while for things to, you know, happen.'

Richard leaned across and handed me my glass. 'Bryce ...' he warned.

'You get there in the end though, eh?' He winked at me, nodding. 'Know I did.'

Harvey frowned and swiped the air at him. 'Cut it out, Bryce!' he said.

'God's sake, Bryce, you didn't, did you?' said Richard.

'Ahm only jokin, y'eejits,' said Bryce. 'Think I'd take a wank in another man's bath water? After youse pair had been in it before me? Christ's sake, all them old pubes floating around and everything.'

He sat back in his chair. 'No way I'd be able to get a stiffy.' He gave me another wink and gulped his wine.

'Where's Grimes?' I said, trying to hurry the thoughts from my head.

'No sign yet,' said Richard.

'His lordship's getting some food ready,' said Harvey.

'Aye, no' too soon either,' said Bryce. 'I'm starving.'

I suddenly realised how hungry I was too. We hadn't eaten all day; the rain had made it impossible. At that moment I heard a clattering sound as Rupert walked in. He was carrying another tray, this one much larger, which I helped him lie carefully down on the table in front of the fire.

'Dinner is served, gentlemen, dinner is served,' he said, straightening up. The tray was full of china bowls filled with a steaming brown stew. I looked more closely and saw cubes of grey meat encased in transparent jelly. The air was filled with a strong, gamey smell that made me recoil.

'Is that . . .' said Harvey.

''Fraid I wasn't left with much after my guests left,' said Rupert. 'All the fresh stuff gone, tins as well.' He motioned towards the bottle of wine. 'Made quite a dent in the old Claret too. Only stuff they wouldn't touch was, er, for the hounds. Used to buy all their grub in bulk, so, loads of it left. Mostly what I tend to eat these days. Tastes better heated up.'

He looked around at us nervously.

'Hope that's alright,' he said. Then he wiped his shaking palm upon his shirt, reached for his collar with his finger, faltered and let the hand fall. The gesture gave me a sudden strange pang of loss and helplessness, and I felt tears spring to the corners of my eyes. I wanted to pull the bowl towards me and eat it and tell him it was alright to be serving us dog food, that he was a good man for letting us stay, that he didn't deserve to be living alone in an ancient, crumbling mansion without his wife. I caught myself, surprised at this sudden well of emotion, and wiped my hand across my eyes.

We think that language binds us, keeps us close, but sometimes I wonder how far apart we really are. We can make a million assumptions from the movement of an old man's hand, most of them probably incorrect. All we have to go on is our own skewed window on the world. We're like hermits living in the attics of big houses on lonely hills, watching each other with broken telescopes.

'All good with me,' said Bryce. He leaned forward and grabbed the bowl, shovelling a fork-load into his mouth. Suddenly he stopped, mid-chew, one cheek bulging with meat, and stared up at the door. Grimes had walked in.

She was wearing a deep-red, velvet dress that ran to the floor. The tight line of the fabric ran from her upper thigh, over her hips and across the tight swell of her abdomen. Her hair was unclipped and fell in curls around her pale shoulders, light ringlets venturing further down towards the small, faint line of her cleavage.

'Well, I ...' said Rupert. 'I do say. You look beautiful. Remarkable.'

She cast a shy gaze around the room. I noticed it landed for too long on Richard. This is when it finally clicked for me, and I wondered why I hadn't seen it before. Ever since the barracks she had behaved differently around him than around the other men. Maybe I had assumed that this was down to his natural military authority, or that sense of easy entitlement he had, but it was clear to me now; she had feelings for him. As this began to dawn on me, my eyes drifted over to Bryce, still mid-mouthful in his pink robe. He hadn't moved a muscle. I heard him gulp his mouthful of dog food and rest the bowl back on the table. As he did so, he caught my eye and I saw him flinch from my gaze.

'Feels a bit tight,' said Grimes, wriggling a little. 'Your wife must have had quite a figure.'

'She did,' said Rupert. 'In her day, yes, she did. Thank you so much my dear, I did so want to see it worn again.'

'That's OK,' said Grimes. 'It's nice to be in something other than uniform for a change.'

She smiled and looked down at the tray of steaming bowls.

'Great,' she said. 'What's for dinner?'

We ate the dog food quickly and in silence. It was better than the rat we had eaten by the stationary lorry, and my own ravenous hunger overpowered the feelings of nausea that washed up and down my throat as I swallowed. When I had finished, I emptied the wine into my mouth and rinsed it around to rid it of the taste, but I had a feeling it would be with me for a few days.

Rupert took the plates back to the kitchen. When he returned, he was holding Alice's stringyphone in his hands. I instinctively stood, stopping myself making a grab for it.

'I found this,' said Rupert. 'You left it in the bathroom. Is it, er, important in some way?'

I felt the others' eyes on me. They had seen Alice and me talking on the stringyphone in the barracks, but I hadn't told them I'd taken it with me when we left.

'It's my daughter's,' I said. 'She left it behind. I sort of … talk to her on it.'

Rupert raised his eyebrows. 'Talk to her?' he said, looking down at the cans and fraying string, turning them in his hands. Finally he nodded, as if he understood. 'Used to play with these as a child. Me and my elder brother Godfrey. Made huge ones that stretched across the lawn. Wonderful fun. Wonderful.' He nodded, then passed the cans back to me.

'You've been carrying them all this time?' said Richard.

'Around my neck,' I said. 'It helps. I can feel them, it reminds me.'

'That's nice, mate, really nice,' said Harvey, putting a hand on my shoulder. He looked around the room. 'Hey, we should sign them, put our initials on them or something, what do you think?'

Grimes and Richard nodded.

'Would you mind, Ed?' said Richard. I shrugged and shook my head.

'Just a mo,' said Rupert. He left through the door and returned a minute later with a short kitchen blade. 'Bit blunt but should do the trick,' he said, passing it to me. I looked at the others.

'You first,' said Grimes. I held the point of the blade between my thumb and forefinger and scratched my initials at the bottom of one can. Richard went next. Bryce, who had said nothing, just looked at me, both hands on the arms of his chair, until the cans and knife arrived in his lap. He took his turn, then leaned across and offered the cans to me. As I took them, he held onto them a little and put his face close to mine.

'I knew I liked you,' he said quietly, and let go.

Then we got very drunk. Rupert brought in bottle after bottle of wine from his cellar, then port, then more of the ancient whisky, then more wine. He told us all about the house in its heyday, about his childhood, the grand parties and famous guests that had stayed. Whenever the conversation began to veer towards asteroids, we each somehow managed to steer it back onto something else. It was as if the subject itself was a friend who had already had too much to drink, and couldn't be trusted to talk in case he said something nobody wanted to hear.

At one point Rupert mentioned the boats and things faltered.

'Where do you think they're headed?' said Harvey.

'Who cares where they're headed?' I blurted. 'I'm not getting on them.'

The room stared at me.

'What do you mean, you're *not getting on them*?' said Richard.

'I'm just not,' I said. 'Why would I? I'm finding my family and getting them out of there.'

Richard put down his glass.

'*What?*' he spat. 'Where the hell do you think you'll go?'

'We were fine in the barracks,' I said. 'Life was simple, we had everything we needed. Safety, shelter, food, water. All we have to do is hold out until things start to get back to normal. We've already started to see the sun coming through the clouds, which means that soon things will start growing again. We could grow vegetables, build greenhouses ...'

'Wait, wait, wait,' said Bryce. He leaned forward and peered at me from where he was standing unsteadily by the fire. 'Veszhtables? Greenhousesh? What do you think this is, *The Good Life*? What's your plan, you gonnae ... gonnae start a fuckin' commune or something?' He gave a hoot and wobbled back on his heels, gripping the fireplace to stop himself from falling into the flames.

'Why?' I said. 'What's wrong with that? Why do we need to leave the country? Where would we go? What's there that's so great? Internet? Television? Department stores? Fast food?'

Richard leaned forward and began counting on his fingers.

'Medicine, clean water, sanitation, midwifery, roads, transport, everything that pulled this world out of the dark ages and took the nasty, brutish and short out of life.' He rabbit-eared his fingers. 'You think that "going back to nature" is going to make your life more enjoyable? You're a fantasist, Ed, and a selfish one. What about your kids and your wife? You think they'd be alright? You think you could really support them and protect them? You probably couldn't even keep a cactus alive, let alone feed your family from a vegetable patch.'

'And what's that supposed to mean?' I said.

'I'm saying society has evolved, Ed. It's not what it used to be for one very good reason: it was shit and people weren't very good at staying alive. We got sick and died daily. Childbirth usually ended in death for the child, the mother or both. Pain, filth, famine and war were everywhere and you were lucky to reach thirty without being stabbed, shot, tortured, decapitated, hung, drawn and quartered, burned at the stake or thrown in a dungeon to rot. People didn't live in some blissful utopia where everyone had an allotment and looked after each other. We *killed* each other because we were starving and terrified most of the time. The last two hundred years have seen us grow, understand, build systems and infrastructures that keep us healthy and happy. We can dive to the bottom of the ocean, fly around the world, go to the moon, Mars, beyond. And all you want to do is go and live in *River Cottage*. We're *not supposed to live in the fucking dirt, Ed*. We're *not*.'

With that, Richard snatched his drink and stood up.

'Not going on the *fucking* boats,' he muttered. He glared back at me, then faced the fire. 'Ridiculous.'

'I could grow vegetables if I wanted,' I mumbled, refilling my glass. Bryce began to laugh.

'Alright, boys, alright,' he said. 'Time out. Ed, don't be a dick. And Dick, get down off your high-horse, you sound like you're running for ... I dunno ... King of ... bloody ... *pfft* ... anyway. Rupert, old chum, old mate, have you got ... got any kinda ... I dunno ... entertainment for this party?'

Rupert looked back at him conspiratorially.

'Funny you should say that,' he said. 'Got just the thing.'

Half an hour later, I was sat next to Bryce on the sofa, half-listening to him talk about tattoos. Rupert had wheeled in an ancient wind-up gramophone and was pouring through a thick stack of LPs. *The Lark Ascending* by Vaughan Williams was playing and through my badly focussing eyes I could just make out Grimes dancing with Richard. She lay her head against his chest. I was aware that Bryce had stopped talking and knew he was watching too. Then I saw Grimes move her hand slowly up Richard's neck and try to pull his head towards hers.

Richard pushed it away and turned to face the fire, leaving her suddenly on her own in the centre of the room. Her shoulders were tight and her hands had clenched into balls by her side; it was the same position I had seen her in when Yuill and Henderson had abandoned us in Carlops.

She turned and said something to Rupert as the music faded to the click and crackle of the needle on the ancient vinyl. 'Of course, my dear, of course. You can sleep through there.' Rupert pointed through double doors to an adjoining room. 'There's a sofa and I've put out some blankets. Usually gets warm in there from this here fire.'

Grimes laid a hand on his shoulder and left, quickly, closing the doors behind her.

Rupert turned to us. 'Think I'll call it a night too, gents, if you don't mind. Should be enough room for you in here. Two sofas over there, another here and . . . oh, right.' He looked back at the arm chair, where Harvey had fallen asleep. He picked up a blanket from a pile by the door and laid it across him. 'Good night, old man,' he said. 'Good night, all.'

We waved him good night and Richard, Bryce and I took a blanket each to our sofas. The comfort of that thick blanket and those deep, velvet cushions was the most I'd felt in almost a year. I stared at the ceiling, sensing time passing and willing away the morning, the time when I would have to get up, go out into the cold and start running again. Then I felt bad for feeling this when we were still so far from Cornwall, and the guilt gave way to urgency and a sudden need to move and be close to Beth, Alice and Arthur. My head suddenly filled with a thousand breeds of panic: the dizzy horror of separation, the implausibility of reconciliation, the physical recoil from the task at hand, the still-present eeriness of the fact that what had happened had happened – *the world had been smashed apart* – the whole strange and alien coldness of it all. My mind began to spin like an engine stuck on full throttle. My heart stuttered and raced, deafening me with the sound of fast-moving blood. I tensed my muscles, fighting for control, until finally my thoughts settled into a kind of low, pulsing sense of doom. My heart gradually slowed too, and I cursed whatever part of human evolution had led to this kind of emotional somersaulting. I thought about what Richard had said. Maybe I was a fantasist. Maybe I was no good. Maybe I couldn't look after my family. After all, I hadn't been doing a great job before the end of the world, so why now?

I think I was just starting to drift off when I heard a spring creak. A moment later I saw Bryce padding across the room with a candle. He paused at the double doors to the adjoining room where Grimes was sleeping, then looked over his shoulder at Richard, snoring soundly in the other sofa. He didn't seem to notice me. Then he turned back to the doors, knocked twice, softly, and went in. I heard low voices coming from inside, Grimes saying something kindly but firmly, Bryce's voice sounding different – boyish and broken, helpless. Then silence, followed by footsteps returning to the door. I shut my eyes as it quietly opened and shut, holding my breath until I heard the sound of the sofa behind me creak once again under Bryce's weight.

I woke to the distant, animal howl. The curtains were open and the room was full of dull shadows. It was still outside; the storm had passed. Richard and Bryce were still asleep on their sofas, but Harvey's chair was empty.

I got up and crouched next to the fire, warming my hands on the embers and enjoying the smell of soot and stone. I should have been feeling worse, given the amount of drink from the night before, but all I had was a dull throb in my temples. My head was clear, my muscles were looser after the bath, and I even felt well rested. I had fallen into a deep sleep shortly after Bryce had returned from his visit to Grimes's room, thinking of the many things that might have happened in there but knowing that there was really only one. I knew it was wrong to take comfort from this, but I did anyway. Other people's problems, even those of your friends, are a great and terrible distraction from your own.

I was thirsty so I made my way out along the dark corridor and through to the kitchen. Harvey was there, piling some of the wood left over from the night before into the stove.

'Morning, Ed,' he whispered. 'Thought I'd get her going early, didn't think Rupert would mind. You want some coffee? I found some in this pot here, looks a bit old but smells alright.'

'Thanks,' I said.

We stood at the window and drank coffee while the morning light grew outside. We watched details of the landscape emerge slowly like drops of watercolour seeping across canvas – trees, fields, hills and fences – all the features of a traditional, rolling English landscape. In the grey shadows, it all looked normal and untouched, so much so that it might have been possible to trick ourselves into thinking that, maybe, the devastation ended here. Maybe, beyond these hills surrounding us, people lived normally, the sun still met the earth, flowers still grew, cities still prospered. Or even – just maybe – what had happened had never happened at all. But then the light grew a little more and we saw dark blights appear – rough gouges in the earth, sections of hillside missing, forests flattened and black, ditches that tore open into hidden quarries of mud. I felt a nameless loss. A grief for something I had never known, a time and a country I could only hope to feel through osmosis, never first-hand.

'Storm's abated, I see.'

I turned to see Rupert next to me, peering through the glass.

'Maybe today's the day to tackle that garden,' he said.

The others came in gradually, first Grimes, already dressed in her dried uniform, then Richard and finally Bryce, booming a loud 'Morning!' as if nothing had happened. I watched him sidle past Grimes without a glance and help himself to coffee from the stove. Grimes herself avoided Richard's eyes and joined Harvey and me at the window.

'I'm sorry, Ed,' said Richard from the table behind me. 'About last night. I had no right to say what I said, I was just, you know … bit drunk, angry, I suppose.'

'That's OK,' I said. 'Maybe you were right.'

'No, no I wasn't. It's your decision, your life, your family. You must do what you feel you must do. It's not my place to tell you what I think is right and wrong. I just …' he began, and sighed. 'I just miss my son. I'm sorry.' He stretched his hand across the table. I shook it and he smiled. 'No hard feelings,' he said.

'None at all,' I said.

'Aaaah, isn't that …' Bryce began. But he stopped when he saw Grimes turning her face towards him, narrowing her eyes and giving a single shake of her head. Bryce cleared his throat and licked his lips, laying his cup down on the table. Grimes turned her head back.

'OK,' she said. 'Once you two are finished cuddling, are we good to go?'

We dressed in our dry clothes and some boots that Rupert had found for us. Mine must have been thirty years old, but they were better than the ones that I had been wearing from the barracks. He found some bandages and plasters for our first-aid kit and we filled our hydration bladders with rainwater from the kitchen tap. Then we thanked Rupert for his help, each shaking his hand at the back door before heading up the drive. I looked back to see him walking to an outhouse, reappearing a few moments later with a rake and a spade. He crossed the yard, dropping first the rake, then the spade, retrieving them both from the gravel and then carrying them both down to the garden. I swallowed down the same feelings I had had the night before, and followed the others back up to the main road.

We made over thirty miles that day, alternating between running and walking every quarter of an hour and stopping for three half-hour breaks to stretch, eat and drink. We set up camp in a service station, where we found a full, unopened box of Mars bars hidden in the corner of an otherwise-empty storeroom, and a vending machine containing three cans of Coke. We celebrated with two portions of noodles, sharing the Cokes and eating three Mars bars each before filling our packs with the rest. We woke to similar weather and travelled almost as well the next day. At some point in the afternoon I felt a wetness in my sock and stopped. My blister had burst, exposing bright crimson flesh beneath a long tear. I strapped it up as best I could with one of Rupert's bandages and carried on. The pain was not as bad as I had expected.

It began to seem that what we were doing might be possible. The weather was cold but we were keeping dry. The road was broken but passable, with no major obstacles. Aside from a little awkwardness between Grimes and Richard, the night at Bartonmouth Hall seemed to have bound us a little closer. Our joints and muscles ached, but the pain became manageable. We were feeling good and making progress. We were settling into a rhythm.

A rhythm that I'm sure would have carried us to Cornwall without incident, had it not been for Jenny Rae.

Jenny Rae's Field

We had been following Jacob's advice, making our way inland and then skirting around the Yorkshire Dales until, three nights after Bartonmouth, we met a town where we camped in a ditch. We saw a fire on a hill that night and decided to start watches, just as we had done in Carlops. The next day we noticed a strange light growing on the western horizon, which we eventually realised was water. Soon we saw blocky shapes rising in the mist before us. These were buildings; the tower blocks and offices of Manchester. It had been over three months since we had seen anything taller than a three-storey tenement barely holding its crumbling bricks together. It felt strange to see human structure again in such concentration – hope and sadness both at once.

We drew nearer to the water. By mid-afternoon we could see that it had made a shore of the western part of the city. We could even see small waves lapping across the dirt yards of industrial estates and against the rooftops of sunken houses. We decided to stop early and stay north of the city, rather than walk into it as darkness fell. We left the road and found a long, natural cave that had formed in a collapsed grass verge. It gave us shelter and a good view of the city, so we set up camp and made a fire.

Our initial surprise at seeing what we thought was a city intact faded as we looked at it more closely. Many buildings were still standing tall, but they weren't what they had been. They were incomplete, their heads lopped off in jagged, diagonal tears. The floors below were windowless, with chunks missing from their corners. My eyes were drawn to the water lapping around the edges of the city, out of place and unsure of itself against its new shore. I saw tiny white specks, gulls moving around on the waves and flapping clumsily up onto high window ledges, the urban cliffs in which they were now making nests. An erosion was beginning, which, I imagined, would result in a beach after enough time. The sand would be made of bones, credit cards, fridges, cars and sofa springs. Dunes would form and grow tufts of grass. The sun might eventually shine on them, a young boy might tumble down them, laughing, rolling in the trillion, trillion fragments of debris and detritus, dust ground from the lives who had once walked the bed of the rolling ocean into which he crashed. The living would run through the dust of the dead, just as they always had done.

Harvey dealt with the fire and Grimes organised the pot. Bryce sat back away from us and took off his boots to rub his ankles. He seemed distracted.

Richard took out the map and studied it.

'I think we're here,' he said, pointing at an interchange about three miles north of the city. He drew his finger down across a mess of roads that spread south east, glancing up at the eerie coastline for reference.

'We probably shouldn't go near there,' he said. 'Which means we'll have to go here.' He pointed to a smaller road going directly through the heart of the city. 'We can be through in a day, follow it south and rejoin the M6 in two or three days …' He traced the road down and jabbed it. 'Here.'

'That means ... Birmingham by the sixteenth,' I said. I did some calculations. 'Nine days to make the final three hundred miles.'

It felt strange to be saying this with confidence. Even a few weeks before, it would have been with hilarity or despair. But what had changed? My body? Was I fitter? Perhaps a little, but certainly not that much after just less than a fortnight of movement. What had changed was my perspective. The task seemed less impossible the more we pushed on. Every mile I conquered was one less to endure. Every night and every morning was another twenty-four hours closer to Beth and the kids. Every hill I scaled was one more than the man who had almost let his family sleep through the end of the world believed he was incapable of scaling. And yet, still he had scaled it. Nothing out there was changing, but everything inside was.

'Let's just concentrate on getting through Manchester,' said Richard. 'Then we'll see where we are.'

We cooked noodles and watched the city as night fell. As the shadow crept towards us from the east, we spotted orange lights flickering in its wake; other fires like ours dotted about the city.

Harvey passed plates round. I ate mine in three gulps and poured the remaining thin broth into my mouth. Bryce took his, moved the noodles around a bit with his spoon and then threw the plate to the ground with a roar.

'Fucking noodles!'

He rolled away from us onto his side and crossed his arms, slamming his head against his pack and grumbling.

'I need meat!' he said.

In the morning, I was surprised to find myself awake before anyone else. It was not yet light but I could see the effects of the sunrise going on behind the cloud. A thin band of light was glowing on the wet horizon. I sat up, stood up, stretched and breathed in the fetid air. We had grown used to the stale smell around us all the time, but it seemed to be getting much stronger now that we were close to a city and the pressure of the cloud above did nothing to help. We knew what it was.

I felt alright, better than I had felt the night before. The tight strain in my legs and back and the sharp pain in my knees and hips were there constantly, but it was as though the all-encompassing tourniquet in which my body was gripped was being slowly released. A small release each morning, but enough to allow me to walk more freely, feel gravity just that little bit less than the day before. I felt a surge of hope with every dim sunrise, and with every surge came a feeling of getting nearer to Beth and the kids. When running, I spent most of the time daydreaming about what it would be like to see them again. The smell and warmth of their skin. The sound of Alice's voice. What our life would be like. Hope became my drug.

I scraped some snow from the ridge with a pan and lit the stove. I sat and watched the small, fierce flame burn, enjoying being the only one awake for a change. The stove radiated warmth and promised me warm liquid. I tried not to think about it, afraid that my good mood was too fragile and might vanish like a butterfly under too much scrutiny.

The water boiled and daylight found the ridge. I made tea and poured it into mugs for the others. Grimes woke up first.

'Morning,' I said. She pushed herself up painfully from the hard ground and pulled up the hat that had been covering her face. She looked across at me, confused. Her skin was pale and her eyes puffy with sleep, the corners of her mouth downturned.

'Good morning,' she said at last. 'You're looking ... well.'

I handed her a mug.

'Don't sound so surprised.'

'I'm not surprised. Just proud. I knew you had it in you.'

The others woke. We drank our tea and headed off, Bryce still miserable and talking only in grunts. Richard studied his route again and led us back onto the road and into the city. I ran with Harvey as usual. After a mile, he looked me up and down.

'What's got into you?' he said.

'Nothing much,' I said. 'Maybe today's just a good day.'

It was not.

The northern suburbs of the city were mostly burnt-out industrial estates. We checked them for supplies and found a supermarket that had been stripped entirely of its stock. Even the store and warehouse had been picked clean. This was not the work of opportunistic looters; there was nothing left, no mess on the floor, no dropped bottles to salvage. Even the tills were open and empty. The whole building had been meticulously emptied by humans who knew what they were doing.

Every place that still stood was the same. We had not seen anyone yet, but the feeling of a human presence, non-chaotic and focused, was everywhere.

The smell became stronger as we ran deeper into the built-up streets. In less than three hours we hit the centre. We crossed the river – now a deep gully with barely a trickle of water flowing in its bed – then stopped when we came to a square.

'We need water,' said Richard. We looked around in surprise as his voice echoed around from the walls of the empty, silent buildings. 'We should take a look in these offices,' he said more quietly. 'Maybe there's some still left in the pipes, vending machines or something.

'Why are you whispering?' I whispered.

'I don't know,' he said. He looked about the square. The buildings were heavily damaged and burned, whole sections torn away exposing needle-like struts and piranha tooth beams. Windows were mostly broken, doors open, glass shop-fronts missing and the contents they had once protected now gone. Nothing left. There were no cars on the road. No rubbish strewn on the streets. I thought of locusts.

'Seems odd, don't you think?' said Richard. 'I feel like … like we're …'

'Exposed,' said Grimes. 'Look up there.' She pointed up to the third floor of what had been a department store, now open to the world. We looked up in time to see movement, something darting quickly behind a wall.

'We're being watched,' she said. 'Come on.'

Grimes led us closer to one of the walls of the square and we jogged along it towards the southern edge, where a small road led away from the open space. We heard a scrape above us.

'Watch out!' said Grimes. A clump of brickwork fell and shattered in a cloud of red dust before us. We looked up and saw the silhouette of a face looking down on us. It disappeared back through a window.

'Come on,' said Grimes. 'We have to move faster.' We heard more scuffles and scrapes above us. 'Now!'

We started to run. As we did we heard voices, whoops and yelps coming from across the street. Then we saw them, six of them, young men leaning out over the edge of a second-storey room, hanging on to broken walls and calling across to the building opposite.

We had crossed a side street to a building that looked like it had once been a department store. The glass doors and windows were gone. Shouts came from inside, and footsteps clattering on metal. Deep in the darkness I saw escalators scurrying with shadows.

'Cross the square!' I shouted, pulling Harvey out into the open with me. We sprinted across the concrete, a pedestrian area of statues that were now splintered and stained with blasts of soot, and benches that were now iron frames with no trace left of their wooden seats.

I glanced back at the department store and saw three boys standing still at the doors. There were hoots and shouts coming from all around us, movement almost everywhere we looked. The boys behind us shouted something and we saw five more shin down from the first floor of the building we were heading for. They ran towards us a little and we stopped, edged back.

'Fucking Rabbits,' said Bryce through gritted teeth.

'Down here,' said Grimes. We followed her down a street that widened out into a strip of disintegrated Georgian shop-fronts. The clamour seemed to follow us, growing louder as we ran. Pipes clanged inside the buildings and shrieks echoed up and down the long street. A large group of whoever was making them seemed to spill out of a collapsed wall and blocked the street ahead. We turned back, took a left and found ourselves blocked again. The line of youths remained still, not advancing on us, just preventing us from going further.

'We have to find somewhere longer and wider,' said Richard as we backed out again. 'Somewhere we can try to lose them.' He nodded up a steep side street. 'Here,' he said. 'I think this leads to a main road.'

We ran up the curved hill and came out on a long, paved road. A group of boys were waiting for us, walking slowly from the right. Two of the groups behind had merged and were following us up the hill.

'Now,' said Richard. 'Left. Run.'

We ran at pace, Grimes far ahead, but we couldn't keep up a sprint. The group behind us was now fifteen strong at least. They were a long way behind, a silent crowd of menace, keeping their distance and jogging slowly.

'Why aren't they catching us up? They look like they could easily outrun us.'

'Shit,' said Grimes, raising her head to the sky and suddenly slowing down. 'Because we're not being chased.'

'What?' said Richard as we caught Grimes up. 'Why are you stopping, come on!'

'We're not being chased,' said Grimes. We stopped at her side. 'We're being escorted. They want us to go this way.' She put her hands on her knees, catching her breath. Behind us, the group had slowed to walking pace. They were no longer making a noise.

'Look,' said Grimes, nodding to our left and right. I saw a few others hiding in the shadowy hollows of the empty shops and banks that had once made up the street. They peered back at us. Grimes looked back at the group behind, who had now stopped and formed a straight line across the street. One of them, tall and gaunt with a red hoody, stood out in front, legs apart and hands by his side. Grimes turned and took a few steps towards him, but the red-hooded boy held up a finger in warning. He shook his head twice, then jabbed his finger ahead of us.

Grimes exhaled and put her hands on her hips. She turned back to us.

'Keep walking,' she said.

'Fuck that,' said Bryce, reaching for the cricket bat he had found in the lorry cab. 'Let's fight.'

'There's too many,' said Richard, bending over to catch his breath. 'What's the point?'

'At least we can take a few out,' said Bryce, but Grimes had reached up and laid her hand gently on his arm. He stopped, looked down at her. Another small shake of her head. He replaced the bat.

We walked silently across the city for two hours, heads down, our herds behind us. Occasionally another cluster of them would appear to our left or right and we would turn obediently down an opposite street. They gave us no directions, said nothing.

Eventually the city gave way to suburbs again. Salt and vegetation began to mingle with the smell of decay.

'They're taking us towards the sea,' said Richard.

We passed through a long stretch of streets which gradually eroded into miles of black wasteland, flattened and burned and littered with plastic, broken bicycles and piles of rubble. We saw some fires burning on this ground. A family sat around one. The father looked back at me through haunted eyes as he warmed his hands on the flame. His wife sat across from him, holding her daughter as she played with some broken relic of a toy.

Our herds nudged us gently across towards some buildings in the distance. It was starting to get dark as we approached them and I felt the pang of another day gone, wasted without progress. Suddenly I felt the urge to bolt. I must have bristled or twitched or maybe Harvey just knew what I was thinking, because he reached out and grabbed my arm to steady me.

'Easy, mate,' he said. 'Be alright. We'll get out of this, you'll see.'

We came to the other side of the wasteland and found ourselves on what looked like a housing estate. The houses were in bad repair and what little plant life had survived in the small, patchy front lawns and between the rusted gates was untended and wild. I saw faces at windows. Some skinny children in oversized winter coats and hats looked up from a game as we passed them on the pavement. Our escorts were close behind us now. They led us down a narrow street and onto another, where some older adolescents skulked in covens along the pavements. One caught sight of us and pushed himself away from the wall he was leaning against. He had a shaven head and a clean face, with a tattoo under one of his eyes. He slunk towards us, eyeballing me. I held his glare as he approached, then he threw out a hand and shoved my left shoulder. I wasn't ready for it and I swallowed a cry of pain as the tendons jerked under the sudden pressure. I continued walking, the boy's frowning face in mine as he walked with his chest up against me.

We huddled into a group and walked slowly down the middle of the road. A girl from the other side of the street strutted out. Her face was thick with make-up and her bare, fat legs showed beneath a long, blue trench coat. She sneered and swung a hand wildly up at Richard's head, plastic bangles rattling as it struck his outstretched arm.

'*Jeeesus*,' said Harvey. 'Hold on a minute.'

I could feel Bryce rattling behind me. My guy was still in my face and the fat girl was walking backwards in front of us, grinning, her hands out above her head, beckoning us on. Jeers and whistles broke out and two boys, maybe sixteen years old, strode out in front of us with their hands in their pockets. They chewed their lips and cocked their heads at Grimes, looking her up and down and grabbing themselves between their legs. One brushed up against her and started smelling her hair. I heard a rumble in Bryce's throat.

'Out of my way!' he yelled, pushing between Richard and me, shoving his palm into the face of the one next to me and making for the boy in mid-leer over Grimes. The boy yelped as he felt a thick hand around his neck and another by his trousers. Bryce hauled him up and tossed him into the gutter, then made for his friend who was already running away down the street. He fell at the feet of four older, skinny comrades, who pulled him to his feet and started making towards Bryce, their shoulders rotating, glaring him down. Jeers and cackles broke out across the gathering crowd as they prepared to see what happened.

A piercing whistle sounded from the top of the street and the men who were advancing on Bryce suddenly stopped and turned. A large woman with cropped black hair stood by the door of one of the houses, feet astride and gloved fists on her sizeable hips. She was at least six foot tall and wore five or six huge cardigans, one on top of the other, a long, purple dress and black boots as high as her chubby knees. Sitting patiently at her feet was a small Jack Russell dog and behind her stood five men smoking. One stood forward. He had the toothless face of an old man, although something told me he wasn't much older than me. He wore a denim jacket cut off at the shoulders, revealing long, sinewy arms. The woman beamed down at the commotion around us and clapped her hands twice above her head as if she was calling back a pack of hounds.

'Enough, boys,' she said. 'Enough.' She started walking down towards us, shooting a dark glare at the girl who had attacked Richard as she passed her. The girl skulked back to the pavement.

'That's no way to treat guests,' warned the woman as she came between Bryce and the five boys. She gave them a look too, and they retreated slowly, eyes still fixed on Bryce. Bryce smiled sweetly and gave them a wave with his fingers.

The woman turned to Bryce and looked him up and down.

'I do apologise,' she said, thrusting a great hand towards him. Deep, hollow Lancashire vowels boomed around the street. Bryce looked warily down at the hand before him, and at the trunk of arm to which it was attached. 'Name's Jenny,' she said, her jaw jutting out from her grinning face. 'Jenny Rae.'

Bryce slowly folded his hand around hers.

'Charmed,' he said, squinting.

The woman held Bryce's hand firmly without shaking it. She nodded once and looked around his face, searching for something, then released his hand and turned to us. I felt like a child returning home covered in mud.

'I am sorry for the escort, really I am,' she said. 'I can't have just anyone walking around the place. Dangerous, see, don't know who you are.' She walked slowly around us, looking at our boots and packs. When she had completed a circle, she puffed a satisfied blast of air through her squat nose.

'Y'look very tired,' she said. 'And hungry. Come with me and we'll get you seen to.'

The woman turned to lead us away, but Richard interrupted.

'Mrs Rae,' said Richard.

She stopped in mid-stride and looked back over her shoulder, frowning. 'Miss,' she said.

'Miss Rae,' Richard corrected. 'I don't fully understand why you felt the need to bring us out to you, and thank you for the offer of food, but we really need to get going. We're on a tight schedule. If you could just allow us to leave, we'll be out of here and on our way.'

Jenny Rae allowed the rest of her body to turn back to face the same way as her head. She looked sideways at Richard, annoyed, lodged her tongue in her cheek, then looked up at the sky.

'Be dark soon,' she said. 'Too dangerous.' She nodded, her mind made up. 'You'll stay here tonight, have dinner, leave in the morning.' She motioned to two boys nearby.

'You don't understand,' I said. Her eyes narrowed as they moved in my direction. 'We're already late, we need to get going now.'

'Late?' she said. 'Late for what?' She fixed her legs apart and craned her neck forward, wobbling on her hips and pulling a ridiculous face. 'Godda date?' she drawled, to great hoots of laughter from the children on the street.

'The boats,' I said. 'We need to get to the boats.'

Her eyes widened ever so slightly at this. She flapped her arm down violently to hush the laughter.

'Boats, is it?' she said, looking down her nose at me, legs still wide in her comedy stance. 'Met some more like you t'other day.' She looked suspiciously between us. 'Wonder if you know 'em?'

We said nothing, although every one of us was now thinking of Yuill and Henderson. There had been no sign of them since we found the abandoned Land Rover before Carlisle. Would they have taken the same route, found themselves in Manchester too, met the same escorts out to Jenny Rae?

After a few moments of silence she puffed indignantly.

'Boats,' she said. 'Alright. Tell you what, you stay with us tonight and we'll give you a lift out of Manchester first thing, make up for a bit of time.'

'Lift?' said Grimes. 'You have a car?'

'A car?' said Jenny Rae, her face frozen in shocked amusement. 'Ha! You don't know the half of what we've got, love. Come on, I'll give you a tour.'

We followed Jenny Rae along the street and out into a closed circle of red-brick, squat council houses, which sat around a small patch of land that may once have been covered in turf. It was now frozen dirt flecked with snow. In the centre, stuck in the hard ground, was a wooden stake about ten feet tall. A few younger children were playing football around it and stopped as we passed, a young boy with badly shaved hair held the football between his hands and watched us walk behind Jenny.

'James …' she said, a low warning in her voice. The child whipped his gaze away from us and threw the football back into the game.

'Ah've always lived here,' she said as we walked around the circle. 'Lived in that house when I was a girl.' She pointed back at a dull green door. 'Then moved to that bigger one when I married.'

More faces at the windows as we walked, families peering out through broken glass and dirty curtains.

'It's never once occurred to me to leave,' she said proudly. 'It's home, always has been, always will be. I've raised my kids here and now it's their home too.' She turned to us. 'Not many can say that these days,' she said, then caught herself, released a terrible hoot of laughter. 'Well, not now anyways, eh?'

She laughed to herself for a while longer as the five of us exchanged looks. We had no idea what kind of person we were dealing with here. When she had finished chuckling, she pointed up to the sky.

'Before it happened, you know,' she said. 'Before them things fell to earth, you couldn't see all this sky, not as much of it anyway.' She traced a finger around the circle of black cloud that hung perpetually above us, smiling. 'Tower blocks,' she said. 'One, two three, four, five of them.' She dotted her finger at spots above the rooftops. 'All around us, blocking out the bloody light. I didn't mind much, it were all I knew, but my dad did.' She cupped a hand to her mouth. 'Didn't you, Dad?' she shouted across the circle to an old man struggling with a key in a door. A plastic bag was looped over his arm. He looked back and grunted something, shook his head and went back to working the lock. She waved him away. 'Deaf as a post.'

A girl in a pink puffer jacket cycled past. She veered in suddenly towards us and made Harvey jump a few steps.

'Watch it, Danni!' said Jenny Rae as the girl pedalled away, giggling. 'They're good kids mostly. We have our problems like anywhere, but we get by.'

'How many people live here?' said Harvey, straightening himself out.

She shrugged. 'Hard to tell, changes all the time, people come and go. Come mostly. About two hundred here, I think, then there's another three we've got across the field, hundred in—'

'Field?' I said.

'Aye, that's what we call it. The field. No man's land.' Her eyes filled with volition. 'It will be one day though. Promise you that.'

More faces, scared, somehow out of place behind the grey netting. She led us around to the opposite wall of the circle and into a tunnel that cut through between the houses. Three teenage boys were huddled at the opening, smoking.

'Jenny,' one said, a broad smirk on his face as they looked us up and down.

'Boys,' said Jenny Rae. 'Go and tell number seventy-three they're having guests tonight.'

'Alright, Jenny,' said the same boy.

'Take their bags as well,' she said.

'That won't be necessary,' said Grimes. Bryce growled.

'I insist,' said Jenny Rae, fixing Grimes with a stare. The boys moved forward. Grimes let her pack fall. We followed, hesitantly.

The boys gathered up our packs and we walked on. One of them muttered something and the other two burst into that horrible, strained laughter that can only be achieved with a teenaged throat. The tunnel was long and low. Darkness was falling fast outside and I felt time moving on. Another day lost, another day further from Beth.

'When it happened I thought we were done for,' she went on. 'All them lights, beautiful really, but they came down so fast. I saw a couple, just small ones I suppose, hitting Ash.'

'What's Ash?' said Grimes.

'Ash Court. One of the towers. Ash, Beech, Oak, Hawthorn and Willow.' She counted them off on her fingers and held them up for us to see. 'I saw the top of Ash explode, then another hit lower down and it started to fall. That's when I ran inside. I thought I was going to be crushed. I thought all the towers would fall on top of us and that we'd all be squashed into the ground. I just held onto my kids and kept my head down, tried not to listen to all the explosions and screams outside. I started praying, got the kids to pray as well, I'd never prayed in my life before! Never even taken them to church! After a few hours, when all the noise had died down, I went outside and the sky was filled with flames and black smoke everywhere. The towers were gone, but somehow ... somehow we were still alright. All this was still here.'

We left the tunnel and came out onto another road with a tall metal fence on the other side. Behind it was a small warehouse, and beyond that was the burned, barren wasteland we had walked across.

'I mean, look at it,' she said. 'Were we friggin' saved or what?'

She laughed. A terrible big, booming, donkey-like laugh, too long and too loud.

She kept laughing as she led us along the road to a short stretch of red-bricked semi-detached houses set back behind small, grassless front gardens. They looked out onto the expanse of empty ground behind the fence. She stopped and turned us towards the view, admiring it like a farmer looking across a well-ploughed field. In the distance, the buildings of the city centre rose out of the mist. Along the edge of the wasteland I could see the crumbling blocks and the new sea lapping against them. We were on the coast, separated from the city by a wide urban moor.

On the other side of the fence, two men in black jackets walked up and down. They held guns. One raised a hand at Jenny and she returned the greeting.

'I don't know what it was like with you,' she said, barely containing her glee, 'but the fires burned for weeks here. We still thought we were dead, that they'd reach us here and we'd burn alive, but they never did. Then there was fighting, a lot of fighting. The city didn't get it too bad, see. It were a mess, lots of people dead, but not as bad as some places from what I've heard, London and that, y'know. It were mostly the suburbs that got it. Everyone who survived – working class, middle class, people from estates and those from the nice parts – we all rushed into the centre to find food. It were chaos for a long time. The police, what was left of them, tried to keep control but there were riots that went on for days. The city centre got more damage from them than the whatdjyamacallits. At first, all the nice folks, middle-class ones like you' – she turned to me – 'they all sided with the police, thought they were going to protect them.' She started laughing again, swung back on her hips. 'Friggin' pigs didn't know what they were doing! All they were doing were protecting themselves. It were chaos. Guns, gas, riot shields, all that nonsense.' She wiped her eye. 'These men and women – the ones you see in suits and high heels, always rushing around dropping their kiddies off at the big schools – they didn't know what to do, running all over the place and trying to hide in burnt-out shops. They weren't used to feeling unprotected, unsafe.

'Couldn't help feeling sorry for them,' she said. She scraped her boot on the side of the pavement, looked at the heel. 'But then a funny thing happened.' She looked up, as if startled by the memory. 'They started coming to us, asking for help, food, water for their kids. Can you believe that? Coming to us?'

More laughter. The more time we wasted listening to her and the closer we got to sunset, the more unsettled I felt. I felt nerves bristling in the others too. I wanted to get away, scale the fence, scramble across the wide, barren plane and get out of the city and on my way. I wanted to run.

When she had stopped laughing, she snorted, coughed, spat and ground the result into the dirt with her heel. Suddenly there was the sound of an engine in the distance and a window at the end of the street turned orange. Grimes spun around.

'Is that . . .' said Grimes. 'Do you have electricity?'

Jenny Rae smirked.

'I heard this story once,' she said, zipping her jacket up and burrowing her hands into her pockets. 'About how the future would turn out. The future back then, you know, not the future now. All the people who know how things work, the people with degrees who can make computers and toasters and that, they'd all live on the hills behind electric fences. Everyone else would live and die in shit.' She turned to us. 'They wouldn't need us any more, you see, wouldn't need our money.'

Another light went on in a house closer to us.

'Funny how things work out, isn't it?' she said. 'Now, who's hungry?' She turned to face Bryce. 'What about you, big lad? What are you for?' She patted his belly twice. 'Balti? Madras? Vindaloo?'

Jenny Rae led us to the end of the street, where we turned left, following the fence. Almost every house had at least one window lit, but halfway along there was a brighter, white light coming from a glass-fronted shop. A queue of people was spilling out of its door and onto the street. Steam and smoke billowed from its windows. I smelled spices and a strange meaty tang on the air.

Bryce almost stumbled. He made a short gasping noise. 'Is that ... is that a takeout?' he said, his voice caught somewhere between anger, hope and joy.

'Aye,' said Jenny Rae, as if he'd asked something ridiculous. 'Where would we be without a curry, I ask you.'

We got closer to the shop and Bryce began walking faster.

'Easy there, fella,' said Harvey under his breath. 'What do you think they're cooking in there?'

'I've never asked that question before,' muttered Bryce, raising his snout to the air like a hound on the scent. He inhaled deeply. 'And I'm not about to start.'

When we reached the front of the shop, the queue was stretching out down the dark street. Cocky, tracksuited teenagers, smoking and hooting and shoving each other in the back, older men and women with pushchairs and beer cans and then, occasionally, a quiet huddle of faces stared out from the line. Dark eyes, pale skin and frightened mouths. Clothes that weren't theirs. They kept their heads down. This was not where they came from.

'Excuse me,' said Jenny Rae as we reached the door. A hole opened up obediently in the queue and she led us up to the shining aluminium counter. I squinted under the bright, fluorescent light, aware that we were being scrutinised by the crowds of people waiting around us, leaning against the tiled walls and the dirty glass behind us. We were only safe here because of the woman we were with.

Behind the counter were two Indian men. One hollered something back to the kitchen behind, noisy with sizzling flesh and clanging metal pans. Another was pushing back a small booklet across the counter to a man next to Jenny.

'No good,' he said, shaking his head. 'You're out till next month.'

The man, in his seventies, thick-set with short, thick white hair and stubble, slowly retrieved the booklet from the counter and slid it inside his thick, black, woollen overcoat. He shuffled around to leave, but Jenny Rae placed a hand on his forearm.

'Give him what he wants, Abdul,' she boomed. 'Just this once.'

The old man looked into Jenny Rae's face.

'Obliged,' he said. 'Thank you, Jenny.'

Abdul shrugged.

'Whatever you say, Jenny,' he said, and shouted the man's order through. He turned to Jenny Rae, scanning us nervously first. 'And what can I get you, madam?'

'Five specials please, Abdul,' said Jenny Rae. 'Gimme a tray of chips and all.'

'No problem,' said Abdul, and then screamed the order back across his shoulder. 'Ten minutes, Jenny.'

We found a place to stand away from the counter while Jenny Rae circulated the shop, talking to the masses that were coming and going. Eyes were on us constantly. Even Bryce avoided them, possibly because of the distraction of the smell of cooking meat as much as anything else. Occasionally a number would be yelled out and one of the waiting hordes would step up to the counter and take their bulging, knotted plastic bag of food.

'This is weird,' breathed Richard, stretching out every word. 'How the hell have they managed to get a takeaway running?'

'I don't care,' said Bryce. I'm eating whatever comes slopping out of those wee foil trays.'

Our order came and Jenny led us out of the takeaway to more mumbled greetings and stares from the queue. She ate her chips as we walked.

'See?' she said. 'We do pretty well here. Electricity, water, food, alcohol, all rationed, of course, but we got quite a good deal in the settlement.'

'Settlement?' said Grimes.

'We had to agree on a rough territory, supplies, that kind of thing,' she said.

'With the police?' I said.

Jenny stopped in her tracks and made a noise in her throat. She stared at me in disbelief, one ketchup-smeared chip halfway to her mouth, then threw back her head.

More laughter. I squirmed as we let it run its course.

'Police?' she said at last, wiping spittle and grease from her chin. 'Police? There is no bloody police. We won!'

'Won?' said Richard.

'Aye, won. The fights, the riots.' She turned her mouth down into a proud snarl. 'We came together,' she said. 'Beat 'em.' She popped the chip into her mouth, turned and continued walking down the street. It was darker nearer the bottom; fewer of the houses had their lights on.

'There were a few of us, you see, from different parts of the city, different estates that had survived. We had what we called a settlement, an agreement. Pretty amicable considering. Everyone got their own territory, their own estates, of course, then bits and bobs around the city where we knew there were supplies, industrial estates, supermarkets, shopping centres that hadn't burned, that kind of thing. Then we got streets and areas of the city itself.'

She turned to us and grinned. Her front two teeth glinted gold in the low light from the houses.

'And you walked onto one of mine.' She raised her eyebrows. 'Lucky for you.'

'And the police,' said Richard. 'Where are they now?'

Jenny gave him a flat look and shrugged. She picked at her molars with her tongue.

'Not a problem any more,' she said. 'Right, here we are.'

She directed a sharp whistle at the fence, now almost hidden in the darkness. We heard a clatter and then footsteps as one of the guards crossed the road towards us. He was tall and broad, head level with Bryce, knew his way around a gym, I guessed. A thick scar travelled the length of his right cheek and met his top lip beneath his nose. He gave us a cold once-over before turning to Jenny.

'Jenny,' he said.

'Guests staying at number seventy-three this evening,' she said. The word "guests" unsettled me even more. I had never felt less like one. 'Keep them company outside, would you?'

'No problem, Jenny,' said the guard. He moved towards the gate of the house we were standing next to.

Jenny strode through it and up to the door, on which she gave three loud knocks. A moment later the door opened and a slim, timid woman in a baggy cardigan looked out from behind it. She looked nervously between us and Jenny.

'Yes?' she said, then 'George?' quietly back across her shoulder. We heard slow footsteps on the stairs behind her.

'Did the boys tell you?' said Jenny Rae, her voice loud and firm.

The woman shook her head. 'No.' A man appeared behind the woman, ashen and concerned. He took off his glasses and let them fall on the string around his neck, peering out at us.

'What's the matter?' he said. He was well spoken, every vowel rounded, every consonant marked. Jenny Rae tutted and rasped in her throat.

'Those boys, I told them, didn't I?' She turned to us, then shook her head and rolled her eyes, smiling. 'I'll murder them one of these days.' She sighed. 'Ah'm sorry, Mrs Angelbeck,' she said, still shaking her head, 'but you have some guests this evening.'

The couple looked us up and down, trying to contain their horror.

'But, b—' the woman began. The man interrupted her with a hand on her wrist.

'It's OK, darling,' he said quickly. 'Of course, Miss Rae. That's no problem, is it? Is it, darling?'

The woman looked up at him worriedly. He seemed to tighten his grip on her arm.

'No,' she said at last. 'No, of course not, no problem at all, er . . . please, come in.' She opened the door wider.

'Ahhhh, thanks, Mrs Angelbeck, that's very good of you,' said Jenny Rae. 'It'll just be for tonight. They can stay in your front room; you don't mind bunking down, do you?' She smiled at us. 'Good,' she said, not waiting for a reply. We stepped into the house, immediately crowding the small hallway and filling it with our own reek and that of the food Bryce was holding. 'Well, then,' said Jenny Rae, turning to leave. 'I'll leave you to it then, oh . . .' She stopped and turned back, holding out her empty chip tray to the woman. 'Put that in your bin, would you?'

The woman stared blankly down at the tray and took it in her trembling hands.

'There's a love,' said Jenny Rae. She turned to the man. 'See you tomorrow, George? Bright and early?'

The man bounced nervously on his toes and offered a small salute. 'Right you are, Miss Rae,' he laughed. 'Bright and early.'

A cold smile slid from Jenny Rae's face as she turned to leave. Richard called after her.

'We need to leave as early as possible.'

'Don't worry,' said Jenny Rae, holding up a hand. 'Someone will come and get you.'

'What about our packs?' he asked.

'I'll see that they're safe,' she answered. 'Enjoy your curry. Get some rest.'

She hooted a laugh out into the cold night, then started off up the street. We stood nervously in the hallway, saying nothing, the stench of curry filling the cold air. The man regarded us, chewing the arm of his spectacle.

'George,' said the woman at last, 'you're hurting me.'

'What?' he said. 'Oh, terribly sorry, darling.' He released her arm and held his hand to his chest, flexing his fingers. He looked back at us.

'My name is George Angelbeck,' he said, offering his hand to us. 'And this is my wife, Susan.'

The woman nodded her head and massaged her arm.

'I'll get you some plates,' she said, walking past us towards a lit room at the end of the hallway. 'Abigail? Can you set the table, please, darling.'

Gull Vindaloo

The Angelbecks' kitchen was long and thin with a small table against one wall. Susan Angelbeck had extended it fully so that it almost filled the floor and provided enough room to sit four people. She lit a candle and placed it in the centre while her daughter, Abigail, a girl who was about to experience what puberty felt like in a post-apocalyptic housing estate where – her manners and posture screamed – she clearly didn't belong, had emptied the cupboards of plates and set them on the table with cutlery. George Angelbeck tucked himself in a corner and watched, sucking the end of his spectacles as everyone found a space. Nobody wanted to take a seat at first and we all stood silently, crammed against cupboards, staring down at the empty table, adrift in social waters which, I'm fairly sure, had never been charted before.

Eventually Bryce broke the stalemate by puffing out a deep, frustrated sigh and grabbing the seat nearest to him. He then went to work on the warm plastic of the takeaway bags and began spreading the foil cartons across the table. Susan offered the remaining seats to us. Grimes and Harvey each took one, Richard and I remained leaning by the sink. George gently pushed his daughter forwards to take the last chair.

Bryce tore the cardboard lid from the last carton and threw it in the remains of the plastic bag with the others. For a moment we all watched the steam rise slowly from the gloopy brown food like smoke from a prehistoric swamp, the candle-light throwing gruesome shadows of the mysterious lumps rising out of the surface.

Once again, Bryce could only stand so much and after a few moments he snatched a bowl and began to spoon dollops of rice and curry into it. When he had filled it he took a fork, hesitating slightly before shovelling a heap of it into his mouth.

We watched him carefully as he chewed, staring straight ahead at the wall. He swallowed with a small shudder, then looked around at the roomful of eyes that were trained on him.

'Not as bad as you think it's going to be, is it?' said George from the corner.

'I've had worse,' said Bryce.

'Abi, darling, take a plate,' said Susan to her daughter.

'I'm not hungry, Mummy,' said the girl. She looked grimly at Bryce as he went to work on his second and third mouthfuls.

'OK, let's go and get ready for bed then. We'll let our … guests … eat in peace.' Susan ushered her daughter out of the kitchen by her shoulders, shooting a look at her husband as she left.

'Night, Daddy,' said the girl.

'Sweet dreams, darling,' said George after them.

We heard them climb the stairs and whisper.

'Do you mind if I …?' said George, pointing at the empty seat.

'Not at all,' said Richard. 'It's your house, after all.'

George sat down and raised an eyebrow at Richard.

'Ah … huh, yes, quite,' he said, spooning some rice into a bowl. 'Our house. Quite.'

'I'm not trying to be rude,' said Harvey. 'But you and your family don't really seem like you belong here.'

George topped his rice with a spoonful of sauce and three slivers of meat.

'Well, we've had to make some adjustments recently, of course,' he said jovially. He sounded as if he was talking about some minor economic downturn rather than the almost-complete destruction of the country. He looked around at us.

'As I'm sure we all have,' he said. He spooned some curry into his mouth. 'Please,' he said, casting his spoon around the table. 'Dig in.'

The wall clock ticked and the candle burned, already halfway down. My legs began to twitch and my foot began to tap. I watched as, one by one, Grimes, Richard and Harvey took a bowl and filled it with the rapidly cooling excuse for food. They moved with painful slowness, as if through mud. Bryce's jaw worked through mouthful after mouthful, the wet squelch of the slurry inside his face seemed to grow louder and louder.

The clock ticked. The candle burned.

'Ed, you should eat,' said Harvey.

'I'm …'

'Huh?' he said. I gritted my teeth.

'I'm not hungry,' I said. Loudly, deliberately.

'Away,' grunted Bryce, his head hanging over the bowl like a pig in a trough. 'Sit yer arse down.'

'I'm alright, really, I'm …'

Grimes slurped something from her lip. 'Sit down, Ed,' she said, not looking up from her bowl.

'Not hungry?' said Harvey. 'We've barely eaten today …'

I slammed a fist on the sink.

'We've barely moved today!' I said, surprised at the sudden thunder in my voice. The room fell silent.

'What are we doing here?' I shouted. 'We've got to get moving! Now!'

George's eyes darted up at me. He pushed back from his chair and took a single long step towards me so that his face was in mine. He was trembling, afraid.

'Keep your voice *down*,' he whispered sharply. He pointed outside. 'There is a guard outside this house. You cannot be heard to say things like that.'

'Why not?' I said. 'What *is* this place anyway?'

'*Quiet!*' he said. 'Quiet.'

There was a knock on the door. George froze, wide-eyed. After a moment he turned and walked from the kitchen.

'George?' came a small voice from upstairs. 'What's happening?'

'Shush, Susan! I'll deal with this.'

'Nice one, Ed,' said Bryce over his shoulder at me.

We heard the door open.

'Hello?' said George. 'How can I help you?'

'Everything alright?' said the guard. 'I heard shouting.'

'Shouting?' said George. 'No, no, just, ah ... laughter, probably, just enjoying the food.'

There was a moment's silence.

'Right,' said the guard. 'Laughter. Any more laughter and I'm calling Jenny, understood?'

'Understood, absolutely,' said George.

The door closed and George walked slowly back into the kitchen. Richard placed his unfinished bowl back on the table.

'Just exactly what is happening here, George? And who is that woman?' he said.

George shook his head, looking frantically around the floor of the kitchen. 'Jenny Rae is a ... a fine woman,' he struggled. 'She's built a strong community, given us homes, protection, work, food ... we ... we really owe her our lives.' He glanced up at Richard and then looked away.

'You can sleep in the lounge,' he said. 'I'm going to bed.'

He left the room. We heard his dull footsteps on the stairs and then the squeak and click of a door closing. Bryce tossed the last empty tray of mystery vindaloo on the pile. We sat and watched the candle burn to its end.

I woke in the night to voices above me. It was pitch black and the distant drone of the generator had stopped. No electricity. No light. No heat. Frozen air and darkness. I was curled up uncomfortably in an armchair, the side of my head resting on an ancient, hard cushion. Everyone else was asleep on the other sofas and chairs that had been crammed into the Angelbecks' small front room.

I sat up so that both ears were free, one lobe peeling slowly back from the flesh beneath it. The voices were coming from upstairs; whispers, a hushed argument. Even in the frosted quiet I could not make out the words, just Susan Angelbeck's high, frantic twitterings steadied by her husband's calm rumble.

Then I heard a word. Then another. Then there was silence and a door closed. I got up and walked over to the window, pulling back the net curtains. I could just make out the shape of the guard outside the house. A puff of smoke billowed from his mouth and disappeared up into the night. I let the curtain fall back and sat back in the chair.

When I woke again it was still dark. Richard was up and dressed.

'It's almost dawn,' he said.

By the time we were all awake and ready, we heard footsteps on the stairs and noises from the kitchen. We went through and found George Angelbeck sitting at the table, rubbing his brow over a cup of black tea. He saw us and looked up, smiled.

'Good morning,' he said. 'There's tea in the pot.'

'When will Jenny call?' I asked.

George gave a little laugh. 'Miss Rae is usually very prompt with her calls. I'm sure she'll be here soon. Please, have some tea while you wait, sit down.'

I remained on my feet, leaning by the sink. Harvey passed me a cup of warm, oily tea which I drank in two gulps. Susan Angelbeck arrived in the kitchen with her daughter, who was dressed in a grey school uniform.

'Good morning, dear,' said George. He stood up, kissed his wife and laid a hand on his daughter's shoulder. 'Right, must be off,' he said. He drained his tea and placed the cup in the sink, then took a coat from the hook and opened the back door. 'See you later.'

'I expect we'll be gone before you're back,' said Richard. 'So, thank you.'

George paused and looked back nervously at his wife.

'Don't mention it,' he said. His cheek twitched once. 'My pleasure. Goodbye.'

'Get some breakfast, darling,' said Mrs Angelbeck when her husband had closed the door. 'There's a good girl.'

'I'm not hungry,' said the girl, looking down at her scuffed, plastic shoes.

'Right,' breathed Mrs Angelbeck. I felt a pain in my cheeks watching her smile stretched permanently across her mouth. 'Well, let's be off to school then.' She took two coats from the line of hooks on the wall by the door, putting one on her daughter and holding the other in a tight fist. She turned to us. 'I'll see you in a little while,' she said.

They left through the back door and I heard her brisk, clipped footsteps disappear up the path outside. We drank more tea. Bryce had started to look through the cupboards for something to eat when the front doorbell rang.

'Let's get our lift,' I said. I walked along the corridor and opened the door. Jenny Rae smiled thinly at me.

'Good morning,' she said. She crumpled her face and squinted her eyes awkwardly. 'Bad news, I'm afraid. Truck's broken down, won't start.'

'Not to worry,' I said. 'Thanks all the same, we'll be on our way now. If we could just have our packs?'

Jenny Rae held a strong, podgy hand against my shoulder, stopping me from getting down onto the path. I eyed the guard still standing at the gate.

'Whoa, whoa, easy there,' said Jenny Rae. She smirked and cocked an eyebrow. 'Didn't say it couldn't be fixed, did I? My boys are working on it, should be good to go by noon. You stay here, have some breakfast. Then we'll make sure you get on your way.' She gave a satisfied nod and turned to leave.

'Our packs,' I called after her.

'I'll get someone to send them over,' she shouted, then suddenly stopped and turned back. 'Oh, and, er, feel free to have a wander if you like. But keep to this side of the square for the time being. For you own protection, you understand.' She leaned in. 'Folk here have had a hard time and they sometimes find it difficult dealing with strangers. They might not understand that you're our guests, see. They might get the wrong idea.'

She gave us each a concerned look. Then she smiled and left, exchanging a look with the guard as she passed him at the gate. Just then we heard the back door open. We walked back to the kitchen, where Susan was depositing her keys on the table and removing her coat.

'Was that her?' she said, without looking up.

'Yes,' said Grimes. 'What's going on, Mrs Angelbeck? Where did your husband go this morning?'

'George?' she fluttered, with a confused smile. 'Why, George has gone to work, of course.' Her face was pale and empty as she navigated her way past us, avoiding our eyes, and hung up her coat. 'Now, if you'll excuse me, I have some things to do upstairs. Please help yourself to tea.'

Susan Angelbeck left the kitchen and went upstairs. We looked between each other.

'This is balls,' said Bryce at last. 'Let's take a walk.'

The guard let us past in that way big men do when they're *letting* you past – chin raised, eyes looking down from their elevated position, a thin sneer creeping onto the mouth.

'This side of the square,' he droned after us, echoing Jenny Rae's orders. We walked up the street, keeping close. It was still early and not many people were about, although I could feel eyes all around us. There was the occasional blur of movement from an upstairs window, the odd flit of curtain. Guards stood at regular intervals along the wire fence to our left. Each one stood or turned towards us as we passed, tracking us until we had moved into the territory of the next.

'Balls,' Bryce repeated to himself as he walked ahead, hands thrust in his pockets and hunching his coat around him. 'Balls, balls, balls.'

It began to drizzle. By the time we had found our way back to the tunnel that led into the main square it was raining heavily. We stopped and sheltered in the overhang, leaning against the wall and looking into the circle of dull red houses with their slate roofs, ragged gardens and broken fences. The tall wooden stake still stood in the centre like some ancient maypole, its ribbons long since lost to the wind.

'What do you think that pole's for?' I asked.

Suddenly a door in the tunnel behind us opened and a woman walked out with her son. He was in school uniform as well, holding a pile of books to his chest. They stopped when they saw us, then the woman ushered her son through and out into the rain without a word. We watched them cross the wet square, the woman protecting her son's head from the rain with one side of her cardigan until they had darted down the tunnel opposite.

'They have a school then,' said Grimes. 'That's encouraging.'

'That depends on what they're teaching them,' said Richard.

Grimes frowned fiercely and looked up at him. 'What's that supposed to mean?'

Richard looked taken aback. He stammered and blinked. 'It means what it means,' he said at last. 'You think they're sticking to a syllabus? Putting them through exams? Getting a good national average?' He gave a puff of derision and walked closer to the tunnel entrance, folding his arms. 'Most of these people never went to school in the first place. Why would they start going now?'

Grimes narrowed her eyes. She walked up behind Richard and cocked her head at him. '*These people?*' she said. Grimes generally had quite a soft accent, definitely Scottish but hard to place when she spoke normally. Now, though, the tight vowels and hard, blunt bite of every consonant told you everything you needed to know. The girl was from Glasgow. 'And what would you know about *these people*?'

Richard glanced back and huffed again. 'You know what I mean,' he said. 'The kids probably knew more about how to cheat the benefits system than they did about algebra or grammar.'

Grimes's frown went up a notch. Her teeth were bared. 'Oh, aye, they're all benefits cheats, scum of the earth, wastes of space, criminals the lot of them. Not fit for society. Not worth saving.' Her lip trembled a little as she glared up at him. 'Not a wee girl trying to do her homework in the toilet because her brother's using her bedroom to deal drugs, or walking to school and passing her dad lying drunk and asleep by the bins.'

Richard glanced down awkwardly at her. 'Not saying there aren't exceptions, of course, just—'

'Not like the nice middle-class kids, eh?' Grimes pressed on. 'Not like *your* people.'

'I'm not saying that,' said Richard. 'I'm just—'

'And *you*,' spat Grimes, jabbing a finger at him. 'What about *you*? What were you doing before this happened? What paid for your house on the hill? What were you doing that was such a big help to society? Insurance? Oil? Banking?'

Richard gave the barest of flinches.

'Banking then,' said Grimes. 'I rest my case.'

'Yes,' said Richard, turning to face her. 'Yes, I made my money. I made my money for me and my family, and I bloody *worked* for it. That's what I did, *work. Hard bloody work*. Something most of these people don't understand.' He threw a hand out to the empty square. 'I deserved what I got because I put the effort in. Why the hell should I feel guilty for that?'

Grimes fixed his glare defiantly. 'There are people who work harder than you have ever worked and don't get a fraction of what they deserve. Believe me, I know. And people who hardly work at all and get more than you ever did too, I'd bet.' She turned her back to him and leaned against the wall. 'It's got nothing to do with work.'

'Who are you?' said a quiet voice behind us. We turned to see a boy standing at the other end of the tunnel. He was small, maybe seven or eight, wearing oversized jeans rolled up at the ankles and a dirty, red anorak. His hair was a tousled mop of blond that hung over his eyes.

'Who are you?' challenged Richard, still riled from Grimes's attack. The boy slunk back a little and put his hands in his pockets. 'My name's Brian,' he said.

'Shouldn't you be at *school*,' said Richard, glancing snidely down at Grimes to make sure he had made his point.

'Little school's on Tuesdays, Thursdays and Saturdays. Big school's on Mondays, Wednesdays and Fridays,' said the boy, as if reciting from a rulebook. ''s Wednesday today,' he sniffed. Grimes countered Richard with a similar look, brushing off his attack and stepping back into the tunnel.

'Hello, Brian,' she said, returning to her softer voice. 'I'm Laura. Where do you live?'

'Are you soldiers?' said the boy, looking up and down at Grimes's uniform, then with confusion at the rest of us. Grimes smiled.

'I am,' she said, then folded her arms and mouthed '*but they're not*' behind a palm.

A shy grin grew on the boy's face. '*Not even the big one?*' he whispered back.

Grimes gave her best incredulous look and shook her head. 'Especially not him,' she said.

The boy looked between us for a while. Then the grin left his face a little. 'Does Jenny know you're here?' he said.

'Yes,' said Grimes. She seemed to be sizing the boy up. 'Jenny knows we're here. What do you think of Jenny? Do you like her?'

The boy frowned and looked away from Grimes as if she had taken a step closer to a line he wasn't comfortable with her crossing. Grimes seemed to sense this and backtracked.

'We were just going for a walk,' she said. 'Would you like to show us around?'

The boy brightened. 'Aye, alright,' he said.

The rain had returned to drizzle and Brian led us around the square. He pointed out houses of other people that he knew, told us about the takeaway and showed us the school, which looked like it had once been a dilapidated nursery. We let him walk ahead, chattering, kicking stones and rattling his fingers along fences.

'Jenny said there was a car here,' said Grimes, in a break between things he found interesting.

'Car?' said the boy. 'There's a garage where there's cars. Do you want to see it?'

'Yes, please,' said Grimes. The boy gave a skip and began to run, leading us down a side street, along a thin alley and out onto a flat area of stony ground. The boy stopped. Across the clearing was another section of fence; the same fence that we now realised surrounded the entire estate. At one end was a gate. Two armed guards stood outside it, looking into the mist. At the other end was a strip of three flat-bricked buildings with metal shutters. One of them was open and we could see a few men in overalls milling around inside by the yellow glow of a work light. There was a tinny crackle of music beneath their voices. The boy pointed. 'There,' he said. 'That's the garage. That's where they fix cars.'

'Sit on their arses more like,' said Bryce. 'I'm gonnae say hello.' He made to step out again, but Grimes reached for him and he stopped. All it took was a touch from her now. He was hers completely.

'We don't want to push it,' said Grimes. 'Let's get back to the Angelbecks' and wait. Is it this way, Brian?'

'Angelbecks'?' said the young boy, leading us back down the alley. He looked back over his shoulder. 'That's where Abi lives. Can I come?'

The boy suddenly bounced from the wide belly of Jenny Rae, who had appeared at the end of the alley flanked by two guards. He gasped, staggered back and stared up at her in shock. She lunged forward and grabbed him by both arms, steadying him and fixing him with her cold eyes. Then she turned to look at us.

'Thought I told you to stay on the other side of the square,' she said.

'It's not his fault,' said Grimes. 'He didn't know. Let him go.'

Jenny Rae turned back to the terrified child. 'What have I told you about strangers, Brian? Eh?' she said. The boy wriggled helplessly in her grip. 'Eh?' she repeated, louder. Then she raised a hand and slapped him hard on the head. He fell to the ground in silence, clutching his ear.

There was a vacuum of shock in which nobody moved or spoke. I wavered on my feet as I let the last few seconds sink in. Then Grimes cried out in protest and leaped forwards to help the boy. I took a breath and followed.

'Get your hands off him,' said Jenny Rae.

Grimes ignored her, already on the ground whispering quietly to the wounded child. I stopped as one of the guards nudged the barrel of his rifle against my chest, pushing me back in line.

'Now,' said Jenny Rae. She motioned to the other guard, who stepped forward and pulled Grimes away. She fell back into Bryce's arms and raised her arms as the guard trained his gun warily in her direction.

'Get up,' spat Jenny Rae. Brian struggled silently for a few seconds, still holding his head, slipping in the dirt. 'Get up, boy!' She yanked him to his feet and hurled him out behind her into the square. 'And go home!' she shouted after him as he ran, head down, his legs spinning beneath him. Jenny Rae turned back to us with her hands on her hips.

'What did you do that for?' screamed Grimes. 'He's only a boy, he didn't do anything wrong!'

'Give us our packs,' said Bryce. 'Then open that gate and let us out.'

The first guard took another step towards Bryce and Grimes. The second one joined him, swinging his gun slowly between the rest of us. Jenny Rae raised a hand to stop them. Bryce growled. 'Fine,' he said, 'keep the packs. Let's get out of here.' He turned towards the gate, still holding Grimes. Two more guards appeared at the opposite end and raised their guns.

'They *will* shoot,' said Jenny Rae. Bryce stopped and looked down at his feet, breathing in and out through his nose like a cornered bull.

'Just let us go,' I said. 'We're not here to cause trouble.'

Jenny Rae narrowed her eyes and took a step towards me.

'I think it's best if you all stay inside for the time being,' she said. 'Safer for everyone, I'd say.'

We were escorted back to the Angelbecks' house, where another guard was made to join the one already stationed at their gate. 'I'll send word when the truck's fixed,' Jenny Rae said, but her sly smile was long gone as she marched away from the house.

We spent the rest of the day drinking tea in the Angelbecks' kitchen. None of us particularly wanted to talk. Eventually I went back into the lounge and closed my eyes, reasoning that at if we weren't moving, at least I could rest. I woke from somewhere north of sleep in a darker room. Bryce was lying against the arms of the sofa, his eyes shut and his thick arms coiled like rigging around his chest. Richard was standing at the window, looking pensively through the curtain at the guards. I walked through to the kitchen and found Grimes and Abigail looking through a book at the table. Harvey was watching them from a chair in the corner. Susan Angelbeck was standing in the small space before the stove, pulling blackened pans and cheap utensils from cupboards.

'What time is it?' I said. Grimes looked up.

'Late afternoon,' she replied.

'What? And no word about the truck?' I said.

Grimes shook her head.

'Laura's helping me with my homework,' said Abigail.

I nodded, furious with myself for having slept for so long. We had almost lost another day.

There were some footsteps on the stairs and George Angelbeck appeared at the kitchen door.

'Good evening,' he said.

'George, we need to go,' I said. 'Now.'

'I agree.' I turned to see Richard standing in the door behind George. 'Those guards have been told to keep us inside. I don't believe Jenny Rae has any intention of letting us go. Mr Angelbeck, please, can you tell us what is happening here? Why are you living here? What do you do for that woman? Why would she want to keep us here?'

Mrs Angelbeck clattered a pan loudly on the stove.

'Now, now,' said George. 'You're jumping to conclusions. I'm sure Miss Rae will get your lift ready before long. It's not easy you know, fixing cars, not any more. It's not as if they can just order parts willy-nilly.' He laughed and held up a placatory palm. 'Things take a bit longer than they're used to, I'm sure you understand. Just calm down and I'm sure you'll be out of here before you know it. And in the meantime, relax, take a rest, put your feet up.'

'I don't want to rest,' I snapped. 'I want to get moving, we should have been past Birmingham by now. We're running out of fucking time!'

I thumped my fist pathetically on the table, holding back at the last minute as I caught Abigail's eye. Her pens bounced and rattled against the plastic.

'Please,' said George. 'Calm down.'

'I will not fucking calm down!' I shouted. 'We're prisoners, can't you see?' I looked at Abigail again. 'Sorry,' I added, crossing my arms.

'Mr Angelbeck,' said Grimes. 'What exactly are you doing for Jenny Rae?'

There was another loud clang from the stove.

'I, er . . .' began George. 'Well, I just, er, you know . . .'

'Oh, for heaven's sake, just tell them, George!' Susan Angelbeck swung around and stared wild-eyed at her husband. In one hand she brandished a spatula. 'Tell them!'

George Angelbeck stopped dithering and looked back at his wife. His throat rippled in a gulp. Then he took a long, quivering sigh and sat down.

'OK,' he said. He fished around in his shirt pocket and pulled out a grey cloth, took off his glasses and began to polish them. 'OK.' He took another sigh.

'I worked as a consultant to chemical companies before,' he said. 'Used to be a plastics expert – still *am* a plastics expert. When we found our way here, to this . . . place . . . she, Jenny Rae, I mean, asked everyone what they could do, you know, what they could do to help.'

He replaced his glasses and sat back in his chair. 'She was looking for people to fix plumbing, rig up systems to collect water, get a generator going, doctors, mechanics, engineers … military.' His voice tailed off and he stared into the space just above the table. Then he looked suddenly up at his wife as if something had just occurred to him. 'Darling, do you mind if I …?' He pulled out a packet of cigarettes and looked up at his wife. She looked away and he lit one, placing the pack on the table.

'Oh, please, help yourself,' he said. We shook our heads as he blew a trembling puff of smoke into the room. 'Right, right, anyway, everyone who could add something to the mix was allowed to stay, taking on the houses that had been left behind by those in the estate who hadn't survived. If you couldn't help, you had to leave and find somewhere else.' He looked out of the window towards the fence, then to Abigail. He smiled. 'The city was still dangerous then, as it is now, especially for children. Most people had to take their chances on the wasteland.'

I remembered the family I had seen as we had crossed from the city, huddled round fires, barely surviving.

'Which put us in a pickle.' He looked around at us. 'Not much call for a plastics expert when running water's your number-one concern, is there? So, I lied. Told them I was an explosives expert. I don't really know why I chose that particular trade, probably because I knew a bit about it when I was younger. I used to be into military history see, read quite a few books about bombs and what have you. With my background in chemistry, I thought that maybe I could just … wing it, you know?' He thumbed the table and looked up for some acknowledgement, then stubbed his cigarette out and ran a hand through his hair. 'It worked. She let us stay, gave us this house. Now I have a job. I work for her. She pays us in food, electricity, protection, education for Abi, everything you want from a society.'

'Everything apart from your freedom,' said Bryce, who had appeared at the door. 'Not exactly free to leave I'd bet, not now you're *on the team*.'

'Explosives?' said Grimes. 'What kind of explosives? What are you doing for her?'

George sighed again and closed his eyes.

'Tell them, George,' said Susan Angelbeck. 'Tell them what you have to do.'

George's face fell. He leaned forward on the table.

'Landmines,' he said at last. 'I'm helping her to build landmines.'

'What?' said Harvey. 'Bloody hell, mate, what does she want with landmines?'

'The settlements, did she tell you about them? After the riots stopped?' said George. We nodded. 'Well, things weren't quite as amicable as Jenny might have made out. Some of the other estates weren't as happy with their lot as the rest. There are still fights over territory, still ambushes at night. We're expecting one any day soon. Jenny wants to protect the estate by laying mines beyond the fence.'

'What's wrong with those big bastards with guns out there?' said Bryce. 'Why can't she just shoot anyone who tries to get in?'

'Her reasoning is that landmines send a clearer message. It tells them that we're organised. Dangerous.'

'We?' said Richard. 'You really are part of the team, aren't you, George?'

He looked around the room at our stunned faces, landing on his wife's. 'I don't want to do this, don't you see? I have no choice. She's a very, very persuasive woman. Each of you would do the same.'

'Would we?' said Richard. 'What if one of those people out there steps on one of your little science projects? A mother? A child?'

'They know not to come too near,' said George flatly.

'You hope they know,' said Richard. 'You hope.'

George stood up and puffed out his chest, turning on Richard. He jabbed a finger in his face. 'Now you listen to me. I'm doing the best for my family under impossible circumstances. What would you do? Take the moral high ground? Put your wife and daughter in danger? Everything's changed, don't you see? We all have to do things now that we don't want to do. I used to do bloody crosswords on Sunday mornings. I used to have milk in my tea. I used to build model airplanes and listen to Classic FM and take my bloody dog for walks. I didn't think I'd end up building landmines in the arse end of the world for someone who should be on fucking *Coronation Street*, did I?'

He shrank back from Richard and leaned against the kitchen work surface.

'Didn't think I was capable of it,' he said, lighting another cigarette. 'Turns out you don't have a clue what you're capable of. Not a clue.'

We sat in silence for a while. The smoke from George's cigarette had formed a thin cloud above the table. Susan stood with her arms braced against the two surfaces at either side of the cooker, as if they might close in on her if she let them go.

'Where do you get the materials to make landmines?' said Grimes.

'The city,' he said. 'Mostly industrial estates.'

'Is that where you were today?' she said.

'Yes,' he said. 'We drove in and found some cabling in an office today.'

Bryce bristled and folded his arms. 'I knew it,' he said.

'*Drove?*' said Grimes.

George seemed unfazed by his slip.

'Yes, *drove*,' he said. 'There is no broken car. We have four trucks and they all work perfectly.' He stubbed out his cigarette. 'I'm afraid you're right. Jenny Rae has no intention of letting extra muscle go when we're facing an ambush from a rival estate.'

Bryce moved further into the crowded room. 'Well, I'm no' fighting for her,' said Bryce. 'Put a gun in my hands and I'll shoot her.'

'She'll find a way of changing your mind,' said George wearily. 'She always does. Look, I'm sorry this is the way things are, but there's nothing I can do about it.'

'There has to be something you can do to help us,' said Grimes. 'A way through the fence? Something about the guards? Their shift patterns?'

'There's nothing I can tell you. And if there was, I'm sorry but I wouldn't risk my family's safety by sharing it with you. Now if you'll excuse me I'm going to get an early night.'

'George,' said Susan. 'What about dinner?'

'I'm not hungry, you eat my portion.'

George picked up his cigarettes from the table and shuffled to the kitchen door. He stopped when he reached Bryce and stared into his chest until he moved. Then he trudged out of the kitchen and up the stairs. Susan returned to her stove and soon after served us a soup that had nothing to do with any kind of meat or vegetable. We ate it silently and then Susan went upstairs too, taking her daughter with her, leaving us alone in the kitchen again.

Dark

None of us felt like sleep. We stayed in the candlelit kitchen and talked in hushed voices about various ways we might escape. Bryce wanted to wait it out, to play along until whatever ambush Jenny Rae was expecting to come our way, then to break out in the confusion. But we had no idea how long that would mean staying. We were already behind schedule and the distance we still had to travel seemed more insurmountable by the minute. Harvey wanted to fake a heart attack, thinking that he would be taken to a doctor and that we might be able to escape in the confusion. He suggested that his own escape wasn't necessary, that he would stay if he had to. None of us was comfortable with that.

Richard's idea was to ambush the guards. We would arm ourselves with whatever we could find in the kitchen and then make enough noise to draw them into the house, overpowering them and stealing their guns so that we could shoot our way past the guards at the fence. It seemed unlikely to work, but it was the best we could come up with. We were discussing the details when we heard a creak on the stair.

We stopped talking and turned to the kitchen door. There were some soft footsteps in the hall and then Abigail appeared at the door. Her face glowed orange in the small candle she was holding, the light flickering across her skin and finding hollow cheeks to cast shadows in where there should have been puppy fat. I opened my mouth to speak, but she held a finger to her lips.

'My bedroom window opens onto a ledge at the back,' she said. Her voice was steady and open, like every child's when carefully stating facts. 'If you walk along the ledge, it leads you onto the roof of a tunnel. If you follow that roof it will lead you down onto an alley that takes you to the lowest part of the fence. It's broken. If you're lucky, you might be able to avoid the guards.'

She looked around at us. 'Follow me,' she whispered. 'And be quiet.'

We followed her up the stairs, keeping our eyes on the small circle of light hovering above us. When we reached the landing she pointed at an open door into a small dark room. She followed us in, holding the candle near to the window while we opened it. Grimes started to say goodbye, but Abigail's finger once again touched her lips.

Getting through the small window was difficult, especially for Bryce, who fell out last with a loud thump onto the bitumen surface below. He grabbed his ankle and held his head down between his legs, stifling the pain. I helped him to his feet and we followed the others down onto the tunnel.

'Was that the same ankle?' I whispered. 'Can you walk?'

'Aye,' he said. 'Shut up.' He shook off my arm and reached into his pocket. I heard a chink as he pulled out a miniature. He tore off the cap and poured it down his throat.

Richard turned back.

'Can't you keep sober for one fucking second?' he snarled.

'Quiet!' hissed Grimes. 'The guards will hear you!'

Bryce raised his middle finger at Richard and put the empty bottle back in his pocket. I looked up at the window and saw

Abigail's curtain fall back into place. I raised a hand to the window, seeing nothing behind the glass.

We walked on down the roof, almost blind in the near-complete dark. The only light came from the distant fires burning on the wasteland and whatever trickles of moon had made it through the clouds.

'Now what?' said Richard when we reached the end. We heard a noise, footsteps rounding the corner and coming to a stop beyond a fence. A beam of torchlight appeared on the ground and scanned the road inside.

'Down!' said Grimes. We fell to the rooftop, hiding behind the red-bricked lip just as the beam swept harmlessly over the top of us. It returned, hovered around us, then swooped away and blinked out. The footsteps began again and disappeared as the guard continued his patrol.

'That was too close,' I said. I moved to get up but Grimes grabbed my arm and pulled me back.

'Wait,' she said. 'Stay down.'

I peered over the rim of the wall. Footsteps sounded again, this time two sets. They stopped and two flashlight beams span around the walls of the houses beneath us. One blinded my eyes and I ducked my head down.

'Shit,' I said. 'I think they saw me.'

I heard a guard's voice. A sentence ending in 'dogs'.

'Christ,' said Richard. 'Back. Back the way we came. Keep down.'

We began crawling along the roof on our elbows.

'Get your face out of my arse,' said Bryce to Richard.

'Believe me, it doesn't want to be there,' said Richard.

'Quiet!' said Grimes.

'Move faster, you fat ...'

We heard barking from the fence, a rattling metal noise and then a scrabbling in the dirt.

'Oh, shit,' said Richard. 'Shit shit shit.'

The sound of dogs grew louder, snorts, pants and two deep and angry barks, the business-like clattering of paws on tarmac, then on brick as the barks stopped and aimed themselves directly up the wall beneath us.

Here here here here here they're here.

I saw beams on the wall behind us.

'Stand up,' said one of the guards below. 'Hands above your heads.'

We stood up slowly, blinded by the beams in our faces.

'Jones,' said one of the guards. 'Go and wake Jenny.'

We stood for minutes under the glare of the second guard's torchlight. Eventually we heard footsteps and voices and then the hideous, unmistakable caterwaul of Jenny Rae's laugh. She stopped beneath us, though we could not see her. She sighed the sigh of a patient headmistress holding an empty can of spray paint.

'Right, then,' she said. 'What's to be done with you lot, eh?'

'Just let us go,' said Richard. 'We just want to leave and be on our way.'

'Yeah ... yeah ...' she said distractedly, a disembodied voice in the dark. I heard a foot tapping. 'Yeah ... what time is it?'

'Just after midnight,' replied the guard.

'Right, right,' said Jenny Rae. More foot tapping. 'Mark, get some men and bring two trucks to the square. Jones, you come with me and this lot. Bind 'em first.'

They tied our hands behind our backs and marched us along the road, blinded by torchlight, the smell and sound of large dogs close by. We reached what sounded like a gate and they led us through, then up an alley. Then I saw where we were. In a few more steps we were stood behind Jenny Rae as she hammered on the Angelbecks' front door.

'Mr Angelbeck,' she shouted. 'Mr Angelbeck, I know you're in there. Come down, please.'

The door opened and George squinted out at us, fumbling with his glasses.

'What's the matter?' he said 'What's going on? What are you—'

'Want to explain this, George?' said Jenny Rae. 'Want to explain how five people got past my guards?'

George Angelbeck shone with horror in the white torchlight. He looked between us and Jenny Rae. Susan appeared in the darkness behind him. I saw Abigail's face by her mother's side. She looked back at me, her brow already creasing in panic.

'George?' said Susan. 'What? Oh …'

'I'm waiting, George,' said Jenny Rae. 'How did these people get out? Eh? I put two guards on the front door, two on the back. None of them saw a thing. What happened? Tunnel out, did they? Fly off the roof? Unless …'

It took a split second for Susan Angelbeck to follow Jenny Rae's eyes down to her daughter, perform a horrifying mental backflip and then step forward.

'It was me,' Susan said. 'I let them out onto the back roof. From Abigail's room, while she was in the toilet. It was me, I did it.'

She lay a firm, gentle hand on her daughter's shoulder and stared resolutely down at Jenny Rae. George was still stuttering in confusion.

'Really,' said Jenny Rae, meeting the woman's eyes. 'Is that so?' She tapped her foot and puffed. 'Fair enough, have it your way. Come with me.' Jenny Rae lunged forward and grabbed Susan by the arm, yanking her out onto the path. Susan stumbled down the steps and shrieked.

'George! Oh, heavens! George! Help me!'

Jenny Rae met my eyes as she hauled Susan past us, her dressing gown open and billowing behind her. 'Follow me,' she said. 'I want to show you something.' The guards pushed at us to follow up the street.

'Mummy!' cried Abigail. 'Daddy! Stop them!'

'What the—? Susan!' George seemed to snap out of his confusion and ran after us. 'Good God, get your hands off my wife!'

One of the guards grabbed him by the arm. Another led Abigail, now wailing and sobbing, onto the pavement.

'It's OK, darling!' cried Susan from up the street. 'Mummy's OK! Don't cry!'

'Wake up!' bellowed Jenny Rae as we past the houses. 'Everybody up!'

Then that laugh, that horrible laugh again. The guards swept their torches around the windows and doors. People were emerging from their houses now, blinking in the flicks of light. We reached the tunnel and walked through it into the square. Two trucks were parked with their engines running, their headlights illuminating the pole in the centre.

'Take that off her. Tie her to it,' said Jenny Rae. 'Face forward.'

Susan whooped in terror as two of the guards pulled her dressing gown from her, then dragged her across the road and began lashing her to the stake with her arms high above her head. Jenny Rae walked to one of the trucks, yelling around the square.

'Wake up!'

'What the hell are you doing?' said Richard.

'Shut up and watch,' said a guard. He smashed Richard in the face with the butt of his rifle, knocking him to his knees. Bryce struggled forwards to help him. A dog growled and another guard knocked Bryce down with his own gun so that he was sprawled with his face on the stone. The guard slammed a boot against his neck.

'Watch!'

Grimes, Harvey and I were nudged forwards to the edge of the pavement. Doors were opening, people coming out of their houses. A crowd formed around the perimeter of the square. Susan hung, blinking, from the pole with her feet trailing on the ground. She searched the crowd and found us. I heard Abigail sobbing behind me. A puzzled smile flickered across Susan's face as she saw her daughter.

'No!' shouted George, struggling in the guard's grip. 'Christ, no! Susan! Let her go, you abominable woman!' I heard another crack and George began to cough.

Jenny Rae searched in the back of one of the trucks and marched back to the pole.

'This is what happens when you betray me!' she shouted, brandishing a plank to the crowd. 'When you go behind my back!' The mumbling crowd became quiet as Jenny Rae nodded around the square, her fierce jaw jutting out in a snarl. 'This is what happens.' She turned her face down to Susan Angelbeck's trembling cotton-clad back. 'This is what happens.'

'God, no,' croaked George Angelbeck, above his daughter's crying.

Jenny Rae swung the plank high above her head and brought it down against Susan's backside. Susan's face crumpled in silent pain. Her eyes bulged in horror and she let out a terrible squeal. The plank came down again, harder this time, and Susan screamed as the full agony of the blow hit the back of her thighs. Then again, and again, and again. Each impact caused a louder scream until Susan became silent, squeaking, writhing against the post, scrabbling pathetically in the dirt with her feet, her body trying in vain to escape each blow.

'Funny how things turn out, isn't it?' shouted Jenny Rae across at us.

'Funny.' Another wallop. 'How.' And another. 'Things.' And another. 'Turn.' Another. 'Out.' Another ...

I can't tell you exactly what happened next. I was aware of Bryce struggling under the guard's boot, of Richard holding his head, of Grimes gritting her teeth and Harvey shaking his head at the ground. Susan's feet were beginning to stop moving quite so desperately and there were murmurs of dissent from the crowd. The blows stopped for a second as Jenny Rae faced the quiet protests. Her face was gleeful and fierce, like a hound interrupted from its feeding. I felt a twitch in my gut, a wave of sickness, a desire to move. Then she grimaced, took a step back and brought the wood down with a sickening crack on Susan's still back. And I ran. I ran towards her, wailing, dizzy with rage. Halfway across the road to the pole Jenny Rae spotted me and glanced over my shoulder. Soon after I felt an explosion of pain in my temple. I don't remember hitting the ground.

Barely conscious. I heard her voice. 'Check his ropes.'

Some struggling and grunts from the middle of the room.

'Get off me, man,' said another voice. Male.

'Secure.' A guard.

'Go on then,' said Jenny Rae. 'Let's get going.'

Oblivion.

I met consciousness again, this time feeling that I had just made an endless climb through thick fog and found myself on a summit I had no desire to be on. It was completely dark, completely still, completely silent. The chair was hard, the ropes cut my wrists and ankles. The blindfold was tight around my eyes and the fabric smelled of other people. The air was still freezing. I coughed. Pain flooded my head.

'Who's there?' said a deep voice opposite me.

'Bryce?' I said.

'No,' said the voice. 'Oh, fuck.' I could hear a smile stretching behind the words. 'It's you.'

Then, once again, oblivion.

The dark does strange things to you. When you're blind, your other senses fill in the gaps. Even in unconsciousness, I felt I had been aware of the others, the noises they made as they struggled against their new bindings, wriggling in their seats, testing the tension on the ropes cutting their skin, trying to crane their necks to rub their blindfolds away with their shoulders. The sounds turned into pictures – Grimes's serious, small mouth, Bryce's cheeks taut and snarling, Richard's crowish frown, Harvey's perpetual smile even as he fought to free himself.

When I came to again, I knew they were there in the room with me, awake. And somebody else too.

'It really is you, isn't it?' said the voice again.

The noises stopped. The faces froze.

'Henderson,' I said.

A puff of air and a gap of silence opening up like a smile told me I was right. The air bristled around me. Different noises now, renewed frustration, now focused on the sixth chair in the room. I swear I remember Grimes's face, though I couldn't see it. I remember it pinching into a point of rage, eyes straining to bulge against her blindfold, lips twisted like a tiny fist.

She was next to me, her breathing becoming faster and deeper, trembling with anger.

'You,' breathed Bryce. 'I'm going to kill you.'

Henderson was definitely grinning. I can't say how I knew; perhaps it was the noises his mouth was making, although he wasn't yet speaking.

'You deserted us,' I said. 'Where's Yuill?'

Another puff of air, still smiling. Now he spoke, the words moving slowly from left to right as he shook his head.

'How the fuck did you make it this far?' he said.

Grimes was still trembling next to me, exhaling fast, furious breaths and shaking her limbs so much I felt they might break. Her chair legs scraped and rattled against the concrete. Bryce was still yelling curses across the room, running out of ways to insult the man who had left us for dead.

'You must have got a lift, right?' said Henderson calmly. He was talking to me, ignoring the noise of abuse and rage building around the room 'You had to, yeah? No fucking way you got here without one. Ahhh, man, was it a chopper? Did one of them choppers stop? Don't tell me, don't tell me, don't tell me … it crashed, right?'

He began laughing, deep and barrel-like. The noise of it seemed to rise up, as if his head was thrown back. Grimes now sounded like an exorcism in full flow.

'Where's Yuill?' said Richard. 'What is going on here? Who are all these people?'

'It did, right? It crashed, didn't it?' said Henderson, still to me. I had a sense of teeth flashing white in the darkness. Grimes had stopped shaking and started grunting, her chair no longer rattling, but banging repeatedly against the concrete.

'Henderson,' I said. 'We need to get out of here. Tell us what's happening. Why are you here, what happened?'

Grimes's chair – it was moving.

'Huh,' said Henderson. 'Work it out for yourself. I'm not … what the … *aaaaaaaagggghhhh*!'

Henderson's deep voice skipped four registers and became a falsetto scream. Grimes's voice was next to his too, a tight, wavering drone of rage but with something else – a slavering sound, wet, as though her teeth were bared.

'Gemmerov! Gemmerov! Gemmerov … *aaahhh* … *gemmerovgemmerov* … *gemmavuckingbitchovmyface!*'

With a final yell, Grimes broke free and fell back, crying out as her chair fell onto the floor. She struggled about for a bit and was still, panting.

'Crazy bitch! She bit my fucking cheek off!' said Henderson between rasps of air and spittle.

Bryce began to laugh and didn't stop for some time.

'Better tell us what you know, arsehole,' he said at last. 'Or I'll work out a way to get her back on her feet, I swear to God.'

'Alright, alright,' said Henderson between grunts of pain. 'Jesus Christ, you fucking maniacs, alright.'

He spat, snorted, spat again, cursed, coughed and spat. He continued this, then took three deep, unsteady breaths.

'Take it you met Jenny, then?' he said. His voice was different now, higher, darker, quicker, no trace of a smile. 'She's the one who runs this place, you might have guessed. She's crazy though.'

'Yeah, yeah, yeah, we know all about her,' said Bryce. 'Just tell us where we are.'

'Lock-up,' said Henderson. He spat again. 'Near the gate.'

'Near the garage?' said Richard.

'Yeah, that's right.'

'There's got to be something sharp in this room to cut these ropes,' said Bryce.

'Don't waste your energy,' said Henderson. 'I've been all over this room, corner to corner. There's nothing here.'

Bryce cursed and stamped his feet.

'What happened to you? To Yuill?' I said.

I sensed another sneer on Henderson's face. He spat a few times more. 'We had to stop the Land Rover, go on foot. The road was all messed up, couldn't drive on it.'

'We know,' I said. 'We found it. We came here on foot too.'

'Shut up,' said Henderson. 'I don't believe you.'

'Believe what you like,' I said. 'What happened to Yuill?'

'Whatever. We went too far west. It got wet, boggy; had to turn back. He started whining, saying we should never have left you lot, that we should go back. He was slowing me down.'

'So you killed him?' I said.

'Nah,' said Henderson. 'We were crossing this bog, trying to find a road. He was moving too slowly, kept getting stuck. Then I heard him crying like a baby way behind me, yelling for my help. I turned round and he was sunk up to his waist, couldn't move. So I left him.'

'You killed him. You left him to die.'

'Whatever way you want to look at it,' said Henderson. 'I don't care, he was slowing me down. I made it to Manchester, met Jenny and her mob, put up a fight and ended up blindfolded and locked up in here. Then you lot turned up. I don't know what you did but you were all stone cold when you came in. I tried talking to you but none of you has moved until now.'

Grimes seethed and kicked on the floor. 'When were we brought here?' she said through her teeth.

'Sometime last night,' said Henderson.

'Last night? What time is it now?' I said.

'How should I know?' said Henderson. 'Late though, it's already starting to get dark.'

'Shit,' I said. 'That means we've been here three days.'

'Seriously though?' said Henderson. 'You made it here on foot in that time?'

I ignored him. He puffed. 'Nah, you didn't,' he said.

Nobody said anything for a minute. All I could hear was Grimes breathing on the floor.

'Do you think she killed her?' I said into the darkness.

'Who?' said Henderson.

'Mrs Angelbeck,' said Grimes. 'I don't know. She was limp when they took her off.'

'No,' came a voice from a far corner of the room. 'She's not dead.'

'Mr Angelbeck?' I said. 'George? What are you doing here?'

'She's very badly hurt,' he said. His voice was low and flat. 'You saw what that monster did to her. They took her to the medical centre. It's just a hut really, but I know the doctor. He looked after her. She was unconscious for a while, but she's not dead. Abi's there too. She went into shock.'

'Why are you here, George?' asked Richard.

'I went to find her. That woman.' I sensed George's face crumple as he spoke. 'I took a scalpel from the medical centre and I went to find her. I was going to kill her, kill her for what she did to my Susan. But I couldn't get close to her. I swiped at her a few times and then those big bloody *apes of hers knocked me down again*!' He started to grunt and struggle. His chair began to rattle and bang. He screamed and then suddenly stopped, panting in frustration.

'I'm an idiot,' he said. 'A stupid idiot. Now I'm locked up here. What will Abi do now?'

'You did what any husband and father would have done,' I said. 'I would have done the same.'

I heard a few puffs of air depart from various noses – Grimes, Richard, Bryce. It made me think of eyebrows twitching.

'What's that supposed to mean?' I said.

'What?' said Grimes.

'I heard you. You all puffed. What did you mean?'

'Don't be ridiculous,' said Richard.

'I know what I heard, what—'

'Ed,' interrupted Bryce. 'It's just … no offence, but you're not exactly father of the year, are you?'

'What?' I said, derailed from everything else that was going through my head. 'What does that even *mean*?'

I knew exactly what it meant.

'Just what he said,' said Grimes. 'I watched you, in the barracks, everyone did. Other dads, other parents, they were always with their kids, looking after them, spending time with them. You … you were just … you seemed to just skirt around the outside. You only went on the salvage runs to get away from your kids.'

'Hang on a minute there,' said Harvey. 'Give the guy a break, won't you? Alright, he might not have been the most engaged of fathers …'

'Jesus, Harvey!' I shouted.

'… but being a parent's hard, you know, especially after, you know, what happened.'

'Oh, aye,' said Bryce. 'And what would you know about it? Have you invented a family as well as your career running around continents?'

Henderson's smile, I felt it, I felt it opening up as my own gut swam with guilt. Wide, white, disembodied teeth.

'Leave him alone, Bryce,' said Richard. 'You're a fat, stinking drunk and you've no right to talk to—'

'That's it, you wanker,' said Bryce. 'Soon as I'm free I'm kicking the living shit out of you.'

The air filled with jabbering, angry, stabbing words, chair legs rubbing against the concrete and skin rasping against rope. And all the time Henderson's Cheshire-cat smile stretched across the darkness, beyond my blindfold, out of sight, somehow as loud as the noise itself.

'I know I'm a bad father!' I said, from nowhere. 'It's true. I know it.'

The voices fell away.

'I never wanted kids,' I said. I kicked at the floor with my bound foot. 'I know how that sounds. I know what that makes me. I know how that makes people *think* of me. I was terrified when Beth went into labour. I know, everyone is, but I was terrified because I knew I was supposed to feel something. When I held Alice for the first time, I was supposed to feel this lightning bolt. "Nothing'll prepare you for it," they all said, all the other dads. "Your life changes, right there, when you see them for the first time, it changes everything, it's like a kick in the balls, your heart just melts, all your priorities change." All that bullshit, all that grinning, saccharine bullshit. I was terrified because I knew it was bullshit, I knew it wouldn't happen for me.'

The room was in utter silence. I felt eyes all around me, searching through rags in the dark, following the ears that led them to seek out my voice.

'Don't get me wrong,' I said. 'I did all the things you're supposed to do. I held Beth tight when she told me she was pregnant; smiled, told her how happy I was, told her how excited I was, how perfect our lives were going to be ... and I wasn't lying, not exactly. I felt all those things, I did, I just ... they just didn't ... when Alice came out, when they handed her to me, with all that blood and shit and sweat everywhere, Beth still howling, still trying to hold onto my hand, when I took Alice, I looked down at her. Her eyes were rolling all over the place, trying to focus, trying to lock onto something, and then they locked onto me and I knew that that was the moment, that was the moment I was supposed to go weak at the knees and start crying. That was when I was supposed to change, to move up a level, transcend from my childhood, become the man, the father. I knew it but I didn't feel it.'

I moved my head around in the dark, moving my ears to try and pick up a sound.

'That's not entirely true,' I said. 'I did feel it. I fell in love with her, I felt all that terrible love flood through me, but it was like an undercurrent to something else. Something … something old. Something that had been around too long. It was like … when those big, wet, unseeing eyes found mine and locked on for a second, it felt like something was saying, *Is this it? Again? We're doing this again, are we? Another child? Another life? Another turn of the wheel? Another struggle?*'

I breathed a while into the still, cold silence.

'Look,' I said at last. 'I know I'm not a great father. I don't … I didn't spend enough time with them, put as much effort in … but that doesn't mean I don't love my family. It doesn't mean I don't miss them.

'For Christ's sake, I carry these two tin cans around my neck every day and whisper into one of them at night, because I believe that Alice might hear me.'

Silence. I felt a strange space around me, no sense of other bodies near me, no feeling of movement or breath, Henderson's smile no longer hanging in the darkness.

'I'm done,' I said, listening. 'You can carry on arguing now.'

Not a sound. No movement. Transparent darkness all around me.

'Hello?'

'These cans,' said Grimes from the floor at last. The room became full again at the sound of her voice, like warm air suddenly filling a cold room.

'What about them?' I said.

'You said "*these* cans",' she said.

'Yes, I did, so what?'

'As in, still hanging around your neck.'

I managed to wriggle my shoulders so that the cans fell into my lap, then rocked the chair enough for them to fall onto the floor.

'They're blunt,' I said. 'I took the sharp edges off for Alice.'

'You'll have to break them, said Grimes. 'Crush them with your boots so that they split.'

I hesitated.

'But . . .'

'Just do it,' said Henderson.

'It's our only chance, Ed,' said Richard. 'Alice will understand.'

I shifted my chair around until my left toe hit the metal, then lifted my heel up till it was almost on top of it. The can spun out and hit the other.

'I can't lift my boot high enough,' I said. 'The rope's too tight.'

'Lift your chair leg then,' said Grimes. 'Use your weight.'

I shuffled across the floor in the direction of the sound the two cans had made until I found them. Then I positioned my front left chair leg next to one of them and rocked slightly to one side. I pushed myself along on the two legs, almost fell and then came down on the other side of the can.

'Shit,' I hissed.

'Try again,' said Grimes. I heard her chair scraping nearer to mine.

I pushed myself up again, rocked too far again, corrected myself, then fell back with a crunch on the can.

'That's it,' said Grimes. 'Now get off it.'

I rocked off the can and heard Grimes scrabbling on the floor with muffled grunts and metallic scrapes.

'Good,' she said. 'You broke it. It's sharp.'

She grunted some more.

'*Mmk*,' she said. '*MBryssse. Mift me ump*.'

'Whit?' said Bryce.

'*MIFT ME UMP*.'

'Lift her up,' said Richard. 'She wants you to lift her up behind Edgar so she can cut through his rope.'

'*MMPH!*' said Grimes.

'Oh,' said Bryce. 'Right.'

Bryce dragged himself across to where Grimes was lying. I heard scuffles and more grunts and then Bryce spluttering, and then felt Grimes's head against my hands.

'*HLMD ME*,' she said.

'What?'

'*HLMD ME!*'

'Hold her head, Ed!' shouted Richard.

I grasped back with my fingers and gripped her chin. It was slippery with sweat and I felt the bird-like bones of her jaw moving in my palm as she worked the can. We balanced like this, Bryce somehow supporting her, me grasping her face, Grimes holding herself up on her elbow trying every conceivable position of the can in her mouth in order to locate the rope with its sharp edge. I lost count of the times she dropped it and we had to start all over again, or cut my wrist or yelled as she cut her own lips. For what must have been an hour we kept going until I suddenly felt a pressure against my outer wrist and a twang as the rope was snagged. Then again, and again, as the metal found its first fray and dug in. I felt the gurn of Grimes's sore face harden into a solid, muscled clench and begin to saw, heard the sound of the rope breaking once, then twice and then felt my hands slip free as Grimes fell to the floor exhausted.

The can clattered onto the concrete.

'Are you free?' she mumbled.

'Yes,' I said, wincing as I brought my hands slowly round from behind my back, flexing my fingers. Grimes let out a low whimper. I heard Bryce whisper something to her, Harvey chuckle, Richard let out a sigh of relief. I'm sure I even heard Henderson whistle. I took off my blindfold but it made no difference to my vision. There was no light, not even a chink through a crack or keyhole. We were sealed in full dark: a black room in a black, starless night. I could see nothing.

And yet I felt them near me. I did. I felt them, they were there; they were always there.

My legs were bound tightly but I managed to free them. Then I went to work on Grimes and helped her to her feet, then Harvey, Bryce, Richard and finally George. We stood and stretched our limbs and fingers.

'So what,' said Henderson. 'You're going to leave me tied up, are you? Escape without me? Good luck with that.' That smile had returned, hanging between syllables, invisible white pearls stretched out in tar.

'What do we do now?' whispered Harvey.

'Door's over here,' said Richard from behind us. 'I can feel the lock.'

'How many guards are there?' said Grimes.

'You asking me?' said Henderson. 'Why should I tell you?'

Grimes brushed past me, stepping towards Henderson's chair.

'Just answer me,' she said. 'Answer me or I'll kick your chair over and bite your throat out, I swear.'

'Two,' said Henderson. 'Always two. It's the ones from the gate, I recognise their voices.'

'OK,' said Grimes. 'We get their attention, wait by the door, break them over the necks with the chairs, got it? They'll have already opened the gate out of the estate.'

'Fucking A,' said Bryce.

'What about the dogs?' I said.

'They'll come in first,' said Richard. 'We need something to bait them.'

Silence.

'Forget it,' said Henderson.

We dragged Henderson's chair so that it was facing the door, as far away from it as we could. He struggled in his ropes as we moved him.

'Don't worry,' said Richard. 'Harvey and Ed will be next to you. They'll get to the dogs before they get to you.'

'Oh, that's alright then, I've got an old man and a fat bastard saving me from two hungry Alsatians. GET ME OUT OF THESE ROPES!'

'Quiet!' hissed Grimes. 'Bryce?'

'Aye,' said Bryce. I heard wood snapping. Bryce passed me a broken chair leg, then passed one to Harvey.

'In the throat,' he said. 'Hard as you can. Twist it.'

'Right,' said Grimes. 'Richard, Bryce, stand with me and George at the door. Are you ready?'

'Are you alright with this?' I whispered to Harvey.

'What do you mean, mate?' he said.

'Killing a dog,' I said.

'Ah, yeah, I've killed dogs before,' he said. 'Nothing to it.'

'What? But—'

'Are you ready?' said Grimes.

'No,' said Henderson. 'Fuck this, fuck all this—'

'Right, let's make some noise.'

Bryce began shouting.

'Ho! Ho there, ya fannies! Outside! Y'English bastards! Y'English cunts!'

Then Richard began shouting too, stamping his feet on the floor. We all followed, shouting and yelling, banging on the concrete, drowning Henderson's protests out.

'Hey!' I shouted, lost for anything else more meaningful. 'Hey!' Louder and louder, watching the black space of the door, hoping that there was some light outside, that we would see it open, see what came through it.

Amongst all the clamour of Bryce roaring, Richard hooting, Grimes's witch-like screams and Henderson's muffled dissent, I heard something else, something familiar – a howl rising up behind it, quieter than the rest. It was partway between an animal and a human, fox-like, primal. A howl that had woken me up every day since Carlisle. I felt like nobody else heard it but me. I knew it was coming from Harvey.

Even as I realised that, I felt the shapes in the darkness again. I felt Harvey looking at me, the howl subsiding as the others still raged on. Somehow I heard his voice speaking quietly to me, yet louder than all the other noise, as if through headphones. I felt his face, his brow crumpled and shining eyes impossibly focusing on me.

You getting this yet, mate? he seemed to say. *Are. You. Getting. This. Yet?*

I barely had time to register this when we heard barking outside. I swung my head to the door in time to see it burst open and torchlight filling the room. Two dogs ran in, salivating, straight for Henderson. I watched them spring, saw Harvey move forward with his broken chair leg. The second dog made it past and landed its teeth into Henderson's kneecap, baring its throat. Henderson screamed. The dog's red eye rolled towards me and I plunged forward, catching it in the neck with the sharp wood. I felt it break through fur and skin, heard shouts and crashes from the door, two gunshots, heard the dog yelp as it detached itself from Henderson's leg, drove the leg in further and twisted it into the dog's throat as it scratched and scrabbled its paws helplessly against the concrete. It twitched twice, gave a slow whine and finally came to rest with a single, quivering scrape of claw on stone.

There was a thump from the door and I looked over to see Bryce straddling one of the guards, a rope around his neck. The guard lay still on his front and Bryce pushed himself up, wiping back the strands of damp, straggled hair that were pasted across his face.

Richard stood looking down over the other guard, a splintered, bloody chair in his hand.

Harvey had fallen back against the back wall, his dog skewered and whimpering at Henderson's feet, its jaw still clamped around his shin.

'Get it off me!' Henderson shouted, kicking at the dog's jaws. 'Get this animal off me!'

Bryce pulled the dog away. It growled and renewed its struggle, weakly, as Bryce pushed the chair leg deeper into the animal's side and twisted it until it too yelped and died.

'Everyone OK?' said Richard.

Henderson howled.

'My knee!'

'Are they dead?' I said. 'The guards?'

'Mine is,' said Bryce gloomily.

'Pretty sure mine is too,' said Richard, inspecting the end of his weapon and then letting it fall to the ground. 'Jesus, I never—'

'Where's Grimes?' said Bryce. 'Grimes?' He picked up one of the torches dropped by the guards. 'Grimes?'

'My knee!' shouted Henderson again.

There was no answer from Grimes. Then a few weak breaths from the corner. We ran across.

'Grimes? Oh, no,' said Bryce. 'Oh, Christ.'

She was lying curled on her side, clutching her belly. Fresh, shining blood moved through her fingertips and was pooling on the floor. Her face was pale and smeared with blood from the cuts made by the can around her mouth.

'One of the guards fired,' she said. 'Hit me.'

'OK,' said Bryce. 'Come on, let's get you up.'

I helped Bryce lift her up and she rested on his knee. Harvey crawled across.

'We'll get you out, sweetheart,' he said. 'You're going to be OK.'

Henderson was panting through his teeth.

'My knee,' he said. 'My knee . . . I think it's come off.'

Richard picked up the second torch.

'Quiet,' he said in Henderson's direction, like a distant father to a mothered child. He strode across to where we were huddled around Grimes and crouched down. The pointed shadows cast by his features were stretched to cartoon-like dimensions in the yellow beam.

'Can you walk?' he said. 'Get up?'

Grimes wheezed. The corner of her mouth flickered and she shook her head. One of the guards' radios hissed static. Grimes looked in its direction.

'You there, Gav?' a voice crackled. 'What's happening? Over.'

'You need to get going,' said Grimes.

'Gav? Over.'

There was a noise from far away. A door banging. An engine.

'Now,' said Grimes.

Henderson was still seething air back and forwards between his teeth, rocking his chair.

'Get me out of these ropes!' he shouted. 'Get me out!'

'You're coming with us,' I said to Grimes. 'We can carry you.'

She frowned at me.

'No, you can't,' she said. 'You can barely—'

'We're carrying you,' said Bryce. He put his hands beneath her arms and hauled her over his shoulders. Outside, a pair of headlights rounded a corner at the far end of the clearing and stopped. The engine revved twice, then the lights began to grow as the truck sped towards us.

'They're coming,' said Richard. 'One truck. Jenny's with them, I can hear her voice. What are we going to do?'

'That woman,' said George. He grabbed a shotgun from one of the dead guards' hands. 'She really must be stopped. Get back.' He motioned to us all. 'Back away from the door.'

We moved back into the darkness of the lock-up as the truck pulled up and stopped. Jenny Rae got out, a guard on either side of her, and stopped in the headlights. Her bulk cast a squat shadow in the dirt as she surveyed the scene with growing fury.

'You,' she said, pointing a finger at Henderson. But before she could continue, there was a deafening shot and I saw something spray from her kneecaps. The two guards swung their guns towards the sound of the shotgun, but George Angelbeck had already reloaded. He shot one quickly and then the other. They fell lifeless to the ground as he stepped into the light and walked over to where Jenny Rae was lying, howling in the dirt.

We followed him out, Grimes barely conscious over Bryce's shoulder. The truck's engine was still running and gate was open out onto the wasteland.

'I suggest you go,' said George. 'Now. Before anyone else turns up.'

'What about you?' said Harvey. 'What are you going to do?'

'Don't worry about me,' said George. 'I'll deal with Miss Rae. We'll sort something out, won't we, Jenny?'

Jenny Rae struggled on the ground at his feet. Between whimpers, I thought I could hear a sound of assent. George looked up at us.

'Go, go on.'

Bryce lifted Grimes into the back seat and lay her across his lap, covering her with a dog blanket. Harvey got in beside him and I sat in the passenger seat next to Richard.

'Hey!' shouted Henderson, still strapped to the seat and bleeding amongst a mess of dead dogs. 'What about me?'

'Good luck,' said Richard, and drove away through the gate.

Darkness. Still darkness, all around, engulfing everything, amplifying every shuddering breath in our throats, every thundering heartbeat in our chests, making everything close in. I had no sense of where we were, how far we were from the city. I could see nothing but yellow triangles cast by the truck's headlights on the hopeless, rocky ground as the engine roared.

I could hear Bryce. I felt his dark bulk in the seat behind and to my left. I heard his sniffs, his grunts, his sobs.

There were noises behind us; Jenny's guards, I guessed, but they weren't with us for long. The sun came up as we hit the city. For a few short seconds we saw it again, the disc of fire straining to be seen behind the clouds, but it fell away like it had done before, abandoning its blaze to the slow seep.

And then we found buildings. And then we drove through empty streets. And I watched Richard grit his teeth and lean forward over the wheel, willing the truck to continue, willing the roads to carry us safely away. And then we found one that led us south. And I listened to Bryce's struggles and I pressed down against my own, which is all you can ever do. And then we drove, speeding south out of Manchester as daylight grew around us.

Church

It was around midday when Bryce announced that Grimes had stopped breathing. I looked in the mirror. He was still cradling her in his lap, stroking her head. His face seemed to belong to someone else; no longer arrogant, no trace of a sneer. We stopped the truck and each made sure. Her eyes and mouth were open. Her pulse was gone.

We buried her. We tried to say some words but there were none to say, and so we carried on. Soon after, the truck ran out of petrol. We let it splutter and stop, then got out without a word. There was a small canvas bag in the back which we filled with the dog blanket and a map we found in the glove compartment. There was half-empty bottle of water as well. And we started to run.

I remember very little else about that day. We never stopped except to fill our water from a dribbling, dirty stream. We said nothing.

I have no idea if what happened had any bearing on this, but that day was the first day that running actually started to mean something for me. I wouldn't say that I enjoyed it, but I started to feel what enjoying it might feel like. I pressed down the pain and found springs in my muscles I didn't know existed. At points I had to hold myself back, keep myself from bounding up a hill or taking a few longer strides to catch up with Harvey. *So this is what it is*, I thought. *So this is why people do it*. I wish that it hadn't been that way. I wish I'd found that feeling in some sunny park somewhere, or halfway up a hill in winter, looking out across a bay with a fire and a family waiting for me at home. I wish I'd found it in any number of nameless fantasies that don't belong to me, rather than scraping across the raw dirt of a burned country, half-starved, blind with thirst and freezing, running from the death of a friend. But that's where I found it. And, yes, I felt guilty for it, but, yes, it felt good.

We noticed that the water was getting nearer on our right. By the time the light began to fade, we were running close to a strange beach of dirt, grass and brick. The new sea was dotted with islands, towers and metal claws reaching up into the skies. A man-made archipelago stretched out as far as we could see towards the smeared horizon. This had once been the north-west of England, the Welsh border, the start of the Midlands – all now drowned in saltwater.

We stopped on a hill. Beyond us we could see flames moving slowly along the shore. They started at a small, dark building and ended at the water's edge. We left the road and walked closer, heard the waves crashing against broken machinery and concrete, beginning their long grind into sand. Then we heard music – a distant, hollow sound that warbled across the bay from the building. It was a church organ.

We found a grass-covered ridge and sat down to rest. The flames were torches carried by people in a procession from the church to the shore. They all wore white dresses. I could see children, families walking with their heads turned down towards the ground. One woman fell to the earth, threw her head up and screamed, then scrambled to her feet and tried to leave the line but was caught on both arms by two others and brought back, where she eventually stayed, head hung, sobbing.

The music was a slow, hymnal drone; deep flutes and woody, reverent descant searching for a melody above. In the sea were three men in black, standing in water up to their waists. Two held larger torches much higher than the rest. The third stood in front of them holding a book. Each member of the procession moved up to meet him, whereupon he would touch them on the forehead, read from the book, move his hand around their scalp and push them down gently into the filthy brine. He read from the book as he held them there. A baptism, I thought. But the hand remained clamped against the scalp and the head far beneath the water until the white dress began to flap in the torchlight and the water began to splash and froth. Occasionally, one or more of the two torchbearers would step forward to help out with a particularly wild struggle. And then the body would twitch and finally lie still and float away with the rest behind them towards the dark horizon, and the next would be beckoned to the front.

We watched it all for an hour at least. In horror at first, then in confusion, anger, sadness and finally restlessness, as the lack of light drove us to think of shelter and safety for the night. Apathy arrives very quickly.

'Idiots,' said Bryce. It was the second thing any of us had said all day. 'Let's go.'

We rejoined the main road and ran until we could no longer hear the terrible music or the crashing of the sea. When it was dark we had reached the borders of a small town, where we found a multistorey car park that was still – barely – standing. We started a fire on the second floor of the stairwell using the wood from a half-burned door. We had no food. A deep puddle had formed in a hole in the concrete. We boiled some of the water in the unbroken can of Alice's stringyphone and shared it out in sips, then boiled some more. Fires started in the distance. They were small, so we weren't worried, but we still kept a watch that night. I took the first. I drank another tin of boiled water and burned my lips on the metal to take away their dry itch. I spoke words into the can after every sip. I stared into the fire and out at the others burning around the demolished town and thought about gravity, about how it holds everything, even things with no weight, like thoughts, dreams, love. Even flames struggle to escape it. Everything is weighed down. Everything is pushed down towards the sea. Everything is kept at bay.

Sometime after midnight I shook Richard awake and he took over. I went to sleep thinking of how it would feel to run through the night.

No White Prophets

I was awake before I really knew it; my eyes were open but my brain was far behind. Harvey was standing at the far corner of the car park and howling into the grey morning mist. I knew now that it was him I had been hearing. He had been the source of the animal howl that had woken me every morning since we'd left Edinburgh. I watched him raise his chin and pull back his arms to open up his chest, then release two strangled, dry yowls. The noise was dampened into fast-dying echoes by the wet stone, but some found its way outside and soared away into the low sky. I sat up so that he would see me watching when he turned. He did and said nothing; he acknowledged me with a quick smile and bent down to the puddle.

We each drank as much as we could of the dirty water, then filled the bottle with it, packed and set off into another gloomy dawn. Harvey tried to make conversation but Bryce and Richard were having none of it. They kept themselves apart, separating themselves from each other using Harvey and me as a wall.

'We need food,' was all Bryce said. There was nothing anyone could say back.

We made our way out through the dull, empty streets of the crushed and nameless town, heading south again. The strange lightness I had felt and kept secret the day before had gone. I could feel and hear the bones of my hips, knees and ankles moving against each other. With every stride, my legs and back screamed that the next would be impossible. My head thumped with hunger and dehydration.

A heavy mist came down around us. The tarmac became broken up and we found that we were no longer running on the remains of a motorway, but on a smaller road with tight bends. We stopped at a car wreck in the ditch. It had been pulling a caravan that had separated and spun into a field where it now lay on its side. We avoided the car – it looked like a family inside – and searched the caravan, finding a dry, crumbled packet of digestives that we shared out silently in a circle. We emptied the contents of the caravan's plumbing into plastic cups and drank it. There was a pool of filthy water in the bowl of the toilet. We drank that too, then we carried on.

The mist became heavier, then became fog. Richard, Bryce and Harvey were turning to ghosts in front of me.

Those days are hard to piece together. I can't say which event followed which, where we slept or which roads we took. We were all over the place. I had little idea of where everyone was at any given time. For long periods of time I was unaware of either thinking or running. I would suddenly come to and realise that I was still moving and still breathing, but that I had lost the others. I didn't know if I was in front of or next to Bryce, if I had fallen far behind or if I had stumbled off the road and was now running in the wrong direction. I would move for miles in the steadily increasing resignation that I had lost them. Then a dark shape would appear and I would surge ahead, fixing my eyes upon it and resolving to keep my concentration. Thoughts became intangible and disconnected. They were like explosions of ash. Each one that arrived lasted only moments before it fell away and disintegrated, as if there was nothing to support it, nothing to hold it together. Eventually I would return into the same deep, oblivious trance where there was no pain, no thought, no memory.

Our rest stops were erratic and frequent. Sometimes without registering it I found myself leaning over, letting the wet mist drip down around my neck and across my boiling cheeks. Other times I would be either retching or hearing someone else do the same. During one stop, I pulled off my right boot and found that the back of my heel had become pulpy and white. I prodded it and a chunk of flesh sheered off, leaving a raw, pink welt behind. The pain was fierce, but distant and momentary. It was as if it – like my thoughts – could find nothing to latch on to, nothing to keep it alive.

On one occasion I opened my eyes and saw that I was lying on the ground by a ditch. I had been asleep. A dull panic swam across me, but I didn't move. I looked around and found Bryce's crumpled boot somewhere on the ground next to me, then the shapes of Richard and Bryce lying sprawled on the dirt. I wondered distantly if they had died. I focused on a clump of grass that was fluttering in the wind in front of me. It was coarse and brown, a stubborn, ugly fist of life still clinging on. There was movement beyond it and I looked up to see a large rook perched on a stone wall. It cocked its head and squawked loudly. Then it raised its black wings and jumped, gliding down to stand next to my head. It twitched its head left and right, inspecting me with its wings folded. I looked up at it, meeting its curious attention. For a brief moment I felt it might speak to me. Perhaps it was a blessing, sent to help me. *Get up*, it would say. *Get up and run*. But then it pecked at my face. Its dark beak was quick and my right eyelid slow to close. A sharp pain funnelled into my brain and I jerked to full consciousness. Then it pecked again, the same eye, keeping its head down and its beak close this time. I brought my left hand around and slammed it down on top of the bird, smashing its neck into the dirt. Its wings flapped and rattled behind and it almost slid from my grasp, but I leaned up, putting my weight on my hand and bringing the other around to help until I was crouching above the bird, squashing it into the ground. Its eye flitted wildly around and its beak worked silently. Blood from my own eye trickled down my face and fell onto the bird's slick feathers. I pushed hard. There was a series of snapping sounds and the bird lay still, its wings caught in one last spasm before curling slowly in like burning parchment.

I sat back on my haunches and caught my breath, looking down at the broken mess of bird below. The right side of my vision was a dark smudge. Pain stabbed at me erratically with every twitch of my eye, as if some vengeful ghost of the bird had already risen to resume its pecking from beyond death. I held a hand to my face and stood up. My knees and pelvis cracked. I woke the others and told them what had happened. Harvey tore of a strip of shirt and tied it in a knot around my head so that it covered my eye.

Then we ate the bird. If we had eaten it raw then I think that might have been the end of us. I think that would have been too much. Eating carrion is one thing, but the experience of biting through feathers and into warm sinews would have drained us of whatever last dregs of hope and volition we still held. We cooked it. We made a fire using Bryce's lighter and some dry wood at the foot of the wall and we cooked it, plucked and gutted. It was foul, although the kidneys had a gamey, rich taste. There was barely enough meat to warrant a meal, but the feeling of having made a fire and eaten anything seemed to restore enough will for us to get moving again. We waited for the fire to die and moved on.

I became aware of him quite soon after we ate the bird. I became aware that I had been aware of him for some time without acknowledging it. At this point it seemed as if my consciousness had sliced into independent layers, countless sheets of awareness, fragile, gossamer thin, each one acting without knowledge of the others. I was none of them. I merely flitted between them like a mote of dust between shafts of sunlight.

He was a presence, barely a person, just a feeling of somebody running near me that wasn't Bryce, Richard or Harvey. He was always somewhere behind my left shoulder, just on the edge of my vision. Although I was moving slowly, he seemed to be travelling at speed, eyes ahead, sleek and wild like a wolf running low to the forest floor. If I turned, he disappeared. Or, rather, he became indistinct. He was like a distant star you could only see if you turned your eyes to the light years of space surrounding it.

He came and went. Sometimes he was close, sometimes he was impossibly far.

'How long have we been running in this fog?' I said.

'Over four hours,' said Richard.

'Are you sure we're still going in the right direction?'

'No,' said Richard. 'I'm not sure of anything.'

The fog became thicker until our clothes and hair became soaked. I sucked at the drips of water running down my face, craving the next each time.

'I don't think this is fog any more,' said Harvey's disembodied voice ahead.

'What is it then?' said Bryce gruffly.

'I think it's a ... a ... holy shit.'

I felt a spade of light and heat slamming into my face. I shielded my eyes, nearly toppled back. I heard the others making noises, nothing intelligible, just the sounds people make when they have no words at hand.

Very slowly, I peeled back my hand from my eyes and allowed them to focus and adjust to what was in front of us.

Blue. Blue and yellow. Sky and sun.

Blue, cloudless sky and bright yellow sun. The entire horizon visible before us, all 180 degrees of it.

We walked without talking. We felt the warmth of the December sun on our faces, tasted fresh air, felt our minds fill with colour, *blue, blue, blue*, felt the pressure drop in our ears. My heart reeled as my senses span into overdrive. I thought it would kill me. But it didn't, the feeling settled and eventually we were just four men walking in the sunshine, struck with awe.

'It was a cloud,' said Harvey. 'We were running in a cloud. Look.'

We looked behind us and saw the cloud we had just stepped out of. Then Harvey raised a finger and pointed ahead.

'But what's that?' he said.

About half a mile in the distance, the shining mud on which we were walking stopped sharply and became a white mass. As we drew nearer, we saw it stretch further and further into the distance, until the entire ground ahead of us had turned into a fluffy, amorphous blanket.

We stopped at the threshold. The ground fell away sharply at our feet.

'That's cloud,' said Bryce. 'Beneath us, that's cloud too. This is a canyon.'

We stood and surveyed the endless white all around us and ahead of us.

'A very big one,' said Harvey.

Richard fell to crouch. The crumpled map hung loosely in his hand.

'Gentlemen,' he said. 'Welcome to Birmingham.'

We sat on the edge of the canyon for a while, trying to dry ourselves in the sun, still marvelling at it, yet growing more and more aware of the fact that we were soon going to be leaving it.

'We have to go down,' said Richard.

'What about finding a way around?' said Harvey.

'We have no idea how big this thing is,' said Richard. 'We could be miles out of our way before we find a way around.'

'How many days until Christmas?' I asked.

'Five,' answered Richard.

'There's no time,' I said. 'There's no time. We have to go down.'

I looked up at the sun one last time and let myself slip down from the edge.

'Ed!' shouted Harvey. 'Wait!'

It was steeper than I had imagined it to be; not a sheer drop, although I'm sure a part of me was hoping it would be, but closer to vertical than was comfortable. I fell, scrambled, bumped along, hitting rocks and debris and trying to stay on my back. At times I left the ground completely, every time feeling sure that I was about to fall to my death, but every time landing back with a heavier thump with mud and scree hurtling beneath me. Something hit my hand and I felt a snap. I tucked in my limbs and shut my eyes and let gravity pull me further and further down into the pit. I heard the others above me, calling, then shouting out themselves as they started to fall. Down and down and down I went, further than seemed possible. Then I hit something hard with my shoulder, span and came to rest on flat ground, staring up into a high sheet the colour of slate.

I blinked. Heard thumps and shouts and voices far away, making quick echoes.

'Ed? Ed? Where are you?

'Ed! Where the ... *ahh* shit!'

'Edgar!'

I tried speaking, but only a thin, H-shaped stream of air left my mouth. There was a sharp pain in my right shoulder and the hand below it felt numb and strange. With some effort, I sat up on my left elbow, looked down.

My index finger was pulled back and pointing straight up at me. The thumb had twisted upside down and hung loosely from its socket like a dead slug. The third finger was out of sight, hiding in a near right-angle beneath the remaining two that cowered together away from the horror of their siblings like two children having stumbled across a family bloodbath.

'H ... here,' I managed at last.

'Ed? Is that you?' Harvey's voice.

'Here,' I said, louder.

'Wait there,' said Richard. 'We'll come to you.'

The voices snapped and repeated like springs against concrete. I fell back and looked up again. Tall dark walls rose up into the cloud, skyscrapers of mud and stone. Some stood on their own, others massed together into long blocks. I felt like I was in a city, yet this was well beneath the surface of the earth.

I heard scrabbles and curses far away. I think I drifted off. At least, I had the sense of time passing without me.

'Ed! Ed! Are you still there?' Harvey's voice again, farther away this time.

'Yes,' I breathed.

'We can't get to you, mate,' he said. 'All these walls, it's like a maze. Can you walk?'

I shifted up again, managed to get to my feet.

'I think so,' I said.

'Good, keep walking then, and keep talking, we'll try to follow each other.'

'Which direction?' I said.

'The one pointing away from where you fell from, mate. Follow my voice, keep talking.'

I saw the ground rise sharply ahead and guessed that it marked the beginning of the canyon wall, so I turned in the opposite direction and walked.

'Over here,' said Harvey, from somewhere far over to my left. 'Actually, Ed, I'm just going to say "here", that OK? You say it too. *Here . . . here . . . here.*'

It was dark, of course, and misty, but I could see the direction the walls were making and followed them round.

'Here . . . here . . . here,' I said. 'Harvey?'

'*Here . . . here . . . here,*' said Harvey. 'Keep saying it, Ed. *Here . . . here . . . here.*'

I followed the walls, holding my mangled hand to my chest, repeating the words like a mantra.

'*Here ... here ... here ... I'm here ... here ... here.*'

Harvey's '*here*'s became softer, further away.

'Harvey? Harvey? Where are you?'

'*Here ... here .... here.*'

'Harvey, I'm losing you, *here here here*,' I shouted.

'*... here .... here ....*'

Eventually his voice faded until it was only a memory in my head – an imagined sound, carved from the silence. I stood still, holding my breath, willing it to return, until even my mind refused to conjure it for me.

'Harvey! Richard! Bryce!'

Nothing. I kept walking, following the walls. It became darker and the mist got closer. I bit back the panic. Then I froze. Then I ran.

The concept of time or distance left me. I kept running, painfully, following the darkness of the wall on my left, listening out for any human sound. I kept talking.

'*Here ... here ... here.*'

I passed boulders, pipes, car parts, bits of road, some human remains, a jumble of industry and life either littered about the wide, muddy streets that had been carved into the prehistoric rock or wedged into the rock itself. I did not even allow myself to think of how this had happened. I just wanted to get out of the maze. Whenever I saw a puddle, I stopped and drank from it, burying my face in the dirt and sucking up the water like an animal. When it became too dark to see, I stopped and fell next to a huge iron girder that was speared into the ground. There was a warmth in the ground that unsettled me. I huddled into the giant metal groove and tried to sleep, gripping the broken can of Alice's stringyphone in my uninjured hand, whispering to myself as I squeezed my eyelids shut.

'Here . . . here . . . here.'

'Here.'

I used to dread being asked whether or not I believed in God. Either answer aligns you with an entirely new set of certainties. Say 'yes' and you're certain of a myth, you say 'God bless you' and mean it quite literally, you commit to a wild insanity of faith. Say 'no' and you're an atheist: confident, assured and certain of the scientific method and all of its own twisted ideas – string theory, infinite universes, emergent consciousness – equally strange, equally alien, each requiring its own version of that insane faith.

I know now that it's certainty itself I have a problem with. Certainty doesn't feel like something we're supposed to have.

It's hard being a human. Most of the time we're just blind idiots seeking joy in a world full of fear and pain. We have no idea what we're doing and on the rare occasions when we get things right, we're just lucky. Our lives are filled with the humdrum, dust and noise with no meaning. And yet they contain moments that seem to mean something, something we can't describe but want to. Those moments leave holes that we want to fill. We want to name them, paint them, teach them, sing them. But we can't. We can't because when we try the hole disappears and all we can see is the imperfect, unrecognisable imprint of our own crude imagination. We want God. We want this life to end, for the curtain to go up and a kind, loving face to smile down on us, a warm voice to call us through and explain everything to us. The hole is everything we don't know and everything we suspect, and we need a truth to fill it.

People often wonder if we see that truth in dark places. Dark places like the one through which I ran. Sometimes people say they do. Others say they see only the darkness.

God is a shape that fits a God-shaped hole. There, will that do?

Do I believe in God? I still don't know. Did I meet him in the canyon? Yes.

Absolutely yes.

'Here,' I grunted, and opened my eyes from a barely visited sleep. I could see. I pushed myself out from the girder, growling as my limbs straightened, rediscovering my shoulder and hand and the more determined version of the pain to which they were both now dedicated. The mist had risen a little. I drank puddle water, every gulp provoking new pangs of hunger in my empty belly. Then I found my bearings and followed the wall again, walking a little until my legs stretched, then began to run.

Again, no sense of time or distance, only the sense of pain from every direction, down, up, left, right, from skin, from bone, from muscle, from gristle, from hunger, from exhaustion, from eyes, ears, nose, tongue, bladder, stomach, legs, arms, hand, shoulder. From outside. From inside. Physical and mental. Pain from the present. Pain from the past. Pain in the future. Suffering and regret with little hope to alleviate either of them.

Only the sound of two cans hitting each other beneath my jacket.

Only the word, the mantra I grunted with every two steps.

'Here ... here ... here.'

I felt a sense of space open up around me; the walls were growing apart. The right one disappeared entirely, then the left, and the sound of my voice and my footsteps no longer echoed. The mist had lifted and I looked ahead at a wide, open plain of mud overhanging with colourless, textureless cloud. I felt soft spots of water on my face, drizzle against my skin.

'Here ... here ... here ...'

It was as this plain opened up before me that I allowed myself to consider what was happening, what had happened – what had *really* happened. There was no shape to the world that I was running through, no detail, just brown flat mud and rain falling from dull cloud. Behind me was full of detail, full of strangeness. Grimes was dead. Harvey, Bryce and Richard had disappeared. I had heard about people experiencing hallucinations when running long distances, imagining things that were not there.

Imagining people who were never there.

Two water droplets that had formed on my cheek bulged and touched each other. The resulting trickle of rain water fell down through my beard, across my cracked lips and into my mouth.

'Afternoon.'

My heart jerked like a sleeping dog's leg. I looked down at my left and saw a man running alongside me. He was small and wore a white smock and sandals. His hair was long and curled, his beard black and cropped. His eyes were pools of cobalt swimming with light. They made everything else seem hazy and ill-defined. I could see more detail in the two small spaces they filled than in all the air around me; planets, suns, nebulas and infinite space.

In his hand he held a bottle of wine. He looked up at me, raised his eyebrows and smiled with his mouth shut.

I turned my eyes forward.

'Here … here … here …'

I heard a bottle being upended and fluid sloshing in glass. Then a gulp and a satisfied exhalation. I glanced back. The man was still there, wiping his white sleeve across his mouth, looking back at me with another sheepish smile.

I frowned, turned away.

I heard his footsteps, the soles of his sandals slapping against the mud.

'Puh!' he said.

I turned to see him shaking his head at me, eyes wide, mouth cocked in a smirk as if to say, *Can you believe this weather?*

'Huh!'

'Tuh!'

He took another swig from his bottle, coughed and looked ahead, eyebrows raised into an innocent, crumpled frown. I turned away again.

When I turned back the smile had disappeared. His face had fallen into deadpan, eyes resolutely on the road. The bottle was gone. His galaxy-sized eyes drifted right and snapped back when they saw me looking, his mouth pursed seriously. He glanced back at me twice, suddenly suspicious of me.

I ran for a couple of minutes, his footsteps always just behind me and to the left. I heard the scuffling noise of fabric.

'Ahem.'

I looked back. A black T-shirt was now stretched over his tunic with writing on the front:

J.E.S.U.S.

The letters strobed and changed colour, cycling through a series of cheap, pixelated animations. They beeped and chirped like an arcade machine. He puffed out his chest, beaming proudly down at the letters as they danced and span. Then he looked up at me and winked, clucking his cheek.

Again, I turned away.

I heard a crunch. Looked back. A large kebab was flapping about in his hand. Meat fell out from the sides and the pitta had a huge, cartoon-sized bite mark in its middle. He was chewing slowly, looking delightedly down at the meat and letting chilli sauce dribble down his chin. He looked up, stopped in mid-chew, his cheeks puffed out like a hamster, then offered me some.

I looked down at the kebab floating in front of me. It would be one step too far into madness, I reasoned, to accept it.

He shook it encouragingly.

'Unleavened,' he said through his mouthful.

'No, thanks,' I said.

He looked disappointedly down at the sandwich, then looked it over. Eventually he curled his lip.

'Probably right,' he said, throwing it over his shoulder. 'Not very healthy. Especially considering, well, you know, we're *running* and that.'

He ran up alongside me.

'So . . .' he said. He bit into a large, dark green lettuce that he was suddenly holding in both hands and chomped down a mouthful. 'I expect you've heard about people experiencing hallucinations when running long distances.'

'And I expect you're going to tell me you're not, that you're, you know . . .' I said, nodding at his still-flashing T-shirt. He threw back his head and laughed, a big, open-mouthed laugh, so honest a sound that the air around him seemed to fill with colour.

'I'm not going to tell you anything, sunshine,' he said, still laughing. He turned his eyes towards me. Blue, luminous tendrils seemed to be streaming from them, reaching out towards me and pulling me in. 'I'd say you've let yourself be told too much already.'

'What do you mean?' I said.

'It means that maybe you should take things on face value for a change, stop trying to unravel them.' He watched me for a while, light pouring from his face.

'You're white,' I said. 'And you sound like you're Welsh.'

'Whatever you say,' he said with a shrug.

'Jesus was supposed to be from the Middle East,' I said.

'Yeah, it's funny, isn't it?' he said. 'Ever wonder why there are no white prophets?' He shrugged again. 'Maybe one day. Anyway, put it this way, you watch telly, right? You know it's not *really* little people stuck inside a box trying to entertain you. You know it's just electrics and that inside, you know you're just looking at lots of different pictures one after the other played really quickly, and you know those pictures are just made out of dots, right? But you're still watching telly, aren't you? You're still watching *EastEnders* or *24* or whatever.'

He turned his eyes forward again. 'Not so much nowadays, granted, but you get the idea. OK, put it another way: everything that happens, happens. In some form or other. Know what I mean?'

I pulled my eyes back to the brown sludge stretching out in front of us.

'Not really,' I said.

'Do you know why people tell stories, Ed?' he said. He waited for me to speak, but I didn't. He sniffed and went on. 'Because the truth doesn't really have any words of its own. They're not enough, see? Stories work ... good stories ... because they make you feel something like how the truth would make you feel if you *could* hear it.'

I closed my eyes, shivered a little at the thought of what was happening to me. The past seemed like a grey corridor fading behind my back, dissolving into blank space and difficult questions, leaving nothing and nobody in it.

'It's all about resonance,' he said. I sensed his giant gaze washing across my shoulders, waiting for a response, but I kept my eyes shut, running blindly in the mud.

'I've got a story if you want one?' he said. I didn't answer.

'OK,' he said chirpily. 'So I knew a woman in India, lived on the mudflats next to the Ganges. Her house only had three walls and even they weren't really what you'd call proper walls, not like you get nowadays. Anyway, so the front of the house opened out onto a deck and the deck ran down into the grass and the grass ran into the reeds and the reeds ran into the water. Over time, the water had risen over some of the reeds and the reeds had grown across some of the grass and some of the grass had grown over some of the deck and into the house.

There was water from the river in her house and everything else in between. Crabs, flies, flowers, toads, spiders, I even saw a fish. Likewise, some of her house was in the river.'

His gaze again, awaiting a word from my mouth that never came.

'See?' he said. 'There's only an outside and an inside if you close the doors.'

'I don't really understand what you're trying to say.'

There was no answer. I turned and he was gone.

I carried on across the plain. Piles of earth began to appear, small at first, then large. When it got dark I found one and burrowed beneath it to sleep. I woke up retching, drank from a puddle and pushed on, alternating between a stumble and a delirious stagger. Halfway through the morning, I felt the familiar presence behind my left shoulder.

'So where are we going?' he said. It took a while for me to find the will to answer.

'You know where I'm going,' I said.

'No,' he said. 'No, I don't mean you, personally, now, with the running and everything. I mean you, everyone. We, I suppose. The human race. Where are you going?'

'I thought you were supposed to tell us that?'

'I already told you, I'm not here to tell you anything you don't already know. In fact, I don't *have* anything to tell you that you don't already know. I'm quite simple really, when it comes down to it.'

'Peace and love, I suppose,' I coughed. Spat. Missed the ground and hit my arm. I wiped a thick string of phlegm from my face. My throat hurt. Everything hurt.

'Sure, why not? What's so funny about peace, love and understanding?' He sang the words and laughed another honest, wholesome laugh.

'Seriously though, where?' he said. 'It's a serious question.'

I laughed, a sad, maniacal laugh that sounded terrible next to his. It embarrassed me and I chomped my jaws shut.

'Where are we going?' I said. 'Look around you!'

He did what I asked, looking up and back and down and ahead.

'What?' he said.

'It's not where we're going, it's where we've gone!' I said. 'This is it, the end. We're done.'

He frowned and pulled back his head into his neck.

'The end?' he said. He shook his head. 'It's never the end, Ed.'

He looked down at his watch, suddenly distracted, as if he had just remembered something.

'Now listen,' he said. 'It gets a bit hard core up ahead, so this is where I get off. Just remember, Ed, don't panic.'

He stretched out his arm and laid a warm hand, full of goodness, onto my shoulder. I felt tears in my sick eyes at his touch. It disarmed me; not because I thought he was real, but because I knew the opposite. I was creating this. I was creating this thing of hope. It was already inside of me, it didn't come from anywhere else.

'Everything's going to be OK,' he said. Then he let his hand fall and he broke off into the mist and disappeared.

'... probably,' I heard him cough in the distance.

And then it was me, just me, running, stumbling, coughing and spluttering in the mud and the mist of a nameless pit. I was in the dark. Alone, alone, alone. Running alone, as I was sure I always had been. How hard did this have to be? How hard to simply exist, to move, to twitch muscles, to think, hope, accept, move, love and be loved.

There was some noise in the distance. Music, I thought.

I hit a rock and my right foot bent outwards. I sprawled into the cold, frozen mud and lay back, wide-eyed and horrified at the new pain in my ankle.

How hard? How hard did this have to be? To live?

And then I was back in Edinburgh, lying on the bedroom carpet and staring up into a shaft of winter sunlight swarming with weightless dust. It was a couple of months after Arthur was born. Beth and I were exhausted, with weeks of broken sleep behind us and nothing but the promise of the same ahead. We had argued fiercely about something ridiculous like the temperature of milk and I had retreated upstairs with Alice. She was toddling about on the other side of the bed, trying out new words, squealing at something. I lay, listening to my breathing with my eyes half-shut while Beth slammed cupboard doors downstairs.

How hard? I thought. *How hard does this have to be? To bring life into the world?*

And then, out of the corner of my eye, I saw Alice looking at me, smiling, her chubby fists at her mouth, realising something, plotting something, excited by a new scheme. She ran across to me and stopped suddenly at my head, gazing down through the light shaft onto my tired, drawn face. Then she bent over and paused, hovering above my head and searching my tired face, breathing little, excited breaths. Then she placed her lips softly on my brow. It was the first time she'd ever kissed me.

I choked on a lungful of icy air and I was back in the pit. I peeled my head from the mud and got to my feet. There was the sound somewhere of somebody howling, me I supposed as my twisted ankle took its first weight. The noise of the music was growing louder. I staggered forward and broke into a limping run towards the sound. And then I was stumbling, gasping and shuddering up a hill.

And then the mist cleared.

And I felt warmth.

And I broke out into bright sunlight, blue sky and a thundering wall of sound.

It was freezing cold and brighter than I imagined anything had ever been. I watched it all through my one good eye. My right was sealed shut with scabs beneath Harvey's bandage. There were people everywhere, crowds, hungry faces, worried faces, lost faces, happy faces, drunken faces, toothless mouths, campfires and makeshift tents of rags and sticks, sizzling meat, smoke and steam, stalls selling food, tattered clothes, families keeping close, traipsing along in what appeared to be a gigantic queue snaking towards a tower of metal, beggars holding out their hands for food, musicians singing and playing, girls half naked and daubed with mud and paint, dancing, eyes closed, lost in something else away from the world, noise and movement all around them. A man in a ragged pinstriped suit and hollow eyes barged past me, spinning me into a fat woman and her child. She growled and shoved me and I fell. I heard laughter, then someone pulled me up and patted me on the back. I staggered on, trying to focus on something in the glare of the new sunlight. Every face that saw me reeled or sneered or looked away in horror. A topless teenage boy walked past in sunglasses, six-pack and pectorals glistening in the sunshine, a grin of white teeth exposed for all the world to see. He had his arms around two girls. One of them looked me up and down, then pulled back her mouth as she saw my hand.

'Whatchoo staring at, mate?' said the boy. 'Oy. I'm talking to you. Cyclops. Hear me? What the fack are you looking at?'

I moved back, but the boy had released his girls and was stepping towards me.

'Ed!' I heard a voice from through the throng and spun my head.

'Oy!' said the boy. 'Look at me when I'm talking to you, you ...'

And suddenly Bryce was there, towering next to the boy, holding a cup of something. I saw Harvey behind him. His arm was wrapped in a sling.

'Ed!' he said. 'Christ, I thought we'd lost you for good!'

Bryce turned his head down to the boy, who had stopped talking.

'You got some trouble here, Ed?' said Bryce. 'Ed?'

The world span again, tumbling down as my head hit mud and my eyes were filled with blue light.

Family

I woke up beneath a blanket in a warm, hard bunk. Light spilled down a wooden wall from a small window above. The room was moving to the sound of water slapping against a bow. I rolled over and saw Bryce sitting on a bunk opposite. I felt relief. I didn't know why at first. It was ephemeral, a floating feeling with no cause or effect. Then I remembered the feeling of running alone, the feeling that I had always been running alone. But Bryce was there. He was right there in front of me, sitting forward with his elbows on his knees, his hands and hair hanging down to the floor.

You're here, I thought.

For a moment I thought I'd caught him in some vulnerable moment, imagining him to be in a kind of bedside vigil. I wondered how long he'd been there like that, worrying, hoping, praying. Then I heard a gaseous rumble erupt from somewhere deep in his throat. He retched and spat. I looked down and saw a bucket between his feet.

'Are you alright?' I said.

He lifted his eyes from the floor a little, then let them drop again. 'Boats,' he whined. 'Fucking hate boats.'

'Boat? What happened?' I said. 'Where are we? What was that . . .'

I remembered leaving the canyon, feeling the shock of sunlight again, the freezing air, spinning around in some ghoulish carnival of noise and light. Bryce retched again. Something came up this time and hit the bucket in a single jet. He gave a moan of relief and sat up to look at me, wiping his mouth on his wrist.

'Why are we on a boat, Bryce?' I said. 'What happened?'

'Uhh,' said Bryce.

'What day is it?'

'Huh ... uhh.'

I sat up and threw off the blanket, rolling my feet off the bunk. 'We have to ... ' I began, but stopped as my right foot hit the floor. I shrieked. I'd forgotten about my newly injured ankle. I clawed for it, remembering as I did so my mangled hand, howled and fell back on the bunk in the grip of two suddenly screaming pain centres. My eye joined the party by beating sharp thumps in the ensuing blood rush, until the entire right-hand side of my body was possessed by pain.

'Wouldn't do that,' said Bryce. 'It's not broken, but it's a bad sprain.'

As the pain subsided, I looked down at my shaking hand. The last time I had seen my fingers, they had resembled a cutlery drawer. Now they were set neatly and bandaged to a splint. My ankle was tightly bound. I felt a tight tape across my eye and suddenly registered the smell of antiseptic. I sat up slowly and placed my feet more carefully on the floor so that I was facing Bryce. I caught my breath. He looked back at me.

'Did I tell you I hate boats?' he said.

'You should be on deck,' I said.

'That just makes it worse,' he said. He looked pitifully down at the pail beneath him. 'I've nothing left to hurl anyway.'

'Tell me what happened,' I said. 'What was that place?'

Bryce took a deep, shuddering breath. 'The place you passed out? That would be the gate. The way in.'

'The gate to the boats?' I said, leaning forward. Suddenly the feeling of water beneath us filled me with hope. I had no idea how long I'd been running alone or how many nights I had fallen into some hollow in the dirt, shivered through sleep and then crawled out to carry on. Was it possible that the canyon we had found at Birmingham stretched all the way down to the south coast? Was it possible that I had run all that way?

'Are we here?' I said, elated. 'Did we make it?'

Bryce's sour smile told me the answer before he spoke.

'No,' he said. 'We're in Bristol. About two hundred miles short.'

'What's the gate then?' I asked.

'The way to the boats,' said Bryce. 'The route to Falmouth. There's a big chunk of the south coast that's smashed up and water-logged. Cornwall's cut off from the rest of the country by a long causeway that starts at Bristol. That's where they built the gate. That's where they decide who gets on the boats.'

'The queue,' I said. 'They were all waiting to see if they'd be evacuated?'

'Aye,' said Bryce. 'After the broadcast and the rescue missions, more people turned up than they expected. More people survived than we thought, I guess. There aren't enough boats, so they're turning a lot of punters away. Oh, and there's a virus as well, a bad one. A lot of people are dying from it without the meds. You have to be tested and given a stamp to even be considered. Plus you ...' he paused and looked me up and down '... you have to be in a certain state of health to get on.'

'What about the people they rescued?' I broke in. 'Beth, my children, Richard's son.'

'The choppers got here first. Everyone on them is guaranteed a place.'

'I have to talk to Richard,' I said. 'We have to talk about what we're going to do.'

'Er, that's not going to be so easy,' he said. He looked uncomfortable, trying to read my expression. 'Don't worry, he's fine, it's just . . . Richard got through. He made it down to the boats.'

'What. How. What. I don't understand.' The words fell out flat and sick.

'We got here the day before you did, Ed. I thought you were gone for good, we all did. Richard managed to talk to a guard, explained the situation, got himself bumped up to the front of the medical queue and got the all-clear. He had a twelve-hour wait in the queue to the gate and then he was through.' He reached a hand forward for my arm, but let it fall back. 'He's going to try to find your family, Ed. He's going to make sure they're OK.'

'I can still make it,' I said. 'I can find the same guard and tell him who I am. They have to let me through to my family.'

Bryce looked down at his bucket, adjusting it with his boot. 'I'm sorry, Ed. The gates closed about an hour ago. They're not letting anyone else through.'

My insides coiled. 'What day is it?' I said.

'Christmas Eve,' he said. He ventured out another consolatory hand, pulling it back once again before it could land on my arm. 'I'm sorry, bud. The boats leave tomorrow.'

We heard a noise above us, some footsteps and the scrape of rope. Bryce looked up.

'Thank fuck, I think we're stopping,' he said. 'Come on, I'll introduce you to the captain.'

Bryce helped me out of the bunk and I limped after him through the cabin. The boat was short and filled with the warmth of family. Coloured and frayed cushions lined the wooden benches in the galley. Next to the stove was a teapot covered by a woollen tea cosy in the shape of a cat's head, and next to this a photograph of an old woman. On the wall above, a child's drawings were pinned across each other on a board: birds with triangular beaks and pink eyelashes, dogs with straight legs and human teeth, people with limbs that only served to support gigantic, circular hands and feet, faces drawn smile-first; everything primary, every stroke started before the last one had been completed. Alice had started to draw the previous spring: endless lines and scribbles, nothing recognisable yet. I felt a sudden need to see her progress and draw pictures like these. A strange and directionless feeling: joy, sadness, hope and envy all at once.

I followed Bryce up the thick ladder to the deck of the boat, relying more on my arms than my legs to lift me. We met the sun, low in the sky but still a shock. It was morning, I guessed. I shielded my eyes and looked up at the bright blue sky, a few wayward white clouds scudding away like lost dogs. I could smell saltwater and stone. I blinked and allowed shapes to form from the glare. We were on a small sailing boat moored in what looked like a makeshift harbour in a small cove. About a dozen more boats – yachts, barges, fishing junks and dinghies – were anchored and tied up against posts on a wooden platform built into the rocks. Bryce staggered over to the stern and leaned against the railing, looking blearily down into the black water.

A man stood at the helm wearing a thick, navy sweater and drinking from a tin mug. His hair was jet black but his beard was dashed with white. I put him somewhere in his forties. A younger woman sat on the bench beside him with her feet beneath her legs. Her hair was a wild stack of dull bronze and rich gold tied back with a purple bandana. A girl of about five sat cuddled beneath her right arm, an older one leaning into her left. All three were huddled together in a sprawl of cardigans, shawls and blankets.

The man put down his mug and looked across the deck at me. He stepped forward so that he stood between me and the girls on the bench and began to inspect the space around my eyes. He offered me his left hand.

'James Grey,' he said, still scanning my face.

I gave him my good hand and he turned it over gently, pulling up my sleeve and looking at my wrists. A bald spot was staking a claim to his crown.

'Any pain in your ears?' he said as he pressed his thumb up and down the soft flesh. He spoke fast with the curves and angles of a broad south-western accent; every vowel stretched apart like a rubber band, every 'r' curving in on itself.

'No,' I said.

'Diarrhoea?'

'What?'

'Vomiting? Neck pain? Does it hurt when you urinate?'

'No, I mean, no more than usual, I . . .'

'Nose bleeds?'

'No.'

'Trouble catching your breath?'

'No.'

He looked suspiciously up at my eyes again. Finally he blinked and nodded. He gave my hand a single shake, then replaced the sleeve and let it drop.

He stepped back so that he was looking at me, not just the bits of me he had previously been interested in, and placed his fists on his hips. 'James Grey,' he said again. He aimed a thumb back over his shoulder at the bench. 'Wife Martha, two girls Jenny and Clare.' The woman raised a hand and smiled. I nodded back.

'Where am I?' I said.

'Just north of Croyde,' he replied, stepping over to the helm and busying himself with a rope. 'Brizzle Channel.' I felt a warm hand grip my shoulder and turned to see Harvey behind me.

'G'day, Ed,' he said. He looked me over. 'How are you doing, son?'

'Fine,' I said.

Harvey squinted a little, careful with his words. 'Did Bryce fill you in?'

I nodded. 'Some of it. I know we didn't make it and I know Richard got past the gate, but I still don't know how I got here.'

'Do you remember seeing us? Before you passed out?'

'I remember seeing Bryce, then nothing.'

'We'd just said goodbye to Richard when we found you. We were about to join the queue ourselves, although I don't think we would have got in. People were already starting to give up and drift away. There was a bit of a party going on by the time you showed up, lots of kids, drinking and all that, arguments, fights, it was getting rough. People'd had enough, I expect.'

He gripped my shoulder again.

'Then you stumbled out of nowhere, Ed,' he said. 'Just fell out of the mist right in front of us. How did you know where we were?'

'I didn't,' I said. 'I had no idea where I was.'

'You looked like death, mate, hell of a mess with your fingers and everything. How's your ankle? Martha got you fixed up.' He smiled and nodded at Martha. She smiled back as she walked past us and climbed the ladder down below deck. 'She's a nurse.'

'How did we get here?'

'James and Martha found us. You were on the ground, unconscious. We were trying to wake you up, shouting for help from one of the medical tents, but nobody came. Too busy, I guess, but then Martha came across, asked what had happened. They were on their way back to their boat and offered to help. We came too.'

'You left the queue?'

'We didn't stand a chance, mate. We were too far back. Besides, it was getting dangerous with all the fighting. We figured it'd be a better idea to come along and make sure you were alright.'

'Thanks,' I said. I shook my head. 'How the hell did Richard get through?'

'He had a good reason. Plus, well . . .' Harvey shrugged. 'You know what he's like. He's probably never queued in his life.'

Martha returned onto the deck and handed me a bowl. I stared at the oily, thick liquid inside it, and smelled fish on the steam rising from its surface. A familiar panic began to churn inside me, the string being pulled taught from my chest.

'Your ankle's sprained,' she said. Her voice was detached. 'It needs rest. Your fingers will fix themselves. Not much I could do about your eye, I'm afraid. It'll heal, but I don't know if you'll be able to see properly out of it again. Like I said to your friends, you're welcome to stay with us until you're well enough to move on. We don't have a lot of space, but we make do.'

'I'm sorry, Ed,' said Harvey. 'We tried.'

I looked up from the broth. Two faces looked back at me. They were full of care and pity, neither of which I needed.

'How far can you get us around the coast?' I said, turning to the helm.

James dropped the end of a rope he was arranging and straightened up. He looked over his shoulder.

'Beg pardon?' he said.

'How far can you get us around the coast?' I repeated. 'How close can you get us to Falmouth?'

He turned and took a step towards me. 'Not sure I follow,' he said.

'Bryce told me that everything directly south of Bristol was a swamp now,' I said.

'That's right,' said James. 'Everything from Plymouth to Southampton, as far north as Glastonbury. Can't be walked on, can't be driven on, can't be floated on.'

'But there's still a thin strip of land that runs south-west from here to Falmouth, where the boats are leaving from,' I said.

'Right,' said James slowly.

'If you can take us south, around the Cornish coast, we might be able to make it across that strip to Falmouth.'

'How?' he said.

'On foot,' I said.

He stared at me, then he buckled his legs and laughed up at the sky. When he had finished, he shook his head. The smile crept from his face.

'You're serious?' he said.

'That's how we made it from Edinburgh to here,' I said.

James looked me up and down. 'So I understand,' he said. 'Not working out so well for you though, is it?'

He took a step forward, folded his arms.

'That coast,' he said. 'It's not the same as it used to be. It's all changed. There's water where there didn't used to be water, rock where there never was before. I wouldn't travel past Padstow. Everything after that, well, it's just too dangerous.'

'If you can get us to Padstow, how far is it from Falmouth?'

'Thirty, forty miles.' James looked at me with his face squinted, as if I was an idiot.

'I could make that,' I said.

He laughed. 'I very much doubt it. It's not just the coast that's changed, it's the land too. The roads are a mess …'

'If they can transport all those people down from the gate, then I can get down too. Is it possible? Can you get me to Padstow before tomorrow?'

'The land is covered with sink-holes and marshes. Whole villages have fallen into the ground, the virus …'

'Can you get me there?'

James sighed, scratched his head and looked up at the sky.

'Wind's good, picking up,' he said. 'So yes, I'd say it's possible. But then what? Even if you make it to Falmouth, do you think you'll just be able to jump on board one of those boats without a pass?'

'Ed,' said Harvey. 'You can't be serious, mate. There's no way you can walk on that ankle.'

'I don't think Ed's talking about walking,' said Bryce from the stern, still looking over the side. 'Are you, Ed?'

I kept my eye on James.

'I know it's a lot to ask,' I said, 'but my family are down there. I have to try to get to them.'

I glanced at Martha and then at the girls, still huddled together on the bench. They looked back at me curiously, as if I was some strange form of entertainment that would hopefully disappear soon.

'You understand?' I said.

'Jesus, Ed,' said Harvey. 'You *are* serious.'

James looked back at me with his head cocked and mouth open, frowning in disbelief. Martha turned to her husband.

'Maggie,' she said.

James turned his incredulous look towards his wife and cocked his head the other way. Eventually he rolled his eyes and shook his head. He walked to the stern.

'Maggie!' he shouted.

A plump woman with grey, straggled hair appeared from the hatch of the neighbouring boat.

'Yiss?'

'Can you look after Martha and the girls for a day?'

The woman craned her neck to look past James.

'Pleasure,' she said. She smiled and waved.

James turned back at us. His face was wild and quizzical, still trying to fathom it out. The boat rocked gently on an incoming wave, bumping the fenders against the bow.

'Right then,' he said at last, tossing his hands up and picking up the rope at his feet. 'Padstow it is.'

'Girls,' said Martha. 'Come with me. We're staying with Aunt Maggie. Daddy will be back tomorrow.'

Bryce walked across to where Harvey and I were standing by the hatch. 'Listen, thanks for getting me this far,' I said. 'And I'm sorry we didn't make it. If I hadn't fallen, maybe we would have been at the gate sooner. Maybe we'd be on a boat by now. I just need … I need …'

'I know, Ed,' broke in Harvey. 'I know.'

'Where will you go?' I said. 'Perhaps you could find somewhere safe around here.'

James kissed his wife and helped her and his daughters onto the other boat. He emptied his cup over the side and began to loosen the moorings. 'Best be going,' he shouted across to us again.

Harvey turned to me and heaved a happy sigh.

'Nah,' he said. 'I don't think so, mate. Reckon we're coming with you. Right, Bryce?'

Bryce grumbled. 'If you want me, I'll be below deck,' he said.

Little Boats

We waved goodbye to Martha and her daughters and I stood next to James as he navigated out of the cove. The wind was strong and southerly and before long we were scudding along under the power of three bulging sails. I had never been on a yacht before; the only boat I had ever travelled on was a cross-channel ferry and a canoe that had capsized and nearly drowned me once on scout camp. I wondered what to do with the exhilaration of moving freely through water with the fresh, salt spray blowing around me. I was blind in one eye, my fingers were broken and every step I made ended in pain. Yet here I was, soon to face another thirty miles on foot. Once again I felt I was in the grip of a decision that hadn't entirely been mine. Something was pushing me, forcing me on, and I doubt it cared for eyes or ankles. I wondered whether hope and exhilaration were the right things to feel at this point.

Bryce was still below deck and Harvey had taken a seat at the bow. I stood next to James at the helm, steadying myself on a post and watching as he gripped and span the wheel against every hurl and nose dive the boat made as it ploughed through the sea.

'We should make Padstow before nightfall with this wind,' he said. 'I'll get you as close as I can. You might even have an hour or two of light to move in before it's dark.'

'Thank you for this,' I said above the wind. 'I'm sure you think we're crazy.'

'Family's important,' he said. 'I'd be doing the same thing in your boots.' He turned his eye from the horizon, looking at me sideways. 'Can't say for sure I would have made it as far as you have, mind.'

'At the gate, were you trying to get on the boats?' I said.

He glanced at the compass and made a quarter turn.

'Nope,' he said. 'We're alright where we are. Our boat's strong.' He slapped the wheel. 'And there's plenty of fish. There are quite a few folk like us living on the channel now. We look after each other, there's a school, a little community. I don't see the need to head off to a different country.'

'What about medicine? The virus?' I said.

He shrugged. 'Take your chances, don't you. There's danger wherever you go.'

'So what were you doing at the gate?'

'Martha was trying to find her sister. We've been going down to the gate every day since it was built, searching the crowds.'

'Did you find her?'

'Nope.'

'I'm sorry.'

'Don't be. Just you find your family.'

A rough wind whipped the sea and sent a squall across the boat. James turned and squinted through the rigging at the western horizon, where a dark band of cloud was growing.

'Looks like we might have some weather,' he said.

I left James at the helm and spent some time walking up and down the deck, putting more and more pressure on my ankle, trying to work through the pain. The wind died a little around noon, although it was still blowing enough to keep us moving. James asked me to hold the wheel while he went below deck. He brought back some mackerel that he had smoked and poured something sweet and alcoholic into two tin mugs that he gave to me and Harvey. Bryce was still below deck, nowhere to be seen. Harvey and I sat at the front of the boat and ate our fish, watching the clouds creep slowly towards us as we rounded a rocky bay. When we had finished, Harvey sat forward and pushed his plate away. He picked up his cup and held it as if it was something warm and comforting.

'So what happened in the canyon?' he said. 'Did you see anything?'

'What do you mean?' I said.

'I mean, did you see anything?' He took a sip. 'Anything unusual?'

'Lots of mist, rocks, weird shapes …'

'No, Ed, you know what I mean. Did you *see* anything?'

I could feel him watching me across the lip of his cup as I struggled for words. Eventually he took a swig and breathed out a great satisfied sigh, wiping his lips on his sleeve.

'You don't have to say, mate,' he said. 'These things are sometimes personal.' He put down the cup and toyed with it on the deck for a while. 'I started seeing spiders somewhere in Victoria. Little ones everywhere, crawling all over the ground and over my feet, running up my legs. I thought they were real at first, I kept swatting at them, trying to get them off. Then I realised they disappeared when I stopped. They only followed me when I ran. And when I did run, they started making noises, little voices calling things up to me.'

He laughed and placed his cup neatly on his plate. Then he looked at me and tapped his head.

'Up here, mate, all up here.'

He sat back against the cabin window and put his hands behind his head.

'Then one day they all suddenly ran off into a forest. But this big one stayed behind. I could feel him crawling slowly up my back and onto my shoulder.'

'How do you know it wasn't a real one?'

'When I looked at him, he smiled. He had a little face, two big human eyes and buck white teeth where his fangs should've been. I ignored him, turned back to the road, but I knew he was there. Every time I looked he turned his head and gave that little goofy smile back. He hopped off a few days later and I never saw him again.'

'Did he speak?'

'Nope, just smiled. But I did meet a Chinaman in the desert who told me about the cobalt he was trying to get back from the moon. He was always in front of me, running backwards. He wanted me to help him, started crying when I said I couldn't fly. There was a girl on Route 1 who told me she was lost. Only little. I'd felt her with me for a while, you know, near me, around me. But then I saw her and heard her. She had a little pinny and a grey cardigan, I remember it was buttoned up wrong. I thought she was real, I really did. I stopped running and tried to get my head together, find my bearings and work out where the nearest town was so I could get her to safety, you know. I asked her where her mummy was and she looked up at me and stuck out her lip. Then she kind of started drifting off into the wind as if she was made of sand, head to toe, all gone. Her and the little stuffed frog she was clutching. Pretty upsetting, that one.'

He stared up at the sail billowing above us, lost in his memory. Then he tapped his head again.

'Anyway, just saying, I've seen a few things myself. I know how weird it can get. We're not really supposed to be on our own, Ed, we're not built for it. Spend too much time running away from reality and that's exactly where you get.'

I heard James's boots on the deck and a rope whizzed behind us. The boom swung slowly across and stopped, shifting the boat starboard. James fastened the sheet tight and returned to the helm.

'Can we help, mate?' shouted Harvey.

'No,' called James. 'But you might have to go below deck before long.' He nodded west. The dark clouds now covered half the sky, shadowing the sea all the way to the horizon.

'I felt like I was coming apart,' I said. 'Like I was lots of little threads unravelling. I couldn't tell where I started and where I stopped. I knew my body didn't want to be running, but I felt like I wasn't my body any more. I knew my mind didn't want to be running, but I wasn't there either. I wasn't my body or my mind or any of the layers in between.'

'But you *were something*, right?'

'Yes, I was,' I said. 'I was there, I was conscious, aware, I just wasn't any of the things I'd thought I was.'

Harvey smiled and looked back at James, then at me. He threw a thumb back at the helm.

'When I was a boy my father told me that life was like being on a boat,' he said. 'You can't control the wind and you sure as hell can't control the ocean. One day it's calm and the next it's a storm and there's nothing you can do about that. All you get is a tiller and a sail and the weather you find yourself in.'

He crossed his arms and puffed through his smile.

'Was he a sailor, your dad?' I asked.

'Nah, he was a shearer, he'd never been on a boat in his life,' said Harvey. 'I lost count of the times he told me that, though. "You're the captain, Harve," he'd say. "Just keep an even keel and watch the wind, you won't go far wrong." Whatever the fuck that means.'

'What do you think?'

He rubbed a coarse palm over the fingers of his other hand.

'I think we like stories,' he said. 'I think we like hearing that we're just little boats lost at sea, all alone, fragile things at the mercy of some darkness we can't fathom, but solid nonetheless – enclosed and separate. It makes sense to think of things being out there.' He waved a finger at the clouds rolling towards us and then touched it against his temple. 'And things being in here. But just because it feels right, doesn't make it true.' He glanced at me. 'See, I drifted apart as well, Ed. I felt it all fall away, just like you. I didn't feel like I was in charge for a while, like I'd ever been in charge. Maybe we're not the captain, not the boat, not the crew, not the cook, not the stowaway, not the rats below deck. Maybe we're …'

'The sea,' I said.

'Yeah. Yeah, I suppose …'

'No, look, the sea. It's moving.'

A great swell was growing off the bow. The surface of the water tipped in our direction, ripples and weed spilling from it as it rose.

'Christ,' said Harvey.

James cried out from the helm and we began to tip. Our empty plates slid slowly across the deck, then suddenly flew off into the sea as the whole boat swung violently over. Harvey fell first, then I followed, both of us landing hard against the rail. I scrabbled up and pulled Harvey to his feet as a heavy spray of seawater hit our faces.

'Getting choppy!' shouted James. 'You'd best get below.'

'You sure we can't help?' spluttered Harvey.

'Best if you don't,' said James. 'I'll call you if I need you.'

We clambered down below deck and I fell into one of the benches at the table. A single bulb hung above it, barely throwing enough light to fill the small galley. I heard Bryce groaning from one of the bunks beneath the foredeck. Harvey sat down across the table, wiping his face with a dishtowel.

'Do you think we'll make it?' I asked.

'Probably,' said Harvey. 'If he knows what he's doing.'

I watched the old man flatten the dishtowel on the table in front of him, then fold it neatly into a square. He boxed it with his hands, then flattened it again and smoothed the surface before setting it to one side. The boat pitched again and the towel slid across the table. I caught it before it fell.

'I saw you howling,' I said, 'that morning in the car park. You stood on the edge and screamed into the sky.'

Harvey ran a hand over his scalp and smiled.

'Yeah, *that*,' he said. 'I was wondering when you were going to ask me.'

'And every morning before, was that you too?'

'Yeah,' he winced. 'I tried to get up before everyone else. Didn't realise you could hear me.'

He leaned his elbows on the table and opened his mouth, but before he could speak there was a thump from above and the boat pitched again. Harvey slid back in his chair and I slumped forward over the table. The timber around us seemed to strain as we bumped on the waves.

'Sheesh,' said Harvey, pulling himself back upright. 'Think he's alright up there?'

We heard footsteps and the creak of the wheel. The boat's movement calmed and we returned to a less-violent angle.

'So what is it?' I said.

'What?'

'The howl, why do you do it?'

Harvey flipped his hand dismissively and crossed his arms. 'Ah, nothing,' he said. 'Just something I used to do when I was running.'

He caught my expression and uncrossed his arms, folding his hands on the table in front.

'It's the sun,' he said. 'I'm yelling at the sun. I used to do it every day in Australia, just as it came up.'

'Why?'

He sighed. 'You don't understand. When you run that far for so long, it's not just spiders and Chinamen and little girls. It's everything. Everything looks at you. All day long that bastard up there beat down on me, all day long, every day from the moment it rose to the moment it fell behind that bloody great horizon. It gets hard to ignore it. You start thinking things are out to get you, watching you, bearing down at you, trying to stop you, resist you.'

His brow furrowed and he chewed his lip. Then he leaned forward again and stared hard into my eyes.

'We're all born screaming, Ed. The moment we pop out our throats open and the same scream bursts out that always has done. We see all the lights and faces and the shadows and the strange sounds and we scream. Life screams and we scream back at it. After a bit of time we learn to be quiet, we learn to muffle it. But life doesn't stop, it just keeps screaming. All. The. Time.' He tapped his finger on the table three times and sat back.

'I reckon it does you good to remind it that you can still scream back once in a while,' he said. 'So that's what I do. I wake up and tell the sun I'm still here. Still screaming.'

We looked at each other for a while. He jutted his jaw and worked his lips seriously like a camel chewing.

'Bet you *really* think I'm a fruit loop now, don't you?' he said.

'Harvey, what really made you run? What happened?' I said.

He blinked at me slowly. Then something seemed to fall in his face. His mouth stopped working and he looked down at his open palms.

There was a jolt. Then a crash from above and James's urgent voice yelling down at us. The boat pitched back and forwards, the hatch flew open and the cabin suddenly filled with wind and water. I pulled myself up and climbed the hatch. James was gripping the wheel as the boat rocked violently on its keel. Behind him, the sky was torn into bright blue across the coast and black, electric clouds bouldering in from the sea, as if the night had come early and was slowly feasting upon the day.

'I'm dropping anchor in that cove,' shouted James. 'This storm's only going to get worse. I can't take you any further, I'm sorry.'

'How far are we from Padstow?' I screamed across the gale.

'A few miles north. Now I need your help. Get up here!'

Getting Bryce up on deck was almost impossible, but eventually we all managed to arrange ourselves on the rolling deck, Bryce hugging a mast and rubbing with his pale brow against the wood as Harvey and I tried to follow the various orders James barked at us, pulling at ropes, winding and unwinding winches, ducking as the boom swung back and forth over our heads. At last, without realising how, I found myself helping James drop anchor in a calmer patch of water that was sheltered behind a rocky outcrop. It was still daylight, although the clouds were trying their best to change that.

'I'm sorry,' said James again as we walked back through the taut rigging to the stern. 'I just can't risk it. I'm heading back. You can come too if you like. If you've changed your mind, I mean.'

'I'd rather get going,' I said. 'Maybe we can make up some distance before nightfall. But thanks all the same.'

James nodded and scanned the sky. 'You've got a couple more hours of daylight, I reckon.' He pointed at a steep, narrow path that wound up the rock on shore. 'Follow that path. Maybe one of the roads south is still there. You'd do well to find shelter as soon as you can, before the storm really hits.'

'Thanks,' I said. 'For everything.'

'Alright,' said James. 'You'd best get ashore. I've no dinghy, I'm afraid.'

I thanked him again, then we jumped in and swam till our boots hit the sand, then waded until we found a small beach. There we sat shivering, catching our breath and watching the boat bob harmlessly on the tide as the blue sky was consumed by darkness.

Ours Alone

This is hard; I'm unsure of everything. Events, places, faces, words, they're all like pages of manuscript blown across a lake. I can't catch the sheets, I can't place them in order. I remember the smell of ozone, the stiff air, the light around us seeming to bristle with electricity. I remember lightning stabbing at the horizon with jagged spears. I remember that the storm seemed to compress and ignite the low light. Our skins, our eyes, the stone path on which we climbed – it all gleamed.

We found the road and followed it, making sure the churning sea was to our right. We began to run. I could put pressure on my ankle, but not for long, so I was doing nothing more than a brisk limp. It didn't seem as if Bryce and Harvey had much trouble keeping to my slow pace either; they had their own injuries to slow them down.

We had travelled about four miles by the time the storm hit the coast properly. The wind bore down upon us with whips of rain, blustering and snapping, trying to herd us back inland. We made it another two miles before looking for shelter. The light had fallen dramatically, but Bryce pointed out a lonely house sitting in the mist on a rocky outcrop and led us towards it.

As we fought through the wind, Harvey pointed out that all of my injuries were on the right side of my body, because I led with this side. Every stride was right foot first, with the left acting as support. He wagered that, if I tripped, I would always put my right hand down to break my fall. Hence the broken fingers. I was thinking about whether you could look at crows more with your right eye than with your left when the ground beside me seemed to shudder and shift. I felt my foot slide on gravel. When I looked, Harvey was gone, replaced by a hole in the ground.

'Bryce!' I fell down to the ground and looked in. Harvey was lying face down and still, about ten feet beneath. The wind blew clods of wet earth onto his back.

'What happened?' yelled Bryce as he scrambled down beside me.

'I don't know, the ground just opened up.'

'A sinkhole?'

'James said the land wasn't safe.'

'We have to get him out,' said Bryce. 'Can you get down?'

'I'll try.'

Bryce held my arm as I lowered myself in. Harvey was out cold. I turned him over and wiped the dirt from his face. He opened his eyes and blinked at me. There was a long cut across his forehead.

'Hello,' he murmured. He touched a finger to the wound and scored its length, wincing as he reached a deep gouge thickening with blood near the top. 'What happened?'

'I'm not sure, but you had a fall. Can you move?'

'I think so.' I helped Harvey to his feet and shouted up to Bryce.

'He's hurt. Can you lift him out?'

'Pass me his arms,' said Bryce. He held down a hand and hauled Harvey up the side, then turned and pulled me out too. Harvey stood groggily in the deafening rain, holding a hand to his head. He looked at us sheepishly.

'Sorry, fellas,' he said.

'Not your fault,' said Bryce. 'Let's get out of this rain.'

We each put an arm around Harvey and helped him the rest of the way to the house. With every other step he'd mumble another apology. 'Sorry, sorry, fellas, dunno what happened, sorry, fellas.'

The house was a small, pebble-dashed cottage with a yard and a garage that backed onto a field and, beyond, the edge of a cliff. There were no lights on inside, no sound of a generator, no candles. Water streamed down in a waterfall from a broken gutter. We hammered on the door, the windows too, but there was no answer. We went round the back and found an open door banging against its frame. White paint peeled from its wood and most of its glass panels were smashed through.

We pulled Harvey inside and closed the door. We were in a utility room. Crumpled and faded clothes hung on a stand in the corner and the stone floor was puddled with rain.

'Hello?' I called.

'He's bleeding,' said Bryce. 'Let's get him inside.'

'I'm alright, just need a sit down, sorry fellas, sorry.'

We pushed a door through into a kitchen. The stench hit us like lead. A man and a woman sat at the table, slumped forward, long dead. The top of the man's scalp was turning green and crumpling like a cabbage. His arms were stretched out before him and I could see blistering pustules up and down his wrists.

'Christ,' said Bryce, holding his free hand to his mouth. 'Do you think it's the virus?'

'Looks that way,' I replied.

We stood in the doorway, covering our faces, Harvey still hanging between us. He gave a groan.

'Do you think it's safe in here? Can we catch it?'

'I don't know. Maybe we already have,' said Bryce.

'The garage,' I said. 'Let's take him there.'

We slammed the door on the kitchen and found a set of keys hanging on a hook in the utility room. Harvey gave a groan as we crossed the yard and his feet stumbled in the mud, trying to get a hold on the loosening ground. The third key fitted the metal door and Bryce pulled it open. We fell inside and I pulled Harvey's legs out of the rain, sitting him up against a brick wall. Bryce began to search the square room. There was hardly any light and most of the space was taken up by a small, battered boat on a trailer.

'Any blankets? Sheets?' I said.

'Sorry, fellas, sorry.'

'I can't see,' Bryce growled. A tin can rattled on the floor. Something made of glass broke as Bryce swept the shelves.

'He's really bleeding,' I said.

'Found a torch,' said Bryce. 'Shit.' He began scanning the room with the watery light. 'OK. Wait . . . here.' He threw over a pile of dust sheets. I tore off a strip and held it against Harvey's brow. His head lolled and he began to mumble something.

'Safe now, Harvey,' I whispered. I wrapped two of the sheets around him and laid his head against the wall. Then I tied a longer strip around his head. The dirty grey fabric darkened with blood but it seemed to staunch the flow. Harvey sighed and smiled at me.

'Thanks, mate. Sorry, fellas.'

Bryce began throwing other things down to me from the shelves – a couple of candles, matches, a dog blanket. Then he stopped and crouched next to me.

'Found these too,' he said. In his hands were two tins of baked beans. He gave one to me and we opened them. I held mine out to Harvey.

'Eat some, Harvey,' I said.

Harvey frowned and waved away the can.

'Nah, I'm not hungry, thanks,' he said. 'You go ahead. Think I just need to rest a bit. Sorry, fellas.'

The storm screamed and hammered the garage door as if the sea itself, filled with some nameless grievance, had risen up over the cliffs and hunted us down. We ate our beans nervously, watching Harvey swim down through his unconsciousness, his face flickering with whatever cruel dreams lay beneath the surface.

We saved some of our beans for him. I lit a candle and we sat beneath the remaining sheets, huddled next to Harvey on either side. Bryce struggled for a while with a roll-up, pushing his last wisps of tobacco into a soaking paper and trying to ignite it over the flame. Eventually he cursed and threw the whole mess on the floor, sticking the match between his teeth instead.

'I'm sorry I dragged you into this mess,' I said.

He didn't answer for a while. 'We choose our own mess,' he said at last. 'Besides, I wasn't doing anything. It's not like I had family of my own to look after.'

'Do you think you ever will?' I asked, surprising myself at the question.

He snorted. 'Not after seeing what you've put yourself through,' he said. 'Too much fuckin' trouble for me. No, thanks.'

'We choose our own mess,' I said.

Bryce smiled. 'Aye,' he said. Then he turned to me, his face softening. 'And your mess isn't so bad, Edgar. Remember that.'

'I know,' I said.

Bryce's eyes glistened for a while in the struggling light. Then he blinked back the weakness and the moment was gone.

'Anyway,' he yawned. He flicked the match away and lay down with his back to me on the cold floor. 'I've not yet met the woman who can handle my shite.'

'I saw you at Bartonmouth,' I said.

I knew I was taking a risk. I don't know why I wanted to push Bryce into talking about it. Maybe – sitting in the cold with the storm outside and Harvey injured between us – maybe I just didn't want another conversation masked in bravado. Maybe I wanted to talk about something honest, and maybe something told me that we wouldn't have another chance to do so.

'With Grimes. With Laura, I mean. You went into her room that night.'

Bryce was silent for a moment.

'I know you did, arsehole. I saw you looking,' he said. I heard his head turn. 'What did you think, I was in there after a shag?'

I didn't answer. Bryce wheezed a laugh.

'You think I fancied my chances?' he said. 'Picking up where that dickhead left off?'

'I didn't say that,' I began.

He laughed again. 'That's funny. Christ, Ed, what do you take me for?'

'I didn't mean anything. Sorry.'

'I mean I wasnae exactly her type, was I?' he said, suddenly angry. 'She was after Richard. I knew that, even in the barracks I knew that.' He settled his head down and shuffled under the blanket.

'So what happened?'

'I just wanted to tell her, that's all. I saw how she looked after she made that pass at him. I just wanted her to know.'

'Know what?'

'Just know.'

I slid down the wall and made a pillow from a bunched-up blanket. I lay in silence for a while until I heard Bryce's rumbling snores. Then I closed my eyes.

When I awoke the metal door was still banging, but less violently. The storm seemed to have moved further away. The candle was almost out but I could still see Harvey's face. The bandage was completely red now. His eyes were twitching and small sounds whistled from his cracked lips.

'Hey? Wha . . . Hornsby? Too far. Not my run, mate, you tell . . . tell Rosie. Give it to her, she'll stamp it for ya . . . yeah nice and dusty.'

I raised myself up on one elbow, trying to listen.

'Real hot one today, gotta watch . . . wha . . .? No, no, no, mate that's not what . . . wha? I said tell Rosie . . . she'll stamp it for . . . I gotta get going, mate . . . letters won't post themselves . . . all nice and dusty . . . Annie? Agnes?'

I watched him wrestle with the tangle of memories in his head. They were his and his alone. They were inside him, trapped and bound inescapably to him. No amount of storytelling could release them. None of them could truly be shared. In the end, I thought, this is how we all end up: running alone through our own wilderness, the landscape of disjointed events that form our lives, with nobody to make sense of it but ourselves. The road is ours, and ours alone.

I still didn't know how much of what Harvey had told Bryce and me about Australia was true. I didn't know if he had been a postman in the bush, if he had fought forest fires, if he had run his routes with his dogs in the New South Wales sun.

'Gotta go … can't stay here … all dark and dead … can't … can't …'

If he had run because his dogs had died.

'Losing dogs,' Bryce had said, next to that roadside fire. The taste of rat had still been on my tongue. 'Hardest fuckin' thing. Harder than losing a person.'

I remember Harvey suddenly seeming to flinch, to close up. I remember feeling something, a brief glimmer of sadness, as if a small trap had shut. Some of the memory he was coaxing into the world had pulled back. It didn't want to fly, it wanted to stay inside.

'Well,' Harvey had said. 'I don't really know about that.'

'All dark and dead … that road … bright and living … Agnes?'

'Everything here was dark and dead,' he had said. 'Everything out there was bright and living.'

'Agnes? Where's Annie? Bring her in, love, it's too hot out there. She got sunscreen on? OK, darling, I gotta go now … I'll see ya later, love you too.'

His words became faint whimpers and his eyes became still. Then he coughed and shifted his head against the wall. I watched his chest moving in the dying candlelight until the flame burned out.

The road is ours, and ours alone.

Happy Christmas

When I woke again the storm had gone, and the small window at the back of the garage was brightening into a square of blue. Bryce was still asleep and Harvey's head was still resting on the back wall. His jaw hung open and his eyes were empty pools turned up towards the ceiling. His hands lay face up on the blanket, fingers curling loosely into his palms. A thin trickle of blood had dried to one side of his face and neck. His chest was still.

Something seemed to contract inside me, like a cord drawn tight around my stomach. I got up, shook off the blanket and staggered back to the door. I stood there for a while, looking down on him with horror. Then I felt my stomach clench again and opened the door, stumbling out into the early morning and vomiting into the dirt.

I wiped my face and steadied myself against a wall that ran next to the garage, looking across the field of mud and the sea below it. The water was calm now and the dark horizon was clear of cloud. The sun was rising behind me, reclaiming the sky with light after the storm's assault. The air was still, only traces of the wind from the night before still whispered about.

I heard a noise from far away. At first I thought it was a voice calling. I left the yard and stood in the road, feeling the warm sun on my face, the cold air on my fingertips. Then it came again. Not a voice, not a human; an animal calling. Again, two this time. Cows. Cattle braying.

I followed the sound for half a mile. The road and every field along it was thick with mud from the rain. As I walked, the sun rose higher and offered me a view further inland. The mud stretched as far as I could see, caking everything. Eventually I found a gate to a field. There was a farm at the top and midway up was a small pen containing five emaciated cows. The farmhouse door was wide open. Between it and the pen, lying face down in the dirt, was a body. I walked up to the pen and stood before the cows. They turned on shaking legs, manoeuvring themselves awkwardly about each other to face me. Their eyes rolled and bulged, their jawbones stretched up to the sky in hoarse bellows.

I opened the pen and stood back. One by one they stumbled out, moving past me in a mass of warmth. They kept close together as they made their way across to a corner of the field. A sparse patch of pale grass was still growing there. They stopped and bowed their heads down and ate it.

I heard footsteps in the wet ground behind me.

'Harvey's dead,' said Bryce.

'I know,' I replied.

We found a spade in the garage and buried Harvey in the field behind the house. The ground was soft and not difficult to dig. We lashed two sticks together and stuck it in the ground, then stood before it, eating the beans we had left for him the night before.

The sun was still rising and we looked southwards, away from the coast. Thirty miles of freshly soaked marsh stretched out between us and Falmouth. It was already mid-morning. My bones felt like stone and my muscles like dried rubber. Pain threatened every movement.

'Is this the end, Ed?' said Bryce.

'It's never the end,' I said.

Bryce sniffed. 'I thought you might say that,' he said. 'I found these in the house.'

Bryce held out a white box with a printed label stuck to its side.

Codeine Phosphate Hemihydrate 30mg/
Paracetamol 500mg

'Happy Christmas,' he said.

Never the End

You want to know how it feels to run thirty miles. You want to know how it feels to run thirty miles straight through mud and across scorched earth, dodging sinkholes and crawling beneath toppled trees, when you've already run the length of the country, when your ankle's sprained, your fingers are broken, you're blind in one eye and you've only had half a tin of baked beans for breakfast.

I'll tell you. It starts like every other run. Before the first step, before the first muscle twitches, before the first neuron fires, there comes a choice: stand still or move. You choose the right option. Then you repeat that choice 100,000 times. You don't run thirty miles, you run a single step many times over. That's all running is; that's all anything is. If there's somewhere you need to be, somewhere you need to get to, or if you need to change or move away from where or what you are, then that's all it takes. A hundred thousand simple decisions, each one made correctly. You don't have to think about the distance or the destination or about how far you've come or how far you have to go. You just have to think about what's in front of you and how you're going to move it behind you.

Of course, codeine helps. We overdosed on it and drank drizzle from a ditch. Then we got our bearings and put our feet to work.

The first ten miles were slow torment. We tried talking about the boats, and about where they might be going, and about Harvey. Each attempt ended in half sentences, and I didn't mention Harvey's delirious mumblings in the middle of the night. My ankle was not as much of a problem as I thought, but my back was, probably from the way I had slept. Splintering pain ran up from the base of my spine whenever my feet hit the earth. I counted my steps, distracting myself with calculations about how many it would take before the codeine kicked in. My bones felt dry and hot. My ligaments threatened to shear like ancient rubber bands with every step. But every step came and went and led to the next one, fresh with its own unique breed of pain.

Mud became less of a problem the further inland we went. Brown marsh became scraggy dirt. There were fields and fences, coarse hedgerows, copses with some trees still growing. We stopped at a stream and drank freezing water until I felt my belly bursting against my belt. We passed through empty villages and took shortcuts through abandoned farms, and all the time a thin, blue line of sea ran along the western horizon to our left, reminding me, pulling me on.

About fifteen miles in, things began to change. A small bird – a starling, perhaps – had been flying ahead of me. I couldn't remember for how long. It flitted between branches of a hedge, waited for me, then flitted to the next. I realised that the painkillers must have taken effect. I felt that something had separated inside. I wasn't numb, just indifferent; the pain was still there but it didn't seem to matter as much. Bryce was ever present, lumbering along beside me. He seemed to have withdrawn too. My attention turned to my breathing, and the sound of air moving in and out of my lungs took centre stage. I looked down at the struggle going on between my battered feet and the ground beneath them and remembered Harvey's appraisal of my gait – that I still led with my right foot, in spite of its injury. I changed this; pushed forwards with my left.

It may have been this or the codeine or any number of other things that triggered what happened next. Maybe some long battle deep within my brain had finally been won, or maybe a hidden reserve of endorphins had suddenly burst under slow pressure. What it felt like was a surrender; something gave up, something that had kept its hold too long. I felt a slow unravelling take place around my shoulders and down my spine. A lightness drew me up and my ribcage filled with cold air. My legs seemed to stretch and flush, as if unexpectedly released from heavy chains. My muscles broke free, my blood rejoiced. Everything within me seemed suddenly to turn in the same direction, like a billion tiny compass needles twitching towards a giant magnet. Everything that had been grinding and grating and straining against each other was now flowing in one single path.

I was running, and my body wanted everything to do with it.

My mind wanted everything to do with it.

That other beast inside you, the one you rarely see? You have it tethered tight. It watches and waits while you mess up your life, fill your body with poison and muddy your mind with worry. For some it takes just one call to free it. For others it takes 500 miles of agony.

But mine was free now, for the first time since I was a boy, running with a grin like a wolf through moonlit bracken. Pain ran alongside me, kindred and beautiful and grinning my grin. *I'll always be here*, it said. *Always, but now we're friends.*

I held nothing back. I took every pleasure I could from the experience and took all the warmth I could from the sun, now high in the clear sky above us. I thought about my wife and my children and ignored the cold shreds of instinct that told me they were already far away, that I was already too late. Instead I thought simple, bright thoughts about a cliff-side house with a small field, of a woman in a garden teaching her daughter how to plant vegetables, of a young boy standing in the sun, gazing up at his father as he sands the sides of an old boat in long, satisfying strokes, of an empty beach and sand beneath small toes and laughter on the water's edge as the sun falls.

Bryce fell behind, then caught up. I felt as if he was riding on my tailwind, with me carrying him effortlessly on whatever boundless reserve of energy I had somehow tapped into. I felt like a child. I was a child; I am a child. Because we don't grow up; we grow over, like weeds over new grass.

I ran with Bryce across dales and meadows and we followed streams and stone walls through ancient forests until finally we broke through a hedge and hit a road. We stopped and caught our breath, swaying, dizzy with adrenalin. We looked up and down the tarmac. It was long and straight and flat with no potholes, an untouched relic – the first unbroken road I had seen since before the strike. A white signpost said:

Falmouth 3 miles

We ran the first two easily. The last was hell.

* * *

'Ships!' shouted Bryce. 'Ships!'

By the time we reached the outskirts of Falmouth, I was running on the last fumes of whatever fuel I had found that morning. I was back to struggling and limping and wincing. The pain had shape-shifted back into its old unfriendly and unfathomable form. Then we reached the top of a hill and my heart exploded with relief. Falmouth Harbour opened up gloriously beneath us. I could hear and see people; I swear I could even smell them, though they were still a mile from where we stood. There was movement – a ship; we were not too late. We had made it. It might take some time, but I would find Beth. I would find her and tell her I loved her and that I had run across the country to find her. We would find a quiet place and I would tell her about my vision of our simple life, and she would understand and say that she wanted that too and we would take our children away from the heaving crowds and find a place to live our lives.

'Ships,' said Bryce again. This time he hesitated. His voice was flatter and his head was turned out to sea. Relief, joy, hope, the strange new energy I had been moving with: everything began to seep slowly away. A line of ten or more ships drew out of the harbour with their bows puffed towards the horizon and their funnels pointing back to the shore from which they were sailing. A roar of voices rose up on the wind like a mourning choir. People filled the dockside, a dark mass of human life pushing, pulling, pulsing, swarming, moving as a single entity in a clamour to reach the gangplank of the one ship still moored; the one ship, the last of the fleet to leave.

I felt my knees tremble and give way. Weight returned like an iron jacket. Gravity grew stronger, doubled, trebled, quadrupled and finally yanked me down to the earth. My face hit the tarmac and I sprawled forward. I heard Bryce's voice. One of the stringyphone cans fell out from my jacket and rolled forward. I grasped for it, missed it and watched it roll slowly away. Road, sky and sea all blurred into one smear of grey as the can picked up speed down the hill.

I felt myself being lifted, then dragged, looked down to see my feet moving beneath me, clawing at the ground as it moved backwards like a conveyor belt. A long string of drool floated out from my lips and wavered on the breeze. I saw the can pass beneath me and bent to scoop it up. Bryce's voice again, distant and urgent.

'We're here, Ed. We made it. You made it.'

The noise of the crowd suddenly closed in around me. The smell of human life hit my nose. Something hit my shoulder, then my other one. A woman laughed, a cackling laugh like a witch, then I looked up and saw only sky. The light was the same electric yellow that we had seen on the beach the day before: charged, static, on the brink of change. Then something hit me. Bryce hit me, open palmed, twice on each cheek.

'Ed!' He shook me, hit me again, clicked his fingers. 'Ed! Snap out of it! Come on! We're here!'

I was awake again, standing upright, breathing, seeing and hearing. But time was slow. Everything moved through sludge. We were at the harbour. The boat was above us. We were separated from the gangplank by a crowd fifty people deep that lined the dock as far as we could see in each direction. People were moving about aimlessly. Some were laughing, some were weeping, some were drunk, others dizzy with hunger, staggering up and down with wide eyes and taut mouths. Everywhere I looked I saw lost, wandering souls and huddled families. The stench was terrible: fear and panic and shit and squalor – the breath and sweat of a million survivors still clawing for some chance of escape from a crumbling country. No medicine, no water, no food, no rest. We were not the only ones to have made it to Falmouth that day.

I jumped as a loud female voice filled the air, airy and pleasant. Speakers rigged to poles rang out a metallic tannoy.

'*Please move back from the dock. The* Endeavour *is ready for departure. Please move back from the dock.*'

'Move back, please,' said another voice, close to my ear. It sounded Dutch or Nordic. Next to us were two men in military uniform. They held assault rifles.

'My family,' I murmured. 'My family are here.'

'You have papers?' said the first.

'Papers?' I said. 'No. My family. They were brought here … I came to find them.'

'You don't have papers, you don't belong here. Move back, please, sir.'

'Come on …' began Bryce, holding his hands up. The second guard moved closer to him, pushing him back with the tip of his gun.

'You don't understand, they were taken …' I began, but I jumped again as the noise of the ship's horn blared across the harbour.

The second guard raising his gun slightly at Bryce.

'Move *back*, sir.'

'No, you don't … you don't… .'

The ship's horn sounded again, longer this time. I heard something else in the long reverberating tail that made me freeze.

'You don't understand, I . . .'

I looked up at the ship. The crowd was dispersing, moving past us, opening up the gap between us and the gangplank.

I knew then I would find her. I didn't believe it or hope it, I knew it.

'SIR, MOVE BACK NOW.'

That sound again. A voice.

'SIR!'

'Daddy!'

I swung my eyes to the boat and a shot of adrenalin pulsed through me. How much that chemistry set inside dictates our perception of the world; my mind and muscles came to life and time returned to its normal speed. There on the deck, with both feet on the bottom rung of the railing, was Alice. She leaned out and stretched a hand towards me.

'Daddeeeee!'

The other passengers didn't see her, too busy finding a place to stand or searching the crowd. She put one foot on the next rung up.

'Alice!'

Then she followed with her next leg. Her waist was now at the top of the railing.

'SIR, MOVE BACK.' The second guard was bullying Bryce back with his gun.

'Alice! No! Wait!'

Her face fixed into a determined frown. She pushed her hands down on the railing and raised another trembling leg.

It slipped and she tried again, this time finding the next rung. I called out and ran, but the guard caught me, pushing me back.

'That's my daughter!' I cried. 'Alice! Get down!'

A hopeful smile crept onto her face. She kept her eyes on me, her only goal to get from where she was to where I was. It was a simple journey; nothing stood in her way but the railing. Then it was just empty space and then me. The freezing sea and concrete thirty feet below was not part of the equation. I watched in horror as she hauled herself up.

'Somebody help her!' I shouted up to the boat.

Then another sound, another voice I recognised. An arm shot out of the crowd and around Alice's chest, yanking her back. Beth's arm. In her other was Arthur. She plonked Alice down on the deck and began to scold her. I saw Alice remonstrating, her fists waving, pointing out into the crowd, jabbering back at her mother's sharp words. Then she stopped and took a deep breath.

'It's DADDDEEEEEEEEEE!' she screamed. Beth seemed to falter, then stopped. She held her finger in mid-wag, crooked like a question mark. Then she turned to the crowd on the harbour. Alice placed her hands on her mother's cheeks and directed them towards me. Beth's mouth fell open.

Then things began to move very quickly. The boat's funnel gave another blast. There was a scuffling in the crowd next to us, raised voices, people moving apart. The guards turned in the direction of the commotion. Mine loosened his grip. I heard some words of warning, then the wet crack of a fist on cheek flesh. A fight had broken out. People were making space for two large men, one of whom was now reeling from a punch.

The guard shook me away, yelled out and ran towards the fight. His partner followed, leaving Bryce and me standing, facing the thinning crowd moving away from the boat. I shot him a look and we ran for it. I kept my eyes on Beth as I pushed through the filthy hoards, ignoring the shoves, the bony elbows digging into my ribs, the angry glares, the growls of disdain. When we reached the bottom of the gangplank I saw that it was sealed off with a white, padlocked gate. Four guards stepped warily forward and one held out his palm. He was tall with a wide jaw and cold, grey eyes.

'Stop there!' he boomed.

'My family are on that boat,' I said. 'Please, you have to let me on board.'

'You have medical papers?' he said.

'No, no, but I'm fine. No virus,' I said. 'Let me speak to them!'

He looked me up and down.

'You cannot board without medical papers,' he said. 'You must go, the ship is about to depart. Please step back.'

'No, look,' I said, pointing up on the deck. 'That's my family there! They're right there on the deck! Beth! I'm here! Please let me speak to my family!'

'Ed!' called Beth.

The guard turned his head to the boat, keeping his eyes on me until the last minute, then flicking them up to where Beth was standing. He saw her calling down and turned back.

'I am sorry,' he said. He shook his head. 'There is nothing I can do. You cannot board without medical papers. You should not even be here. Now, please, get back from the boat.'

The other three guards moved cautiously towards us and raised their guns.

'You don't …' I began. 'I just … I just …'

'Ed!'

'Daddy!'

'Sir, please step back.' The guard raised his head and stood tall. I fell back into the crowd.

'I just … just …' I looked up at Beth. She was crying. I felt an elbow in my back.

'Watch out,' someone grumbled.

'Just …'

I had been aware of Bryce somewhere behind me. He had been quiet and the guards hadn't paid him much attention. Now I felt him close by, heard him splutter something, felt his breath on my neck, sensed his frustration, sensed his hackles rise. His throat rumbled, then he snarled, then he grabbed me with both arms. The guards stepped back in fright. The first raised his gun. Bryce pulled me to his face and he planted a single, fierce kiss on my cheek. I felt myself rising up above the crowd, then swing down into them. Bryce hurled me with a thundering roar. And then I was flying, flying high over the astonished faces of the four guards beneath me, my legs and arms flailing as I sailed over the gate and landed on the metal gangplank with a crack from somewhere in my leg that I chose to ignore.

I scrambled to my feet and turned to the crowd. I was halfway up the gangplank. Cheers and shouts came from all around, from the boat and from the harbour. I searched for Bryce, but the crowd had begun to thicken again, turning to the boat to see what was going on. The guards were at the gate, trying to open it. One was fumbling with a set of keys. He dropped them and the others cursed. I saw my chance, turned and ran up to the deck. There was another gate at the top, too tall to climb. The crowd of passengers stepped back from it as I rattled it, trying to open it, but it was locked. Beth was further up the railing to my left.

'Help her through!' I shouted. 'Help me reach her.'

The crowd shuffled about, pushing her along with Alice clinging to her dress and Arthur gripping her neck, laughing as he saw me. I hung from the gate and reached out a hand. Beth took it and I pulled her to the gate, reaching both arms through and holding her face in my palms.

Beth and I met one Christmas when we were both living in London. We were at a friend's party. I was twenty-seven and single, she was a year younger and had just broken up with someone. She was pretty and funny and we cornered each other, avoiding everyone else and stealing their champagne when they weren't looking, laughing at their faces as they tried to drink from empty glasses. She called me her 'partner in crime' and I phoned her the next day, arranging a date for some time in the New Year. I spent Christmas with my parents, she with hers in Dundee. We texted each other, each alert from my phone bringing the same jolt of excitement, each message more and more sexually charged. I would excuse myself from whatever meal or game or film I was enduring with my family and go and sit on the toilet, thumbing through the history of our conversation again and again, imagining things.

We met as planned and I took her to dinner in a Polish restaurant where they served vodka instead of wine. We got drunk and kissed and she let me sleep with her in her bed, although it was two weeks before we made love. 'Partner in crime' became our private joke for everything, including sex. It was how I proposed to her and it even made it into our vows when we got married, when I faced her in a small church and saw only her glowing face and the bright red bouquet she was holding, bathed in a blur of noise and light, all the rest of the world draining away, so distant and inconsequential next to her.

I don't know what happened between then and now. We never stay constant, no matter what we promise; the world has its way of pulling you about the way it wants. But some things pull you back to where you were before. Like a woman's face through the bars of a gate.

I held her head in my hands and felt that same draining of reality. The crowd's jeers and whistles, the sound of the guards struggling to unlock the gate behind me, the clamour of the passengers on the deck: it all seeped into a far-away hum and all that was left was Beth's face, smiling, wet with tears, full of love. She claimed all of my senses, all of my time, all of me. I felt so ashamed and sorry; sorry for leaving her in the barracks, sorry for not looking after her more, sorry for everything I didn't do as a husband, a father, a friend. All I had for her was 'sorry'.

'I'm sorry,' she said. Her eyes creased.

'What?'

'I'm sorry we left you at the barracks, I thought it was our only chance, they said they were sending more helicopters. They had medicine for Arthur. I'm sorry, I'm so sorry.'

'You're not the one who says sorry,' I said. The gate shook at the bottom of the gangplank and Beth looked across my shoulder. I turned and saw one of the guards shout something up at me in a language I didn't understand as two of his cohorts struggled with the lock on the gate. I turned back to Beth. She was frightened.

'It's OK,' I said. 'It's alright, I came to get you, to take you home.'

She tipped her head sadly and put a hand through the bars to stroke my cheek.

'There is no home, Ed.'

'I know.' I laughed. 'I know that now.'

There was a jangle of keys on concrete, the guards' angry voices as they argued with each other. A small group at the front of the harbour crowd laughed.

I took a deep breath and the smell of her hair came with it. Memories of London, our first night together, the flight we had taken to Rome on our honeymoon when I'd leaned in to watch her sleep, holding her head close in the delivery room, skull to skull as Arthur squeezed into the world.

'I'm sorry,' I said. 'I've not been what you deserve. I've been … I've been lacking.'

The passengers on the deck had formed a small semicircle around Beth. Some of them were looking nervously back to the stern. People further back were making way for more guards moving up the boat towards us.

'No you haven't,' she said. 'Don't say that.'

'I have and I'll change. I will. All I want is you.' I held my hand to touch Arthur's gleeful face and smiled, then looked down at Alice, looking up at me with that dark look of hers. 'You and these things here. I'm just sorry it took the end of the world to make me see that.'

Beth smiled and something peaceful glinted in her eye. She reached around my neck and pulled me in, pressing my forehead against the bars and needling my eyes with her own.

'This is our world, Ed,' she said. 'Me, you and these things. It doesn't matter what happens out there.'

All of my senses. All of my time. All of me.

'Daddy, what happened to your eye?'

I looked down at Alice. She swayed, a single filthy bunny gripped in a fist. I knelt down and reached in to touch her brow.

'A bad birdy,' I said.

'Does it hurt?'

'A bit.'

'Can you see?'

'I can now.'

She frowned suspiciously. 'You could have a patch,' she said. 'Like a pirate.'

'I have something for you,' I said. I reached inside my coat and pulled out one end of the stringyphone, breaking the string in my teeth and holding out the battered can for her. She took it and grinned.

'Now I can talk to you,' I said. She went to speak but I saw the crowd move behind her and a guard burst through.

'Step back from the gate,' he said.

'Please,' said Beth. 'This is my husband. You have to let him on board.'

'Papers?' said the guard. I shook my head and leaned it against the bars. 'Then you must get off. Please, move back.'

'You have to,' said Beth. She swung round to face him, furious. 'You have to. We have children.'

'Not without papers. I'm sorry. Now please step back.'

I heard keys in the gate behind me, more shouts from the crowd. The gate rattled.

'Then we're getting off,' said Beth. She reached through and grabbed my good hand. 'We're coming with you. Open the gate.'

The guard on the boat looked unsure, nervous. I thought of the house on the cliff, the vegetable garden, the boat. A possible life. A fantasy life. On the deck, behind Beth, I saw a nurse treating a child. There were stacks of fresh bottled water, clean laundry, warm blankets, food, relief on every face. I didn't have to look behind me to see the difference in the faces at the harbour.

Everything here was dark and dead. Everything out there was bright and living.

'No,' I said. 'You stay here. I'll come to you.'

Beth blinked and a tear ran down her face, but she didn't argue. She understood.

'Step back now,' snapped the guard on deck. I heard the gate open behind me and a disappointed jeer rose from the crowd, boots clattering on the gangplank.

You want to find the big line, the words that tie everything together, the phrase that speaks the world and all that's in your heart, but you're holding tightly to a railing and your hands are tired and time is running out and all you have are words and a set of feelings you don't fully understand. All you ever have is cards, a mixed deck, shaking hands and no clue how to deal them. So you reach for anything that might work. You try to resonate. You reach for something to say, a story, a memory, anything.

'Alice kissed me,' I said.

'What?'

I felt the metal floor shudder behind.

'We'd been arguing about milk. We were tired. You were downstairs, angry, slamming doors. I was upstairs, lying on the bedroom floor and Alice came over. She kissed me. Right here.' I touched the space above my wounded eye. Beth shook her head, confused.

'It was wonderful,' I said. 'It's wonderful.'

Three hands grabbed my shoulders.

'You're wonderful.'

They pulled my body back and my hands left the gate. My heels dragged and the boat fell down out of my vision. My head hit the metal twice and they tossed me onto the harbour floor. The boat's funnel blared and I heard water moving. I lay still and stared up into the electric sky. Strange, worried faces framed the dying daylight. I kept my eyes open, refusing to blink.

Sennen

You want to know the truth. You want to know if what happened happened. I'll tell you what I believe.

I believe that there are three bodies buried in the field behind the house in which I live. I believe that two of them were the strangers who lived here before me and that the third was an old man named Harvey Payne who once ran across Australia. I believe that somewhere north of Birmingham lies the body of a soldier named Laura Grimes, that a man named Richard Shore is safe with his son on a boat to South Africa. I believe that I lost a six-foot-eight Scotsman with waist-length hair named Bryce Gower in a crowd of emaciated refugees on the Falmouth dockside.

Now, having written this down, I can see how you might believe otherwise. And you might find your own version of the truth in that. But we choose our own truths, we choose what to believe. Beliefs are just little stories we tell ourselves to make life easier. So you enjoy yours and I'll enjoy mine.

I stayed at Falmouth for a day or two, trying to find Bryce in the camps people had set up. Nobody had seen him. There was a small riot as the last support vessel left, but nobody really had the energy to see it through. I watched it disappear over the horizon, then everyone drifted away. I found my way back here, to the house we had stayed in the night before our run to Falmouth. I sheltered in the garage for a day or two, then decided to risk moving inside. I used blankets to shift the bodies of the young man and woman at the table. From their clothes, I guessed they had been in their twenties and I noticed that she had been pregnant when they died. I didn't spend too much time thinking about that. Then I buried them in the field next to Harvey.

I've been here for two months now and I'm showing no signs of illness, so my guess is that I'm safe. I'm getting quite good at fishing. I found a line in the garage that I take down to the rocks when the tide is high. I don't know what the things I catch are called but I can eat most of them. I found a pool up the road that's filled with rain, so that's where I get my water. And the weather's getting warmer. I'm surviving.

It took a month for my ankle to heal. Now I wake before the sun every day and head out along the path around the headland. I run for two or three hours, or as long as I can manage. I found a music player in a kitchen drawer and a stack of batteries that fit it. I don't recognise half the songs and the display is broken so I can't see what they're called, but there's one I like to listen to when I run. It starts like a long train coming out of a tunnel, then explodes into deep, grinding guitars and distant drums. There's a male singer who sounds like he's calling back from some other place, some halfway desert between reality and dream. There's a part about him searching for something with his good eye closed, which seems appropriate to my condition. Although my own eye has healed, it's still blind and it doesn't look great, so I patched it up properly with some black fabric I cut from a coat. Maybe Alice will think I'm a pirate when I moor in Cape Town.

The song ends with the singer howling a long refrain about being on his way. This is appropriate too; I am a man with a boat, after all.

It needs fixing and I don't know what I'm doing, but I guess the couple had been trying to do the same thing before the strike because I found a few books in the house that are helping. The mast is a concern and I have no idea if it floats. I'm trying not to think about how I'll get it down to the water, or about how far I have to travel on seas and around coasts that may have been crushed beyond recognition. These are all just details.

I feel as if my soul has woken up from a deep, dark sleep and that, as long as I keep moving, as long as I keep running, it won't go back. I don't know where we're going. I don't know what will become of us or where civilisation will end up. But I know where *I'm* going, and that's good enough.

When I've caught my fish and worked all I can on the boat, I sometimes set out on another run before sunset. Then I come home and eat and read books from the dead couple's shelves. Before I go to sleep I whisper words into a tin can etched with five sets of initials.

This isn't the end. It is never the end. I still live and I still dream of my family. I miss them so much sometimes that the pain of love and the pain of running converge and become a single bright thing clenched in my fist like an atom. This morning, as the sun rose, I ran up the steep path from the cove and remembered a day on our doomed Cornish camping trip that I had somehow forgotten. The sun had come out and we had driven to Sennen Cove, a beautiful white beach next to Land's End. We'd been for a walk along the cliffs and had stopped on the sand, running from the tide, dancing and laughing as the sun set. I remember feeling Beth's growing bump beneath her dress, watching her smile in the orange light as Alice kissed her cheeks. I remember falling in love with her for the hundredth time.

I could feel them behind me as I ran up the path this morning. I felt Beth's breath on my neck as I pounded my feet into the sand. I swear I caught the scent of my son's head on the breeze and heard Alice's laughter twinkling like the light on the tide before disappearing into the morning air. They were there with me. I felt them.

At the top I turned and faced the sun. Then I held out my arms, and into the screaming heat of that distant fireball rising above me, I screamed right back.

Acknowledgements

I would like to thank the following people, each of whom helped make this book happen – Dennis Coughlin, Catriona Vernal, John-Paul Shirreffs, Bob Ross and my father, Norrie Walker.

Also, thanks to everyone who supported the Thunderclap, especially Mel Young. Thanks, Mel!

This book is dedicated to my children and my wife, Debbie, without whom this book simply would not exist. Thank you, my love and *partner in crime*.

All characters appearing in this work are fictitious. Any resemblance to real persons, living or dead, is purely coincidental.

Oh . . . apart from Jacob (thanks, Tobias).